CORPUS
CHROME, INC.

Corpus Chrome, Inc.
© 2013 by S. Craig Zahler

Published by Dog Star Books
Bowie, MD

First Edition

Cover Image: Bradley Sharp
Book Design: Jeremy Zerfoss

Printed in the United States of America

ISBN: 978-1-935738-53-4

Library of Congress Control Number: 2013956047

www.DogStarBooks.org

CORPUS CHROME, INC.

By
S. Craig Zahler

DARK STAR
BOOKS

Dedicated to my mother, Linda Cooke Zahler, the supportive and intelligent woman who took me to bookstores when I was a kid and told me what science fiction should be. Thank you.

PART I:
ANCHORED TO THE DEAD

SPRING, A.D. 2058

Chapter I
The Tarnished Trophy Wife

"Your husband believes that he is trapped in fiction," the German doctor said to an anxious seventy-four-year-old woman. "On most days," he specified, "your husband believes that he is confined within a cinematic world, a celluloid film."

Her mottled hands huddled together like worried crabs, Mrs. Jennifer Albren pursed her lips, rubbed them with her dry tongue, opened her mouth, contemplated a question, and then exhaled a long breath instead of words.

The doctor slid his magnetically buoyed chair to the table and leaned forward. "Do you understand what I am telling you?" he asked, his voice cloying and childlike. Small emerald eyes on either side of his upturned nose awaited an answer.

"He thinks that this is a movie—that everything's fake. Right?"

"That is correct," confirmed the doctor. "And he has been in this delusional state since his dawn, three weeks prior to today."

"Did you explain to him what happened—how he was resurrected and with the cryonics and everything?"

"He was informed. Still, he continues to ask for the director." A lavender light illuminated in the air and vanished, followed by a trilogy of chimes, each a major third higher than its predecessor. "Your husband's shepherd has arrived," said the doctor, pointing a finger that looked like a pencil at the wall behind Mrs. Albren.

The old woman swiveled around.

A plump black man with a neat beard and an olive tweed suit emerged from the wall. The magnetically buoyed armchair within which the shepherd sat glided across the room, half a meter above its shadow on the blue carpet. The transcended wall held the shape of his silhouette for a moment (through which Mrs. Albren saw a waiting area with foam-rubber hammocks and a woman adding soy to her coffee) and then closed over, healed by crackling nanobuilders.

"Good afternoon. I'm Mr. Johnson," said the shepherd, his deep voice comforting, like an old song. He took the septuagenarian's right hand in a big soft palm and shook it warmly.

"Hello."

"I am Edward's shepherd, and have had sessions with him every day since his dawn." His deep voice stirred her latticework earrings, upon which ninety-sided diamonds sparkled like rain.

Mrs. Albren asked, "Is he going to be okay?"

"Doctor Kreussen explained to you the disorientation that your husband is currently experiencing?" He tilted his head toward his left shoulder, as if the inquiry were an air bubble that would threaten his equilibrium until it was popped with an answer.

"He told me that my Edward thinks he's in some movie."

"Indeed, indeed, indeed." Mr. Johnson righted his head.

"You explained what happened," the woman asked, "with the cryonics and everything?"

"Slowly and in great detail every morning for the last three weeks, I have explained the tortuous path that led him—"

"Torturous?" She fearfully recalled how Chinese men had tied knots into their prisoners' intestines during the Beijing Conflict twenty years earlier.

"Tortuous, not torturous," explained the shepherd. "It means convoluted or winding. It has nothing to do with torture."

"Oh. I didn't…I didn't get to college," confessed Mrs. Albren. More than fifty years later, her academic history embarrassed her like a piece of parsley stuck between white front teeth.

Mr. Johnson continued, "Edward Albren isn't the only resurrected performer to suffer from this particular psychological schism, which we call Schipmann's Syndrome after the first man who had it."

"Schipmann thought he was in a movie, too?"

"He believed he was in a theater play. Whenever somebody tried to explain his condition to him, he said, 'Those aren't the lines.' Like Schipmann, your husband was dead for a longer period than most of the people we have re-bodied…and we have found that there is some correlation between length of absence and ease of recovery."

"Thirty-nine years ago, my Edward died," said Mrs. Albren. "He was forty-six." She remembered the call she had received that day, and how the life she had led afterwards always seemed dimmer, slower. "It's gotta be pretty weird, waking up in that thing—especially when you think you're never gonna wake up ever."

"It is incomparably strange," said Mr. Johnson, flinging his chair around the crescent table so that he sat beside Dr. Kreussen. Upon the blue rug, the shadows of the two Corpus Chrome, Incorporated employees merged like reunited turtles.

Dr. Kreussen said, "It is standard practice for us to require a reorientation test score of at least seventy percent before a resurrected individual is exposed to people from his or her first life. As you might imagine, the experience can prove traumatic for the re-bodied person."

He allowed Mrs. Albren a moment to imagine traumas.

The doctor resumed, "We strive to have the re-bodied person well acclimated to his or her mannequin before such exposure, but—" He looked at the shepherd.

Mr. Johnson pressed his large soft palms together and said with great kindness, "We have done what we can to reorient Edward, but have failed. Your husband continues to maintain that he is in a movie. And unfortunately, there are restrictions regarding how much time we may spend on any one patient."

"Corpus Chrome, Incorporated can only manufacture eight thousand mannequins a year," Dr. Kreussen stated, "and at this point, there are close to one hundred and thirty million cryogenically preserved minds worldwide."

Fear like a cold squid wriggled in the septuagenarian's stomach. She said, "He'll get better," and nodded authoritatively.

"Not without changing our tactics," opined the shepherd. "This is why we've called you here today. Our hope is that an interaction with you, the most significant person from his first life, will effect a change in Edward, an acceptance of what is. There are risks to such an encounter, but we have exhausted all other options."

Mrs. Albren felt something wet drip upon her folded hands. The shepherd plucked a handkerchief from his olive tweed suit, leaned over and handed it to her before she realized that she was crying.

"I'll talk to him." She wiped her eyes with the silken fabric; the cloth warmed, and the fluid turned to powdered salt.

"Wonderful," said Mr. Johnson. Beside him, Dr. Kreussen remained inscrutable.

"Will you come with me?" Mrs. Albren asked the shepherd. "When I talk to him? Please?"

Mr. Johnson shook his head minutely. "It is better if I do not accompany you. I fear that my presence will only reinforce the continuity of his delusory state. He believes I'm a stand-in."

She managed to articulate the word "But," before fear lodged the remainder of the sentence in her throat.

"I will be just beyond the polarity curtain," said Mr. Johnson. "You may call for me at any time."

Dr. Kreussen added, "There is nothing for you to fear: We have locked his motor controls."

"You turned him off?" asked Mrs. Albren, befuddled.

"Partially," the doctor said in his thin child's voice. "He can see and hear and speak, but his limbs are offline. He cannot move."

"Why? Did he try to hurt somebody?"

The doctor and the shepherd exchanged glances that seemed grave.

"No," said Mr. Johnson. "He...Edward...has only proven to be a danger to himself."

"How? What did he do?"

Mr. Johnson hesitated, and the German replied, "He cracked open his head. Twice."

Mrs. Albren envisioned her handsome husband (eternally forty-six in her mind) slamming his skull against a brick wall until gore erupted.

"The damage has been repaired," clarified Dr. Kreussen.

"Oh. Okay," said the unnerved old woman. "How long will he last? If we can straighten him out?"

"Our scientists believe that most brains will survive longer in a mannequin than they would have in a healthy body. A total lifespan of one hundred and twenty years—perhaps more."

"That's a lot."

"Have you have seen the chromium mannequin model 8M?" asked the shepherd.

"Yes. I saw it on m.a."

"Wonderful. Though you should refrain from referring to the mannequin unit with the word 'it' in front of Edward."

"You're right. I will."

"Wonderful," responded the shepherd. "Would you like to speak to him today… or do you feel that you need some time to prepare yourself for the visitation?"

Terror and hope coursed through her blood in dueling currents. The old woman rose from her chair and said, "I want to see him now—it's been long enough. But first I need to change my clothes."

* * *

Ice lights that were embedded in the ceiling cooled and illuminated the royal blue hallway and its two occupants, Mrs. Albren and the shepherd. They walked east.

"This is what I was wearing when Edward proposed to me," said the tall lean woman. "I brought it in case I got to see him today. He always said it was a head-turner." She smiled as she remembered the compliment. Although the gold and lavender dress tugged at the four and a half pounds she had gained in the last five decades, she was proud that she had not fattened, as had so many of her friends (especially the widows who showed their nude bodies to nobody but doctors). "I used to wear high heels with it." The septuagenarian glanced with contempt at the designer-label foam-rubber shoes adorning her feet.

"You look very nice," said Mr. Johnson. He sucked air through a mint vapor tube wedged between his thick lips, and produced a trilling B-flat.

Mrs. Albren looked up from the serpentine veins that covered the backs of her hands. "Is there anything I should do? Stuff I should talk about? Or not talk about?"

"You should not focus overly on friends or family members who have passed away in the interim."

"Okay."

The passageway split into two; with a paddle-like hand, Mr. Johnson motioned for them to continue to the left. Iridescent numbers, spaced six meters apart, glowed upon the living walls on either side of the sky-blue hall.

Mrs. Albren smelled gelatin and chrome in the air as she proceeded. "William and Jana are still alive, though William has slowed down a bit these last years. I'll talk about them."

"That sounds like a good topic for discussion."

"What else should I mention? There were those wars between the Indians and the Chinese, and that mess in Korea. Glad the Global Senate put an end to that sort of thing."

"Major historical events are good topics. They will help give him a sense of time elapsed."

The iridescent numbers diminished.

Mrs. Albren ruminated for a moment and said, "The New York Yankees have won the World Series nine times since he died. He won't like that—he liked the Pirates. But I paid attention so I could tell him whenever I saw him next. In the afterlife or wherever." She was fully aware that she was rambling, but since silence made her anxious, she continued. "I don't really care for baseball. I'm not sure what the point is. It's just a ball. Do you like baseball?"

"Not especially, no." Mr. Johnson's kind eyes appraised her face for a moment. "Would you like a softener?"

"I don't take drugs. That's why I still have my figure, even if some of it sags a bit." She giggled in a girlish way that belied her years and betrayed her anxiety.

Mr. Johnson stopped in front of the living wall numbered 784.

Mrs. Albren's heart thudded as though she had just climbed five flights of stairs in twice as many seconds, and her throat became dry. The shepherd reached his hand into the wall; the fleshy extremity disappeared as if in opaque water. Three musical tones rang in the hallway.

Mr. Johnson withdrew his hand and said, "Please pass through. The waiting area is on the other side."

Mrs. Albren strode through the malleable part of the living wall and entered a brown alcove, where she saw a suspended leather couch, a water sphere, a table with two movie sheaves, a mote aquarium and, on the far side of the room, an orange polarity curtain that was a meter taller and wider than was she. The shepherd strode beside her. Behind them, the Mr. Johnson- and Mrs. Albren-shaped wounds in the living wall were healed over by crackling nanobuilders.

She nodded her head at the orange polarity curtain and asked the shepherd, "He's through there?"

"Indeed, indeed, indeed. A nurse placed a chair in his room for you—situated directly in his line of sight."

"Because you shut off his motors?"

"Precisely. You may move the chair forward or backward if you'd like, but you must remain on the same axis. He can't turn his head, but he can refocus to different distances."

"Okay."

"I shall observe the encounter on that," he said, pointing to the mote aquarium that floated before the couch. "Unless you object?"

"Please watch. Let me know if I mess anything up. Should I…is he ready to…?" She let her sentence trail away with a look at the curtain.

"Please proceed. The curtain is open."

On long thin legs that had been warped by horse saddles, the passage of time and a predilection for sitting Indian-style in Japanese restaurants, Mrs. Albren approached the door.

The moment her right shoe pressed a sensor in the rug, a chime rang on the far side of the curtain. A voice that sounded like the rich baritone of a mote aquarium announcer said, "I'm stuck."

Mrs. Albren hesitated, looked at Mr. Johnson (who was seating himself upon the suspended couch) and asked, "Is that Edward?"

"Indeed."

"It doesn't sound like him."

"I'm stuck," called the voice from beyond the orange veil.

"That is the standard-issue male voice for model 8M. His software has yet to be tuned to the particulars of his speech patterns."

"You'll do that if he gets better?"

"We will."

"Okay."

Mrs. Albren looked at her foam-rubber shoes, righted the strap on her left shoulder, inhaled deeply and stepped toward the polarity curtain; the fabric furled itself into the top of the frame, retracting like an exhausted party favor. The septuagenarian walked into the room beyond.

The oval-shaped chamber was adorned with sepia wallpaper that depicted windblown flowers, falling leaves and flying birds, all moving fluidly in serene loops of action. Lit by three ice lights that floated beneath the ceiling was a model 8M chromium mannequin. The inert machine, clothed in a light blue hospital gown, sat upright in a bed. An empty wooden chair stood on the floor two meters beyond its flesh-colored toes.

Unable to do anything else, Mrs. Albren stared. The curtain unfurled behind her; its sound was a dull rumple.

"Who's here?" inquired the mannequin. According to Mr. Johnson and Dr. Kreussen, this inert, chrome-plated machine with gelware extremities and the voice of a stranger was her resurrected husband.

"I know somebody's in here with me," the machine said. "I can see your shadow. Or is that the boom microphone?"

Mrs. Albren saw that her shadow had fallen upon the back of the wooden chair. "Edward?"

"Who's there?" asked the mannequin. The strange voice was hostile.

Mrs. Albren walked to the chair, sat down and looked at her husband. The mannequin's hairless face (like its hands and feet) was made of flesh-colored, touch-sensitive gelware; two inscrutable lenses stared forward from between the mask's unblinking eyelids. She tried to think of something to say to the machine, her husband.

Buried larynx speakers inquired through an unmoving mouth slit, "Mrs. Glawski…is that you?"

A fist squeezed Mrs. Albren's heart; she clasped her knees with the throbbing tips of her fingers and damned the tears that burned her eyes unshed. She tilted her head down, the inexorable progress of time her loathed foe.

Unable to speak, the old woman shook her head in denial. When her voice finally returned to her, she said, "My mother died twenty years ago." She lifted her face and gazed upon the mannequin. In a small voice, she confessed, "It's me. It's Jennifer."

The mannequin stared forward, inscrutable. Mrs. Albren smiled, hopeful, yet aware that the expression would emphasize the wrinkles she had acquired during the thirty-nine years since he had last seen her. The apertures in the mannequin's ocular wells dilated; pristine lenses slid in their housings, mechanically arranging light for the human mind within.

"This fucking movie just keeps getting worse and worse."

In that instant, Mrs. Albren was destroyed.

Chapter II
A Murderer's Encore

Alicia Martinez, wearing a black business suit and hard shoes, hurried up the stairs, down a passage, through a living wall, past seven perplexed peers (and a mote aquarium filled with warfare), and up the high hall, bearing an anger that would soon explode in a deluge of vitriol.

"How dare they!" the thirty-three-year-old woman shouted, while the muscles in her legs carried her heated thoughts and two clenched fists to the living wall outside the executive meeting chamber of Steinberg, Goldman, Taliq, Shabiza and O'Brien, LWC. She thrust her right hand forward, and the unyielding surface jammed her fingers. "Unlock the goddamn wall!" She slapped the palm of her left hand against the barrier.

Alicia Martinez had blazing words with which she intended to lash these unconscionable men.

Three pitches rang in the air; the wrathful woman strode through the living wall and into the beige executive chamber.

Seated in buoyed chairs were the three active partners of the firm, Morton Goldman, Safan Taliq and Paolo O'Brien, and two assistants whose hands were clasped to the studded hemispheres embedded in the oaken table. Sunlight poured in through the wide oval window, obliquely chiseling the conspiracy and warming the plush, spice-scented leather upholstery.

Alicia spat at her employers, "What the hell do you think you are doing?"

"She's angry," O'Brien said to Taliq.

The Arabic man shrugged, causing his viridescent suit to scintillate.

"Morton," Alicia said to her former mentor, "you don't have a problem with this?"

"I have lots of problems," Goldman replied, motioning to the artificial hair that concealed his previously bereft scalp.

"This's exactly why people don't like Jews."

"They don't?"

Taliq nodded in agreement with Alicia's claim, and Goldman feigned shock.

"Morton! Don't you dare make light of this."

"If you are going to make anti-Semitic remarks, I'd prefer you called me Mr. Goldman."

Taliq and O'Brien laughed—every Jew thought he was a comedian—and Alicia saw white crackling fire. For a moment, all the words that she knew were obliterated by her private inferno, and the physical urge to do violent things clouded her thoughts.

The partners looked nervous beneath their calm exteriors.

"Have a seat," said Goldman, motioning to an empty chair.

"That won't change anything," she said, as if accepting a chair might intimate accedence.

Goldman flashed the palms of his big hands and nodded his artificially decorated pate.

"Please sit, Mrs. Martinez," said Taliq, whose thin-lipped mouth was embedded in a silver goatee that was a perfect equilateral triangle.

Alicia sat in the proffered leather chair, smelled its luxurious scent, and was irked by how comfortable it was. (The avenue of anger had many detours.)

"Have some water," said Goldman.

"Don't you dare pretend that this isn't wrong. Really wrong."

"First, water. Take a moment to calm yourself, and then let's discuss the particulars of this case. We will listen to everything you have to say."

Paolo O'Brien, calm, handsome and thirty-one (two years younger than Alicia, but already a partner in the firm), poured a glass of water, walked it around the table as if it were an elderly person and placed it in her hand. She drank, set the glass down and opened her mouth to speak.

Goldman started first. "Corpus Chrome, Incorporated is our client. We have worked for them exclusively for eight years. They paid for this room. They paid for these chairs. They paid for this building and the water currently traveling down your esophagus. They pay all of our salaries, at a rate fifty percent above those of our contemporaries in international litigation." He looked at the flickering fingers of the assistants. "And they pay for the transcriptions of all of our meetings."

"I'll say what I came here to say," replied Alicia, a crease of anger upon her forehead like an auxiliary frown.

"Undoubtedly," said Goldman. "I just wanted you to pause and consider the permanency of your words." His eyes went again to the assistants. Their typed reports were fifty pages long each day (after editing) and extraordinarily detailed; the lightning readers employed by Corpus Chrome, Incorporated could assimilate a full day's information in less than five minutes. (Visual, audio and mote recording took far longer to appraise.)

"There are other jobs," Alicia said, righteously burning, "ones that do not involve an unethical law firm, contracted exclusively to an immoral corporation."

"You left out the word 'evil,'" said Goldman.

O'Brien laughed.

Alicia wondered if the kind and caring man who had been her mentor ten years ago still dwelt somewhere within this Morton Goldman.

She doubted it.

"This situation with Derrick W.R. Dulande is deplorable," said Alicia. "How can the firm even consider getting behind this idea?"

"We are not 'getting behind this idea,'" Goldman said, musically reshaping her statement as if it were a balloon animal. "Corpus Chrome, Incorporated has decided to re-body a man executed by the state of Florida thirty-two years ago. We are exploring the legal restrictions and obligations for CCI, because they are our client."

Alicia venomously replied, "If you ply your courtroom theatrics on me, I will smash this glass and make you eat the goddamn shards."

Goldman raised an eyebrow.

Taliq's lacquered nails tapped the folded arms of his scintillating suit, and his face was dark and wary.

The woman continued, "Derrick W.R. Dulande is a murderer and a rapist."

"Was," Goldman said.

The remainder of the water slapped his face.

Alicia slammed the empty glass down upon the wooden table, shook her head and glanced at the assistants' flickering fingers. Did they describe how Morton's red face shone with moisture, as if burnished; how contempt roiled beneath his seemingly aloof gaze; and how droplets beaded in his thick black eyebrows?

The Jew took a handkerchief from his blue jacket and wiped his wet visage until the cloth had absorbed and evaporated the insult. Calmly, he said, "This is precisely why O'Brien has his name on the door, and you do not. It certainly isn't because he's more capable."

O'Brien's face was inscrutable: It was impossible to tell if he felt that he had been insulted. Taliq suppressed a smile. Alicia hated the Arab.

Goldman resumed his lecture, his voice deeper than it had been a moment ago (another courtroom affectation). "Derrick W.R. Dulande's parents had his brain submerged in liquid nitrogen less than twenty seconds after he was pronounced dead in order to minimize the possibility of brain damage."

"That would've been a pity."

"Mr. Dulande is in the top point-one percent of healthy candidates for resurrection. CCI has decided to re-body him, and they will. This is private enterprise: There are no laws—inchoate or implied—governing which cauliflowers CCI may choose and which sit in the icebox. Our work in this particular case is merely due diligence."

"Perhaps there should be some laws governing CCI," said Alicia. "Hoarding and monopolizing resurrection technology isn't terribly ethical."

Goldman said, "CCI created the interface, and we represent their interests."

Alicia shook her head. "Morton...this is wrong. Thousands of people—individuals who could benefit society—better deserve a second life in that mannequin. Jesus Christ, anybody does! This is exactly why the Global Senate put a ban on cloning—so private organizations couldn't play God." She calmed herself, but the vitriol remained. "There could not be a worse, less ethical choice than Derrick W.R. Dulande." The name sat like early-morning saliva upon her tongue. "Why? Why now, and why him?"

"His mother has bone cancer and will die within the next few months. She wants her son to be re-bodied."

Alicia inquired, "Exactly how much money does Mrs. Dulande have?"

"Twenty-nine billion globals," said Goldman.

"Christ."

"CCI asked for ninety-seven percent of the Dulande estate in exchange for the mannequin. Mrs. Dulande accepted the offer this morning. That was when we were notified."

"This is absolutely disgusting."

Goldman continued as if she had said nothing. "CCI specifically requested the services of our top attorney: They want you to make sure that the injunctions are killed and that this deal is properly—and expeditiously—closed. Dulande's legal team has already drafted a contract."

Alicia was speechless: Her incredulity momentarily knocked the legs out from beneath her anger. She could not stomach the thought of working at a firm that would facilitate this indefensible deal, much less apply herself to it personally.

Before the clicking fingers of the assistants and the narrow eyes of his two partners, Goldman formally inquired, "Alicia Martinez, do you feel that you will be able to facilitate this deal to the best of your abilities, wholly and without bias?"

Horrified, the woman looked at her former mentor and contemplated which ethnic and personal epithets to fling at him before she stood and forever left the firm. She was about to spew the vitriol of the righteous when Morton Goldman winked at her. The flashed eyeball escaped the attention of everybody else in the room.

Taliq said, "We will put Klein and Sing on this case if you decline. Their record is not as impressive as yours, but they are good."

"I will facilitate this deal," she said to the active partners of Steinberg, Goldman, Taliq, Shabiza and O'Brien, LWC. "We all have to do things we find distasteful, and I know that this is important to the firm."

Alicia felt that her clandestine obstruction of this odious deal would be the first time she had truly done anything to better the world since her days as a public defender. A piece of buried detritus warmed within her chest: the dull coal of pride.

The satisfied manner in which Morton Goldman clasped his hands together and reclined in his scented-leather chair showed her that he felt exactly the same way.

Chapter III
The Elasticity of Cat Vertebrae

Champ Sappline, his shadow stuck to his feet, crossed the street and approached a metal door, which was housed within a wooden frame that had been painted over so many times that it looked like molten candle wax. Bolted to the wall with violence was a placard that read:

> This Building Has Been Classified Antique (SO-3100L24-54-X), and the Owners are Not Responsible for Any Injuries Sustained Herein, Whether Caused Directly or Indirectly by Antique Conditions.
>
> All Persons are Required to Fingerprint an Agreement of Burden Acceptance Prior to Ingress.
>
> Any Person Who Enters Without Compliance is Trespassing and has Voided His or Her Legal Claim to Remuneration (and Will be Fined).

Champ pressed the tips of his right thumb and index finger to the obsidian-glass ovals beneath the waiver. The door buzzed like an irate hornet and slid into the floor, where something cracked.

The forty-two-year-old man walked into the mail alcove, which smelled like dust, animals and pizza. He looked for an elevator, but instead saw an unclean and narrow stairwell.

Mentally, he cursed Candace.

The blonde man pulled long hair back from his handsome face and began to climb the stairs of the old Nexus Y apartment building.

Mote aquariums, barrage metal, string jazz, bounce, dogs and live human arguments resounded behind closed doors that were equipped with scratched lenses and customized print locks. Champ plucked a Purpureal tube from his blue jeans, raised it to his lips, sucked a trilling B-flat and tasted cardamom. The mist was not powerful enough to impair behavior (the manufacturers took their psychotropics to the exact edge of legality—a little further each year), but it was strong enough to pat him on the back and say, "Well done, sir!" He then replaced the vapor tube in his jeans.

Sweat beaded above his upper lip as he climbed the third flight of stairs, and he grew lightheaded, almost as if the air had thinned during his twenty-two-meter ascent. Champ's foam-rubber boots squeaked upon something viscid; he looked down and saw the circular stain left by a suicidal pizza that had landed face-down. (The coroner had apparently decided to remove—and eat?—the carcass.)

The blonde man ascended the fourth flight of stairs, crossed a landing covered with broken eggs and silver paint, climbed the fifth and walked into the sixth-floor hallway.

The passage was illuminated by blue sunshine that struggled through a trio of grimy skylights. Upon the nearest of the clear plastic panes lay the splayed corpse of a turkey pigeon, whose head had been splashed with bleach. Champ looked away from the murdered bird and down the long hallway, the green walls of which looked like the icing of a dismal Christmas cake.

The blonde man wiped sweat from his face, double-tapped the lily in his right ear and said, "Play: Memo." He heard his own voice say, "Seventy-two Gregs Street; apartment six-twelve; owner, R.J. the Third."

Champ strode down the hall (which, for some reason, was far quieter than the others in the building), stopped in front of the door marked 612 and tapped the chime placard. He wiped the sweat from his brow, breathed and waited. The lens housed in the metal door hissed; its iris narrowed, and glass planes shifted.

"Are you Champ Sappline?" inquired a man with a loud tenor voice that matched the one in the audiad.

"I am. Are you R.J. the Third?"

"You are early."

Champ triple-tapped the lily in his ear and heard a demure woman's voice say, "The time is thirteen fifty-eight." His appointment was at fourteen.

"I'm sorry," said Champ. "I can wait."

There was no response.

The blonde man fidgeted, shifted his weight and swallowed spit while he stared at a scratched lens for one hundred and twenty slow seconds.

"Enter!" ordered the tenor voice.

The fleximetal door slid into the ground and revealed an obese gray Persian cat. Although the audiad had mentioned nothing about pets, there it was—haughty and shaped like an abundant bag of garbage.

"Architect," R.J. the Third called from farther within the apartment, "please escort Mr. Sappline into the common area." The cat eyed the intruder derisively and strode away, its tail stuck in the air like a middle finger. Champ followed the beast down the copper hall; the animated posters on either side of him exhibited blossoming explosions, bone-crushing karate kicks and burning brassieres in two- to five-second loops, depending upon the thickness of the poster. The blonde man did not know much about collectibles, but he knew that these were valuable pieces.

The cat led him into a square room that was nearly ten meters wide; the walls were painted metallic gold and the floor was covered with thick silver carpeting. Seated upon a fur couch was a tall slender man with protuberant eyes, red cheeks, a large nose (thrice pierced) and messy black hair. He wore silver shorts and a matching shirt, both monogrammed "RJ # 3." The feline walked before the man's bare feet and redistributed its tonnage, apparently sitting. The man's toes disappeared beneath the fat cat.

"Hi. I'm Champ Sappline."

"I am R.J. the Third," the seated man said with musical flourish, as if he expected applause. He looked at the cat upon his toes and then up at Champ. "Architect does not appear to hate you." The twenty-five-year-old pointed to an inflatable chair that rested beside the mote aquarium and said, "You will sit."

"Danke," Champ said as he sat.

"It is a very difficult thing—to determine if a person is trustworthy," said R.J. the Third, shifting his toes beneath the feline. "Why should I rent the room to you, hmmm?"

"I'm reliable. And I can pay four months' rent in advance."

"How about friends? This isn't a place for parties."

"I don't have any friends."

"Why not?"

"My wife got them all. Even the ones who were mine."

R.J. the Third became uneasy. "Wife?"

Architect, sensing its owner's displeasure, swiveled its pumpkin to face the interviewee. The beast's head turned twenty degrees further than cat vertebrae typically allowed, although it was possible that the body had shifted somewhere deep within the blubber.

"You're married?" pressed R.J. the Third, cat eyes demonically agleam at his feet.

"Not anymore. She left me."

"Oh." R.J. the Third relaxed, and Architect's head swiveled away. The tall skinny man in silver posited, "So you're depressed, single and friendless?"

"I wouldn't disagree with that assessment."

"Terrific. What do you do for a living?"

"I'm a garbage man."

"That isn't going to make you popular."

"Nope."

"Anything else?" asked R.J. the Third.

"I did some stand-up comedy for a while, but it didn't work out."

"You don't seem humorous."

"Most people agree with you."

R.J. the Third leaned over and grabbed Architect; limbs sprouted obliquely from the furry mass; a purr like tires redistributing gravel emanated from deep within the bloated beast. The skinny man in silver stroked the feline between its ears and inquired casually (as if to trick Champ), "What did you think of the mote aquarium experience *The First and Final Rocket?*"

"I haven't seen it."

"What!?!" R.J. the Third cried out in disbelief; Architect did not know what to do with its paws, but there was flapping. "It was a huge hit! Enormous!"

"I haven't had a mote aquarium in almost a year."

R.J. the Third's bulging eyes lit with horror, summarily replaced by something that looked like grief. "I'm sorry to hear that," he said.

Architect looked dolorously at the window, as if the creature had just been diagnosed with cat cancer.

"I don't miss it all that much," defended Champ. "I like movie sheaves more. I just flip through those when I'm bored."

"Movie sheaves," said R.J. the Third, derisively. "Are you a great supporter of all the dead, two-dimensional arts? Novels? Cave paintings?"

Champ had learned to tolerate rudeness during the latter years of his marriage, and thus replied with well-concealed irritation, "I haven't read a book since I was in college."

R.J. the Third nodded, placated by this information. "It is unfortunate that you have not seen *The First and Final Rocket*." The wan timbre of his voice caused Architect to lower its head and flatten its ears, disheartened. "Unfortunate."

The conversation sank into a ponderous silence.

Champ thought of the storage niche that awaited him if he did not find a new place to live, and inquired of his host, "Does this part of our discussion have any bearing on whether or not you'll rent the room to me?"

"Tremendous bearing."

Architect haughtily raised its chin.

"I'm just looking for a room—we don't need to be pals. I work lots of nights and we probably won't see all that much of each other. I'll respect the rules."

R.J. the Third shook his head in refutation. "I will need to know far more than that if you are going to take up residence in my apartment."

"And this m.a. movie—"

"Experience! Mote aquarium experience."

"My opinions on it will let you know whether I'm a suitable tenant?"

"They will."

"Will you show it to me? *The First and Final Rocket*?"

R.J. the Third's mouth became slack, and his eyes widened. Architect looked at its master as if the man had just malfunctioned.

"That is a brilliant idea! I will show you this landmark work, this zenith achievement in the history of the arts (including all those dead ones you prefer), and afterwards, continue and conclude the interview. You should know this ahead of time: *The First and Final Rocket* is a life-altering experience that will change you, thoroughly and irrevocably."

"How long is it?"

"Six minutes."

"Great."

R.J. the Third whistled a C-sharp and said, "Darkness!" The windows became opaque, and the room plunged into night. Another C-sharp pierced the silence and was followed by the command: "Play: My meisterwerk!"

CHAPTER IV

THE FIRST AND FINAL ROCKET (A SCIENCE-FANTASY MEISTERWERK BY R.J. THE THIRD)

"Full volume! Maximum brightness!" cried the popinjay.

Architect's eyes sparkled as it gripped the fur couch with excited paws.

Champ spun the inflatable chair around to face the mote aquarium, which was one of the largest that he had ever seen. It was a two-meter wide, one-meter tall and one-meter deep frame of black bars that housed thousands of micromagnetic engines. The device heated up with a dull whir, radiating the smell of hot copper.

Three hundred thousand magnetized pixels sprayed into the viewing stage, luminous motes that were red, orange, yellow, green, blue, indigo and violet. The haze coalesced, took the form of a comet, and then flew to each of the rectangular cuboid's eight corners like a parakeet trying to escape a cage.

"That's the test pattern," said R.J. the Third, didactically.

The luminous motes converged to form

> *Buddha. The porcine deity was clothed in a sumo diaper and a fedora; he held a double-barreled sawed-off shotgun in his right hand and the hair of a dripping severed head in his left. Buddha pointed the weapon forward and fired.*

"Pause," ordered R.J. the Third.

The smoke and sparks froze in midair, just outside the gun barrels. "Before the narrative begins," the host said, "I want you to see how beautiful a properly-calibrated mote aquarium can be. This image has no background, so you can look at it from all angles." He motioned for his guest to rise and inspect the unit.

Champ stood and walked toward the mote aquarium, his patience almost exhausted. Buddha was as clear as reality itself—even up close, the pixel sculpture had no errors or limitations in resolution. The garbage man circled the unit and saw that the fat deity was just as fully rendered from behind, and when he looked through the top of the cuboid, he descried gentle creases in the big man's superb fedora. Champ knelt and looked up through the bottom of the unit: The soles of Buddha's splayed feet (victims of fallen arches, apparently) and the diaper that covered the sacred groin in between were also sculpted without error. (A notice of copyright inhering in R.J. the Third had been embossed on the Asian's right heel.)

"Gorgeous, right?" inquired the host. "Inspect the muzzle flash."

Champ withheld expletives and surveyed the puff of smoke frozen before the weapon's dual barrels.

"Do you see the pellets in there? The shotgun pellets caught in midair?"

"I do."

"In order to capture that level of detail, the unit must refresh flying pixels six hundred times per second—ten times faster than the human eye can even discern."

"Amazing," said Champ. (He felt that this must be the appropriate response.)

"Touch them," implored R.J the Third. "The pellets."

"I thought you weren't supposed to touch a mote sculpture."

"That is the case with inferior units. It's fine with this one—unless you are wearing a ring or have metal inside your hands. You don't, do you?"

"Nope."

"Go ahead." R.J. the Third nodded his head like an emperor.

Champ cautiously slid his right hand into the mote aquarium and toward the muzzle flash frozen in front of Buddha's sawed-off shotgun. Nine tiny spheres, each one-tenth the circumference of a green pea, pressed against his extended fingertip and then burst into white flashes of light. Champ jerked his hand from the unit. The smears of light contracted and again became nine shotgun pellets— the sculpture was fully restored.

"They call it childproofing," said R.J. the Third. "Lots of m.a. sets were ruined by toddlers reaching in and touching things—to say nothing of the frequent pornographic accidents—so Tante Werks developed a model that could cope with tactile intrusions. The flying pixels are bonded and spatially retentive."

Champ returned to his chair and sat down, commenting, "It's incredible." (He did not understand why people took pride in the technical achievements of others.)

"Resume play," said R.J. the Third. The explosion reverberated in the seventy-two speakers embedded throughout the apartment;

the flash of gunfire dispersed. Buddha spat on the ground, cracked open the sawed-off shotgun and flung the shells behind him, where they disappeared—

beyond the perimeter of the mote aquarium.

Upon the bottom of the stage were the words:

Vengeful Buddha Presents...

A Science-Fantasy Mote Experience
Conceived, Wrought and Controlled by
the Extraordinary New Talent:
R.J. the Third

The pixels dispersed with a bright flash that made Champ wince, and then rendered

a speeding white rocket. Blood dripped from a crack in its nosecone as it pierced clouds. In the rocket's wake, amidst sidereal spirals and plumes of exhaust, appeared the title The First and Final Rocket.

The pixels dispersed and then rendered

a bathroom. A handsome black man of forty set his four-year-old son into a bathtub. The boy looked up at his father. The boy's eyes glowed; the father's eyes glowed.

The boy flapped his arms and splashed water. The father raised his index finger, shook his head and said, "Arthur. Don't splash." The boy stopped splashing. The father said, "Good boy." The boy smiled.

"I brought you a present," said the father. The word

"present" echoed five times in the boy's mind. The father raised a small box that was tied with a red bow. The box glowed. The boy's hands glowed. The boy said, "Let me have it." The father said, "You forgot something." The boy ruminated. The word "present" echoed five more times in his mind. The boy looked at his hands. His hands shone brilliantly. He looked at the box with the ribbon. The box shone brilliantly. He looked at his father and said, "Let me have it." "You forgot something," said the father. The boy looked at his glowing hands and at the glowing present. The word "present" echoed three times and stopped. "I know. Please let me have the present." The father smiled; his teeth glowed. The boy smiled; his teeth glowed.

The father set the box on the edge of the bathtub. "Can I get it wet?" asked the boy. "It is waterproof," said the father. The boy said, "Waterpoof," and untied the ribbon. He lifted the lid and looked inside the box. The boy cried out, "It's a little man!" Inside the box was a translucent man filled with wires and doodads; he was fifteen centimeters tall. "It's a homunculus," said the father. "Honcles," repeated the boy. "Homunculus," said the father. "Honcles," repeated the boy. The father laughed and said, "Honcles."

The boy scooped Honcles out of the box. Honcles kicked his feet and flapped his arms. The boy giggled; the father laughed. "Put him in the water," suggested the father. "He won't drown?" asked the boy. "No. He's waterproof." "Waterpoof," said the boy.

The boy put Honcles in the water; the homunculus floated, buzzed and then began a perfect breaststroke across the bathtub. "He can swim!" said the boy. "Put him on his back," said the father. The boy flipped Honcles over. Honcles did the backstroke across the bathtub. "How does he work?" asked the boy. "Science," said the father. Honcles reached the perimeter of the tub and turned around. He swam freestyle. The boy said, "I want to make science." "A person who studies science is called a scientist." "That's what I want to be!" shouted the boy.

The pixels dispersed and then rendered

a book-filled study. Arthur, twelve years old, walked into the room. He wore a light blue uniform that said Science Academy.

Arthur opened a drawer and withdrew Honcles. Arthur set Honcles down on the table. Honcles' left arm spun backwards, and the toes on his right foot twitched. Arthur took out his microsurgery kit.

Father came into the room and asked, "What are you doing to Honcles?" "Repairs," answered Arthur.

The pixels dispersed and then rendered

Arthur, seventeen years old, and Father, with gray hair. They sat in the living room on the couch. On the mote aquarium, an astronaut walked across orange rocks. A woman announcer said, "Ralph Jasper is the first man to walk on Mars!"

Father looked at Arthur and said, "I wish I could walk on Mars." Arthur shook his head and said, "I know from private calculations that Mars is covered with lava." "All of it?" asked Father. "All of it," replied Arthur.

Father pointed to the mote aquarium stage and asked, "Then how can he walk on it?" Arthur answered, "He isn't walking on it. No man can walk on Mars." Father was confused; he scratched his gray hair with black fingers. Arthur said, "They are lying to us." "The astronauts?" asked Father. "No. The government and the elder scientists." "Why would they lie about Mars?" asked Father. Arthur frowned and said, "I don't know." Father scratched his gray hair.

Arthur said, "I want to build a rocket so that I can visit outer space and learn the truth." Arthur's forehead glowed. Father asked, "How long will it take to build?" Arthur answered, "Seven years." Father said, "I will help you." Arthur's eyes glowed; Father's eyes glowed.

The pixels dispersed and then rendered

Arthur, twenty-four and strong, and Father, old and white-haired. They stood in the garage of their house; they looked up at a white rocket that was twenty meters tall. On the side of the rocket was painted its name: Truth.

"It looks good," commented Father. Arthur said, "Thank you for helping me." "You're welcome." Arthur's eyes glowed; Father's eyes glowed.

"Let's go," Arthur said, "I want to see outer space." "We should eat dinner first, in case we are gone for a long time and can't get hot meals." Arthur nodded and said, "Okay."

They walked into the house.

They walked up a hallway that was covered with pictures of Mother and waved to them.

They entered the kitchen and sat at the dinner table. A white monkey brought them each a big bowl of spaghetti and meatballs. To the monkey, Arthur said, "I want grated cheese." The monkey did not move. Arthur repeated, "I want grated cheese." The monkey did not move. Father said, "Please give Arthur some grated cheese." The monkey grated imported cheese over Arthur's spaghetti and meatballs. Arthur said, "I was thinking about the rocket and forgot to say please." Arthur laughed and Father laughed; their teeth glowed.

The white monkey took the empty dishes. Father said, "We should probably use the bathroom before we go into outer space." Arthur nodded in agreement and said, "You can go first." Father went first; Arthur went second.

They walked into the garage. Arthur leaned a wooden ladder against the nosecone of the rocket. Arthur said, "You go first. There is one last thing I need to get." Arthur hurried from the garage.

Father climbed the ladder to the rocket's door, which was eighteen meters from the ground. Father reached over and typed the code. The door slid open. He went into the nosecone; the room was conical. Father climbed into one of the pilot seats; his back was horizontal and his feet were in the air. He looked through the windshield and saw the ceiling of the garage. Father buckled his seatbelt and waited for his son.

Arthur entered the nosecone and typed in the code. The door slid shut. He took the seat next to Father and buckled in. Father saw that Arthur held Honcles in his right hand.

"Ready?" asked Arthur. Father's eyes glowed; Arthur's eyes glowed. Father said, "Yes." Arthur pressed the ignition. The engines roared. Truth *shot through the garage ceiling. The windshield filled with blue sky and scattered clouds. The rocket shook.* Father took Arthur's hand and said, "I'm scared." Arthur squeezed his father's hand and said, "So am I." Arthur's belly glowed; Father's belly glowed.

The rocket rumbled. Clouds flew past the windshield. Seven birds dispersed.

Two fighter jets pulled up alongside Truth. "Land this rocket ship!" said a fighter jet with a crackly voice. "Right now!" demanded the other fighter jet. "No!" Arthur and his father yelled together. "We will shoot you down if you don't land!" said the first fighter jet. "Pronto!" added the other fighter jet. "Go ahead and try!" replied Arthur.

Arthur said to his father, "You steer while I handle this." Father leaned over and grabbed the steering wheel. Arthur took out two joysticks.

The fighter jets fired ten missiles at the rocket. Arthur used the joysticks and shot ten anti-missiles that neutralized the threat. The fighter jets fired a flank barrage. Arthur shot back an anti-flank barrage. The fighter jets fired three anti-aircraft warheads. Arthur shot back three anti-anti-aircraft warheads. The fighter planes gave up.

Father pointed at the joysticks and said, "You're good with those." "Thank you." "I'm very proud of you." Father's heart glowed; Arthur's heart glowed.

Truth *sped towards space. The blue sky darkened.*

Ten defense satellites converged ahead of the rocket. The

satellites shot lasers. Arthur spun the rearview mirrors around. The lasers were deflected. The satellites exploded.

Truth *sped towards space.*

A mechanical bird landed on the windshield and yelled, "You can't go into outer space!" Arthur replied, "You can't make us to do anything—you're a mechanical bird." "The Global Senate sent me!" yelled the mechanical bird. It showed Arthur documentation. "We're going," said Arthur, firmly. "You can't!" "Why not?" "Because!"

Father turned on the windshield wiper. The mechanical bird caught the wiper with a talon and broke it. The mechanical bird pecked its beak against the windshield. A small piece of glass chipped off. The mechanical bird pecked the windshield again. A small crack appeared. Honcles sneaked into an air-conditioning vent.

"That damn mechanical bird is going to compromise the integrity of this ship!" cried Arthur. The mechanical bird raised its beak for a final assault. Honcles, now outside, threw his arms around the mechanical bird's neck. The two machines fell off the windshield. Arthur screamed, "Honcles!"

Truth *sped towards space.*

Arthur wiped tears from his eyes. Father said, "Honcles was a hero." "He was."

Truth *sped towards space.*

Arthur said, "We're almost there." Father said, "You should make sure your seatbelt is secure." Arthur checked his buckle and said, "It is."

The rocket plunged into a gelatinous wall. "This doesn't feel like space," remarked Father. "No, it doesn't." Truth *plunged through kilometers and kilometers and kilometers of gelatin. Arthur saw a satellite stuck in the gelatin. Father saw a toy helicopter and a bottle rocket and a wrench. The windshield was covered with slime. The engine rumbled.*

Truth *transcended the gelatin and splashed into green water. "It looks like space is underwater," observed Father. "Seems like it,"* said Arthur, confused. "Will the ship work in water?" "Yes. Truth *is* waterproof." "I taught you that word." "You did," said Arthur.

The rocket sped through the green water.

Giant air bubbles drifted past the windshield, left to right. Father pointed to the right and said, "That way must be up. It's where the bubbles are going." "We'll follow the bubbles," said Arthur.

Written upon the stage was the following:

Truth *followed the bubbles for seven months...*

The words dispersed.

The rocket sped through the water. There was no air. There was no space. There were flooded moons, flooded asteroids, flooded planets and some suns surrounded by millions of kilometers of boiling water.

Arthur pointed through the windshield to a moon made of copper and said, "I see some lights on over there. Maybe they'll know what happened to the universe." "Good," said Father. "I'm getting sick of food pellets."

Truth *landed on the copper moon.*

"We'll need to wear helmets so that we can breathe underwater," Arthur informed his father. They put on air helmets. "And we'll need to leave through the airlock so that the ship doesn't get flooded." They exited.

An alien with four heads drove a submarine up to the rocket ship. The alien got out of the submarine and swam toward Arthur and his father. The alien extended a tentacle to each man and shook appendages. "Are you hungry?" the alien asked with four mouths. "Spaghetti and meatballs would be nice," suggested Father. "I can make some in my submarine, though it's difficult for me to eat spaghetti." "Why's that?" asked Father. The alien waggled his tentacles. "These." "Oh." Arthur and his father entered the alien's submarine.

"What happened to the universe?" asked Arthur. "It got flooded," the alien said with the three mouths that were not eating salad. "Did the Earth government do it? The elder scientists?" The alien lowered its four heads and said, "No. It was my race. We flooded it by accident." The alien chewed salad in two mouths and with the other two said, "We put a bubble around the Earth to protect it."

Arthur said, "We flew through that bubble when we left the planet. We could've popped it!" The alien shook its heads and said, "It's fifty kilometers thick—you can't damage it. The fabric heals up when something passes through." Arthur asked, "How long has the universe been flooded?" The alien answered, "For the amount of time it takes your world to swim three billion laps around the sun."

The alien brought the humans spaghetti and said, "I told your Earth leaders all about it so you wouldn't bother with spaceships."

Arthur sniffed. He did not want to cry, but his eyes filled with tears that he could not control.

Father asked the alien, "If the leaders knew, why didn't they tell us? Why didn't the leaders tell us the truth!"

The alien pointed a tentacle at Arthur's tears and said, "Because the truth would make everyone very, very sad."

The stage turned black.

R.J. the Third whistled a C-sharp and said, "Sheer."

The opaque apartment windows became translucent. Daylight poured in and assaulted dilated pupils.

Champ squinted.

"What did you think?" inquired R.J. the Third.

"Not very realistic."

Architect, teeth bared, paws extended and claws unsheathed, leapt toward the critic, hissing like a snake.

CHAPTER V
THE BIFURCATION OF A COMPOSER

Sitting upon a buoyed stool in a Running Turtle coffee bar, Lisanne Breutschen awaited the arrival of her date. In the glass wall opposite, she appraised herself. A dark blue overcoat hid the beige silk suit that draped her petite wiry frame, and her pale skin glowed at sleeve ends and collar. Mounted upon her sinewy neck was a face wrought in angles: square chin, prominent cheekbones, large nose and high forehead, above which short blonde hair shaped like pencil-tips pointed in all directions. Her overall appearance was boyish, yet still feminine enough to garner the attentions of straight men who were not brave enough to explore their sublimated attractions to their own gender and in her saw a heterosexual solution. The thirty-eight-year-old woman thought she looked like a ghoul.

For the thousandth time, Lisanne wished that the mirror image was not reflected parallel light, but the deceased person that it resembled—her identical twin sister, who had succumbed to pancreatic cancer two and a half years ago.

She focused past her reflection.

Outside Running Turtle, foam-rubber cars and vans jostled, bumped and jockeyed to get to and through the intersection. A six-wheeled ladybug bumped into a box van, the latter's driver cursing from behind his soundproof window. The traffic orb changed from green to yellow, and three cars sped through the intersection until a red light glared. A padded stopwall shot up from the road, and the foremost ladybug bumped into the risen obstruction. Vehicles on the perpendicular avenue awakened, a flickering deluge of orange, yellow, blue, black, red, orange, blue, black, red, blue, green, white, green, and silver.

Traffic in Nexus Y was rubber-weapon warfare.

The petite blonde looked away from the window to the coffee menu that was embedded in the table. Since Ellenancy's death, Lisanne had developed a taste—and ultimately a need—for the stimulant-loaded ichor: The caffeine- and dexaprine-laced beverage helped enliven her moribund mornings.

She pressed her right pinkie finger to the espresso-cup icon and tapped it four times. In the box at the bottom of the menu was the price: 42 globals. (Her new habit was expensive.) The woman put her fingertips to the placard, and soon the word "Accepted" scrolled across the screen, chased by a cartoon turtle on a motorcycle. At the bottom of the menu was the ubiquitous flat taxation notice: "12% of this Payment has gone directly to the Global Senate."

Three seconds later, she heard a click and looked up. An aluminum turtle, feet and head waggling, descended from the ceiling and landed upon the table. Nestled in the flattened top of the oblate shell was her steaming quadruple espresso. She took the porcelain cup.

The turtle said, "Danke, Lisanne Breutschen," and magnetically levitated back into the ceiling. Many people were irritated by automated service, but Lisanne preferred it. She was not at all interested in exchanging false pleasantries with bringers, salespeople, hosts or waiters, and nothing made her feel quite as lonely as that moment when some stranger—a paid appendage of a mercantile unit—pretended to be her friend in order to encourage sales.

The petite blonde sipped the espresso that the turtle had given her; the taste was of caramel, clove and rust. Caffeine and dexaprine warmed the spaces between skin and bone.

With her free hand, Lisanne triple-tapped the lily in her ear. A demure woman said, "The time is twenty-thirteen."

Her date was tardy.

Lisanne would stay until she saw the grains of her espresso, and not one millisecond longer.

"I'm sorry I'm late," Osa called across the coffee bar, plucking an errant twine of black hair from her mouth as she hurried to the waiting woman. "Sorry about that," she added, and then threw herself upon a buoyed stool.

"You were late the other time we went out," remarked Lisanne, coolly.

"I'm never on time—I've always been a late person."

"The correct adjective to describe a person who is always late is 'discourteous.'" Lisanne set the espresso down; porcelain clacked upon the table like an exclamation point.

Osa blinked as if struck. "It's not a crime to be late. Things come up. Stuff can happen—especially in my line of work."

"Of course 'things come up.' I am tardy perhaps one in twenty times. But you said you were always late—that being tardy is your typical behavior."

"I can't help it."

"That is nonsense. Being punctual is a choice—the considerate choice—unless remedial math is beyond your comprehension. You simply figure out how much time it takes you to get somewhere and then give yourself a little extra time, should some unforeseen delay occur."

"You're harsh."

"And you have been an inconsiderate diva both times I've met you. Your time is not more valuable than mine."

Osa closed her slack mouth and said, "Should I go? Is this…like an impasse for you? Punctuality?"

"Is it within your power to be considerate of others?"

"I'll try to be on time."

Lisanne frowned.

"I'll be on time," corrected Osa.

"That is the proper answer."

For the first time since Osa had arrived, Lisanne allowed herself to see how gorgeous her date was. The woman's long face and tall stature revealed her Scandinavian origins, while her raven-black hair (braided with sapphires), dark eyes, sharp nose and sepia skin displayed her Indian ancestry. Her unique beauty was an enthralling physical force (one that had probably shielded her from many much-deserved criticisms throughout her lifetime).

Bright white teeth were framed by painted lips into a smile. "That was quite a tirade," said Osa.

"Time is life. I take it personally when people are blithe about murdering little bits of mine."

"Um…you accused me of being a diva?"

Lisanne grinned. "We should go—our reservation is at twenty-one sharp."

Osa smiled mischievously and said, "Wouldn't it be ironic if your tardiness lecture made us late for dinner?"

"I budgeted time for the lecture."

* * *

The cab driver, a nineteen-year-old Brazilian man with gold-dyed dreadlocks, inserted his vehicle between a ladybug and a box van, nudged each aside and sped toward a yellow traffic orb.

"If you slam us into a stopwall, we will get out and I shall dispute the charge," Lisanne said to the cabbie's hair. (The tendrils reminded her of an orchid that she had once watered in the Cuban Republic.)

The cabbie thumbed the brakes, and the speeding car lurched. Pseudopodia gripped the waists and shoulders of the women in the backseat; inertia tilted their heads. The vehicle halted. In front of its rubber fender, a padded stopwall leapt from the road like an upside-down guillotine.

The cabbie turned around and asked Lisanne through the clear plastic partition, "Are you famous? You look familiar."

"Please mind the road."

"We're stopped now—just like you demanded. Tell me who you are. C'mon."

Lisanne did not reply.

"A woman like that," the driver said, pointing to the tall beauty, "doesn't go out with a woman like you unless you're famous or rich."

"I think she's beautiful," said Osa

Lisanne felt her cheeks redden and, for a moment, saw herself as an attractive woman rather than a thirty-eight year-old ghoul.

"Does she pay you to say that?"

Osa pushed the release button. Pseudopodia retracted, and she flung the door, saying, "Let's go."

The women climbed out of the car. Osa slammed the door, leaned over, grabbed the cab's side bumper with her strong hands and said, "Help me."

"You aren't going to—"

"Help me!"

Lisanne leaned beside the tall beauty and curled her fingers around the vehicle's side bumper.

The cabbie looked at the women. "Don't you dare!"

The women heaved, and the tires nearest them lifted from the ground until the car stood on its side. Pressing their palms forward, the women shoved, and the vehicle toppled onto its roof. The driver, still inside the capsized foam-rubber cab, spewed epithets in five different languages.

Osa remarked, "I always wanted to know how to say 'bitch' in Portuguese."

* * *

"I cannot believe what we just did," remarked Lisanne. "That was barbaric."

Her pulse thudded as she strode from the nether level of a multi-tiered sidewalk, through a living wall and into the firelit reception area of Motile. Flowers grew like tree roots, downwards from the ceiling, adding a luxurious scent to the maroon-wallpapered room. A host in a burgundy tuxedo stood behind a wooden lectern on the far side of the room.

Osa emerged from the living wall and replied, "That asshole brought it on himself. He deserved it."

Lisanne did not actually agree with Osa's assessment of their reprisal—they had carried a verbal dispute into the realm of physical action—but capsizing the cab had been more satisfying than she ever would have expected.

The petite blonde said, "I have never done anything like that before, not even with—" She still had a problem saying her sister's name casually, and so completed the statement with the word "—anyone," which did not quite fit.

A wooden orb with four knobbed spokes floated toward the women.

Lisanne helped Osa out of a gray-green slickwax coat. The garment underneath was tailored to the Swedish-Indian American's tall curvilinear form: a black sleeveless dress with a sapphire-bejeweled neckline that plummeted like a rapier to her navel, and a spiral hem that wound from her thighs to her ankles.

"That is a very beautiful and very flattering dress," complimented Lisanne.

"Danke."

The petite blonde set the overcoat upon a spoke, and the orb swiveled to present a free arm for the next garment.

Osa helped Lisanne from her blue trench coat.

"That is a very nice ensemble," the tall woman said of her date's stylish—albeit unspectacular—beige silk suit.

"Danke."

Osa briefly appraised her date's torso: The apparel did not in any way obscure the fact that Lisanne had flattened her breasts. (The petite blonde felt that it would be better for her date to have a moment of disappointment now rather than later, when a startled hesitation or a furtive glance or a minute frown might prove hurtful.)

Unaffected by the revelation, Osa flung Lisanne's coat upon the orb. The machine fled like a haunt with manifold pockets and flapping arms.

"Miss Breutschen and Madam," the English host said, "good evening and welcome to Motile. Please follow me into the dining room." He turned around, strode into a large cornucopia fresco and vanished.

Osa took Lisanne's hand, which was an unexpected (but not unwanted) connection, and the women walked forward. Crackling nanobuilders scattered before them.

The burgundy dining room was lit by quartz chandeliers, around which hybrid flowers grew down toward the seventy guests who filled every single table, excepting the one in a sequestered corner to which the host led the new arrivals. Eyes flickered like struck matches at the petite blonde and her tall companion, and conspiratorial whispers eddied in all directions.

"Does this happen whenever you go to places with rich people?" inquired Osa.

"I believe that they are discussing your dress and how divinely it sits upon you."

The tall woman squeezed a 'thank you' into her date's hand.

At the table, the host withdrew an upholstered wooden chair for Osa, and slid it beneath her as she sat. He then seated Lisanne and presented each guest with a sheaf menu.

"Would you prefer waiter service this evening, Miss Breutschen?"

"My companion and I are capable readers."

The host grinned. "Very well. Dial your food whenever you are so inclined: The bringers will see that you dine undisturbed." The man bowed respectfully and walked away from the table.

Lisanne glanced at her date: Osa seemed simultaneously excited by and wary of the elite environs.

"I feel like I need to talk quietly in a place like this," whispered the tall woman. "Like regular conversation would shatter the champagne flutes or something."

Lisanne surveyed the room and saw a dozen eyes retreat from her gaze like falling stars. "I do not often dine in establishments such as this, but the chef here is superb."

"I haven't had much animated food."

"Jing Duck LePierne-Chawpa-Fan is an innovator in the field. The walking courses on screen six are divine."

"I'll check them out," said Osa, though she did not look at her menu. Instead she stared across the table, directly into Lisanne's eyes, for a long moment. "Can I ask you a question?"

"Of course."

"Why am I here?"

"Why are you in this type of restaurant? Is that your question?"

"No. I'm asking why I'm here with you. Why is Lisanne Breutschen taking me out to dinner?"

"I enjoyed our first date and wanted—"

"You aren't gay."

Lisanne had not at all anticipated her date's declaration and was momentarily stunned.

The tall beauty continued, "I did a search after our first date. You were married twice. Both men. You lived with another man for a year in Hamburg when

43

you and your sister were first becoming famous. You had several high-profile romances. All of these relationships were with men."

"Many people are attracted to both genders," replied Lisanne.

"Of course, but you don't even seem to be bisexual—at least according to what I've listened to and seen. So…sitting here with you—in a place like this—up here in your stratosphere—I felt like I needed to say something. To ask."

"I have been with women before," replied Lisanne. "Does that make you feel more comfortable?"

"Not really. You are particular about punctuality, and I am particular—very particular—about people I might get emotionally involved with. I don't want to be some experiment for you."

"Is that why you think you are here?" asked Lisanne. "As an experiment?"

"Who knows why rich people do anything?"

Lisanne leaned forward and looked into Osa's dark deep eyes. "I am very attracted to you."

"Have you ever maintained a serious long-term relationship with a woman?"

Lisanne hesitated, but answered truthfully. "I have not."

Osa nodded, her eyes scrutinous. "Do you see why I'm asking you this? Why I question your motives?"

"I understand your apprehensions."

"I was planning to ask you after dinner, but this place—these people—I just had to say something. I couldn't wait."

Lisanne looked at the maroon carpet and nodded slowly. "My feelings are difficult to verbalize—I am not sure that I fully understand them myself—and they will sound…strange."

Osa silently awaited a better answer. It was clear that the evening would not continue until her fears were allayed.

Lisanne looked into her date's suspicious eyes and nodded her head. "In graduate school, I had an affair with a married woman who was a professor at the university I attended. Three years later, while on a tour in Europe, my first husband and I invited another woman into our bed. She and I continued to see each other privately and this ultimately led to the end of my marriage, though the relationship with her ended not long afterwards. Since then, I have found myself in relationships with men. No—I should not phrase it so passively. I chose relationships with men and have more good memories than bad ones."

"So what's different now? You get tired of football and screwing?"

"My sister died two and a half years ago. Since—" Lisanne's voice cracked. "Verflucht...I will not cry." She paused for a moment and gathered herself. "I miss talking to her, and I miss the things we made together."

Disbelief widened Osa's eyes and lips. "You're looking for a replacement for her? That's why you're taking a woman out to a romantic dinner? Do you realize how—"

"I am not looking for a replacement," Lisanne said, her perfectly modulated voice six decibels louder and meaner than she meant it to be. "Ellenancy and I were the Sisters Breutschen: We created sequentialism and together reshaped the landscape of modern music. There is no possible replacement for her as a person in my heart or as my creative partner. But there is an emptiness." She looked at Osa's face and there saw a beautiful but inscrutable mask.

Lisanne continued, "Since Ellenancy's death, I dated two men. Both relationships were light and ended in a matter of months. More recently, I dated a woman for six weeks, and although we were not well matched, she helped me realize that the thing I most needed in my life was a strong female presence. That is what I am looking for."

Osa silently ruminated upon what she had just heard.

Exposed and vulnerable, Lisanne waited for a response. She wondered why she had revealed so much to a tardy woman who capsized cars and shouted across rooms, but did not find an answer.

Osa shook her head. "This sounds like a very bad reason to skew your sexuality. And also...a little bit like incest."

Lisanne's cheeks burned scarlet.

"I'll call you, if I can digest it."

Before the surviving Breutschen sister could respond, the tall Swedish-Indian American rose from her seat, strode from the table, and—in the long black dress that was a benediction to all onlookers—walked through the living wall.

Genteel whispers rippled throughout the dining room, and a few beefy men coughed.

Lisanne looked at the sheaf on the table before her, and in its obsidian surface saw her own reflection, and the second person who was always there.

* * *

Later that evening, seated alone in the back of a cab and clutched by pseudopodia, the petite blonde said to the hunched Japanese driver, "Please take Fulton Street across town and proceed north." The suggested route was a circuitous one to her apartment in Central Park.

"Hai." He nudged a ladybug out of the way and guided the foam-rubber vehicle onto Fulton Street.

Ten minutes afterwards, she saw the cylindrical skyscraper that was the Corpus Chrome, Incorporated Building. One kilometer underground, sealed within an autonomous cryonic capsule, lay the frozen brain that was more similar to her own than any other in existence.

CHAPTER VI
THE RENTER'S GAMBIT

Claws and teeth bared, the obese feline hissed venomously as it sped toward Champ Sappline's face. The furry meteor knocked his upraised palms aside and smacked into his nose. Cartilage snapped. A spike of pain lanced his face, and he tasted fur. Thorns that were the beast's claws harassed the garbage man's ears and cheeks and chin while its needle teeth pierced his left eyebrow. A furry tail shot up his nose and triggered a violent sneeze.

The scientific foe known as gravity combated Architect's tenuous grasp and pulled. The fat feline fell from Champ's head.

"Um," R.J. the Third said as his pet thudded upon the carpet.

Uninterested in the carnage that it had wrought, the cat returned to its master.

Something red dripped from above, and soon, Champ realized that the source of the fluid was not the ceiling but his left eyebrow. Like a score of marathon runners who had just heard the starting gun, beads of blood traversed his stinging face.

"Do you have fleshtape?" inquired the savaged guest.

R.J. the Third—who was surveying various points centimeters above, below and upon either side of Champ's eyes—nodded and said, as if from a great distance, "I'll retrieve some fleshtape. Do you have any allergies?"

"No."

"I shall be back presently."

The popinjay in silver arose from the fur sofa and strode across the room toward a door that was adorned with an icon of a toilet that had its lid raised. Quietly, the fleximetal barrier slid into the floor, revealing a rose-hued enclosure, which R.J. the Third soon entered. The door shut behind him, its icon now depicting a closed toilet.

In the den stood Champ, his face a constellation of throbbing punctures.

He looked at the malicious culprit, but the bloated cat did not return his gaze. Instead, the beast looked at the turned-off mote aquarium as if awaiting an encore showing of *The First and Final Rocket*, or its sequel, or anything more interesting than a stupid bleeding man.

The injured party (also known as Champ Sappline) took the lily from his ear, pointed its lens at his face, double-tapped and said, "Camera: Record." The device beeped once. He extended his arm, panned the lily across his sundered visage and repeated the process from a lens distance of twelve centimeters for a more detailed view of the injuries. "Save to vault," said the garbage man. "Save to public reservoir." The lily beeped twice. Satisfied, the garbage man placed the transmitter back into his ear and bled.

The bathroom door slid into the floor, and R.J. the Third emerged, carrying a clear medical box. Architect trailed its master like a rolling boulder.

The popinjay knelt beside the garbage man and set the kit upon the silver rug. Inside the box were two tiny spray cans of sterilizer, a Perfect brand thermometer, codeine candy (with nauseous side effects to discourage recreational use), ultrasprin, antitoxin shots, vomit pills, chewable penicillin, spermicide capsules, vasectomy-in-a-bottle, abortion capsules, three coils of fleshtape, one container of gore putty and a Smart-stitch brand miniature sewing machine.

Lathered with sweat, R.J. the Third stood and inspected Champ's injuries.

"Do I need stitches?"

"No. It's mostly punctures and a couple of cuts; there aren't any significant lacerations."

"That's a pretty cute ministitch. I've never seen one that small."

R.J. the Third withdrew a four-centimeter-tall spray can that was labeled 'Germicide' and said, "Shut your eyes and hold still."

Champ closed his eyes and heard erratic hissing. The burning wound on his left ear cooled; his left eyebrow stopped throbbing, and the rips in his cheeks turned to ice. A terrible taste like brine and old socks filled his mouth.

"Yuck."

"Keep your mouth shut!" admonished R.J. the Third. The spray can hissed once more near each wound, and soon, the sterilized injuries became numb. "You may open your eyes."

Champ complied. Opposite him, the popinjay seized a coil of fleshtape from the medical kit and poked the vacuum seal, which belched. He plucked the starter, tore off a five-centimeter strip, stuck it on the garbage man's left ear and soon applied similar-sized chunks to the victim's other wounds.

R.J. the Third inspected his patient, nodded his head and gestured across the den. "You may use the bathroom to deal with aesthetics."

"Fine."

Champ stood up, wobbled momentarily (at which point R.J. the Third put gloved hands on his shoulders), said, "I'm fine," and walked across the silver carpet toward the toilet icon. The automated metal door slid into the floor, revealing a monochromatic rose bathroom. There, the garbage man trod upon porous linoleum until he reached the sink, where he stopped and looked into the mirror. Blood (mostly dry) decorated his face and neck like a doily, and patches of brownish-red fleshtape adhered to his wounds. His nose was askew.

"Shit."

"Please use the disposable cloths," R.J. the Third requested from the other side of the closed door.

Champ pulled a paper towel from the wall slit, held it beneath the faucet and wiped blood from his face and neck. He shouted when he accidentally poked his nose.

"Are you okay?" asked R.J. the Third.

"Yeah. Just touched my nose by accident. I think it's broken."

"It looks quite broken."

Champ moistened a second towel, wiped away the remainder of the blood and dropped the pink, red and rust-colored disposables into the chute that led to the building's containment tank. He then exited the room and returned to his seat in the common area, where his blood had already been wiped (or licked) off of the inflatable chair.

"Would you like some juice," R.J. the Third inquired, "or a protein drink? I have one with an iron supplement."

"I'd like the room you advertised," Champ said with precision.

The demand did not surprise R.J. the Third.

"The waiver on the front door won't protect you from any claim I make on these injuries," added the garbage man.

"I am aware of that."

"I want the room, and I want a discount."

R.J. the Third looked at Architect and said, "Bad cat!" This was the first time the feline had been reprimanded, and it huddled in globular shame. The popinjay looked up at Champ and said, "Please describe this 'discount.'"

"I get the first year for free."

"That is absurd!" shouted R.J. the Third, his eyes bulging dangerously. "Outrageous! Comically naïve." He guffawed thrice to illustrate his point. Architect, delighted, rolled on its back and pawed the air. "No lawsuit would yield thirty-six thousand globals, or even half that amount. I already have a lawyer in my employ—my cousin (who provided the voice of Fighter Jet Number Two in *The First and Final Rocket*)—and I am certain—quite certain!—that he would limit my liability to proven medical costs and thereafter delay the payment of those for three years, at which point you would get the first of ten small annual installments."

Champ dropped the litigious posturing (largely because his adversary was far more knowledgeable on the subject than was he) and said simply, "I'm the injured party here, aren't I?"

"You are—and I'd rather not have hostility between us—but I will not allow myself to be gouged. Other than your magnificently idiotic comment about *The First and Final Rocket*, you seem like the best candidate for the room."

"How about you cover my medical costs and give me three months for free?"

"That sounds fair," acceded R.J. the Third. "I'll have my cousin draft the contract by tomorrow."

Champ appraised his spherical and recumbent attacker and asked of its master, "Is Architect an altered cat?"

"No, but he's empathically conditioned to my moods. The Global Senate shut down altering a few years before he was born."

"How'd he get so big?"

"I was depressed for a while after my mom died. I slept a lot, but he binged." Architect stood up, waddled on bowed legs and affectionately rubbed his nose against R.J. the Third's left knee. "He's slimming down."

Champ surveyed the common area. "Where's the room?"

"You didn't look at it when you were in there?"

The garbage man was confused by the question. "In where?"

"In the bathroom. I thought I heard you open the trapdoor."

Champ hoped that he had misheard the man. "The room you're renting is accessed by a trapdoor in the bathroom?"

"It's quite novel, I assure you."

"Maybe I'm missing something here…but wouldn't a trapdoor from there just lead to the fifth floor?"

"It's more complicated than that."

"That's already pretty complicated," said Champ, frowning.

"The ad described the room as eclectic," defended R.J. the Third, who then looked at Architect and said, "Stay." There was a minute shifting within the aggregation of fur, fat and overtaxed bones that signified a redistribution of weight to the beast's hindquarters. "Let me show you to your dwelling," the popinjay said to his guest.

The duo walked toward the toilet icon; the fleximetal door retracted into the floor, and they then entered the rose-hued bathroom.

R.J. the Third kicked aside a sponge-wool bathmat, revealing a hinged trapdoor.

"Great," said Champ. His spirits sank to new depths as he contemplated the idea of living beneath a bathroom.

R.J. the Third yanked the burlap twine that functioned as the trapdoor's handle, and the flap yawned wide upon creaking hinges.

Champ peered inside. "Is that a rope ladder?"

"An excellent one. Go down and take a look." R.J. the Third ostentatiously motioned for his guest to descend the ladder.

Champ was mortified by the fact that he was not too mortified to examine the room.

51

He descended into darkness. The moment that his feet hit the floor, an amber light illuminated, and he saw that the room was a kitchen. Beside an empty spice rack lay a new mutable mattress that looked rather comfortable. A mote aquarium sat atop an ancient gas stove, and a refrigerator with no door was filled with sweaters, mittens and corduroy pants.

"That's my winter clothing in the icebox," R.J. the Third remarked from the bathroom above, his voice huge and reverberant. "I shall remove my belongings prior to your residency. You may use my old m.a. if you wish—it still works."

The room was saturated with the smells of grandfathers, yet it was larger and cleaner than Champ had expected it to be. One small window faced an alleyway, and on the opposite wall stood an old hinge door, which had been welded shut and also barricaded with mismatched (and sloppily affixed) wooden planks.

R.J. the Third climbed down the rope ladder, wiped dust from the soles of his bare feet and looked at Champ. "Do you like it?"

"It's fine. But how is this not the fifth floor? You live on six, and this is down one flight."

"Physically, this is the fifth floor. Technically, this is the sixth floor. We acquired it in fifty-three."

"What are you talking about?" said Champ, utterly perplexed. He pointed to the sealed-off door and asked with rising perturbation, "And what the hell is that barricade for?"

"There is a war between the fifth and sixth floors of this building."

"War?"

Chapter VII
Lanced

A private air shuttle owned by Steinberg, Goldman, Taliq, Shabiza and O'Brien, LWC floated over a landing ground in northern Florida. From the aircraft's undercarriage, a foam-rubber car dropped like an egg from a hastily snatched hen. Magnetic repellers hummed, ensuring that the vehicle's twenty-meter fall was neither faster nor more impacting than that of a parachutist. Within the descending vehicle sat Alicia Martinez, a sheaf-filled attaché case on her lap.

She ruminated.

The air shuttle flung back whence it came the moment the wheels of the foam-rubber car touched the pavement.

"Mrs. Alicia Martinez has landed," Isaac said into his lily as he sped the vehicle toward a multi-tiered causeway. The young man, an efficient driver and clerk (and Morton Goldman's nephew), glanced at the sheer face of his passenger in the bottom corner of the windshield and asked, "Mrs. Martinez, would you like to eat something prior to your meeting? I have a list of highly rated restaurants that feature your favorite foods and also guaranteed service times."

"It's too early. I'd rather eat after the meeting."

"Yes, ma'am," he said, like a soldier. "I shall drive to the mansion directly."

"Danke."

Alicia ruminated.

Mrs. Dulande had almost died last night. Prior to the episode, the wealthy widow's doctors had estimated that she had three or four months to live; now they spoke of her life in terms of days.

Every person at Steinberg, Goldman, Taliq, Shabiza and O'Brien, LWC was very, very, *very* aware that had the woman died, their client, Corpus Chrome,

Incorporated, would have lost nearly twenty-five billion globals. Alicia had volunteered to fly out to Florida the next morning, review the document with Dulande's legal team, and, once it was approved, witness the fingerprinting.

Looking through the window at the sunlit city flitting past, she ruminated.

In her attaché case, Alicia Martinez carried two versions of the contract.

The contents of both voluminous sheaves were identical and letter-perfect, but for one discrepancy—a small-print clause created by Mrs. Dulande's rather mediocre legal team (Wittigan, Nyung-Jones and Hostler) that did not allow Corpus Chrome, Incorporated to seize any portion of the Dulande estate until after the re-bodied murderer had been declared mentally capable. Two weeks ago (when Mrs. Dulande was far healthier), the old woman's attorneys had inserted the clause to hasten the resurrection; but if Mrs. Dulande died prior to her son being declared capable, the clause would inadvertently create a window during which the Dulande estate would have no legal claimant. In this period of limbo, the notoriously aggressive Florida State inheritance attorneys could seize the unclaimed billions with talons outstretched, happy to redistribute the hoarded old money into their myriad social programs (minus the twelve percent the Global Senate claimed from all transactions).

In the first contract, the Dulande attorneys' error remained uncorrected, and because the small-print clause was not an actual change, it was not highlighted for review and would likely be overlooked by its authors. In the second contract, Alicia had deleted the faulty clause and in its place detailed a secure escrow account in which the money would be held until Derrick W.R. Dulande was declared mentally capable (a relative thing, in his case).

Houses and buildings swept past; a ladybug and a box truck nudged each other in and out of the right lane as the conflicted woman ruminated.

If she killed this deal, there was a very good chance that CCI would terminate its relationship with the firm and sue them for negligence. A lot of decent people with whom she worked would suffer, and several lives might be ruined.

Alicia had discussed her dilemma for three ulcerative nights with Sammy, her thoroughly wonderful husband. He said that he would support her decision either way, but he did not offer any advice. There was pain for her in either choice, and he did not have the stomach to guide her toward one agony or the other.

The righteous decision would throw her life, Sammy's life and Alicia Jr.'s life into upheaval, and hurt many other people for whom she cared. But the alternative, allowing CCI to re-body this loathsome man, was an injection of poison directly into the veins of her soul, and an act that rendered any claim that she had ever made about bettering the world a risible and empty vocalization.

Buildings sped past, and she ruminated.

The conflicted attorney imagined her four-year-old daughter seated in front of a mote aquarium, watching a news broadcast of the historic case—the one in which her mommy gave an executed rapist and murderer a second life.

Alicia made her terrible choice.

"Fuck them."

"Pardon me...?" inquired Isaac.

"I was just talking to myself."

The driver steered onto an off-ramp, guided the car to an intersection and thumbed the brakes. A stopwall lurched up from the ground; opposing traffic sped past, right to left. Alicia felt disembodied...as if she were watching someone else—a strange but familiar woman—throw her entire life onto the altar of her beliefs. She was scared for this woman, but she cheered for her.

"You'll show those assholes."

Isaac pretended not to hear her.

* * *

The road ahead led to a ten-meter-high granite wall that stretched beyond seeing in either direction, and in the exact middle of the forbidding barbican roared a waterfall. Alicia recognized the famous entrance to the Dulande estate, and felt a mixture of contempt and awe regarding the ostentatious display of wealth. When the car was less than half a kilometer away, she descried two occupied nests of bald eagles atop the wall; the birds' white heads and hooked beaks were unmistakable even from a distance.

The car sped toward the waterfall, and the thunderous cascade grew, filled the windshield and parted.

Beyond the barbican, Isaac navigated a driveway that wended through orange groves, an avocado orchard, a deciduous forest and a coniferous forest. The road became a marble bridge that leapt over a pit occupied by skulking white lions.

"This is obscene," remarked Alicia.

The car sped past ninety crescent-shaped ponds filled with fish that sparkled like costume jewelry.

Then the vehicle wended its way through a grove of golden weeping willows within which scores of white deer flitted.

Alicia found the grounds stunning and appalling—and wholly divorced from mankind. It was easy for her to imagine how Derrick W.R. Dulande—genetically imbalanced and raised as a god by holiday parents—had become something inhuman.

The mountainous blue-gray Dulande mansion filled the windshield. Upon its marble façade sat three hundred prismatic windows; their etched panes cast shaped rainbows into the air.

"What assholes," opined Alicia.

Double doors, seven meters tall and made from burnished redwood, opened on automated hinges, and a buoyed skiff with a gold balustrade emerged from the mansion, driven by a man in a blue-gray suit. The standing pilot flew the vehicle towards Alicia (apparently the Dulandes had an ultramagnetic network buried beneath the tuffgrass) and extended his right arm in salutation.

Alicia decided to hate him.

Isaac thumbed the brakes, and the vehicle halted. "Have a good meeting, Mrs. Martinez."

"Danke."

Alicia pressed the release button, and the pseudopodia retracted from her waist and shoulders. Isaac opened the door remotely.

The attorney stepped outside and was struck by moist Florida sunlight.

"Konnichiwa," said the handsome skiff pilot. The craft, suspended half a meter above the tuffgrass, glided toward the attorney.

"Konnichiwa," replied Alicia.

"My name's Olaf Jarle. I am the senior executive vice president of the mansion's interior staff."

"That's more like a butler or a maid?"

The man forced a smile and replied, "I oversee all duties that affect the interior. How much do you weigh?"

"Fifty-three kilos."

"Are you wearing any free metal?"

"No. And the contents in my case are shielded."

Olaf twisted the lift dial counter-clockwise; the platform sank and settled upon the ground. The handsome man motioned for her to stand beside him.

Alicia stepped onto the skiff, where she gripped the gold balustrade with her right hand and held her attaché case with her left. Olaf twisted the dial clockwise; the tuffgrass dropped away.

The craft wobbled.

With a look of consternation upon his face, Olaf inquired, "Are you certain that you weigh only fifty-three kilos?"

"Yes." Alicia was positive.

"Well, this is odd. Perhaps the skiff needs to be recalibrated?" The handsome man tweaked the dial another notch in a showy manner, unnecessarily furrowing his brow in feigned befuddlement. Soon, the platform levitated to the proper flying height—half a meter above the ground—and stabilized. "Please mind your balance," he said as he tapped the top of the guidescreen. The fans embedded in the back of the platform whirred, and the craft surged forward.

Wind chilled the sweat upon Alicia's face as she glided toward the burnished redwood doors.

"Cutthroat Cheung awaits you in the parlor."

The attorney did not like any of the information contained in that sentence. Soon, the redwood doors swung wide, and the skiff glided from the sunshine into the comparatively dark entrance hall.

"Why is Cutthroat Cheung here?" Alicia asked, as her pupils tried to arrange and identify the dim shapes that sped past.

"He is the head of Mrs. Dulande's legal team."

Apprehension prickled the attorney's nape. "What happened to Wittigan, Nyung-Jones and Hostler?"

"They were fired this morning," said Olaf, as if the news were of trifling interest.

Alicia's stomach sank, and she squeezed the balustrade to steady herself.

Wittigan, Nyung-Jones and Hostler had handled all of the Dulandes' contracts for the past three decades, and—more importantly—they had authored the flaw in the document that was its undoing. A pair of fresh eyes—especially the evil onyx slits of Cutthroat Cheung—would have a far, far greater chance of noticing the faulty clause. The abrupt termination of Wittigan, Nyung-Jones and Hostler indicated that their error had been descried—very likely by the loathsome lawyer who had replaced them.

For the second time that day, Alicia Martinez made a terrible decision: She would facilitate the deal.

The skiff glided past one hundred and twenty marble pillars, each wound with a spiral of gold. For some reason, the vast enclosure smelled like rose water.

"Is this not a marvelous home?" asked Olaf.

Discomfited and preoccupied, Alicia nodded.

"You look pale. Are you feeling ill?"

"I'm just awestruck."

The skiff glided through a room with green parrots, a room with red parrots, a room with blue parrots, and then five galleries, the walls of which were covered with Renaissance artwork. Alicia imagined Derrick W.R. Dulande in a model 8M chromium mannequin, walking these halls, admiring oil paintings and listening to talking birds, while the bodies of the women he had raped and killed rotted in their graves.

"The parlor is northeast of here," Olaf informed his passenger (who was annoyed that he used a compass direction inside of a house). He then tapped the top right side of the guidescreen, and the skiff veered in that direction.

Oriental rugs scrolled underneath the craft as it flew toward an open entranceway.

The room beyond was awash with bright sunlight that rippled weirdly.

Olaf tapped the center of the guidescreen thrice and twisted the dial counterclockwise; the skiff slowed, sank to the rug and landed.

Alicia stepped out of the craft and strode into the parlor. The burnished-wood walls of the room were covered with landscape paintings that featured boats and lighthouses and waterside tableaux. Reclining upon a satin divan on the far side of the room was a man who wore a dark green suit and glossy shoes.

"Seize it," rasped Cutthroat Cheung.

A black man, whom Alicia had not noticed, grabbed the handle of her attaché case and pulled it from her grip.

"Give me that!"

The woman reached for the purloined item, and the thief swung it beyond her reach; she swept her open palm at his face, and he retreated to safety.

Suddenly, the black fellow pointed something at her face and said, "I am a pol—"

Alicia lunged at the man. A light flashed in her eyes, and a screaming headache erupted in her skull. She stumbled into darkness, unable to see anything but the luminous blue skull that shone in her mind's eye.

"You fucking lanced me! What the—"

"I am a police officer acting within full jurisdiction of the law," said the black man. "The migraine pen I lanced you with was set on one skull. If you come at me again, you'll get two skulls. That'll put you on the floor and make you soil yourself."

Alicia's sight returned, but the skull seared into her retinas was superimposed over what she saw. She looked at her squat assailant: He wore a black uniform and a police badge that transmuted from a clenched fist to an outstretched helping hand twice each second. His grips were tight upon her attaché case and the migraine pen.

"The afterimage will go away in about twenty minutes," informed the officer.

"I can't believe you lanced me. That attaché—"

59

"Any attempt you make to reclaim this property will result in an obstruction charge, and any physical contact with me not initiated by me will be considered an assault."

"On what legal grounds can you seize my goddamn attaché case?"

The rasped reply came from the other side of the room. "The attaché case is property of your firm, as are the documents therein."

"They transferred the rights to you?"

"Temporarily."

"Why?" asked Alicia, rubbing her temples.

"I accused your firm—and you in particular—of obstructing the deal," said Cutthroat Cheung. "Your firm denied my allegations and yielded control of all related documents as a show of good faith. You may call your colleagues if you doubt me."

Alicia did not need to check with the firm. "You could have simply asked me for it."

Cutthroat Cheung did not respond to this suggestion.

"I have personal property in there as well," she essayed.

"What property?"

"Personal."

"Is it imperative that you retrieve these articles directly? If so, the officer and I will sort through the contents, and you can identify your—"

"Forget it."

From the divan across the room, Cutthroat Cheung rasped, "Please join me," as if a dim sum cart were about to roll by with steaming bundles.

Alicia strode across the Grecian rugs. The sunshine that lit the enclosure poured through the ceiling aquarium in rippling veils, and the shadow of a stingray drifted alongside her like a bat familiar.

Cutthroat Cheung motioned for her to sit upon an uncomfortable wooden chair opposite his luxurious divan.

Pallid and uneasy, but with hate in her eyes, Alicia sat and faced the rasping lawyer.

The Chinese fellow, supine upon the divan, observed her coolly. His dark green collarless suit emphasized the red scar that laterally bisected his neck, and his narrow, gruesomely pockmarked face admitted no identifiable human emotions. He was a very rich man and could have fixed his epidermal anomalies, but he chose not to—perhaps for effect, or perhaps because he did not at all care about his appearance.

"Why are you so protective of your attaché case?" he asked.

"The Chinese own too much already."

Cutthroat Cheung did not reply, but instead looked to the far side of the parlor. Alicia followed his gaze. Near the entrance of the room, the officer placed her purloined property upon an antique table, dialed a code into the lock and twisted the release nodule. The attaché case buzzed discordantly, flashed red lights, honked eight times and burped.

"She changed the code," explained the policeman, rather unnecessarily.

Cutthroat Cheung looked at Alicia. "What's the code?"

"There are only ten trillion possibilities."

From across the room, the officer inquired, "Should I try to get this thing open?"

"Do not. Forced entry would jeopardize the contents." Cutthroat Cheung returned his attention to Alicia. "Do you refuse tell us the code?"

"It's not all ones or zeros."

The rasping lawyer leaned over and pulled a legal sheaf from an accordion folder. "This is the contract I drafted this morning," he said as he placed the document into the woman's hands. "Screen sixty-three shows the most significant change."

Alicia dialed to the aforementioned page. The faulty clause had been replaced: There would be no window for the state to seize the inheritance.

Cutthroat Cheung rasped, "If your documents are unavailable, we may use this contract to close the deal."

Alicia said nothing. The shadow of a swordfish slid across the floor and over Cutthroat Cheung's folded hands. In the passing darkness, a partial afterimage of the migraine pen shone in Alicia's mind—the skull's giant white teeth.

For twenty-six minutes, she scrolled through sheaf screens, carefully and expertly reading every word. The document was precise. Everything seemed in order, until she reached page seventy-eight.

"This isn't what my client agreed to." The division of the Dulande estate had been altered: Corpus Chrome, Incorporated was to receive ninety rather than ninety-seven percent.

"Those are the terms of the new contract," said Cutthroat Cheung.

"CCI will not agree to this."

"That is the only contract I have." The Asian fellow looked meaningfully at her attaché case upon the table. "Provide another one or I will submit this to your firm while you concoct reasons why you are here without a contract."

Alicia knew that she had no option but compliance. Quietly she said, "I'll open the case."

The woman stood up and walked across the room, where the officer leveled his migraine pen at her face while she typed the code, twisted the nodule, opened the attaché case and selected the corrected document.

Instantly, the policeman claimed the other contract.

Alicia walked over to Cutthroat Cheung and put the amended sheaf in his hands. He scrolled through the screens in half the time it had taken her to peruse his contract, fingering the ropy scar on his neck in a way that seemed almost sensual. Upon the rug between them slid the shadows of three eels swimming in tandem.

Cutthroat Cheung set the contract upon his lap, nodded and extended his right hand; the policeman handed him the other sheaf.

"That's the previous draft," she said weakly.

The rasping lawyer scrolled directly to the faulty clause and looked at it for the duration of time that it took him to caress his scar twice. "Both contracts are locked and ready to print," he said, "and both bear today's date." The Asian fellow looked up at the woman and asked, "Do you wish to utter more lies, or shall you end it there?"

Alicia knew that her career was over. "Fly in somebody else to witness this deal—I won't have anything to do with it."

"Fine."

Cutthroat Cheung, unconcerned, leaned his head back, looked at the fish in the ceiling and double-tapped his lily. "Connect me to Steinberg, Goldman, Shabiza, Taliq and O'Brien." The shadows of tiny fish slid over his face like bacteria seen through a microscope.

Alicia rose from her chair and turned toward the door; her stomach sank at what she saw.

Recumbent in a magnetically buoyed bier at the parlor entrance was Mrs. Francine Junille Dulande, the withered, one-hundred-and-six-year-old matriarch of the sprawling estate. An attendant in medical green stood on either side of the transport.

Alicia looked away from the ancient woman, circumvented the bier, strode into the hall and there looked for the skiff that had carried her hither. The craft was absent.

"I called Olaf: He'll be here soon," the old woman said from behind Alicia. "May I speak with you for a moment? Please?"

Alicia turned around, and the attendants spun the bier so that the old woman faced her directly.

"I'm sorry," said Mrs. Dulande.

Alicia said nothing. She would neither accept the apology nor display her anger—either reaction would give the ancient enemy some satisfaction or relief or closure, and Mrs. Dulande deserved none of these things.

Inscrutable and removed, Alicia observed the dying woman.

Upon the bier's gelatin cushions, and beneath an aerating plasma blanket, which had been decorated with a giant cursive *D,* lay Mrs. Dulande, curled on her side like a cold animal, her compressed spine bent like a cane, her skeletal right hand clutching the rail, and her other digits secreted in the front pocket of her silken blue robe, the surface of which had a sheen similar to that of her sagging skin, which was itself two dozen times pierced by autonomous fluid engines that inhaled her old blood, spat it through twenty levels of filtration and returned it to the green veins that wound through her tissue and muscle into her pale head, which had bright blonde hair, ears that had been cut and reshaped to hide the woman's age, a corrected nose, and an almost imperceptible coating of sheer facial fuzz.

The crone shivered.

Agonized blue dots shone within the congregation of wrinkles and focused on Alicia. "I'm sorry about what just happened to you," creaked Mrs. Dulande. "What happens to a person of integrity in this world."

"I'm uninterested in your sentiments."

The buried eyes appraised Alicia for a moment. Three fluid engines sucked blood from the woman's right shoulder and spat it back into her body. A valve upon her downy nape hissed like a locomotive engine.

Mrs. Dulande shuddered and then cleared her throat. "I understand why you think harshly of me."

Alicia turned away from the grotesque thing that lay before her and looked up the hall for the summoned skiff.

"You have a child of your own," said the ancient matriarch. "A four-year-old girl, correct?"

Alicia was surprised that Mrs. Dulande knew anything about her.

The dying woman continued, "Every mother makes an exception of her child. That is what it means to be a mother."

Alicia faced her adversary. "Your son is an abomination."

Bones clicked as Mrs. Dulande nodded her pale head in agreement. Two fluid engines withdrew dark blood and returned it to her system, bright and medicated. "You have no idea how Derrick's crimes have burdened me," whispered the old woman, her blue eyes sparkling.

"If you'd mothered him properly, this might not have happened."

"I know."

"And Jessica Reynolds-Tam, Lana Pearlman and Rena Takahata might still be alive."

"I know." A tear plopped upon the gelatin cushion beneath the old woman's head, and a feeble anger constricted her right hand. "My-my Derrick…he was…a terrible person."

"Then why are you bringing him back?"

"People change and—"

"He didn't," said Alicia, indisputably.

"I doubt that there could be a more transformative experience than dying."

Alicia saw the skiff speed up the hallway, guided by the handsome hands of Olaf.

Mrs. Dulande continued, "That's my hope—that he will be…better. Better than he was." A fluid engine administered two cubic millimeters of dexaprine

64

into her spine, and she nodded her head.

At that moment, the inchoate plan in Alicia's mind crystallized.

"My hope is different," the attorney said, her voice strong and clear. "My hope is that I can appeal this case on behalf of the families of the victims and have your son executed a second time."

Horror filled the mucoidal eyes of Mrs. Dulande. "You can't. The courts—they will never allow it."

"There are no precedents for any of this, but I will do my best to set one."

Alicia turned away and boarded the skiff. When she was ten meters off, she heard the sound of the old woman sobbing, and found herself moved to tears despite her anger.

Chapter VIII
The Joys of Incest

Lisanne stepped from a foam-rubber cab and strode toward the entrance of The Pinnacle, a one-hundred-and-ninety-floor turquoise and patina skyscraper that was located directly in the middle of Central Park. (Since the destructions of the Empire State Building and One World Trade Center, this structure and the Corpus Chrome Incorporated Building had become the two most recognizable parts of the Nexus Y skyline.) The surviving Breutschen twin soon arrived at the entrance, pressed her fingertips to the placard and walked through the central living wall, exchanging damp blue dusk for a mustard-colored lobby that was dry and smelled of lemongrass.

She walked past the head concierge and six attendants (they did not greet her because she had informed them that she did not engage in small talk) and was surprised to see, seated upon a plush gelbench, the supremely beautiful American woman of Swedish and Indian descent who had walked out on her three nights earlier.

Osa looked up and said, "Hi." Her slickwax overcoat was beaded with precipitation from the flash storm that had swept through Nexus Y twenty minutes earlier.

"Hello," replied Lisanne, guardedly.

Osa looked down at her fingernails. "Can we…um…talk?"

"Of course. There are a number of bars and cafes within the building, and about twenty restaurants that—"

"I'd rather go someplace private. It's already awkward enough."

"We could talk in my apartment," proffered Lisanne.

The tall beauty nodded. "That would be fine. Is it the penthouse, or something like that?"

The petite blonde owned three floors of The Pinnacle (two of which were recording studios) but did not want to seem pompous, and so said modestly, "I have a nice space."

"Okay. Let's go there."

They traversed the mustard lobby and reached a bank of twenty-six elevators. Lisanne touched her fingertips to the wall, and a fleximetal door retracted.

The quiet women walked forward and sat in foam-rubber seats that faced each other within the graduated glass elevator. Silently, the fleximetal door sealed the enclosure. Pseudopodia secured their waists, and a female voice with a light French accent said, "Resident L. N. Breutschen: floor one hundred sixty-eight. Rate of ascent: medium."

The elevator shook, and the green park fell away.

"I'm sorry about running off the other night," announced Osa. "I was just... overwhelmed. I had no real right to question you that way. To question your...your...."

"Authenticity?"

"I had no right. It was unfair to judge you like I did. And rude."

The canvas of tuffgrass outside shrank. Tall buildings encroached upon its perimeters like advancing armies.

It was clear that Osa was not done speaking—her long fingers twirled in her lap continuously as if shaping invisible taffy.

The two women transcended forty floors in silence.

Looking at the park, the tall beauty resumed, "Lots of dykes I know started to explore women because of bad experiences with men—really awful shit—when they were little or teens or whenever. Your reasons for your feelings—for wanting to connect with a woman—aren't less legitimate than anybody else's. Even if it seems a little weird, you're self-aware and are moving toward something you miss—something positive in your life that's now gone."

"You have thought about this."

"Yeah," said Osa, as a score of buildings sank behind her shoulders.

Lisanne remarked, "I thought it was sweet when you accused me of incest."

The window of Osa's lips framed a smile. "Thank you for not being a bitch about this."

"I have been on very few formal dates in my lifetime—none with women— and I do not know how to go about it. I was probably too candid."

The sinking skyline was abruptly eclipsed by the woman of Indian and Swedish descent as she leaned forward and pressed her lips to those of Lisanne. Carrying the flavors of lime, cranberries and vodka, the tall beauty's tongue slid into the petite blonde's mouth. Lisanne's ears crackled from the elevation change, and her entire body warmed. Reaching up, she touched Osa's smooth cheeks with her fingertips. Hands that were both strong and delicate ran through the pencil points of her short blonde hair.

When the women pierced the clouds, the chute turned white.

* * *

The mattress exhaled.

Dressed in a black negligee and matching socks (her feet were always cold), Lisanne lay upon her side; the weight of Osa's nude body pressed into her back, radiating warmth.

The mattress inhaled air fragrant with the smells of spice candles, and the sleeping surface rose two centimeters beneath the recumbent women.

Lisanne always had a difficult time falling asleep with a new lover beside her: She perspired inexplicably and was seized by odd itches throughout the night, as if her system was creating antibodies in an attempt to fight off a foreign invader.

The mattress exhaled air into the candlelit room, and the surface of the bed sank two centimeters.

Osa lay about Lisanne like a beautiful fortress. The tall woman's anxieties had been dispelled by the long, unhurried night of lovemaking, and now she slept deeply. At present, the petite blonde did not feel like a ghoul.

The mattress inhaled and rose two centimeters.

Lisanne relished how creative and free the experience of being with another woman was—the lack of directionality was so unlike being with a man, where things inevitably led to a specific culmination. With Osa, there were no issues of timing, nor was there a defined goal: Their explorations had lasted for three tactile, wandering hours and multiple climaxes.

68

The mattress exhaled, and sank two centimeters.

Lisanne felt: warm air issue from Osa's nostrils into her short blonde hair, heavy breasts press upon her back, two hearts beat in slow aquatic syncopation, and the curve of the tall woman's hip against her buttocks. The Swedish-Indian American was tall, and her presence was gigantic.

"I'm glad you don't want to use toys or artificials," remarked Osa, awake but groggy. "They're not really my thing."

"I am not interested in replicating heterosexual intercourse when I am with a woman."

Osa kissed her nape.

"I thought you were asleep," said Lisanne.

"I was, but I've never slept on a breathing bed before, and it keeps waking me up."

"I can turn it off—or lower the respiration rate."

"Don't. I like waking up beside you."

A hand slid underneath the hem of the petite blonde's negligee and along her stomach, and stopped at her flat chest, where a moist index finger feathered her right nipple until the bud stiffened, and she could feel her pulse within it. Long warm legs twined about Lisanne's right thigh, and Osa began to sway, her nexus damp.

The discussion had ended.

In the candlelit silence, bodies and eyes communicated.

* * *

Bright morning light poured through a sunburst-shaped window, illuminating the bedroom.

With terrific aches throughout her body, Lisanne walked toward Osa, who was still abed. The long beauty was wholly hidden beneath a beige cashmere blanket, which hewed closely to her hips and shoulders.

"Guten Morgen," Lisanne said to the curvilinear heap.

Osa grunted.

"I have made breakfast for us."

Again, the covered figure grunted.

69

"I do not speak cavewoman."

From beneath the blanket, Osa complained, "It's bright in here. I can deal with the breathing bed, but morning sunlight is definitely out."

Lisanne whistled a C-sharp and said, "Pinhole." The meter-tall malleable window narrowed to a hole three centimeters in diameter. "It is safe to come out."

"Danke." Osa pulled the covers from her squinting face and looked around like a newborn kitten unsure of the world into which it had been born. "Um…can you get me my clothes? They're kind of dirty, but I can't really eat breakfast nude."

Lisanne put a folded silk robe on the mattress. "Wear this."

"I don't think it'll fit—you're probably a size zero or something."

"I am, although I prefer to wear size two." The petite blonde pointed to the robe on the breathing bed and said, "That is a six long. I had it delivered while you were asleep."

Osa glanced at the garment and looked up, grinning. "That was really, really sweet. Thank you."

Lisanne pointed to the toilet icon on the east wall. "There is a bottle of toothscrub beside the sink."

"Great." The tall beauty sniffed the air and excitedly inquired, "What's for breakfast?"

"Eggs, salmon, crab cakes, dill cheese, black toast and veal sausage."

"Danke, Fraulein."

* * *

Lisanne sipped a quadruple espresso while Osa drank a peach mimosa. Outside the glass picture window, the sibling cities of Nexus Y and Brooklyn sat like children's toys at their feet. Two birds, a hasty cloud, an escaped balloon and a police airborne riot wagon sped past the pane, casting brief shadows upon the glowing faces of the women.

"I need to be in the studio in a couple of hours," said Lisanne. "A barrage metal band scheduled a session today."

"Can I watch you produce? It's okay to say no—I'd just love to see you work sometime."

"You would be a distraction."

"For who—I mean, for whom?"

"Everyone with eyes—especially me." The petite blonde thought of the other woman's hands gripping her ankles…of straddling her strong thighs…of her taste.

"You're blushing," said Osa.

"The espresso makes me warm."

"Now you're blushing more."

Underneath the buoyed table, a long foot sluiced up Lisanne's calf and across her inner thigh. Osa grinned as if she were aware of—yet not responsible for—her foot's actions.

* * *

After they had twined once more, the two women clothed themselves, exited the apartment that wore their scents and descended to the mustard lobby.

The pair stopped in front of the living wall that led outside and looked at each other: The moment was pregnant.

"Shall I tap a cab?" inquired Lisanne.

"I'm going to walk around the park for a while—I've got today off. And tonight." This last statement was emphasized.

"The recording session will go well past midnight."

Osa looked disappointed, but did not say anything.

The petite blonde took the tall beauty's right hand. "There is no way I will enjoy a night with these egomaniacs as much as I would another evening with you, but I do not want to set a bad precedent with us."

Osa clapped her hands to the sides of Lisanne's face and kissed her as a male teenager might—suddenly and forcefully.

The tall beauty pulled back, smiled, turned around and walked through the living wall, pleased by the other woman's rather significant usage of the first person plural.

71

* * *

Lisanne tilted her head up, eyeing the giant in the wolfskin jacket who stood before her. "I know you think that you can record this music live in the studio, but you cannot."

"We play it that way all the time," said Eater of Your Eyeballs, a frown upon his granite-studded face. "Don't tell us what we can or can't do."

"That is exactly what I'll tell you. I let you try it your way, and the results are not good enough for a true-definition spherical recording, nor are they anything that I will put my name on."

Lisanne could tell that Eater of Your Eyeballs wanted to call her a cunt, but his mutterings were unintelligible.

Intestinal Noose put his hand on the irate guitarist's arm and said, "This is why we hired her."

Eater of Your Eyeballs growled in defeat, picked up his nine-string guitar (from which dangled an embalmed bald rat that had a nail in its head) and walked through the living wall.

"I'm sorry, Miss Breutschen—EYE's kind of temperamental," said Intestinal Noose, tying his steel-dyed hair back into a ponytail. The drummer seemed like a shy, effeminate boy who found confidence and masculinity in his fashion choices and musical identity.

"We need to record the drum tracks first," Lisanne informed the percussionist.

"Okay."

"Your eleventh and twentieth tom-toms are not correctly tuned."

"I'll fix them," said Intestinal Noose as he walked through the wall into the suspension sphere, where his drum kit sat upon the intersection of four catwalks, surrounded by amplifiers that pointed up, down, left and right.

King Cancer, Unspeakable Intentions and Satan's Amazing Father entered the mixing room, vapor tubes wedged in between their fingers and lips; the young men were uniformly distinguished by granite studs, wolfskin jackets, black jeans and steel-dyed hair.

Lisanne pointed at the short lead singer. "Do not inhale vapors—they will affect your vocal cords."

"Sorry, Miss Breutschen," said King Cancer. He secreted the offending tube and, accompanied by the bassist, entered the suspension sphere.

"I'm a really big fan of your music," Unspeakable Intentions said to Lisanne. "So's Satan's Amazing Father."

"I am pleased that you enjoy my work."

"I studied sequentialism in music school—my thesis narration was on you and your sister, and I even wrote a piece of sequentialism, though I'm sure you'd hate it. I don't know if you can tell, but you're a big influence on our music."

"I hear the influence." Lisanne had heard a few purloined melodies as well, but found that they sounded charming in the context of barrage metal.

"Are you going to do more pieces—by yourself?" he asked, oblivious of how personal an inquiry this was.

"I do not know," answered Lisanne, honestly. She then looked through the window into the suspension sphere and remarked, "You boys need to tighten up the departure section in 'The Sound of Twelve Men Getting Crushed in a Soviet Printing Press.'"

"Yeah—that's where we came apart." Unspeakable Intentions left the room and joined his metallic comrades within the sphere.

The band practiced the rather difficult bit of polyphony in which the four guitarists played completely different riffs in different time signatures that interlocked once every twelve seconds.

"Eater of Your Eyeballs is late at the joining," remarked Lisanne into the microphone that fed into their earplugs.

The man cursed.

"Play it again from the top," she ordered.

The petite producer watched the seven men expel their furies as the tall beauty's eyes and lips and hair and neck and arms and hands and fingers and nipples and nexus and buttocks and thighs and feet and toes pulled at her thoughts.

Lisanne yearned wonderfully.

CHAPTER IX
GARBAGE AND WAR

A foam-rubber car bounced off the front of the thundering orange and green garbage truck, veered into a bubble moped and bumped into a box van. Mikek cackled as he watched the accidents accumulate upon the frontview, rearview, and sideview octagons that comprised his bugview windshield.

"That wasn't nice," said Champ, seated in the sucker's seat directly behind the driver, observing the carnage.

"I ain't nice," admitted Mikek. "You can even ask my momma."

"Don't really need to ask anybody."

Of the three men with whom Champ sucked garbage, Mikek was the smelliest, the fattest, the rudest and the meanest, yet somehow, he was happily married and the father of two irrefutably lovely girls.

The driver eased the steering staff to the left, and the garbage truck turned onto Ninth Avenue.

"You see her?" said Mikek; he pointed a stubby finger adorned with silver hair at the bugview windshield. "You see that dairy?"

Champ looked at the indicated octagon and saw a brunette woman clothed in tight-laced jeans and a leather vest. "I see her."

"I'd hit her with the truck." This was the phrase that the porcine driver uttered whenever he wanted to compliment a woman.

"I'm sure she'd be flattered."

"Run right over her." Mikek clapped his hands together and then reclaimed the steering staff. "Flattened."

The garbage truck sped up the street, and the woman shrank in the rearview octagon until she became indiscernible pixels. A red light on the dashboard map blinked, indicating a full canister.

"Shit on shit," said Mikek, who was never happy about sucking garbage. He thumbed the accelerator, jerked the steering staff and nudged a foam-rubber ladybug out of the way. The fellow then snorted, satisfied by the small car's discomfiture, as if he had just attained some long-sought revenge.

"People're always making garbage," complained the driver.

"Yup."

The truck swept past a yellow traffic orb and toward a loaded orange cylinder, which was two meters tall and half as big around. Mikek steered the vehicle into the niche beside the receptacle (he was an expert driver) and thumbed the brakes.

Dressed in a bright orange suit and hard boots, Champ opened his door and walked to the rear of the truck, where he dialed his passcode into the 'Dissolvent Authorization' placard, grabbed the nozzle of a juice hose and dragged it to the canister.

"Any bodies in that one?" the plump fellow asked, and then laughed. Sergio had found a corpse in a canister three months ago, and the grisly discovery had inspired Mikek to utter this joke several times a day.

Champ lifted the flap and surveyed the garbage. Bottles, wipes, a diaper, candied broccoli, soy bits, vapor tube boxes and the smell of garbanzo beans filled the receptacle. He then shut the flap, inserted the nozzle into the sprinkle valve at the top, twisted the lock, and dialed up one liter of juice.

The hose jerked briefly, like the death twitch of a snake, and fluid shot into the canister. A few pieces of metal crackled defiantly as the dissolvent broke down the disposable and biodegradable trash, but ultimately, the juice won all of its battles against rubbish.

The fans at the top of the receptacle whirred and sucked up the fumes. Champ plucked the sibling hose from the truck, pulled it to the canister, locked the nozzle to the bottom valve and waited while the garbage was rendered into what was variously referred to as twat piss, diarrhea, shit serum, shit sauce or—by polite garbage men—soup.

"Hurry it up," prompted Mikek, who was restless by nature.

"I'm not an alchemist."

The canister light illuminated. Champ walked to the rear of the garbage truck and turned on the straw; the soup was sucked into the vehicle's containment tank where it was stabilized with an antacid.

Twenty seconds later, he unplugged the hoses, locked the canister valves, replaced the nozzles and clambered back into the vehicle.

The garbage truck prowled.

Champ found the simple acts of condensing, consolidating and disposing of waste satisfying in a way that his executive job at Golden Opportunities had never been. His ex-wife had been appalled when he explained his philosophy to her over the phone, but he was not lying about how he felt. His job, his derided occupation, made an actual, physical difference in the world. If he could not make people laugh for a living, at least this job effected some positive change in the world.

"A lot of twat piss in that one," said Mikek, tapping the gauge on his dashboard. (The quantity of reduced soup varied significantly, depending upon the contents of the canister.)

"Yup," said Champ, satisfied.

* * *

Twilight in Nexus Y was a jumble of buildings, people and vehicles etched in gold by the falling sun. Upon Tenth Avenue, the plasticore garbage truck menaced, dragging its long blue shadow.

"Look at that one!" said Mikek, pointing out a curvaceous woman. As the vehicle passed the walking object, she flashed across a lateral octagon and then appeared in a rearview. "I'd really like to run her over," he said, "maybe even show her the axle a second time." A stubby finger tapped the rearview octagon, and the woman's buttocks were magnified.

Champ looked away, embarrassed.

Mikek whistled. "I'll be running over that thing in my dreams."

The man in the sucker's seat had no reply worth uttering.

A red light blinked upon the dashboard map.

"Shit on shit."

The driver reset the screen to standard bugview, coughed, sucked on the vapor tube, gauged the traffic, said, "So many foes," and nudged two ladybugs aside. "It was better when we only did pick-ups at night." He motioned expansively at his two-, four- and six-wheeled adversaries.

"The canisters fill up too quickly," remarked Champ.

"They should make more...though I guess this helps us get some overtime," said Mikek, arriving at a stalemate with himself.

Wheels whined as the driver flung the vehicle into a niche.

Champ exited the truck and noticed a score of people on the sidewalk, all of whom were looking in one direction. Following their gazes, he saw the façade of an antique bookstore.

"Hurry up," Mikek prodded, "we need to get going." Thursday evening was the end of the professional workweek, a time during which women went to parties and clubs and bars in alluring outfits that the driver needed to appraise. "It's important that we're on the road."

Champ walked the nozzle to the canister, locked it in the valve, assessed the garbage (vapor tubes, drink bulbs and soy wrappers that smelled like hamburgers) and dialed up half a liter of juice. As it squirted, he looked back at the gaping throng.

"It's coming out!" said a little girl.

"Don't say 'it,'" admonished the child's father. "There's a man inside that thing."

From the living wall of the store emerged a chromium mannequin, model 4M. The re-bodied man wore a brown suit that covered over most of his steely surfaces, yet left his flesh-colored gelware hands and face exposed; tucked underneath his right armpit was a hardback book. His lenses appraised the people watching him.

"Are y'all starin' 'cause I've got a mechanical body or 'cause I bought a book?" asked the re-bodied man, his voice tuned to a syrupy southern accent that was supposed to replicate what he sounded like in his first life. The expression on his rubbery gelware visage was an approximation of a grin.

"What are you reading?" asked an inquisitive young man.

The mannequin held up the novel. *"The Gunfighter Who Chewed Bullets,"* he said. "A classic I never got 'round to readin' the first time."

The re-bodied man waved amicably and turned west; the sun flashed upon his lenses, and the optics retracted into his head until they were shaded from flares. He walked off, his gait a wide swagger.

For the last decade, myriad stories about resurrected people had been featured in the news, yet there were only about sixty thousand such individuals worldwide. This was only the fifth time Champ had seen one in person.

As he watched the chromium Southerner amble down the sidewalk, Champ thought of his own deceased father, whose brain was a cauliflower in a Bronxland cryonics vault. The rumination made him uneasy and a little sad.

"Suck up that twat piss," prompted Mikek.

Champ attached the straw to the canister and dialed on the garbage truck's inhaler; while the vehicle ingested soup, he watched the mannequin walk into and disappear behind the living wall of a shop called "Botanist Exotique."

The crowd dispersed, and the canister gurgled.

* * *

The garbage truck fell atop its sibling, the booming impact resounding throughout the compartment. Soon, the upper vehicle's axle twisted, locking into the slot in its brother's roof, and a loud clank reverberated. Mikek flung open his door, grabbed the ladder that led up to ground level and began to climb. Champ then exited the truck, climbed onto the catwalk, connected the garbage truck's urethra to a valve in the wall and dumped the soup into the sanitation block, where it would be condensed, hypercondensed, frozen, crated and eventually dumped in outer space.

The garbage man climbed up the ladder.

Mikek was waiting for him up there, dressed in jeans and a Hawaiian shirt. "Wanna get a beer?"

"Danke, no." Champ accepted the driver's invitations occasionally—about once every other week—so that he would not give offense.

"See you Saturday."

Champ clenched his right hand and pressed his knuckles to those proffered by Mikek.

* * *

An unfunny comedian who stood upon a buoyed dais told jokes about airplanes and abortions, but few people within the darkbar paid any attention to him. One person laughed, but it was in the middle of a joke and was unrelated to the bald man's neurotic monologue.

Drunk and alone in the corner of the establishment, Champ recalled his own failed attempts at standup comedy and his busted marriage. The inebriated garbage man then made a decision that sobriety—or the advice of smart companions— would have precluded. He double-tapped his lily and said, "Connect to Candace." Flutes played in his right ear, and as he listened to his ex-wife's outgoing music, anxiety sat in his stomach like a water balloon.

"Hello, Champ," said Candace, her thin voice betraying mild apprehension.

(The two of them had not spoken in three months, and their last conversation had been unpleasant.)

"Hey there," said the garbage man with forced nonchalance.

"What is it?"

"I just wanted to let you know I found a place. To live. I found a place in the city on Monday."

"In Nexus Y? You can afford that with your…job?"

"It's a sublet." (Champ neglected to inform her that the room was a kitchen acquired in an ongoing intra-building war, and that it was accessed through a trapdoor in a bathroom.)

There was a pause that had no possible positive interpretation.

"Do you have a roommate?" asked Candace. The timbre of her voice told him that the expression on her face was one of mild revulsion.

"Yeah, but he's okay. We leave each other alone."

There was another pause, at the end of which the woman inquired, "Is this what you want?"

"It's a pretty good-sized room."

"That's not what I mean. Sucking garbage, getting drunk—I can tell you're drinking right now—and dealing with roommates? At forty-two? My father says you can still work for him at an executive level—"

"I don't want to work for Larry."

"Because of what happened to us?"

"Please don't describe your adultery like…like a rainstorm or-or some uncontrollable event that 'occurred'—that 'happened,'" said Champ, aware that he sounded bitter.

"I didn't mean it that way, but okay—fine—I'll rephrase the question: Are you turning down a cushy and lucrative position at my father's company because I cheated on you and we got divorced?"

"No."

"Seems like you are."

"You've got it backwards. The only reason I ever worked for Larry was because… because it was an easy way to provide us with the life we wanted—the life you wanted. As far as jobs go, I can't think of anything worse—anything emptier— than talking to rich people all day about where they should put their large sums of money so that they can get just a little bit richer. I hated it."

"So being a garbage man's better? Sucking soup in that bright orange suit is better?"

"The suit doesn't bother me at all. It's funny, but-but I never really think about what I look like when I'm working." (This statement was true, though not something that he had known until the moment that he uttered it aloud.)

There was a long pause.

"Candace?"

"I'm here," said his ex-wife, somberly.

"I just wanted you to know that I got a place. I felt like I should tell you."

"Okay."

Champ heard some muted foreign voices through the lily. "Where are you?"

"Kyoto."

"With Alan?"

Eventually, Candace replied, "Yes."

Jealousy lanced Champ, but he kept it from his voice. "Have a good time."

"Danke. I should be going."

The moment when they used to say "I love you" had arrived.

"So…uh…good-bye," proffered the garbage man, fumbling and weak.

"Bye. Take care of yourself."

"Sayonara."

The solitary drunk tapped his lily, sank into a fourth thermomug of hops-heavy Belgian ale and tried not to think of Alan and Candace, nude and intertwined, their silhouette a single flailing entity upon a rice-paper screen.

* * *

Impaired but upright, Champ fingered the "Antique Conditions" placard on the front door of the building within which he dwelled. He entered, climbed the stairs and stealthily crept past the fifth floor.

Looking over his shoulder for hostiles, the garbage man fingered his identity and typed in his code. The fleximetal sank into the ground, and he hastened into the apartment, shutting the door behind him.

Safe from foes, the inebriate walked past the animated posters and across the silver rug of the common area until he reached the bathroom. The door did not move, and soon, he noticed that toilet icon had its lid down.

"Shit on shit," Champ grumbled as he slumped upon an inflated recliner.

Architect sluggishly emerged from beneath the sofa, looking as if it were recovering from a night of feline debauchery. The only time that the garbage man had seen the cat behave in this languid manner was when its pompous master was asleep.

Champ returned his attention the fleximetal door, suddenly wondering who was behind it. Had the fifth-floor adversaries reclaimed their former kitchen and annexed the bathroom as well?

Suddenly, he became nervous.

The garbage man looked around the room for a weapon. Although the intra-building war was characterized as "Class II: Nonviolent; Humiliation and General Discomfiting," he did not know if perhaps the current occupant was the individual who intended to change the bloodless conflict into a bloody one.

Champ rushed into the kitchen, grabbed a fork from the wall dispenser and returned, clutching the four-tined weapon in his right hand.

He waited, listening at the door, but whoever was in the bathroom was very quiet.

Architect looked at him as if he were an idiot.

The toilet icon lid lifted, startling the garbage man. Fleximetal slid into the floor, and a topless woman whose nether region was covered by a green towel emerged from the bathroom. A lifelike tattoo of a snake sat like a gigantic wound upon her skin: Its rattle encircled her navel, its body climbed in between her breasts, its neck wrapped around her own and its head sat just below her chin. The woman's patina-dyed hair was pulled up in a tight knot, excepting a braid upon which sat two lacquered serpent skulls. It looked like she was about twenty-three years old.

The tattooed woman stopped when she saw Champ and then eyed the utensil that was clutched in his right hand. "¡Oye! Why you have this fork?" Her Spanish accent was heavy, and her tongue had been surgically cleft at least twice. "What you doing with that?"

"I didn't know…who was in there. In the bathroom." The garbage man looked at the fork, which was clutched in his right hand like a talisman, and then back at the tattooed stranger. "Are you from the fifth floor?"

"No, no, no." The woman inspected the inebriate's face for a moment. "You the new one, si?" She pointed a viridescent fingernail at his bruised nose. "You the one the cat beat up. The garbage man."

Champ lowered the fork. "That's me."

"You are not what I thought." The tattooed woman clicked the pearls that adorned her tongue tips as she appraised the blonde drunk. After some consideration, she said, "You do not seem pathetic."

"You're sweet."

"It is open for you now," said the woman, pointing to the bathroom. "You may make mierda or go to sleep."

"Thanks." There was an awkward pause, during which time Champ tried not to glance at the woman's breasts or tattoo or forked tongue. "Are you R.J. the Third's girlfriend? Something like that?"

The woman cackled. "I am not with him."

"I would've been surprised," remarked Champ. "I thought he was gay."

"Only during winter."

"That makes sense."

"I rent the hall closet from him. I am saving money to buy my own place in Brooklyn City when I graduate herpetology school."

"Herpetology?" repeated Champ. "Don't they already have the cure?"

"It is the science of amphibians and reptiles. I study them."

"Sounds dangerous."

"That is a ignorant thing to say."

"I don't mean to defame cobras or crocodiles."

"They are wonderful creatures."

"A lethal kind of wonderful."

The woman did not find the garbage man's remarks amusing.

"I'm sorry," he said, "I didn't mean to offend you. I'm an irritating drunk. I tried to do some stand-up comedy once, but all I did was annoy people."

"It is okay. Most peoples do not understand me. My father—in Madrid—he called me bruja."

"That means bitch, right?"

The student flinched. "No. It means witch."

"Sorry."

"When I left Spain, he gave me a broom."

Champ started giggling, and across from him, the woman frowned. This was a historically awkward conversation, he thought as his eyes (despite his efforts to thwart them) surveyed the student's serpent tattoo and three-pronged tongue and full high breasts.

"R.J. the Third gives me discount—it is half-price if I never wear shirts."

"That's quite an arrangement."

"Buenas noches," the woman said, and then walked toward the copper hall, revealing the tattoo of a snake skeleton that ran up her spine. The image was detailed and shaded with such precision that it looked as if it were a real, tangible thing floating outside her skin.

"My name's Champ."

The student left the room without responding, the soles of her bare feet squeaking upon the wood in the adjacent hall.

Champ walked toward the toilet icon, and as the fleximetal slid into the floor, he heard the herpetology student cry out.

"Snake girl?"

"¡Ladronas!" the woman shouted into the hall. "¡Hijos de putas! ¡Ladronas! ¡Ladronas!"

"Serpenta?" he inquired, drunkenly giggling.

The herpetology student raced back into the common area. "This is not a funny joke—they steal the closet! ¡Los cincos! Los cincos have took my room!"

The tattoo of hammers driving nails resounded from the copper hallway.

"We need to stop them!" shouted the student. "They making un barricade."

"Should we get R.J. the Third? I don't really know the rules."

"¡Pollo amarillo!"

The woman raced to the homeowner's door and slapped the chime placard; bells sounded within the bedroom.

"For what reason has my slumber been disturbed?" R.J. the Third ostentatiously inquired.

"They taking hall closet!" cried the student. "The fives!"

The door sank into the floor and R.J. the Third, wearing a silver robe and matching underwear, emerged; his black hair was askew and his bulging eyes were saturnine.

"Flank me!" ordered the popinjay, striding across the common room. The herpetology student, Champ and the spherical cat followed the roused man into the war zone.

"It is set on one skull," R.J. the Third said as he slapped a migraine pen into Champ's right hand.

The platoon halted before the closet. Upon the other side of the hinge-door, hammers fell, pounding nails.

"He's drunk," the herpetology student said of the garbage man.

R.J. the Third snatched the migraine pen from Champ's right hand, said, "Crapulous fool!" and gave the weapon to the herpetology student. The garbage man was pleased that he would not have to lance anybody.

From a large pocket in his silver robe, R.J. the Third withdrew a black cylinder adorned with a blue face that had a wavy mouth and mismatched eyes. The popinjay expediently connected a tubule to the can's spigot and—through the space between the door's bottom and the floor—slid the nozzle into the closet.

"You have ten seconds to vacate the closet before I gas you!" R.J. the Third said to his enemies.

The hammers hesitated, and Champ heard a muffled discussion.

"One!!!" shouted the popinjay, who thereafter paused dramatically.

The enemies redoubled their efforts, pounding nails, and the herpetology student clutched the migraine pen in her right hand.

"Two!!!" R.J. the Third called out as he pressed the can's ignition. Gas sprayed into the closet, followed a moment later by three heavy thuds. "Once the vapors dissipate," the popinjay said to his tenants, "we shall need to clear the battlefield."

"Toss them down to five?" asked Champ.

"Affirmative. We don't want them to regain consciousness up here—that's hangover gas and they're going to be nauseated."

The herpetology student handed the migraine pen back to the popinjay.

"Comrades, we have won out the day," announced R.J. the Third. "Tomorrow, libations!" Architect purred at the man's big feet, the sound like that of boulders rolling down a gorge.

CHAPTER X
SPOKEN INTENTIONS

"Unspeakable Intentions recommended it to me," said Lisanne, sitting down upon the leather sofa, a bulb of red wine cradled in her right hand.

Osa, recumbent on the couch, stretched her robe-draped legs across the blonde woman's lap and sipped from a cylinder of jasmine tea. "Which one's he? The bassist?"

Lisanne swallowed the floral wine, savored its ghost and shook her head. "Satan's Amazing Father is the bassist. Unspeakable Intentions plays counterpoint guitar."

"Is that the shy one—the one with a crush on you?"

"No. Intestinal Noose, the drummer, has a crush on me. Or more precisely *had* a crush on me that ended the moment you appeared in that cutaway outfit." Warmed by the memory, Lisanne tipped a splash of wine into her mouth; spices pricked her palate and the perimeters of her thoughts. "You left seven salivating admirers in your wake."

"You can keep them," said Osa, flicking her long fingers dismissively.

"No thank you. It is challenge enough keeping them in tune and on beat."

"Should I have worn something more modest? Did it make you uncomfortable?"

"As long as you are in a safe environment, you should wear whatever you want to wear."

"Even if you're not around?" inquired the tall beauty, as she played her toes upon the silk pajamas that covered the petite blonde's thighs. "I can wear a cutaway? Or a threadform?"

"As long as you are in a safe environment."

86

"Georgia wouldn't've let me do that." (Osa's ex-mate was a possessive (and occasionally violent) singer in a shriekpunk fusion band.) "You wouldn't be jealous if I wore that dress when you weren't around?"

"I would not be jealous," Lisanne replied evenly.

"Not even if other people are looking at me?"

"Looking is an impersonal action. People have the right to look at whomsoever they want."

"And if they flirt with me? That's okay too?"

"Flirting is different: Flirting is interactive and may lead toward physical and emotional connections," stated Lisanne, aware that she sounded like a scientist.

"So that would make you jealous? If I flirted with some other woman?"

"It would."

It had been three weeks since the women had first shared a bed, and they had not yet discussed the parameters of their relationship.

Osa took Lisanne's free hand and looked into her blue eyes. "So…we're exclusive, then? We're monogamous?" There was some anxiety underneath the tall beauty's smile.

The petite blonde set her wine bulb upon the table, leaned over and kissed the other woman, tasting her cool jasmine mouth. A strong fist pounded in her ribs as she withdrew, and when she finally spoke it felt as if she were setting the words directly into her lover's eyes. "Ja," said Lisanne. "We are monogamous."

"I'd been wondering…." said Osa.

"As had I." Warm relief coursed through the muscles in the petite blonde's back and neck. It was clear to her that she was already falling in love.

"You're blushing," said Osa.

"It is the wine," replied Lisanne, quite unbelievably. She then pointed to the mote aquarium and said, "We need to watch this tonight: It is on a limited reservoir."

"I hate when they do that."

CHAPTER XI
THE HOMEBOYZ OF BROOKLYN BOROUGH
(AS EXPERIENCED FROM A WARM COUCH)

Lisanne whistled a C-sharp and said, "Darkness." The dusk sky disappeared from the windows. "Load: *The Homeboyz of Brooklyn Borough.*'"

The stage of the mote aquarium filled with luminous pixels. Lisanne played her fingertips across Osa's feet and ankles and over the curves of her calf muscles while the motes—propelled by micromagnetic engines—flew to all eight corners of the set.

"Medium volume and medium brightness," instructed Lisanne.

"How long is this?" asked Osa, the flashing colors of the test pattern giving her hundreds of faces.

"I believe it is double length."

"Twenty minutes? It better be good."

The motes rendered

a panda bear. The animal doused itself with gasoline.

To the right of the soaked animal were the credits:

Burning Panda Presents…

A Period Mote Experience
Conceived, Wrought and Controlled by
the Award-Winning Master:
Jefferson Sheinwald-Jones

The credits dissolved.

The panda flicked a lighter and burst aflame. Three yelling koala bears with red firemen's helmets on their heads ran at the burning bear with hoses.

Three hundred thousand pixels dispersed and then rendered

an aerial view of Brooklyn borough. A sprawling topography of high-rises, brownstones, streets, cars, ponds and green parks.

"Your set's really, really nice," said Osa.

The mote aquarium's voice-activated pause froze the flying pixels in midair.

"I can see my building," added the tall beauty, pointing to a brownstone upon the sculpture. "Or at least, the one they built mine on top of."

"I see it," said Lisanne, nodding her head. "Resume play."

The pixels were reactivated.

The cars in the streets scrambled in all directions, bumping and careening, until they successfully spelled out the title, 'The Homeboyz of Brooklyn Borough.'
A cumulus cloud covered over the city.

Atop the white and gray curtain was the following information:

In the year 1986…

The luminous pixels dispersed and then rendered

a bad area of Brooklyn Borough. Two teenage boys—one black and one Puerto Rican—walked up the street. They each wore gigantic white sneakers, blue parachute pants, white undershirts and thick gold chains. "I am Scraz," said the black teen. "I am Rodrigo," said the Puerto Rican teen. Scraz raised his hand in the air, and Rodrigo slapped his palm against it. "We are homebrothers in Brooklyn borough," declared the teens in unison. "Back before Brooklyn was a city," added Rodrigo, winking.

"Let's go have us some corndogs," suggested Scraz. "Word," Rodrigo replied, "I love them corndogs."

"Unspeakable Intentions recommended this to you?" Osa inquired, her voice freezing the pixels.

"He did."

"As a joke?"

Lisanne admonished Osa's feet with a gentle swat.

"For some reason, for the first time in my life, I'm in the mood for corndogs."

Again, toes were chastised.

"Resume play."

The teens walked down the sodium-lamp-illuminated street. Scraz put a gigantic stereo on his shoulder and yelled, "It's time to blast the ghetto!" "Word," agreed Rodrigo.

Chapter XII
Bereft

Steam loaded with nanofilter drones hissed through tiny cracks in the purity tanks that hung from the ceiling of a subterranean room, the walls of which were covered with lichens. Alicia Martinez, in black, sat before a table upon which rested a verispectragram, a truth-descrier that looked like a miniature white metropolis. Behind the apparatus, clad in a one-piece gray uniform akin to the type janitors wore, was a humorless and hairless man of thirty. The room smelled like heated copper, incandescent light bulbs and fungus.

"What is your name?" asked the hairless man.

"You know my name," Alicia said into the floating, cilia-covered sphere that was tethered by a superconductive thread to the verispectragram.

The inquisitor said, "Some of my questions might seem arbitrary, desultory or redundant, but each one has a specific purpose and must be answered. What is your name?"

"My name's Alicia Esther Martinez."

The crystal cylinder that was nestled within the body of the machine turned blue.

"Are you married?"

"I was." The crystal cylinder turned blue. "That's why I'm here." The crystal turned lavender. "What the fuck does that color mean?"

"I ask that you answer only the specific questions that you have been asked," advised the hairless man.

"What does lavender mean?"

"It means that the analogue larynx within the machine has recognized a partial truth."

"I hate these machines," said Alicia, pointing at the verispectragram. The crystal cylinder turned blue, and nearby, spume hissed from the purity tanks.

The hairless man asked, "When was the last time you saw your husband alive?"

"Three weeks ago. The seventh of May." The crystal cylinder turned blue. Alicia thought of Sammy at the kitchen table, and she thought of her precious girl Alicia Jr. beside him. She recalled the terror in their eyes and the tears upon their cheeks and the things upon their heads. A pit larger than the universe opened up in her belly.

The inquisitor proffered a handkerchief, but the woman did not accept the cloth.

"Would you like a moment to gather yourself?"

Alicia laughed humorlessly and said, "I'd need a goddamn century to do that." The crystal cylinder turned lavender. "This thing is irritating." The crystal turned blue. "Ask your damn questions. I'm ready." The crystal turned magenta.

"I understand that this will be very painful for you, but please describe the event in detail. I may interrupt you on occasion to inquire after specifics."

The woman nodded. It felt as if she were standing on the surface of the moon, freezing, cosmic dust shooting through her body, and if she dared to open her mouth, her soul would be drawn out into the vacuum, followed by her guts. The famously intelligent and articulate individual named Alicia Martinez had been abandoned by the English language.

She was bereft.

The hairless man said, "I suggest that you start with the lunch prior to the event—there might be something relevant there…and it is an easier place to begin."

"Fine." Alicia inhaled and began, "I had a lunch meeting with Saul Feldman and Werner Kereich. I've known these two since law school, and—unlike me—they'd never moved into more profitable, less morally compelling litigation. Our immediate goal was to drag Derrick W.R. Dulande before a jury the moment he was granted autonomy, and have him put to death for a second time. After that, we wanted to establish some sort of legal framework for resurrection—we already had a lot of ideas for the jurisprudence. Toward the end of lunch, I got a call from Sammy—"

Alicia was bereft.

The universe expanded in her stomach.

"Please continue," prompted the inquisitor.

The woman cleared her throat. "Toward the end of lunch, I got a call from Sammy. He said that Mrs. Dulande had been pronounced dead—it was all over the news. This was only three days after I had been in her mansion. I thanked him for the information and told Saul and Werner about it.

"We ordered martinis.

"We paid for our food and drinks separately—these guys are frugal, and I was newly unemployed—and we left the restaurant."

Alicia thought for a moment. "I got an intercity cab and shot the tube to Brooklyn. The driver was an Asian guy, maybe Thai or Malaysian or Vietnamese. One of the darker ones that can grow a beard. I don't remember his name, though it had a lot of y's and th's in it. He pulled up in front of my building, and I tipped him."

"Why did you do that?"

"I was happy with how the meeting with Saul and Werner had gone." The crystal cylinder of the verispectragram turned magenta. "Fine. I was in a good mood because Mrs. Dulande was dead." The crystal cylinder shone blue.

"I walked up the stoop," she continued, "fingered the placard and went inside."

"Which type of waiver is the placard? Antique Conditions?"

"It's not a waiver— it's a Historical Preservation Agreement."

"Please explain what that is."

It was clear to Alicia that her inquisitor had not spent much time in Brooklyn City. "The HPA protects the brownstone portion of the building, which was built in the twentieth century. Sometimes, even earlier."

The hairless man nodded for her to continue.

"I walked up into the lobby, which used to be the roof of the original building. Near the elevator there's a bird coop where they keep some cockatoos, white ones, and a canister with seeds. I fed the birds."

"Were there any other people in the lobby?"

Alicia thought for a moment. "No."

"Is that typical in such a large building?"

"It was fourteen-thirty on a Tuesday—I imagine most people were still at work or in school or doing whatever it is they typically do."

The hairless man nodded for her to continue.

"For a couple of minutes, I watched the birds crack the hulls of the seeds and pick out the meat with their black tongues. I didn't have…I had no idea what was happening upstairs." The crystal cylinder shone blue.

"The elevator came—the one in the middle—and I got in and pushed number seventeen. I called and tried to connect with Sammy, to let him know I was almost home, but he didn't answer."

"Would you like a glass of water before you continue?" inquired the hairless man, the timbre of his voice weighted with a low note of sympathy that had previously been absent.

Alicia did not know whether or not his subtle emotional display was genuine.

"Keep your water. Let me get through this."

The inquisitor motioned for her to continue.

"I arrived on the seventeenth floor and got out." The crystal cylinder shone magenta. "Why's it doing that? I live on the seventeenth floor and got out." The crystal cylinder shone magenta. "Why the hell's that thing calling me a liar? That's where I live."

"Magenta, like lavender, indicates a partial truth," informed the hairless man. "Can you think of any reason why this statement might contain false tones?"

Alicia ruminated for a few seconds. "I live on floor number seventeen, but it's actually the sixteenth floor because of some idiotic aversion to having a floor number thirteen." The crystal cylinder shone blue.

The hairless man said, "The verispectragram can sense sublimated falsities amongst our general, casually considered truths."

"That'd be impressive if it weren't so goddamn annoying. This's hard enough—talking about what happened."

A gout of steam sprayed from the purity tank, and the lichens on the walls stank sweetly. The inquisitor waited for the woman to continue.

"So I walked down the hall," resumed Alicia. "I saw a neighbor—this bearded guy who's always walking around in shorts and sandals like a homeless man who somehow owns an apartment. Probably, he inherited it. He's carrying a plastic hydroponics kit filled with reefer and basil. He said, 'Have a good day' to me, and I said, 'Take a bath.'

"He went into his place, and I was alone in the hall. I reached my apartment—my family's apartment—touched my fingertips to the placard, dialed my code and walked through the living wall.

"I went into the den and saw that the m.a. was on—some cartoon that Alicia Jr. likes with a vampire dog. I mean, she liked."

Alicia's vision blurred, and in her wet eyes, the hairless man became an impasto stroke of paint. "There was an open shipping box on the floor," she continued, "but I didn't pay any attention to it at the time.

"I went into the kitchen and there they were…seated at the table with sandwiches on their plates. I still didn't know what was happening. Sammy said, 'Wait!,' and my daughter said, 'Mommy!' and then I saw it—the device attached to the side of her head—a piece of metal shaped like a horseshoe crab with vials of fluid on its back. A line of blood ran from underneath it down her neck. Her eyes were red from crying. There was one on Sammy's head too.

"I ran for Alicia Jr. to rip the fucking thing off, but Sammy yelled, 'Stop! It'll kill her if you try and take it off!' and I stopped. I've never felt so small, so fucking insignificant, so terrified in my entire life. I dropped to my knees and threw up.

"And then my lily rang.

"The caller was identified as the late Mrs. Dulande.

"I didn't understand what was happening—she was dead. But the lily kept ringing, and I took the call.

"The voice on the line said, 'Sit down with your family and listen to me.' It was her voice. It was Mrs. Dulande, unquestionably.

"I sat down, because what else could I do? I looked at my daughter—she was crying again—and at the thing attached to her head, at the vials that stuck out of its back filled with carbonated acid. 'What do you want?' I said into the lily, and the voice replied, 'This is a recording.'

"I sat there. Completely helpless.

"Dulande said, 'Look at your family, Mrs. Martinez,' and I looked away from them. 'Look at them and know that they suffer because of you.' I just stared at the floor, sick. 'During the latter years of my long life, years filled with far more agony and medication than joy, the only thing that balanced me was the hope that my son might someday live again and do something righteous, find redemption… or at least be happy. When you and I spoke, you declared war upon that hope. Cruelly. Maliciously. You threatened the one thing that made my existence and my coming death bearable.

"'Allow me to illustrate true hopelessness.' I looked up, and the plungers in the vials shot down. I yelled, running at my daughter, and Sammy grabbed the device from her head and yanked it off, blood and acid spraying everywhere. But it was too late. My husband and daughter fell out of their chairs, hit the floor, acid bubbling inside their—"

Alicia lost her voice, cleared her throat and continued. "My daughter looked up at me. The shape of her head started to—"

With a shaking hand, the woman took the proffered handkerchief and wiped the tears from her face. The cloth warmed, evaporating the fluid.

"The last thing I said to Sammy was, 'How could you let this happen to her? How could you!' I-I-I wasn't thinking." Alicia looked at her right hand, the skin of which was scarred by the acid that had dissolved her daughter's mind. "I regret that accusation—dumb and illogical and mean—more than anything I've ever said in my entire life."

The crystal cylinder shone blue.

Alicia sniffed, shaking her head. "That was the last thing he ever heard—that terrible accusation. I loved Sammy." The crystal cylinder turned magenta.

Fury filled Alicia, and she lunged at the white machine. Pseudopodia clasped her waist and wrists, restraining her, as two hairless women in gray hastened into the room, armed with migraine pens.

"Please calm yourself, Mrs. Martinez," said the inquisitor.

Alicia glared at the verispectragram and resettled herself.

The hairless man waved his peers away. As they departed, the extruding pseudopodia retracted, releasing their grip upon Alicia.

"Continue your account whenever you feel capable of doing so."

"Why did that fucking machine say I didn't love my husband?"

"It did not turn red, which is the indication of a falsehood. It turned magenta."

"I know—but you said that that color indicates a partial truth."

"This is a very common reading, Mrs. Martinez. With rare exceptions, love—as defined ideally in our consciousness and by society at large—is not purely realized. When people speak of love for another adult person with whom they have had various experiences, the machine almost always registers a partial truth. This is one of several unfavorable insights proffered by the verispectragram that resulted in it being barred from courtrooms, despite its accuracy."

"But magenta's worse than lavender, right? Closer to red—to a false reading? But-but Sammy and I had a very good marriage: I loved him deeply." The crystal cylinder shone magenta.

"I suggest that you continue your account," advised the hairless man. "This result is neither extraordinary nor germane, and it does not in any way affect our appraisal of you."

"It is very goddamn important for me to understand why that thing shows magenta when I say I love my husband. Can't you understand that?"

Water dripped from the purity tanks onto the concrete floor, and the hairless man nodded his head. "I understand why it matters to you."

"What color does it usually show when a person says he or she's in love?"

"The device typically displays lavender or, if the person is in the first blush of love, deep indigo. The only pure results that I have ever seen are when a parent speaks of his or her love for a child that has not yet learned to talk."

"Why did it show magenta for me?" asked Alicia.

"There are many possible reasons. For instance, in your account of the event, you blamed your husband for what—"

"But I was out of my mind at the time," protested Alicia. "I regret saying that." The crystal cylinder shone blue.

"Do you hold your husband partially responsible for what happened? Do you believe that he could have done something more than he did to save himself and your daughter?"

"He opened the package and those things leapt out. They move as fast as a person can think. Maybe faster." The crystal cylinder shone blue. "He couldn't do anything more than he did—I don't hold him responsible."

The crystal cylinder shone red.

Behind the machine, the hairless man said nothing.

Alicia Martinez stared at the luminous refutation, but did not remark upon it.

"Please resume your account whenever you feel capable of so doing."

"They were dead on the kitchen floor," Alicia continued, "their heads were…" She was unable to verbally articulate the expansion and subsequent collapse of their skulls. "I was starting to black out when the voice in my ear, Mrs. Dulande's voice, said, 'You and your associates will be killed if you pursue a case against my son. Inform them and any other like-minded individuals that death awaits those who come after Derrick W.R. Dulande. My son will be re-bodied and have a chance at life, if not redemption. I died, clasping this hope firmly to my breast.' The recording ended. I heaved bile and passed out.

"I woke up, disoriented, and had a moment where I thought I'd dreamt everything that had happened." Alicia shut her eyes and tilted her head forward. That brief period of disorientation had been the last time that she had felt something other than rage or despair. "But then I opened my eyes and saw. They were there…on the floor. Dead. It was all real."

The woman opened her eyes. "I called the police. An airborne riot wagon was at the window in six minutes, and eight officers climbed in. I told them everything, but there was nothing to do. That spiteful old crone was guilty, but she was dead and nobody else could be connected to the double homicide. Derrick W.R. Dulande was still in the mumbling phase of recovery and in no way responsible for anything that his mother did.

"What a fucking family.

"I called Saul and Werner. It was hard to talk—I kept breaking down—but I told them they had to drop the case immediately. They protested until I explained what had happened to me, to my family. They believed in the case—in our cause—but there're lots of causes and they didn't want to die for this one. They still had families and lives to live.

"I felt so fucking helpless," Alicia admitted, "like-like a baby thrown into the arctic."

"I know," said the inquisitor, nodding his barren head. There was genuine empathy in his voice and in his eyes.

"I had no family, no job, no belief in the law whatsoever, in society or anything. I needed to do something—something that was real and something that was substantial—or I would kill myself, end it all, because this fucking world is so awful. It's a place where a company like Corpus Chrome, Incorporated can exist, presiding over life and death, and where people like the Dulandes can murder people from behind walls of money. I hated it. I hated it violently."

The crystal cylinder shone blue.

"That's why I'm here," declared Alicia Martinez, eyeing the hairless man in gray.

"Many of the people in our organization share your hatred."

Chapter XIII
Holy Shits

Awake for three minutes, Champ Sappline sat up on his malleable bed within the purloined kitchen below R.J. the Third's bathroom. The garbage man yawned, stood, stretched, pulled his long blonde hair behind his ears, picked up a bottle of toothscrub, squirted two cubic centimeters into his mouth and swished the viscous paste around. Anti-plaque nanobrooms and fissure-sealing nanoplasterers prickled his teeth, tongue and gums until he spat the foam out into a mug, which rested upon the table that he had found last week on the sidewalk.

A knock upon the ceiling startled him. "You are going to get sandwiches with us or no?" the herpetology student inquired through the partially lifted trapdoor.

Champ looked out into the alley and exchanged glances with an unhappy brown and black turkey pigeon that was nestled beneath a fire escape landing on the opposite building, where spikes and razor wire adorned ladders and balconies, garnering bird corpses, gloves, rust and trash bags. (The war over there had been a "Class VI: Violent; Limited to Appendages" conflict for almost six years, according to R.J. the Third. Two people had lost fingers and one person had lost a hand and some toes [and because it was above Class III, the police were occasionally involved.])

"You awake?" inquired the herpetology student. "It's late and we leaving."

"I'll be up there in a minute," said Champ. "I just woke up."

"Muy bien."

The trapdoor shut, and a moment later, the toilet flushed.

Champ, wearing jeans and a yellow t-shirt that read AVAILABLE AT A DISCOUNT, and the herpetology student, clothed in a turquoise vinyl outfit, followed R.J. the Third, resplendent in silver, down the stairs.

As they reached the fifth-floor landing, the popinjay halted and suggested with feigned nonchalance, "Let us linger for a moment."

"I'm pretty hungry," said Champ.

"Tengo hambre tambien."

"I too have hunger," R.J. the Third said, "but there is an opportunity here—a triumph to claim for the glory of floor six!" The fellow scratched his two-pronged goatee (grown a week ago so that he might "appear more intimidating to his enemies within the building") and then tapped his index finger upon the three nose rings that adorned his right nostril. "Through the living-room floor," he whispered, "I discerned the unmistakable tattoo of hard-soled shoes within the apartment below us. It is an established fact, that the enemy only dons such footwear when he intends to leave his dwelling."

A wicked glimmer in his eyes, R.J. the Third cupped a hand beside his right ear. The reports of hard-soled shoes dimly echoed within one of the apartments.

"Hark!"

The fleximetal door marked 506 slid into the ground. From the open portal emerged a seventy-eight-year-old man in a plaid suit. The moment he saw the trio from the floor above, he shoved his hands—which were splattered with silver paint—into his pockets.

"I saw my mark upon thee!" said R.J. the Third, pointing derisively at the old man. "Thy hands show thee as an interloper! Thou art discomfited!"

Champ and the herpetology student pointed derisively at the old man; they did so unenthusiastically, yet remained respectful of war protocol.

The shamed septuagenarian retreated into his apartment.

"Victory," R.J the Third cried, "and sandwiches!"

* * *

Champ and the herpetology student followed R.J. the Third into an erratic rain that smelled of algae, walked east for three blocks and proceeded north for two.

The triumvirate circumvented a person who wielded a giant umbrella (to whom the popinjay said, "That's dangerous and rude!") and crossed an avenue by going between two raised stopwalls that dammed the foam-rubber traffic.

Soon, they arrived at a building façade that bore the name, "Sandwedish."

R.J. the Third said, "Sponge!" to the living wall a moment before he plunged inside. To the right of the entrance, a drain tube shot the rainwater that it had claimed from the popinjay into the gutter. The tenants followed, calling out, "Sponge." Nanodrones extricated rainwater from their hair, skin and garments as they transcended.

Smells of sautéed herring dominated the tea-green and teal establishment and elicited a growl from Champ's stomach as he and the other sixth-floor victors passed benches, upon which dozens of people chewed, bit and clasped crispy savories.

"You have never dined at Sandwedish?" asked R.J. the Third, leading his tenants toward a counter that was shaped like a planetary ring, within which stood three men who looked as if they were Scandinavian and deadly serious about sandwiches.

"No," said the garbage man.

The herpetology student shook her head.

"Fools!" proclaimed R.J. the Third, garnering more than a couple of glances from strangers. "The sandwiches here are life-changing. You have been wasting your lives. I pity you." He shook his head dolorously. "I am glad Architect is oblivious of your negligence."

"What do you recommend?' asked Champ.

"The herring and lingonberries with horseradish paste on potato bread is superb and their signature dish. The deer sausage with rosemary-fennel sauerkraut, potato paste and rabbit jerky on a seeded pumpernickel loaf is a sandwich beyond—far beyond!—the adjectives of mortals."

"I'll get those," replied Champ. "I'm hungry and they both sound good."

"I am pleased by your decisions." R.J. the Third then eyed the herpetology student and said, "The mushroom pâté with cornichons, pickled olives, caper berries and breaded shallots is what I recommend to you. Unless you plan on forgetting that vegetarian gimmick of yours."

"I am vegetarian," stated the woman.

"Vegetarians are bogus! Frauds! The history of the entire human race contradicts the herbivorous way." The popinjay's face was inflamed with the passion of the righteous. "The flesh-rending teeth that you used to utter that silly proclamation contradict such a choice in a most ironic manner. You may deprive yourself of meat in the stultifying vegetarian style, but you—as a member of genus homo erectus—are no more herbivorous than a person seated upon an airplane is a bird!"

"I am vegetarian."

"It is fortunate for you—very fortunate!—that the mushroom pâté sandwich is terrific. My treat!"

R.J. the Third went to the counter. "Guten Tag, meine Freunde!"

"He once date a girl in New Queens who was vegetarian," the herpetology student said to Champ. "He still angry at her."

"Okay."

R.J. the Third gesticulated histrionically as he placed his order—which seemed to be for no fewer than twelve sandwiches—and Champ contemplated for the twenty-fifth time in as many days whether or not he enjoyed the company of the grandiloquent jackass with whom he lived. A moment later, he was still undecided.

The herpetology student flicked her three-pronged tongue at a vacant table. "We sitting there," she informed Champ.

"Sure."

The tenants sat beside each other, and the woman's vinyl outfit squeaked.

Champ's opinions of the herpetology student were mostly positive. He appreciated her blunt manner and vibrant presence, and he thought that she was physically appealing, even though he knew that his attraction to her was not reciprocated. At a darkbar two weeks earlier, she had informed him that she did not like "blonde mens or mens with long hair or garbagemens or mens whose first names begin with the letter C." (The odds really seemed to be against him here.) During the platonic evening that followed, he had learned what she did like: amphibians, reptiles, grappa and tall black men. By the end of the night, she had promised to set him up with a friend of hers, and he had accepted her pity.

"You sleeping late today," the herpetology student said across the Sandwedish table. "You have the hangover?"

"I'm not hung over."

"You was singing when you came in last night."

"Was I?"

"Yes, you was. You no remember?"

"No." Champ had gone out drinking with Mikek after they had stacked the garbage truck; the remainder of the evening was a wet watercolor memory. "Must've chewed ethanol-hydrate to prevent a hangover."

"You are a drunk."

"Drink enthusiast."

(At the counter, R.J. the Third—for reasons unknown—was pantomiming the way a deer walks to one of the sullen sandwich makers.)

Champ asked, "What was I singing?"

"That song where it say, 'I am waiting for you to come back' over and over again, though you add some words about Candace and also some bad words."

The garbage man dimly remembered the uncouth and embarrassing performance. "Was I good? At singing? Did I show promise?"

"You should stick to the jokes that make nobody laugh."

R.J. the Third pushed a buoyed tray that supported five open sandwiches and seven vacuum-sealed specimens to the table. "Al is going to join us," he announced.

The herpetology student took her mushroom pâté baguette from the ziggurat of sandwiches. "Gracias."

"De nada, amigita."

"Who's Al?" asked Champ.

"He's the senior vice president of my fan club."

"You have a fan club?"

"There are currently four groups of R.J. the Third devotees, but Al's group is the only one I have chosen to officially recognize. Sixty percent of the members are technically-proficient Negroes—that is my target audience—and one of them is my broker."

"That's helpful."

104

The popinjay set a clear glass device upon the table, clicked a button on its circular base and said, "Connect to Al." Pixels sprayed into the pyramidal stage and rendered the tiny bust of a plump black man who wore a t-shirt adorned with the officially licensed logo for *The First and Final Rocket*.

R.J. the Third double-clicked the base, and the pyramid began to rotate.

The tiny bust swiveled toward the popinjay. "Hello," said Al, his voice clogged with phlegm.

"Hello, sycophant." R.J. the Third pointed the tip of his herring-and-lingonberry sandwich at Champ and the herpetology student as if it were a rapier. "These distinguished masticators are my roommates."

Al's miniature face (and the lens beneath it) swiveled past Champ and the herpetology student and again faced R.J. the Third. "How come she's got a shirt on?" he asked. "I thought you had a deal with her."

"I do, but the deal only affects her apparel when we are inside the apartment."

The herpetology student noisily crunched her sandwich in protest.

"What's wrong with the guy?" asked Al. "The one with long hair?" The tiny bust swiveled toward Champ. "You look depressed."

"I'm just hungry." The garbage man bit into his venison sandwich, and pumpernickel crackled. Chewing, he tasted eleven complementary and two contrasting flavors.

"Is that thing good?" asked Al. "Sure looks good. Sounds good."

The lily in Champ's ear beeped. A demure female voice said, "Incoming call: Reorientation Office." The garbage man chewed, pondering over the identity of the caller, whom he did not recognize. It seemed like the communication must be work related.

"What's happening?" asked Al's profile, peevishly.

R.J. the Third replied, "The depressed gentleman has received a call."

"I'm going to take this," announced Champ. "It's business."

"Incoming call: Reorientation Office," the demure voice in his ear repeated.

Clutching his delicious sandwich, the garbage man rose from the bench, walked toward the living wall and double-tapped his lily. "Um, hello?" he said through a mouthful of food.

"Good evening," said a fellow with a rich and soothing voice. "Am I speaking with Mr. Champ Bradley Sappline?"

Champ swallowed chewed food, inhaled a few flakes of crust and began to cough. Darting over, R.J the Third put a lemon-flavored suck bottle in his hand. The garbage man drank and mouthed the words 'Thank you' to the jackass whom he had just then decided that he liked.

"Yeah," Champ croaked into his lily. "I'm him."

"Are you currently driving a vehicle or working with dangerous tools?"

"Nope. Neither." The garbage man coughed once more and inquired, "Is this about that seminar on garbage man etiquette? I'll go next time, I promise. Really. I know I've missed it fourteen times, but next time I can almost guarantee that I'll try to make it."

"This is not related to that matter."

"What're you calling about?"

The man with the soothing voice said, "I recommend for you to go someplace private and seat yourself. I could wait on the line or I could call you back. The information that I am about to tell you will dramatically impact your life."

"Let me get outside," said Champ, concerned that he was about to be fired or reprimanded for something that Mikek had done. He then walked through the living wall and stood beneath the shop's overhang, where he was shielded from the rain.

"Okay," said the garbage man

"Are you settled?"

"Yeah. Yes."

"My name is Mr. Johnson, and I am a shepherd in the Reorientation Office at Corpus Chrome, Incorporated. I am calling to inform you that your father has been selected for resurrection."

Stunned by what he had just heard, Champ stared at the sandwich in his hand. A moment later, he asked the dripping venison, "Are you sure?"

"Indeed, indeed, indeed."

The garbage man felt as if he were a buzzing insect. Juice dripped from his sandwich, and fennel sauerkraut dangled. With great profundity, he said, "Holy shits."

Mr. Johnson laughed. "You aren't the first person to say that."

"Um…how does this work?"

"I'll tell you. May I record this conversation?"

"Should I get a lawyer first? What do people usually do?"

"You should hire a lawyer to review the three-party contract, but this conversation is of no legal consequence. The questions are simple and designed to alert our attorneys to potential conflicts, and to give me an idea of the kind of reception that the re-bodied individual will receive."

"Go ahead, then. You can record."

"Wonderful."

A woman's voice said, "The following conversation is being preserved for clerical purposes and is not in any way legally binding." A pleasant chime rang once.

Mr. Johnson asked, "Do you, Champ Bradley Sappline, object to the resurrection of your father, Eagle Jack Sappline?"

"No. I don't object."

"Wonderful. In a word, phrase or sentence, how would you characterize the relationship that you shared with your father?"

"Um." The garbage man thought of the last time that he had seen his father: They had gone to a 3-D movie in Midtown about a prison riot in which a group of armored policemen swept in, executed all of the inmates and then jailed scores of judges and defense attorneys. Nine years old at the time, Champ had found the violence terrifying, particularly the quintuple decapitation sequence, which he vividly remembered more than three decades later. His father had laughed and cheered throughout the entire picture.

"Might I suggest some words that people often use to describe such relationships?" inquired the shepherd.

"Sure."

"Loving. Nurturing. Respectful. Supportive."

"Nothing that positive."

After a pause, Mr. Johnson said, "Let me go down the list," and then suggested, "Hateful. Destructive. Vitriolic."

"Better than that—but he was a fireman more than a father. My mom divorced him when I was five and moved us to Buffalo because of her boyfriend, so I didn't see that much of him before he was killed."

"I will describe your relationship with him as 'estranged but amicable.'"

"Sounds accurate," said Champ, though he knew that Candace would have disagreed. (She had described his relationship with his father as "the source of many of his problems, especially his blue-collar outlook and his fears of abandonment.")

Mr. Johnson said, "Wonderful. Under these circumstances, Corpus Chrome, Incorporated will be able to proceed apace."

"Sounds good."

"At your earliest convenience, you and I should have a meeting in which we discuss your father's general reorientation and his obligations to CCI once re-bodied. When will you next be available?"

Champ mentally reviewed his work schedule. "I have Sunday and Tuesday off."

"Tuesday at…fourteen will work. I'll toss a datemark in your vault with my contact information."

"Danke. Thank you."

"You are very welcome. Congratulations, Mr. Sappline, and have a good—"

"Wait," blurted Champ. "I have a question—if that's okay? Something I've been wondering since you told me what was going on. Can I ask?"

"Certainly."

"I'm excited about all of this—and grateful—but I don't understand it. I mean—why'd you choose him? He was a fireman. He wasn't rich or a scientist or a famous artist like most of the people who get picked. He fought fires."

"Eagle Sappline is an atypical choice," the shepherd admitted, "but I don't know why he was chosen."

Champ thought that Mr. Johnson sounded earnest.

"Have a good evening," said the shepherd.

"You, too."

Champ Sappline tapped his lily and stared at the rain, thinking of his father. Like the precipitation, his memories were separate and unclear refractions of light.

Once again, the garbage man said, "Holy shits."

CHAPTER XIV
A LITTLE SIBLING RIBALDRY

"So that's where my sister pretends she's a man," said Tjorbn Karlsson, pointing an index finger that was adorned with two white gold rings at Lisanne's breathing mattress. "Unless it's the other way around?" The tall handsome fellow faced the petite blonde and arched an eyebrow. "Ahem, ahem?"

"Neither of us is 'pretending to be a man,'" Osa said to her brother, "though that isn't any of your business."

"Miss Breutschen is wearing a suit," Tjorbn observed, "but it's still feminine. This whole situation's confusing."

"Feel free to slap him," Osa said to Lisanne.

"I can withstand abuse." Grinning like a reptile, the handsome fellow presented a peninsula-sized sideburn to the petite blonde. "Go ahead and smack me. I deserve a slap. Help me out."

Lisanne committed no violence.

"I'd like to see the rest of the apartment," Osa's father prompted from outside the bedroom. He then cleared his throat meaningfully.

"This is part of the tour," the tall beauty called through the open door. "There's nothing in here that'll embarrass you."

From the hallway, the older man replied, "I'm not comfortable going in there. You kids can do whatever you want, but I don't need visual aids to paint the picture. No thank you."

Tjorbn walked over to the drawer panel. "Where do you guys keep the toys? Gelatin man parts? Tongue propellers and those furry little animal heads?" He touched an up arrow, and a drawer extruded from the wall, smooth and silent like a mortuary slab.

"Close that," demanded Osa.

The bronze man investigated the contents of a deep drawer, exhumed one of Osa's large black brassieres, looked at Lisanne's flat chest and dropped the garment. "I know who wears that."

"Don't be an asshole."

"Did you move in?" Tjorbn asked his sister as he appraised socks.

"No, but I stay here a lot."

"Cyclops must be lonely. He's been suicidal ever since you had him neutered."

Osa punched Tjorbn in the shoulder, a forceful blow that would have propelled Lisanne across the room.

The handsome fellow guffawed. "You're weak."

"No wrestling," Osa's father admonished from the hallway.

Tjorbn tapped the up arrow on another drawer, one that was filled with Lisanne's panties.

The petite blonde whistled a C-sharp and said, "Darkness." Suddenly, the bedroom plunged into artificial night.

Osa's father asked from the hallway, "Why'd the lights go out in there?" Receiving no response, he cleared his throat and said, "You kids should come out of that bedroom."

* * *

At the dinner table, Tjorbn was better behaved, and Osa's father was far more relaxed. Mr. Rikard Karlsson was a reserved and quiet sixty-four-year-old fellow who had a long icy face, and like many Swedes whom Lisanne had met, he was fair-skinned and rose to a rather high altitude. The absent mother, an Indian woman from Calcutta who had died ten years ago, was the source of the Karlsson siblings' fiery demeanor, dark hair and sepia skin.

"It tastes like the chicken was made in a real tandoori."

"Danke, Mr. Karlsson," replied the hostess. (Osa had told Lisanne to address her father formally. The petite blonde had asked why, and the tall beauty had explained, "It perpetuates the illusion that he's still an authority figure.")

110

"The curries were delicious," praised Tjorbn.

"Danke. I am glad that you enjoyed them."

Mr. Karlsson said, "My wife used to make curries like these, but she was Indian and naturally adept. You're German American, correct?"

Underneath the table, Osa's bare foot slid under the bulbous cuff of Lisanne's right pant leg—a clandestine suggestion that delayed the petite woman's response for a moment. "American German. I was born and raised in Berlin."

"My first wife was German." Mr. Karlsson looked down at the ancient beer stein that he had brought from home, washed by hand in Lisanne's sink (using only hot water) and dried with a special chamois. The long fellow drank a mouthful of beer and added, "She was smart and graceful, but very strict."

Lisanne maintained a neutral expression.

Osa guffawed. "So's Lisanne. You should've heard her chastise me for being late on our second date." The tall beauty smiled hugely. "That's why I told you guys to be in the lobby at nineteen-thirty even though the invitation was for twenty-thirty." To her mate, she confessed, "My whole family's tardy. Don't kill us."

"Did you keep them in the lobby for an hour?"

"We went to the bar on the fiftieth floor," replied Osa.

"That was why I tasted vodka on your lips."

Mr. Karlsson cleared his throat.

'Oops,' Lisanne thought to herself, as Osa took and squeezed her hand.

There was a seven-second lull in which Mr. Karlsson folded his cloth napkin into the shape of a Viking boat, Tjorbn sped three ice cubes in a rapid circuit of his Scotch glass and Osa ate a steaming bite of curried rabbit. Lisanne enjoyed the moment of silence that she shared with the family and felt that it connected her to her mate in yet another meaningful way.

Tjorbn swallowed a mouthful of Scotch and spat out an ice cube. "That guy's giving his speech tonight—that executed guy that CCI brought back."

"Derrick W.R. Dulande," said Mr. Karlsson.

"That's his name."

The sexagenarian shook his long head. "I remember when he was executed—I was about Tjorbn's age." He drank a mouthful of beer, lowered his blue eyes and fingered the scrollwork upon his ancient stein. "It was wrong to bring him back. I don't believe in the death penalty—perhaps because I grew up in Sweden—but that one deserved the injection if ever any man did. He was remorseless, maybe… maybe even evil if there's such a thing."

"That's tonight?" asked Osa. Lisanne recognized both revulsion and excitement in her mate's voice.

"Yeah," said Tjorbn.

"I've not heard about this," said Lisanne. The men looked at her as if she had just waggled a neon tentacle. "I've been locked in the studio for the past six weeks."

"And with me," Osa added, "and we haven't been watching the news."

Mr. Karlsson coughed loudly.

Osa pointed to the bedroom. "We've been in there."

The sexagenarian clapped his hands to his mouth to contain the explosive coughs that followed. Across from him, his progeny shared wicked-children grins.

"I am interested in watching this speech," said Lisanne. "Osa, please take your family to the living room—I'll join you once I've slotted the dishes."

"I'd offer to help, but I'm afraid it would seem insincere," said Tjorbn, a moment before he was punched by his sister.

* * *

In the kitchen, Lisanne slotted a dish into the horizontal aperture of the wall unit, listening to the distant baritone voices of Tjorbn and Mr. Karlsson as they discussed a sports team. The petite blonde thought of her own father and mother and sister, all of whom were deceased. Soon, she returned her mind to happier thoughts and inserted another plate.

Amidst the sounds of men's chatter and the thrum of the wall unit, Lisanne discerned the soft pad of sock-covered feet. A shadow slid across the floor and draped her as she inserted forks into the utensils port.

Lisanne turned to face Osa.

"I love you," said the tall beauty.

Lisanne nodded, her heart racing. There had been intimations and allusions, but neither of them had actually named the blossom until that moment.

"I have loved you for four weeks," replied the petite blonde.

They kissed.

Osa leaned forward. Lisanne felt the wall press against her back, and soon, their chests were flush. Each woman slid a thigh between the other's legs, and the kiss deepened.

In the other room, Mr. Karlsson was seized by an uncontrollable coughing fit.

Chapter XV
Three Transubstantiations

"These koi fish are lovely," said the white woman. "I saw them at the Met Annex."

A fifty-year-old Japanese man who was clothed in yellow and blue familial robes replied, "Nishikigoi is the correct name for these fish." Junichi Daisuke (like most people) disliked reporters. "Koi just means carp. These are not ordinary carp."

"Nishikigoi," repeated the woman, with an accent that he found laughable. "Is that correct?"

The Japanese man walked away from the reporter and circled the elephantine aquarium—a ten-meter-in-diameter glass tank that was suspended in the air by micron wire and filled with filtered water. This immaculate vessel was to serve as the central backdrop for Derrick W.R. Dulande's resurrection speech.

The frown on Junichi Daisuke's face became more significant when he thought of the re-bodied murderer.

Within the floating pond swam three hundred and eighty-two nishikigoi, which had been culled from the collection of two thousand that the Japanese man maintained in the Living Annex of the Metropolitan Museum. He had transported the chosen fish to the gala room last evening, but many of his favorites had not been included. There were plentiful golden Yamabuki Ogon, pure white Hikari, spotted Bekko, skunk-patterned Kumonryu, and copper Kawarimono, but his supervisor had told him not to transport any Gin Matsuba, Goromo or Kohaku to the event. Nobody had explained to the caretaker why these three types of brocaded carp had been excluded, but they had one thing in common, one visible trait that separated them from their peers. Decorating all of their bodies was the color red.

Junichi Daisuke presumed that the arrangers of this event (a committee within Corpus Chrome, Incorporated) wanted to exclude the crimson fish, which might bring to mind blood, in particular that which had been spilled by Derrick W.R. Dulande during his shameful first life. The red that colored nishikigoi was a brilliant one, and the natural patterns upon Kohaku fish looked almost exactly like spattered gore.

"Pardon me," said two Chinese Americans as they bumped past the Japanese man. The pair then ascended a scaffold and affixed four more centimeter-sized lenses to the ceiling. Junichi Daisuke had counted over one hundred and forty such devices positioned throughout the gala room—above, below and on every wall. Tonight was the first time that his nishikigoi were going to be captured in real-definition, and he was pleased that the whole world would have a chance to see their splendor.

The Chinese Americans climbed down and walked to the tank, where they lingered, observing the graceful fish within. The younger man said, "These're really pretty."

Junichi Daisuke asked, "How come you do not see the lenses when you watch m.a.? They are everywhere, and they are green." He pointed to the tiny glass beads that winked upon every surface of the gala room.

"The green gets isolated and masked out."

The older man saw that Junichi Daisuke was confused and added, "Like green screens in old movies."

"Then why are there not holes in the image where the lenses were?"

"Pixels are smeared over the holes, automatically," said the younger man. "Anything that doesn't look right, an image architect can correct."

"Xie xie," the Japanese man said to the Chinese Americans.

Nodding respectfully, the pair walked toward a floating cart that was loaded with equipment.

The small Japanese man watched the fish swim through the clear water and wondered why a copper Kawarimono that he had named Akihabara seemed both sluggish and confused.

* * *

Junichi Daisuke, four catering chefs, three dendrologists (who had overseen the installation of the golden weeping willows that stood behind the nishikigoi tank), and eighteen unhappy police officers sat behind the stanchions, facing the wooden dais upon which rested three oak chairs, none of which looked comfortable. Twenty reporters from the same number of countries sat upon plush divans to the right of the raised area.

From the living wall emerged a female pastor who was clothed in dark green vestments, her silver hair withheld from her kind face in a tight knot upon the top of her head. She was soon succeeded by a small Indian man who had a brown suit and a humorless face. Together, they walked toward the dais.

A chromium mannequin, model 8M, then emerged from the wall. The re-bodied man had light brown hair and wore a black suit and tie, a gray shirt and a generic face. His hard-soled leather shoes clacked upon the tile floor as he strode toward the dais.

Junichi Daisuke felt the caterers, dendrologists and police officers grow tense. The nishikigoi stirred as the machine approached them, and soon, they fled to the far side of the tank, repulsed.

Pride filled the Japanese caretaker.

The ordained woman in dark green walked to the middle of the dais and announced, "I am Pastor Svetlana Graekow-Jacek." Her subtly amplified voice reverberated throughout the gala room. "I'd like to remind all of the reporters present to withhold their questions until after Mr. Dulande has spoken."

A reporter called out, "Why're you speaking on his behalf? Mr. Dulande's a Catholic."

"Mr. Dulande is no longer Catholic," replied the pastor.

An awkward silence sat in the room.

"Good riddance," said one of the policemen near Junichi Daisuke.

The reporter asked, "Why has—"

"Please withhold all of your questions until after Mr. Dulande has spoken," restated the spiritual woman, equitably.

The reporters remained quiet, and soon, the pastor and the Indian man seated themselves upon two of the three uncomfortable oak chairs.

Hard soles clacked upon wood as the chromium mannequin that contained Derrick W.R. Dulande's mind ascended three steps and walked to the center of the dais.

A policewoman near Junichi Daisuke pressed her right palm to the razor gun on her hip and tapped its polymer shell.

"I'll give you five hundred globals," said her partner, facetiously.

"I'll do this gratis."

Derrick W.R. Dulande employed his iridescent lenses and looked upon the gathering. His gelware mask was inscrutable.

"I haven't come here to apologize," announced the re-bodied man. His subtly amplified voice resounded and decayed within the gala space.

People shifted uncomfortably. Junichi Daisuke heard several policemen snort.

"I, Derrick Wilfred Raymond Dulande, do not offer apologies, because the things that I did in my first life were and are unforgivable. To ask the friends and families of Jessica Reynolds-Tam, Lana Pearlman and Rena Takahata for forgiveness would be a thoughtless and uncaring request. I don't deserve forgiveness: I was mean and loathsome. I did awful, disgusting things to these three women and to the hundreds of people who cared for them. I committed these foul deeds in a deliberate manner, and I fully deserved the death sentence that I received.

"Nicolai Dhanikov, Po-Li Fan, Osama Bin Laden and Adolf Hitler had far better motivations than did I.

"As I stated earlier, I haven't come here to apologize."

Junichi Daisuke saw that everyone in the room was confused by the re-bodied man's words. All of these people had expected to hear contrition.

"I have come here to tell the human race what I've learned." The mannequin's eyes retracted deep into his head. "I have come to tell you what I know of Hell."

Reporters shot up from their seats as shouts, solicitous hands and derisive remarks flashed across the entire room.

The re-bodied man was silent.

A moment later, the small Indian in brown stood up, walked beside the mannequin and said to the assemblage, "If there's another interruption, the media will be asked to leave."

The assemblage quietened and soon became silent. Coolant ducts hummed, stirring the golden branches of the weeping willows.

The reporters and the Indian man reseated themselves, and Junichi Daisuke surveyed his fish; Akihabara was still behaving peculiarly for some reason.

The re-bodied man interlaced his gelware fingers in front of the second button of his black jacket. "Hell is not an imaginary place," he resumed. "It is not a place of pitchforks or grinning daemons.

"It is a real, physical place, one that we look at every day.

"Hell is within our sun."

Several people in the room laughed. An officer whispered, "He's totally nuts."

Like the people around him, Junichi Daisuke thought that the re-bodied man was insane. Only a score of the sixty-one thousand resurrected subjects had remembered anything from the years during which they had been dead, and all of these recollections had been vague, inconclusive amalgams of faces and light, dismissed by scientists as hallucinations that had occurred just before and after death.

Derrick W.R. Dulande continued, "The great majority of you, perhaps every single person watching me right now, will dismiss my experiences as dreams or malicious fabrications or manifested psychoses, but the fact is that I went to Hell and have returned.

"From what I've witnessed, I will conclude that there is no heaven. There is no utopian realm that is the opposite of what lies within the sun. Heaven was created by mankind to give us hope in a vast and senseless universe. Heaven is a fantasy.

"For you to understand my journey, I must first tell you what I have learned about the human soul.

"Every single living human being is two connected but separate entities: a physical body and a spirit body. The spirit body is a living and tangible thing, a symbiotic creature, but it exists in a dimension that is separate from what we know as reality.

"The reason that scientists have never been able to figure out exactly how the mind works is because so much of it is in that other dimension.

"Dreams, artistic inspirations, spirituality, premonitions, intuitions, abstract correlations and sense memories are byproducts of our symbiotic relationship with our spirit bodies.

"I'll wait until you stop laughing."

The mannequin paused until the cacklers quietened.

"The spirit bodies of most human beings dissipate when the physical body dies.

"When philanthropists, artists, doctors, lawyers, priests, rapists, rabbis, animal slaughterers, child molesters and thieves die, they all simply end, unless they are cryogenically preserved, in which case they are stuck in a limbo between existence and absolute obliteration.

"Whether preserved in a cryonic vault or allowed to decompose naturally, all murderers go to Hell.

"When I committed my first murder—when I strangled Lana Pearlman in twenty-nineteen—my spirit body changed and became a permanent thing in that other dimension. It became something capable of transubstantiation and even multiple transubstantiations. My soul became something that could journey to Hell.

"Vile killers like myself go to Hell. Soldiers who kill in war and are celebrated as heroes go to Hell. The man who pushed the button for the injection that killed me will go to Hell. Doctors who euthanize patients go to Hell. A policeman who kills a serial killer goes to the exact same place that the serial killer does.

"Charles Manson, despite what people did at his behest, did not personally kill another human being and so did not go to Hell, nor did Isabelle Xia, despite her part in the destruction of the Empire State Building. A sweet old woman named Roberta Saunders who lost control of her car and accidentally killed a child was forever condemned to Hell."

Two of the policeman near Junichi Daisuke left the gala room. Another officer muttered, "Fuck this nonsense," and departed soon afterwards.

The mannequin watched them leave and resumed, "There's a scientific principle at work in the dimension or dimensions of souls—the place where our spirit bodies live. This science does not at all recognize what we conceive of as right or wrong, any more than molecules do. But for some reason, the act of killing another person—and indirectly, its spirit body—differs dramatically from any other thing that a human being can do. This act changes the chemical makeup of the killer's spirit body so that it can leave the phantom moon.

"Perhaps this is a safeguard, something that isolates the killer's spirit from the other spirit bodies so that it won't infect them.

"I'm not sure.

"I know that most of you will disregard my tale of dual transubstantiations as a malicious fantasy, but I will tell it anyway.

"This is not a pleasant story

"I was about to be executed. I said good-bye to my mother."

Derrick W.R. Dulande stood upon the dais, silent and inert, his face neutral. Junichi Daisuke and the assemblage stared at the abruptly frozen mannequin, concerned that the machine had malfunctioned.

Suddenly, the re-bodied man moved his left hand. "I was secured to a gurney. They slid needles into my arms. They pumped thiopental through my veins, and I went into a coma.

"They injected the toxins into my paralyzed body.

"I faded and died.

"I wake up inside a lunar body that orbits the Earth. From this dimension—or overlapping cluster of dimensions—the Earth looks like ten or eleven overlapping violet spirals…but still, I recognize it.

"The moon I'm in isn't our moon. It's made of some matter that's unlike what we interact with, but it coheres and has energy.

"It might be dark matter, or maybe something entirely different.

"The interior of this shadow moon is hollow and pocked with billions of craters. Within each of these concave areas is something that looks like a glowing squid.

"I understand why you're laughing at me," the re-bodied man said to several chuckling reporters.

When the room was again quiet, Derek W.R. Dulande continued. "These glowing squid-like beings are iridescent gray and seem very, very large, though I have no reference point to gauge exactly how big. They are covered with nerves and creases that remind me of the exteriors of human brains.

"Every single one of these squid-like beings is anchored to a person on Earth: These are the spirit bodies I mentioned earlier.

"When a human being goes to sleep, the squid connected to that person opens its eyelids a millimeter, maybe two. The lights of the other squids shine upon these partially open eyes and create dreams, abstract associations, artistic inspirations and a sense of spirituality for the anchored person.

"A few squids have their eyes wide open: These are tethered to men and women who are insane.

"I'm not sure how I understand all of this, but I do the moment I see it. Instantly.

"All of you gathered here today or watching this on your mote aquariums at home have spirit bodies in this shadow moon."

Several people laughed at the comment.

Derrick W.R. Dulande let the sound decay. "I rise out of my crater, as if pulled by a magnet. I fly toward a hole that is bright with multicolored sunlight. When I try to cover my eyes, I see that my limbs are curved gray tendrils like those of the other inhabitants, but—since I'm a murderer—I don't glow like they do. I'm drawn through the hole.

"The gases in my body swell in the vacuum of space. I bloat, expanding bigger and bigger until I burst.

"But I don't die.

"My exploded squid body, a mass of tangled gray gore, speeds toward the sun.

"The sun grows as I fly toward it. The only thing that keeps me sane is that I know this is all a dream—that I'll wake up soon and be human again.

"I pray that when I wake up, I'll be a kid or a teenager and not have murdered anybody. That I'll be good.

"To mark the passage of time, I start counting stars. By the time I reach one million, I know for certain that I'm not dreaming, that no dream goes on for this long. I flail my burst body to no avail. I can't change my course or wake up or do anything.

"The sun fills the horizon ahead of me.

"I plunge into Hell.

"White fire dominates all of my senses. I have no idea whether I am stationary or flying at relativistic speeds. I'm oblivious of everything but continuous solar explosions.

"I am alone.

"All I can do in this nuclear limbo is contemplate my horrible life and the people whom I hurt: the victims, the families of the victims and my own mother and father. For two months, I ponder a minor argument I once had with my dad. Regret consumes me. For one full year I think with despair of a time when I was a child and called my mom a bitch."

The mannequin tilted his head down and shook it from side to side. "For every second of seven straight years I ponder the murder of Rena Takahata.

"And somehow, I know that I am damned to the sun for its entire life cycle. That is my sentence. I will be there when it turns into a red giant, and I will be there when it turns into a white dwarf, and I will be there when it cools. I can't touch or create or interact with anything. I can't learn or discover anything.

"I will be alone with the memories of my tiny horrible life for more than six billion years.

"That is Hell," stated Derrick W.R. Dulande with finality.

The room was quiet.

Junichi Daisuke and those around him pondered the elaborateness of the resurrected man's hallucination.

"When my brain was thawed," the re-bodied man resumed, "my spirit body returned to its crater within the shadow moon and reconnected with what remained of my physical body.

"But still…"

The re-bodied man shook his head. "That perdition is what awaits me when this brain dies." He slid his gelware hand through his light brown hair. "Six billion years of isolated agony."

Derrick W.R. Dulande raised his head and looked at the assemblage. The Indian man in brown and the female pastor stood up from their seats as the reporters (several of whom were grinning) dialed through the sheaves upon which they had typed their questions throughout the speech.

"Mr. Dulande will take two questions from each reporter and then conclude the conference."

Junichi Daisuke gasped when he looked at the suspended aquarium behind the mannequin. The copper Kawarimono that had been acting strangely was floating at the top of the tank, dead.

The fish's belly swelled and erupted with a squeak. Tangled piscine remains splattered the far side of the tank's surface.

A flash of metal launched itself from Akihabara's guts, arced over the Indian man and impacted Derrick W.R. Dulande. The mannequin toppled forward, slamming onto his knees and gelware palms. Attached to the side of his chromium head was a metal horseshoe crab that had four fluid vials on its back. Junichi Daisuke had no idea how this strange machine had gotten into Akihabara's belly.

The pastor and the Indian man hurried across the dais as Derrick W.R. Dulande reached for the device that drilled into his head.

Plungers sank, shooting serum.

The re-bodied man shrieked, popping two of his throat speakers. Static melded with an aluminum wail.

Throughout the room, people covered their ears.

Green fluid and bubbling brain matter dripped from the sundered head of the kneeling mannequin.

Junichi Daisuke, nishikigoi, dendrologists, police officers, catering chefs and reporters watched Derrick W.R. Dulande's molten mind eat through the dais.

Several people clapped.

CHAPTER XVI
HEROIC INTENTIONS?

Champ Sappline leaned back in his chair, displaying his yellow t-shirt, which read IF YOU THINK THIS SHIRT IS YELLOW, YOU'VE GOT PISS EYE. "I saw what happened with that Dulande guy last week," the garbage man said to the fellow on the other side of the desk. "That was awkward, right?"

Mr. Johnson snorted and replied, "That's a bit of an understatement." The amiable black shepherd with the soothing voice plucked a piece of fluff from his olive tweed suit and put it into the dispose hole.

"Do they know who did it?" asked Champ. "Who killed him?"

"Currently, no."

"I can't believe anyone's taking what he said seriously. Our souls are squids in a crater in some hollow moon and they'll float into the sun if we kill somebody? I mean, how can anyone take that shit seriously?"

"Only a few thousand people are taking it seriously, and they are ostracized and unbalanced people whom nobody else takes seriously."

"Yeah," the garbage man said, "but when I was watching, I got an idea about why CCI chose to re-body my father." He nodded and shrugged. "Resurrect a decorated fireman, put him in a station, get him in the news doing good deeds—a positive CCI story to counterbalance the grief you're getting because you gave a mannequin to Dulande."

"As I've said before," Mr. Johnson replied, scratching his neat beard, "the resurrection choices are made on a floor of this building to which I've never even been. Regardless, Dulande is dead and our commitment to re-body Eagle Sappline remains."

Champ placed a sheaf upon the desk and slid it to the shepherd. "My lawyer said that the contract looks good." (R.J. the Third's cousin had examined it for him, gratis.) "My fingerprints are on it."

"Wonderful," said Mr. Johnson, sliding the sheaf into a slot in his desk. "Do you read books?"

"Nope."

The shepherd nodded and double-tapped the lily in his ear. "Send Mr. Champ Sappline the audio version." The fellow then dialed off the device and returned his attention to the garbage man. "I put an audio file in your vault. Please listen to it before our next meeting."

Champ was not a fan of homework. "What is it?"

"Three narrated transcripts, each of which details the reunion of a resurrected person with his or her loved ones."

"I'll check it out."

Doubt played upon Mr. Johnson's face. "Reorientation for re-bodied people who have been gone for decades is often very difficult. Please listen to the files."

"I will, I promise. I'll tap them when I'm sucking garbage next week."

"Wonderful."

Chapter XVII
The End of Spring

Clothed in a loose brown blouse, beige slacks and matching heel slippers, Lisanne walked past myriad blue cubbies and a dozen adjustable-height drinking spigots. Soon, she descried a living wall marked '115' and walked through it, entering a round room within which sat two dozen eleven-year-olds in baggy blue uniforms. Standing in front of the Brooklyn City children was their instructor, Miss Karlsson. The tall beauty wore the same type of baggy blue uniform as her students.

"We have a special visitor joining us in our interaction session today," announced Osa, gesturing with a long arm at Lisanne. "This is Miss Breutschen."

Twenty-four heads swiveled, tilted back and focused upon the guest.

"Say 'Guten Morgen' to Miss Breutschen."

"Guten Morgen, Miss Boychin!" roared the congregation.

The sound hit Lisanne like a wave, and she winced.

"Snapdragon," said Osa.

A chubby Chinese-American boy looked up at the teacher.

"There's no need to yell."

"Okay!"

"Where should I sit?" Lisanne saw an empty bench at the rear of the room and pointed to it hopefully. "There?"

Osa shook her head. "I'd like for you to actively participate in today's congregation."

"She's scared!" yelled Snapdragon.

"I am not," said Lisanne, inexpertly hiding her apprehensions. She had not been confined with a group of children since she was one herself, and she did not know what they were capable of doing. The undertow of regression infantilized her. "I'm not scared."

Osa suppressed a guffaw. "Please come to the front of the room, Miss Breutschen."

"Miss Boychin's gettin' all red!" observed a black girl.

"She is," agreed the instructor. "What is that type of reaction called?"

Thirteen children said, "Blushing."

Snapdragon yelled, "Gettin' red!"

"Yes," Osa replied, "Miss Breutschen is blushing."

Lisanne's cheeks burned scarlet as she walked over to Osa and looked murderously into her beautiful face.

Turning to the congregation, the instructor asked, "Why do people blush?"

The roar of simultaneous answers ended the moment that Osa put an index finger to her lips. Lisanne was impressed by her mate's authority over the children.

The instructor said, "Answer only when I make direct eye contact with you. Why do people blush?"

Osa looked at a short blonde boy.

"Because they burped at the table and didn't mean to do it."

Osa looked at a black girl.

"'Cause they got caught stealing peppermint cookies."

Osa looked at Snapdragon.

"She wet her pants."

"I did not," Lisanne clarified to the congregation. The petite blonde wanted to flee and hide in the bathroom.

Osa again suppressed a guffaw. "Those are specific reasons why a person might blush, but how does a person usually feel when he or she blushes? Answer only when I make direct eye contact with you."

The children silently awaited the teacher's gaze.

Osa looked at a chubby Latin girl.

The child chewed her lips and furrowed her brow and shook her head, ruminating furiously.

"It's okay to say, 'I don't know.'"

The Latin girl said, "I don't know."

127

Osa looked at a small black-haired girl who had an artificial right leg that was made out of polymer plasticore.

"People blush when they're embarrassed," said the child.

"Autumn is correct. People blush when they're embarrassed."

"Is she your mate?" inquired Autumn, pointing to the guest.

"She's my mate." Osa kissed Lisanne on the cheek.

"Kiss her, Miss Boychin!" coaxed Snapdragon. "Kiss Miss Karlsson on the neck!"

"Behave," admonished Osa.

The boy gripped his desk, gyrating with excitement.

"Snapdragon is very immature," Autumn informed Lisanne. "He's been crazy ever since he had his puberty."

The petite blonde had heard her mate speak of this particular girl as the most advanced child in any of the school's supplemental social courses for home-schooled youths.

Autumn looked at Osa and inquired, "Why'd you embarrass her if she's your mate?" The prodigy shook her head. "That's not very nice."

"Although I found it a little funny, my goal wasn't to embarrass Miss Breutschen, but to include her in our congregation. I'd like for all of us to interact."

"But she's so damn old," observed the small blonde boy.

Osa eyed the youth supremacist. "Reggie. Try to avoid calling a person 'old,' since it can hurt someone's feelings, and it means different things to different people. Miss Breutschen is thirty-eight: To you she might seem old, but to a person who is seventy or eighty, she would be considered quite young."

The blonde boy nodded his head. "Gotcha."

"Does anybody have any questions for Miss Breutschen?"

"Who's in charge?" asked the skinny black boy. "Which one of you is the leader?"

"There is no leader," said Lisanne. "There are things Miss Karlsson wants to be in charge of and there are things that I want to be in charge of. We share."

Autumn commented, "Sounds like a kibbutz."

* * *

An hour later, the congregation filed out through the living wall, and Osa and Lisanne were finally alone.

The tall beauty kissed her mate properly upon the lips and hugged her. "I'm sorry. I hope that wasn't too embarrassing for you. Did you like them?"

"They are very entertaining."

Lisanne looked through the ellipsoidal window that faced onto Prospect Park. Floating gardens and abstract topiary circled the green landscape, casting shadows like fast-moving clouds upon the tuffgrass, where brigades of children in baggy blue one-piece suits ran chaotically. Several students climbed plasticore steps that led to a fenced-in tier of swimming aspic.

The petite blonde remarked, "That uniform seems like the type of thing that children laborers would be forced to wear in an old film about a futuristic dystopia."

"I'll quote the institution's mission statement," defended Osa. "'The loose one-piece outfit is designed to diminish prejudices begat by discrepancies of gender, physique and class. Later in life, when the one-piece-wearers are more sophisticated and have entered society, they will have a greater aptitude for assessing individuals meritoriously, rather than superficially.'"

Osa unhooked a solarcel from the mote aquarium and added, "The other thing that the uniform offers home-schooled children is an immediate sense of community. When they first get here, they see a group of kids wearing the same exact uniform that they have on, and they realize—in a visual way—that they belong to a society much larger than just their family and the people in their apartment building."

"There is a logic there," admitted Lisanne.

Outside, Autumn scampered up plasticore steps and ran upon the surface of the aspic pond, sinking centimeter by centimeter until she was overwhelmed by the viscous mass. Snapdragon bounded after her.

Lisanne remarked, "I understand why you are so exhausted on Mondays and Wednesdays."

"Yeah. And the committee's talking about giving me extra sessions on those days. I said, 'Expect lots of field trips.'"

Outside, Snapdragon landed in the aspic beside Autumn. Slime splattered.

"Is Autumn always going to have an artificial leg?"

"No, but it's safer to transplant a real one after she's stopped growing. They're re-balancing her blood now." Osa looked outside at the slime-covered girl. "She's pretty great, huh?"

"She's obviously the smartest, but Snapdragon is my favorite."

Osa waved her hands in the air as if she were shooing flies. "Enough work talk. What'd you plan for this weekend?"

"We're going to New Orleans."

Stunned, the tall beauty stared at her mate. "Um…tonight?"

"Yes. Our shuttle's at sixteen-thirty. Everything's booked."

"I thought we were going to have dinner or see a concert or something like that."

"On Sunday we will have known each other for exactly three months: I want us to celebrate our first season together."

"Oh…wow…um…I haven't packed," remarked Osa.

"You have new clothes waiting for you in our hotel room."

"I'll need to ask my neighbor to walk Cyclops."

"I've already taken care of that."

Osa's smile was enormous. "Celebrating our first season together?" she said, shaking her head in disbelief. "You, Lisanne Breutschen, are as sentimental as you are meticulous."

"We need to leave school in no more than eleven minutes."

"A smidge more meticulous."

* * *

The gondolier, a twenty-two-year-old Creole of mixed parentage who was dressed in a mustard cloak, guided his vessel up Bourbon Canal, the central waterway in the French Quarter of New Orleans. Seated in the middle of the craft beside Osa, Lisanne leaned her head against her mate's shoulder and inhaled the spice-scented air.

The tall beauty raised a beaker to the petite blonde's lips. Lisanne sipped the sweet mixture of lime, absinthe and cardamom, swirled it in her mouth for a delicious moment and swallowed. Festoons with purple, gold and green lights adorned the mossy building façades on either side of the avenue and hung across the night sky like frozen fireflies. The variegated bulbs were perfectly mirrored in the dark water, and the reflection created the illusion that the gondola was not afloat upon a canal, but flying in the center of a tunnel that had been decorated with myriad sparkling motes.

The vertiginous depths pulled Lisanne forward, and a smiling, multicolored face rose up from the reflected sky below. A long arm pulled the dizzy woman back into the craft, securing her.

"Don't fall in," warned Osa.

"Danke." Lisanne clutched her mate's sinewy balustrade.

"Absinthe is strong. Be careful."

"This is beautiful," Lisanne said and then looked at her mate. "You are beautiful."

"Thank you. And thank you so, so much for arranging this—you know I've always wanted to come here." Osa pressed a kiss to Lisanne's forehead. "This is wonderful."

A cluster of college kids roared and drank upon the third floor of a building directly above a sheltered gondola dock, and a girl in a bikini, hands clapped to her mouth, ran to the rail.

Lisanne looked away. Behind her, nauseous splashes were followed by a grim groan.

"Wouldn't want to fall into this water," remarked Osa.

"Nor would I."

At the back of the craft, the gondolier said, "They send out eau trolls every night." His Creole accent turned his words into bubble gum.

"What's an eau troll?" inquired Lisanne, tittering.

("You're really drunk," whispered Osa.

"A little.")

"She's a submersible," the gondolier said, "that collects junk from the water and keeps her clean. Excrement, bottles, beads, fried oysters and microscopic things—she filters them all and puts them into different stomachs in her belly."

He swept his fiberglass paddle in a wide arc. "This is as clean as your New York drinking water. Cleaner, maybe."

Concentric rectangles of colored light grew, surrounded the craft and diminished. Lisanne pulled Osa's arms around her like a shawl.

The gondolier steered away from a floating shanty that lay directly in the middle of the waterway. A giant bronze crawfish wearing a toque lounged upon the roof of the shack. Crimson lasers shot from the crustacean's eyes, and red neon whiskers twirled madly.

"Mmm. That smells delicious," remarked Osa.

Lisanne inhaled, and the aromatic confluence of gumbo file, cayenne pepper, mustard seed, cumin, garlic and bay leaves elicited a buried memory from long ago. "I'm almost certain that I walked on this street when I was a child," she said to her mate.

"It was a famous one."

Curious, the petite blonde faced the gondolier. "Pardon me."

"Oui, Madame?"

"When was the city submerged?"

"I was a little boy." The Creole stroked the water with his fiberglass paddle as he ruminated. "Twenty thirty-nine it began, though it was not all like this—some areas were flooded and others still dry. In forty-five, they decided to turn it into a water town and flooded it all."

"Merci," said Lisanne.

The crawfish-surmounted shack receded.

"When's our dinner reservation?" asked Osa. "That place made me hungry."

"I made it for twenty-two-thirty."

"What time's it now?"

The petite blonde withdrew her lily, put it in her ear and tapped it thrice. A woman's voice said, "The time is twenty-one forty-six. You have one new priority message from caller Mr. Johnson in the Reorientation Office."

Lisanne's stomach dropped.

"Mein Gott," she whispered. "Mein Gott." Her mouth became dry.

"What?" Osa looked at Lisanne. "What is it?" There was fear on the tall beauty's face.

"Sie haben zurückgerufen." Lisanne's eyes filled with tears, and the purple, gold and green lights swelled in her vision until their luminous edges touched and formed new colors. "Sie haben mich zurückgerufen," whispered the shocked woman.

"English, please," implored Osa, frightened and clutching her beaker of absinthe.

"They called. The Reorientation Office called back! There is only one reason why they call." Tears of joy poured down Lisanne's face, and she laughed, her eyes sparkling with a hundred colors.

"I don't know what that means," said Osa, confused by her mate's hysteria.

"Corpus Chrome, Incorporated is going to re-body my sister!"

Osa was stunned.

"They are going to bring her back to life," cried Lisanne. "They are going to bring Ellenancy back to life!"

"That's wonderful," said Osa. "That's really great."

Lisanne hugged her mate fiercely. "Mein Gott, mein Gott, mein Gott!" She laughed and wept, pressing herself into the tall beauty's chest.

Osa wept.

Her tears were different from the ones that were being shed by her mate.

PART II:
THE BATTLE FOR THE EMPIRE STATE

SUMMER, A.D. 2058

Chapter I
An Airborne Riot Wagon and the Little Reprobates

"This is your last chance!" the fifty-two-year-old policeman shouted at a dozen eleven-year-old children, all of whom were clothed in baggy blue uniforms. The morning sun shone behind the Jamaican-American officer like an interrogation lamp, and his police badge transmuted from a clenched fist to an outstretched helping hand twice each second. "Put your hands up, you little reprobates! Put them up or there'll be trouble!"

Eleven of the children raised their hands and (delightedly) awaited incarceration. The twelfth child said, "Don't talk to us that way. We didn't do anything wrong."

Snapdragon was annoyed that Autumn always had to spoil things. "Man!" he complained. "It's just for fun. Don't take everything so liberally."

"'Literally' is the word you mean. And I don't think it's fun when an authority figure abuses his power and calls us names."

"All right children, put you hands down." Lieutenant Vashan Mumbe knelt on the tuffgrass beside the little objector and inquired, "What's your name?"

"Autumn Tannstein."

"When we go up, would you like to sit up front?"

"Of course. One can see more."

"Who should sit beside you?"

"Snapdragon needs to sit beside me."

The chubby Chinese-American boy did a crescent kick of joy and fell over. He stood up, wiped tuffgrass from his buttocks and violently cheered.

Lieutenant Vashan returned his attention to Autumn. "Is he your friend?"

"He gets into trouble. Miss Karlsson told me to watch him."

Snapdragon did not recall the instructor ever telling Autumn to monitor him, but that was what the girl said whenever anybody asked why they were playing together. (For a moment, the boy contemplated the possibility of a secret meeting in which the matter had been discussed.)

Lieutenant Vashan smiled at Autumn, stood up and walked to the airborne riot wagon, an eight-meter-long cigar-shaped vehicle that was a little taller than the policeman and the exact same color as the tuffgrass upon which it sat.

"How come it's all green?" asked Reggie.

"This is the camouflage function," said the policeman.

Snapdragon said, "But I can see it right there. Everybody can."

"Let me explain how it works. The airborne riot wagon is covered with magnetized light pixels like the ones in your m.a. sets. They can change color and brightness to whatever we want them to, but they can't make things totally invisible be—"

"That sucks," remarked Snapdragon, thoughtfully.

The policeman continued, "Particle camouflage can't make things totally invisible, but it can change the color and brightness of the A.R.W. so that it's very hard to see. It depends on who's looking at it and from what angle."

Lieutenant Vashan kneeled to the level of the children. "This A.R.W. is the same color as the tuffgrass right now, so if you were looking down at the park from above—like from a shuttle or jetcopter—it would blend in with the tuffgrass."

The children nodded.

"But since you're on the ground, you can see it clearly because the background for you is not the tuffgrass, but the park, the sky and some trees and buildings."

The policeman clicked the closed-circuit acorn in his left ear and said, "Iris, give her a hop."

Telescopic legs loaded with combustion relay springs detonated, launching the vehicle into the air. Eleven of the children cheered. Gravity soon overpowered the inertia of the hop, and at an altitude of five hundred feet, the ship began to fall. Hull engines burst alight, keeping the craft in the sky like a buoy.

"Now watch me blend it in." Lieutenant Vashan clicked his acorn and said, "Match: sky."

The craft disappeared; only the flames of its hull engines were at all discernible in the blue vault. Eleven of the children clapped.

"The A.R.W. is camouflaged to us, but someone flying over it could see it very easily. They'd see a blue shape floating over the green park."

Standing up, the policeman clicked his acorn. "Iris, bring her down."

The hull boosters darkened, and as the airborne riot wagon sank from the sky, a dozen five-meter-long hydraulic supports unfolded from the bottom of the vehicle. Snapdragon felt the tuffgrass shake as the craft landed. A moment later, the twelve insectile appendages retracted into their nooks, whirring.

Lieutenant Vashan clicked his acorn. "Match: Country night; cloudless; stationary." The motes that covered the vehicle darkened, and upon the faux night sky, stars twinkled.

The policeman pressed his fingertips to the craft's black surface, and a fleximetal door retracted into the floor, revealing white padded walls, inflatable benches, human-sized containment cylinders and a dozen floating head clamps. A ramp extruded from the portal.

"Get into the wagon, you little reprobates!"

Ten children scampered into the back of the vehicle. Snapdragon followed directly behind Autumn as she climbed up the ramp and entered with dignity.

Pseudopodia extruded from the bench, tickling the Chinese-American boy as they clasped him. He giggled, even though he was aware that this was not a mature behavior. His young guardian was directly beside him, her regular leg and her special one swinging pendulously.

On the bench in front of Snapdragon sat Lieutenant Vashan and Sergeant Iris Smith, a white thirty-year-old woman who held the steering scepter. In front of the adults was a huge bugview windshield.

"Let's go!" Pinto said from the holding cabin where he and the other ten children sat on inflatable benches, clasped by pseudopodia.

Sergeant Iris tapped the windshield; the poly-perspective octagons were replaced by a natural view of trees, bushes, fields, running children and the buildings beyond the western perimeter of the park.

Snapdragon looked over at Autumn, and his pulse quickened. Whenever he imagined putting his lips on her cheek or rubbing against her or licking her hands (or Miss Karlsson's neck), his heart began to thud like it did during kung fu class or when he stayed up late watching violent mote aquarium experiences that depicted the many beasts and crazy people who could come and rip out his heart or suffocate him with a pillow or turn him into a blind wolf or replace his eyes with crab apples or teleport his blood out of his body into glass cylinders in an underground vault on the moon where the vampires lived after the humans had completely ruined planet Earth.

"We're about to hop," Officer Iris said into her lily, her voice booming from the grids in the rear of the wagon, emboldened with reverb, thickened with bass and stripped of its gender. "Is everybody ready?" inquired the sexless deity.

"Yes!" eleven of the children cried out.

This time, Snapdragon was the noncommittal exception: He had never been in a flying vehicle before, and he was scared. The boy did not want to appear cowardly in front of Autumn and the police officers, but all that he could think about was a mote aquarium experience in which a bunch of cops ran into an airborne riot wagon, shut the door and launched themselves directly into the bottom of a spaceship that was covered with spikes.

Lieutenant Vashan said into his lily, "I am going to count from three down to one. After the number one, you are all going to shout, 'Hop!' and Officer Iris will launch us into the air." His voice was also sexless, reverberant and emboldened with bass frequencies. "Does everyone understand?"

"Yes!"

Snapdragon began to sweat.

Autumn looked over and asked, "Are you scared?"

The boy did not reply.

"It's perfectly safe. There's no need to worry."

Snapdragon nodded his head, terrified.

Lieutenant Vashan said, "Three. Two. One."

The students yelled, "Hop!"

Officer Iris stomped the jump pedal with her right foot. The ground outside dropped away. Snapdragon sank in his seat. Great oaks slid from trunk to treetop. Apartment windows raced down the windshield; buildings sank as if demolished. Suddenly, the airborne riot wagon crested the skyline. The western expanse of Brooklyn City, the sun-struck East River, the solar-panel barbican that surrounded Nexus Y and the skyscrapers beyond sat like a diorama outside the craft.

Five hundred feet in the air, the airborne riot wagon stopped.

Gravity overtook the vehicle, and it began to sink. A few children yelled; Snapdragon became queasy. The tallest Brooklyn City buildings rose toward the craft.

Sergeant Iris ignited the hull boosters. Thuds resounded beneath the craft, followed by the crackling of flames.

The airborne riot wagon paused, suspended in midair.

In the corner of the windshield, Snapdragon saw a blinking green word that he did not recognize from his studies. Pointing at the confusing conglomeration of letters, he asked his neighbor, "What's that say?"

"Equilibrium," said Autumn. "It means balance."

"I know the definition of eaglelabia," defended Snapdragon. "I just couldn't read the word from here."

"The next part of our field trip is very, very serious," Sergeant Iris said with the deity's sexless voice. "We are going to the Empire State Building Memorial."

All of the children became quiet and serious.

Snapdragon's stomach knotted. Half of the students in the congregation had stayed in the building with Miss Karlsson because their parents would not allow them to go to the memorial.

"Lieutenant Vashan Mumbe will tell you all about it. He was there when it happened."

The fifty-two-year-old Jamaican American stared out of the windshield; his smile had vanished.

Sergeant Iris tapped a thrust button. The airborne riot wagon sped forward, and Snapdragon sank into his seat. Building tops flew past.

The Asian boy straightened himself and glanced at Autumn, who looked scared. "What's wrong?" he asked.

"Do you know anything about what happened to the Empire State Building?" asked Autumn, her voice thin and weak.

"They exploded it."

"Yes, but that was after a lot of really, really bad things happened." The Jewish girl shook her head. "This's going to be scary."

"I watch scary stuff all the time," boasted Snapdragon, omitting the deleterious impact that these experiences had upon him. "I even watched 'The Bare-Handed Surgeon of Beijing.'" He neglected to mention that he had slept in his parents' bed for the two weeks that followed, fearful that a midnight vasectomy or hysterectomy or mastectomy awaited him.

"But those are fictional," said Autumn. "They're not real. What happened at the Empire State Building is real."

Snapdragon grew nervous; he could taste heartbeats in his throat. The eleven-year-old Chinese-American boy suddenly wished that he were amongst the children who had stayed with Miss Karlsson.

Chapter II
The Battle for the Empire State

The airborne riot wagon sped between the ivy-covered fiber-metal skyscrapers, which had been erected atop historic Brooklyn Heights brownstones. Snapdragon inspected the buildings' windows.

Autumn shook her head. "You aren't going to see any naked women."

"That's not what I'm looking for," he replied as he scanned for nudity.

"It's not your fault. You had your puberty."

"Okay." The boy openly scanned for nudity.

Sergeant Iris pressed her steering scepter to the right; the craft swiveled, caught a western wind and arced over the solar panels that lined the near shore of the East River. A red fire wagon shot past the left side of the craft, pulling twelve tanks of water behind it.

"Must be a big fire," Snapdragon said to Autumn. "I hope they put it out or that it's a school." For a moment, the boy pondered his admission. "Don't tell Miss Karlsson I said that."

Autumn, preoccupied, did not respond.

The airborne riot wagon shot past the solar barbicans on the west side of the East River, over the wall and into Nexus Y. The craft turned north.

Snapdragon saw: skyscrapers, birds, an animated billboard for "The Ugliest Newlyweds," a stone park with a circular fountain and a big white arch, another airborne riot wagon, two jetcopters, an American flag, a Pizza Overlord skyfloat (a giant pie where each pepperoni was filled with two hundred cheese pizzas [all of which were fake and hollow]), and thirty new blue buildings that seemed identical except for their street numbers, which were bright and silver.

Sergeant Iris thumbed the brake and pushed the scepter forward; the craft slowed, relinquishing altitude. Gray buildings and steel-fiber skyscrapers slid past, each decorated with an American flag that was animated by the wind of the flying vehicle.

Snapdragon looked at the traffic below. Foam-rubber ladybugs and box vans jostled each other along Fifth Avenue, and a stopwall shot up from the road, creating a route for the contrary vehicles on Twenty-Third Street. Pedestrians and vending carts swarmed the blue-gray sidewalks.

Lieutenant Vashan said, "I want everybody to look up ahead."

Snapdragon faced forward and saw a twisted, blackened mass that rose thirty meters from the ground and culminated in stalagmites of tortured steel. His heart pounded.

The airborne riot wagon's shadow was absorbed by that which had been scorched as it flew toward a gray platform.

All of the children were silent.

* * *

Upon the observation dais, Snapdragon, Autumn and the other students stared up at the blackened fangs of the wreckage.

Lieutenant Vashan faced the eleven-year-olds. "I'm going to give you a little history and then tell you what happened and what I saw."

He motioned to the six and a half stories of molten wreckage and continued, "The Empire State Building was constructed nearly one hundred and thirty years ago, during nineteen-thirty and thirty-one. At that time, it was the world's tallest skyscraper and an icon of and for this country.

"I want all of you to look straight up."

Snapdragon gazed at the blue sky, which was scratched with white clouds.

"Suspended up there is an American flag. Does everybody see it?"

One after another, the children responded, "Yes!" or "I see it!"

A moment later, Snapdragon located the flag; the floating icon had silver stripes, onyx stripes and an ivory box that contained onyx stars. "I see it!" he proclaimed, blood rushing to the rear of his tilted head.

"The Empire State Building used to be as tall as that." The policeman let the children ponder the edifice's immensity. "For more than a century, the space in between that floating flag and the wreckage down here was filled with people."

Snapdragon lowered his head so that he would not get dizzy.

"In twenty-forty-five, President B.R. Gregs was elected. His main goal was to fully commit our nation to the Global Senate, the unified world government that we now belong to. Most of the country supported him—he was elected by a massive majority—but those who were against him were very outspoken about how joining the Global Senate would hurt our economy, military, culture and independence.

"A week after his inauguration—that's when he becomes the president for real—President B.R. Gregs announced that he was going to a summit—a meeting—in Berlin in early July to fully commit our nation to the Global Senate. His supporters applauded him, and his detractors hated him more than before.

"Most of the people who opposed America committing herself to the Global Senate were peaceful people who held protest rallies and made speeches and wrote letters by hand.

"But some of the people who didn't want us to join the Global Senate were extremists. Extremists are people with very strong opinions different from the majority, and extremists are people who will hurt other people to make a point.

"The most infamous extremist group was led by Isabelle Xia and Nicolai Dhanikov, a married couple from Montana. Have any of you heard of these two people?"

A couple of the children nodded, and a few shook their heads; Snapdragon did not commit himself either way.

"In nineteen-eighty-two, Nicolai Dhanikov escaped the USSR—what Russia was called back when it was our rival—and came to the United States, a thing that was called defecting. He became a surgeon here and for the next four decades practiced medicine. Eventually, he settled in Montana where he met Isabelle Xia, who had escaped persecution in China where her entire family had been tortured and killed when she was a little girl.

"They were married the day Isabelle Xia turned eighteen. Nicolai was sixty-three at the time."

"Gross!" exclaimed a blonde girl who was named Terri.

"In twenty-thirty-five, Xia and Dhanikov created a group called Americans Against Globalization—A.A.G.—that spoke out against U.S involvement with the Global Senate, which was Europe and most of Asia and Africa at that time. The federal government—that was the big government in charge of the whole country back then—was aware of A.A.G. but was not afraid of them, because people who held rallies and spoke publicly and wrote letters were not the ones the big government was worried about. The government was worried about the people who did things in secret. It turned out that A.A.G. was a façade—"

Pinto's hand went up.

"It turned out that Americans Against Globalization was a fake group which Xia and Dhanikov used to recruit extremists for their secret organization, which was called Protectors of the Fifty. Protectors of the Fifty wanted to make sure that America never, ever joined the Global Senate."

"Why'd they think it was so bad?" asked Snapdragon.

Sergeant Iris replied, "Xia and Dhanikov were born in countries with bad governments, but they were able to leave those places and come to a different country with a different government—America—and be safe. They did not want all of the countries connected in one huge government, because if that huge government ever became bad, then the whole world might become like the places where they grew up."

Lieutenant Vashan continued, "Most Americans wanted us to join the Global Senate, but there were millions who opposed it. Still, there is a gigantic difference between speaking out against something and doing what the Protectors of the Fifty did.

"On the Fourth of July, twenty-forty-five, while President B.R. Gregs was at the important Global Senate summit in Berlin, the Protectors of the Fifty took the Empire State Building. It's still unclear exactly how they did this—how they infiltrated it so thoroughly—but we know that they had people on the observation roof, armed with razorguns and migraine pens, and also soldiers on every single floor of the building, as well as some dressed up like policemen at ground level. There were approximately thirteen hundred terrorists in the building, and exactly seventy-nine thousand eight hundred and forty-two innocent people.

"The terrorists who were disguised as policemen sealed the lobby doors and put putty explosives on the hinges, and the ones on each floor confiscated lilies, slapped blockers on all the computers and shot paint bulbs on the lenses of every single camera and against every single window. By the time I arrived, the building and the people in it were cut off from the outside world, and every window was covered with black paint.

"Xia and Dhanikov hung a large fabric screen on the side of the building that we're facing right now."

Snapdragon and the other children looked at the wreckage.

"On it was a message telling us not to enter because the doors and windows were wired to explosives that they had attached to the hostages. It was signed, Protectors of the Fifty.

"Nothing else happened that day, but the whole world watched.

"The next day, the words on the banner changed. It said, 'President B.R. Gregs must not commit the free United States of America to the Global Senate. He must leave the Berlin summit at once.'

"The president made an announcement from the Global Senate Conference Building in Berlin. What he said was, 'I will not speak with terrorists.'

"Immediately after his response, a window opened on the tenth floor of the Empire State Building. A woman wearing a rubber bodysuit and a padded helmet was thrown outside. She plummeted, screaming, and slammed against the sidewalk. Her spine and legs and arms and ribs and pelvic bones were shattered, but she lived for twenty minutes, because the rubber suit held her body together and the cushioned helmet protected her skull. She yelled, 'They're going to kill my whole family if the president doesn't leave the summit! They're going to kill them!' She said this over and over and over until she passed out and died. Her name was Nicole Dorne."

Snapdragon imagined the woman, crushed and suffering inside of her rubber bodysuit, and suddenly, he felt nauseated. Autumn reached out, took his hand and squeezed it.

"The banner changed, saying, 'The president must leave the summit NOW.'

"The president ignored the terrorists, which was and is American and Global Senate policy.

"The next day, three kids younger than you—Sara Dorne, Stevie Dorne and Sassy Dorne—and their father, Matthew Dorne, were thrown from the building's tenth floor and hit the pavement. They were wearing the helmets that protected their skulls and the rubber suits that kept them from bleeding out, and the terrorists had given them painkillers so that they'd remain conscious for a longer period of time...though they felt everything by the end. The nation watched this man and these three children die for nearly an hour.

"The mayor and the federal government filed a broadcast injunction—a stop sign—against the media, which stopped them from showing more deaths.

"The president spoke to the United States of America and said, 'I will not speak with terrorists. Their killing will amount to nothing.'"

"Didn't he care about all the people?" asked Pinto, angrily.

"He cared." Lieutenant Vashan paused and looked at Sergeant Iris with his sad eyes. "He definitely cared."

A moment later, the Jamaican-American policeman returned his attention to the children. "I was in the bomb squad back then. We helped the firemen inflate foam mattresses around the perimeter of the building, though we knew that it wasn't going to help."

"Why'd you do it?" asked Terri.

"It's important to do something at a time like that—something other than just stand around and watch innocent people die. But it didn't change anything— Protectors of the Fifty dropped the next victims from the fiftieth floor and the effect was the same. Their insides were smashed and they survived for short periods of time. Eventually, our doctors euthanized...um...sped up the deaths so that the victims wouldn't suffer.

"For three weeks, people fell from the building—two or three every hour, twenty-four hours a day. During this period, President B.R. Gregs joined our nation to the Global Senate.

"Then things got worse.

"A metal canister was dropped from a window onto the mattresses. The initial fear was that it was a bomb, and everybody cleared the area, except for the bomb squad officers, who were in impact suits. The fabric screen was blank, and we had no idea what was in the canister. I was sent to assess the threat.

"It was a metal thermos that did not appear to be or contain an explosive. I untwisted the top and looked inside, and it looked back at me. It was filled with eyeballs."

Snapdragon's lower lip trembled, and he fought against tears. Autumn wiped her leaking eyes. Pinto and Keshara and Peggy and Dariuz and Terri cried.

"I almost threw up, it was—" Lieutenant Vashan paused and shook his head. "It was one of the worst moments of my life. I was shaking as I walked back to the chief, and when I showed it to him, he did throw up. There were fifty eyeballs in the thermos, each surgically removed from a different person.

"A few minutes later, the fabric screen said, 'You will receive ten canisters a day until the president withdraws our nation from the Global Senate.' That amounts to five hundred eyes a day.

"President B.R. Gregs continued to ignore the terrorists.

"We received canisters for two weeks.

"During this period there were an unknown number of suicides inside the ESB. People cut their wrists or refused to eat or suffocated themselves. There was a conflict on the sixty-fifth floor, an uprising, but all of the hostages were executed and dumped onto the street, their genitals mutilated or cut off.

"The president did not change his position.

"Things got worse.

"Hostages were hung from windows by their own intestines. The holes in their stomachs were sewn shut so that they would live for hours—and some lived for days—dangling upside-down by their guts. An airborne riot wagon tried to rescue one of these people and was shot with a sticky bomb and destroyed."

"Why didn't the president do something?" demanded Pinto.

"What the heck was he waiting for?!" shouted Snapdragon.

"On August sixteenth—almost seven weeks after the event had begun—President B.R. Gregs called a summit with the Global Senators and the mayor of Nexus Y and the governor of New York. At that time, it was estimated that more than seventeen thousand people had been mutilated or killed by the Protectors of the Fifty.

"The mayor and the governor proposed the idea of a temporary U.S. withdrawal from the Global Senate, but everyone feared that would only prolong the hostage situation. And doing something like that—giving the terrorists what they wanted—also went against both U.S. and G.S. policy and opened the door for more terrorism worldwide.

"At that meeting, the president and the G.S. decided to storm the Empire State Building.

"My cousin and my father were in two of the one hundred and seventy-four airborne riot wagons that made up the assault team. When they were preparing themselves, I said good-bye to them. My cousin was optimistic and said she would survive and see me again, but my dad just put on his gear and shook my hand. He didn't seem very hopeful.

"All of these men and women are heroes.

"The eighteenth of August arrived.

"It was raining. The outside of the Empire State Building was covered with dangling corpses and a few people who were still dying. I was with the bomb squad on the ground, inside one of the lightning tanks.

"I watched the airborne riot wagons surround the building. Gangways shot to the walls. Officers crashed through the windows, and explosions threw them back outside. Scores of officers fell to their deaths while more stormed inside. It was an example of the best of mankind confronting the very worst.

"There were one hundred and two floors of warfare in that building. The terrorists had nothing to live for, so they used lava grenades and poison gas bulbs and oven bombs that killed everybody, including themselves.

"The moment that Isabelle Xia was shot and killed, Nicolai Dhanikov detonated the bombs that the Protectors of the Fifty had planted throughout the building.

"The world ended for a moment.

"All I could see was pure white. All I could hear were screams and static. My tank was kicked four blocks from ground zero. We spun end-over-end until we slammed into a building. I threw up and blacked out.

"My captain woke me up a few minutes later.

"We were trapped in our lightning tank—it had been crushed and melted—but we lit forge-axes and got out. Smoke and dust filled the air and black glass was all over the ground. A strong wind cleared the air and we saw what had happened."

Lieutenant Vashan pointed to the agonized foundation of the Empire State Building.

Snapdragon wiped tears from his eyes with his fists; Autumn pressed her face to the boy's shoulder and wept silently like an adult.

"Seventy-nine thousand eight hundred and forty-two hostages died. One thousand nine hundred and twenty-two police officers were killed. Six hundred and eighty-four people in the immediate area also perished.

"President B.R. Gregs resigned the next day. He felt that he was no longer emotionally equipped to be our Chief Representative in the Global Senate. Vice President Samantha Luther replaced him.

"Two days later, former President B.R. Gregs committed suicide."

Chapter III
Paternal Impulses (Kick the Stars)

Holding a spool of udon in one hand and a sauce vial in the other, Champ Sappline looked up at the one-hundred-fifty-story building in which he would presently be reunited with his long-dead father.

The façade of the cylindrical chromium edifice was segmented like bamboo into five thirty-story sections. Excepting the black panes of the one hundred and second, one hundred and fourth, and one hundred and tenth floors, which were dedicated to the Empire State Building, One World Trade Center and the Twin Towers, its windows were one-way glass that matched the metal. Affixed to the surface of the building by the soles of their feet were two hundred seventy defunct mannequin prototypes. The extruding androids faced up, frozen mid-stride on a spiral journey that wound around the cylinder from the pavement to the sky.

Clothed in brown slacks and a collared green shirt and wearing a tie for the first time since his ill-fated sojourn to Madrid (which had been his final trip as a married man), Champ sat upon a spongy bench and sucked udon that was flavored with garlic, miso, shiso, shiitake and shrimp powders. He sipped sesame glaze from the sauce vial as he chewed the lubricated noodles.

Eating, the garbage man pondered his failed marriage, a nearby turkey pigeon, his roommates, his home below the toilet, tasty flavor-injected udon, the war in his building (which had just escalated to "Class III: Violent; Shoving and slapping"), Mikek's smells, the mundane woman to whom the herpetology student had introduced him on his birthday who did not want to see him again even though she thought he was "very good-looking," and the weird fact that he was now five years older than his father.

Champ opened the sauce vial and set it before the black beaks of two turkey pigeons. "Enjoy," he said, tossing the emptied udon spool into a garbage canister from which he had sucked soup more than fifty times. Standing upright, he straightened his tie and looked at the Corpus Chrome, Incorporated Building. Repressed anxieties burgeoned inside of his chest.

The lily in his right ear beeped, and a demure female voice said, "Incoming call: R.J. the Third."

Double-tapping the device, he answered, "Yeah?"

"I wanted to wish you good luck."

"Danke."

"Your father is welcome to occupy the bathroom that our next door neighbors just insurrected from floor five. I believe it comes with a plunger."

"He has a room at the firehouse. CCI wants him there—it's part of the deal."

"That's understandable." The popinjay clicked his tongue twice and added, "Do not hesitate to ring or rouse me to discuss your reunion. I am interested on a personal level, and also as an auteur."

"I'll give you a call after."

"There's somebody else who wants to say something to you—"

A piteous mewling sound that could only originate in a morbidly obese cat caused Champ to end the call. The anxious fellow then dragged on a Purpureal vapor tube, and the uplifting (albeit calming) combination of chemicals patted him on the back, saying, "Well done, sir!"

Pulling his long blonde hair behind his ears, the garbage man walked toward the one-hundred-and-fifty-story temple of resurrection.

* * *

On the seventieth floor, Mr. Johnson, clothed in a beige tweed suit, motioned with a paddle-like hand toward the sky-blue passage on the right. Champ veered into the indicated hall, where the two men proceeded in tandem.

"Did you listen to the files I put in your vault?" inquired the shepherd.

"I listened to one of them—it was pretty depressing."

Mr. Johnson declined to comment upon Champ's negligence.

After passing a dozen iridescent numbers, the shepherd said, "You'll be pleased to know that your father is doing quite well. He has scored quite highly on his equilibrium, manipulation and recognition tests."

"That's good. Maybe—because he was a fireman—he was more prepared for death than most people?"

"Perhaps," said the shepherd in a manner that indicated he did not agree with the garbage man's hypothesis.

"Seven forty-two, right?" asked Champ.

"Indeed, indeed, indeed."

Three strides later, the pair stopped in front of the living wall marked 742. Champ felt a chill prickle his skin, as if he had just stepped from a warm shower into a cool draughty room.

"Would you like a softener?" asked the shepherd.

"Nah," the garbage man said as he raised his vapor tube. "This's fine." He sucked Purpureal; a trilling B-flat lanced the quietude, and positive sentiments combated his anxiety. Soon, the invisible hand patted him on the back, saying, "Well done, sir! Very, very well done!"

Mr. Johnson reached into the wall and dialed a code beneath the surface; three musical tones rang within the hall.

"The waiting area lies beyond," said the shepherd, motioning his guest forward with a nod.

Champ walked through the nanobuilders and into a brown alcove that was furnished with a suspended leather couch, a water sphere and a table that upheld two movie sheaves and a mote aquarium; on the far wall hung an orange polarity curtain.

For a moment, the garbage man wondered if he were dreaming.

Mr. Johnson entered the room, and behind him, the wound of ingress was healed over by crackling nanobuilders.

Champ motioned to the polarity curtain. "He's behind that, right?"

"Indeed, indeed, indeed."

The garbage man stared at the orange fabric; anxiety threatened the positive state that had been engineered by the caffeine, ginseng and dexaprine mist, which he still tasted on his tongue.

"I'll be right here on the couch if you need me," said the shepherd.

"You're gonna watch, right? On that m.a.?"

"That is standard practice. Eagle's interactions with people from his first life are important and will affect how quickly he is granted autonomy. If you are opposed to my witnessing—"

"No, no. You can watch. I'd like you to let me know if I say something bad or if he malfunctions or something."

"I shall, though a malfunction is a very, very unlikely occurrence."

Champ took one step toward the curtain and balked.

Mr. Johnson pulled a reticule of lozenges from his blazer, plucked a slim pink ovoid and handed it to the apprehensive garbage man.

"Danke." Champ put the softener upon his tongue, where it dissolved and was instantly absorbed. "Tastes like a radish," he said as his pulse slowed, and his respirations quietened. The room grew dimmer, and the tightness of his shirt collar no longer bothered him.

Dialed down fifteen percent, Champ walked toward the polarity curtain. The fabric furled into the top of the frame, and three musical chimes heralded his arrival in the adjacent room. He entered a spacious, oval and ice-light-illuminated enclosure, which was covered by sepia wallpaper that cycled loops of horses alternately leaping over hurdles and shrubs.

"Over here," said an unfamiliar voice.

Champ turned to the right and saw a model 8M chromium mannequin standing beside a magnetically buoyed pool table. The blond-haired machine wore blue jeans, white socks and a red t-shirt that said NEW YORK FIRE DEPARTMENT, and held in its gelware hands was a glossy wooden cue. The re-bodied man silently appraised his visitor; lenses shifted within eye sockets like spyglass parts.

"Daddy?" quavered Champ, who had not uttered this word since his father's funeral thirty-four years ago. "Dad?" he said with adult pretensions.

From the unmoving mouth slit came the words, "That's you, huh? You're Champ?"

The garbage man nodded, the corners of his eyes wet and burning.

"You're a grown-up," observed the mannequin as his gelware hands rested the cue upon green felt.

The re-bodied man walked toward his son.

Suffused by a wave of unanticipated melancholy, Champ bit his lower lip and hugged the mannequin. Filling the garbage man's nostrils were the smells of warm wires, plastic, copper and gelatin.

Eagle clapped his hands upon his son's back and patted him like a baseball coach. "It's good to see you."

"Uh-huh," Champ responded, "you, too."

Soon, the Sapplines withdrew from each other and stood face to face. The re-bodied man was slightly taller than his water-based offspring.

Eagle's gelware face wrinkled, grinning. "You look a lot like me. Well...like I used to."

"I don't have many pictures."

The apertures within the mannequin's eyes opened, and the secondary lenses slid forward. "If you cut that hair to a man's length and were more muscular, you'd look just like I did."

"Thanks."

"It's good you took after me," informed Eagle. "The men on your mother's side were all wimpy. She had a cousin Nestor."

"I barely remember him."

"He ain't the kind of guy you want to look like. Wanna shoot some pool?"

"Okay," said Champ, thinking that death had not diminished his father's bluster.

The mannequin walked toward the magnetically buoyed table. "They asked if there was anything I wanted to practice my motor skills with, and I always liked pool."

"I remember." Champ glanced at the buoyed table and inquired, "The magnets don't mess with the mannequin?"

"The robot's only chrome on the outside. Most of it's cheap stuff—plastic and foam, like a toy or something. And they said there're anti-magnet thingies inside that shield the parts from other magnets."

"Okay."

"Did I ever take you to play pool?" asked Eagle. "You were kind of young for that sort of thing." The mannequin fished pool balls from the bank and set them within the wooden rack.

"You took me once. There was a championship game in your pool league, and I was in town, so you brought me. I remember eating popcorn and pretzels out of a bowl that smelled like beer."

"Sorry about that." Eagle set more balls into the stable. "Did we win? My team, did we win?"

"You guys won."

"That's probably why I don't remember it too good. We partied a lot when we won. I liked to get wrecked."

"You got wrecked," Champ confirmed, "and so did the other guys. And there was a woman there, too. She made me hold her cigarettes a couple of times."

"Probably Steph. The guys and gals in the firehouse liked to share her, pass her around." Eagle dropped a red ball amongst its peers and looked at his son. "Should I not say stuff like that? I'm not sure how this's supposed to go—between us. You're a grown-up now, but I'm not sure what's inappropriate or whatever."

"Don't worry about it."

"Kick the stars."

Champ had not heard anybody use this expression in earnest in over two decades. Eagle lifted the rack and pointed to the triangulated balls. "I'll give you the break."

"Danke."

"'Danke?' You become German while I was dead?"

"That's just what people say."

"'Cause Hitler was so charming?"

"I'm not sure why." Champ ruminated for a few seconds. "Maybe because the Global Senate's based in Berlin." He picked up the cue, squeezed the shaft and appraised its alignment: The stick was balanced.

"And why aren't they calling it New York anymore?" asked Eagle.

"It's still New York, but after Brooklyn became a separate city, the mayor pushed for a new nickname. Like Manhattan or the Big Apple, but more international."

"The Big Apple never made any sense. I never eat apples."

"I believe that that name came from a horse racetrack that was here."

"Which makes even less sense," remarked Eagle. "I ran out of chalk, so you can use that baking soda the janitor brought." The mannequin pointed to a cup filled with white powder.

Champ dabbed the cue's tip, shook off the extra, walked to the edge of the table, set the slender end between his thumb and index finger and drew the shaft back with his right hand.

"Your mother's still around, right?" asked Eagle.

"Yeah. Lives with some guy in Colorado."

"That homo with the little dogs?"

"Not James."

"Good," remarked the mannequin. "I wasn't a perfect husband or anything, but that guy pissed pink."

"She divorced him when I was twelve, lived with some other guy for a few years—a health nut who once asked me for a stool sample—and then she married the food engineer who patented the pork-chop loaf. She's still married to him, though they don't seem to like each other a whole lot."

"How's she doin' otherwise?"

"Seems fine on holidays."

"You guys aren't close?"

"Eh."

Champ thrust the shaft forward. The cue ball cracked the pointillist triangle, and colors sped pell-mell to the rails. Three spheres shot into pockets.

"Nice break," said Eagle. "You gonna be solids? You got two solids in already."

Champ appraised the table and shook his head. "Stripes. The positioning is better." He drew an imaginary vector in the air, said, "Eleven, banked, into the side," and lanced the named ball into the promised pocket before the puff of baking powder had settled.

"Kick the stars," exclaimed Eagle. "You're good."

"Thanks."

Champ drew a vector in the air, said, "Ten ball, corner pocket," took and made the called shot.

"Does she know that they made me into a robot?"

"I wasn't sure you'd want me to tell her." The garbage man paused and looked at the mannequin's neutral visage. "Do you want me to tell her?"

"No rush, I guess. Unless you think I should? Didn't talk to her too much at the end other than scheduling your visits."

"There weren't that many of those," remarked Champ.

Eagle was silent.

The garbage man called and made his next shot. Throughout the oval room, the clacking of pool balls seemed louder than it had a moment ago.

Champ said, "Seems like there're other people you'd rather contact than your ex-wife. I got some numbers in my vault—guys from your old firehouse who're still around." He was fully aware that his father's most meaningful relationships were with these men. "I called to let them know what was going on with you."

"Kick the stars! Which ones are still around?"

"Pedro Cheung."

"That ox! Glad he made it."

"Butch Silverberg."

"Bagel Butch? Helluva Jew."

"Bill Lords."

"The way he partied? That's a surprise." Eagle ruminated for a moment. "He's gotta be at least eighty—he's a bit older than the rest of us."

"He sounded a little slow, but he's still breathing. Your old mentor Potato O'Boyd is still around. He's still working for FDNY—he's a Fire Chief."

"Potato made it!" A gigantic smile creased the mannequin's face, almost burying his lenses in gelware. "Kick the stars! That's the best! Who else? Did Brett Brickman pull through? That guy pulled me out of two collapses, and I introduced him to the gal he left his third wife for. The rump on that woman." A sound like a piccolo flute emerged from the mannequin's larynx speakers.

Perplexed, Champ looked at his father.

"That's the sound this thing makes instead of a whistle," Eagle explained, "since the lips don't move and it doesn't breathe or anything."

"Oh."

"Did he make it? Brett Brickman?"

Unsure of what he should or should not say, Champ looked at the polarity curtain. No guidance emerged from the adjacent room.

"Brickman…isn't around anymore," admitted the garbage man.

The mannequin's generic face became neutral, expressionless, and the ocular apertures narrowed. Eagle Sappline stood silent and unmoving.

Champ set the cue on its rubber bulb and leaned it against the table. "Dad?"

The mannequin did not respond.

Champ looked from Eagle to the polarity curtain, but received no guidance from the shepherd. The garbage man then strode around the table towards his father.

"You okay?"

"That's too bad about Brickman," said Eagle, his body inert.

"Sorry. I know you guys were close—he was really upset at your funeral." Champ vividly remembered the untidy scene: Brett Brickman had walked up to the cosmetically restored (but brainless) corpse, yelled, "I told you it was gonna collapse!" and punched the coffin again and again and again until the wood buckled and his knuckles were bloody, at which point a woman clapped her hands to his right arm and pulled him from the dais and from the church out into the snow where he yelled, "That goddamn fool!" while tears poured down his face.

Eagle said, "Considering how we all lived—and what we did for a living—I'm surprised we've got this many still dancing."

"The guys want to have a get-together when you're granted autonomy."

"That'd be great. I'm not sure how I'll get wrecked inside this thing, but I'll figure something out."

Champ imagined Mr. Johnson highlighting that portion of the conversation. "Uh…I feel that CCI would frown upon you purposely damaging the mannequin."

"They gave it to me, right? Seems like if I want to get smashed, then that's just up to me."

"Dad…they're monitoring this conversation."

"Well, I'm not looking to break it or anything. I just wanna have some fun."

The polarity curtain furled, and Mr. Johnson strode into the room. Champ's muscles tightened.

"Hey, Johnson," said Eagle.

"Good afternoon."

"I'm-I'm really sorry about what my dad said," blathered Champ. "He won't damage the mannequin unit once he understands how valuable it is." The garbage man looked at his father and prompted, "Will you?"

"I like to party."

"Dad!" Champ was exasperated.

"Don't go hysterical."

More irate than he had been on that morning two weeks prior when a foe on the fifth floor shoved him into a wall that was covered with wet green paint, Champ shouted, "Don't be glib—this is important!"

Mr. Johnson laughed heartily. "Don't worry: We have consciousness-altering devices that will engineer the states your father desires."

"You do?" asked Champ, incredulously.

"Yes."

"Kick the stars!" shouted Eagle.

The shepherd resumed, "And, unlike caffeine, alcohol, marijuana, lift, dexaprine and cocaine, these devices—they're called tweakers—do not in any way damage the brain."

"CCI is incredible," announced the re-bodied man.

Champ asked, "Why do you have things like that?"

"Generally speaking, the life a person lives within a mannequin is supposed to be a continuation of that individual's first life. Many of the artists we revive rely on such mental states for their livelihood, and people with dangerous, high-pressure jobs—like firemen or soldiers—often require a greater degree of intellectual relief in between duties to achieve their peak performances."

"He's totally right about that," Eagle said to Champ, "one thousand percent correct."

Relieved that his father's crapulous ambitions were permissible, Champ shrugged.

Mr. Johnson grinned and addressed Eagle, "I'm not allowed to give you tweakers until you're granted autonomy, but I will note your interest and put in a request for paisley brain, aquatic thoughts and warp speed."

"Those. Sound. Awesome!"

The shepherd flicked a paddle-like hand at the pool table, said, "Please continue," and walked out of the room.

Champ reclaimed the cue and pointed its tip at a striped ball and a corner pocket. "Fourteen in the corner." He sighted the shot carefully (an enemy sphere sat at the edge of the path) and thrust the shaft. The cue ball sped from the puff of baking powder, nicked the green six and caromed wide.

"Crap." Champ handed the cue to the mannequin.

"I thought you were gonna run the whole damn table on me."

"I'm not that good. I just got lucky with the break."

"You know how to shoot," Eagle said as he powdered the cue's tip. "How'd you get so good?"

"We had a parlor with a pool table. My wife and I."

The mannequin looked up. "You're married?"

"I was."

"Oh." Eagle appraised the arrangement of balls upon the table for a moment and said, "I'd've been surprised. You look like a bachelor."

"Thanks," said Champ, perturbed.

Eagle knelt so that his head was level with the table, closed the aperture in his left eye socket and narrowed the one behind his right lens. "I can get more things in focus when I do this. Bigger debt of field, they said."

"I think you mean depth of field."

"I'm not a scientist." The re-bodied man nestled the slender end of the cue between his index and middle fingers and drew back the shaft with his left hand. "Why'd she leave you?"

Nettled by the inquiry, Champ replied, "Why do you assume that she left me?"

"Don't go hysterical. I can tell. Your mother left me, and lots of guys at the house had busted marriages. When a guy talks about his ex using the word 'we' like that, he's still holding on to something. I did the same thing when your mom put me in the trash can."

"It's hard to imagine how that ever came to pass."

A weird chirping noise issued from the mannequin's mouth slit.

"What the hell was that?" asked Champ.

"A laugh, supposedly. So why'd she dump you?"

"Take your shot." The garbage man was annoyed and did not want to discuss his failed marriage with his father.

"You were always real sensitive," remarked Eagle. "I remember how scared you got at the movies."

"*Ninety-Eight Years in a Chinese Torture Camp* and *Behold the Gutted* might not've been the most suitable choices for an eight-year-old."

"No need to get grumpy." The re-bodied man swiveled his expressionless gelware face away from his son. "Maybe I shouldn't've brought you to those kinds of movies," he said, "but they're the kind I like, and I wanted to take you. As a firefighter, you learn to just do things when you want to, not wait around, because...well, you know why. The stuff in those movies is all fake, anyways."

"It looked real to me. *Grizzly Bear Root Canal* gave me nightmares for a year."

"That's a great one," enthused Eagle, obliviously. "Especially when that bear gets his teeth back from those rednecks."

"Take your shot," prompted Champ.

"Four in the corner pocket." Eagle thrust the shaft forward, and the stick glanced off the white sphere. "Nuts," he said of his miscue.

"You can go again," offered Champ.

"Bullshit."

"Really, just set it back and—"

"Those aren't the rules," Eagle said as he thrust the stick into Champ's hands. "Your turn."

The garbage man indicated a ball and a pocket with the cue, lanced, succeeded, walked to the other side of the table, pointed out the striped nine's destination and drove it home. Missing his next shot, he handed the stick back to his father.

Eagle knelt and appraised the felt surface, shutting one iris and narrowing the other. He then stood upright, set the wood, drew the butt of the stick and thrust. The cue ball hopped ten irrelevant centimeters and spun in place.

"Nuts."

Concerned about the dual miscues, Champ asked, "Is this normal?"

"Hell, no—I used to be good. I was the best player on the team except for Potato O'Boyd."

"But have you been able to make shots since they brought you back? Since you've been in the mannequin?"

"Some," said Eagle. "I'm not as good as I used to be, but I've done a lot better than this. I think I'm doing worse 'cause you're here and I've got more things to keep track of than just shooting."

Unsure what his father meant, Champ eloquently inquired, "Um....huh?"

"It's different in here." Eagle slapped a gelware palm to the red FDNY shirt that covered over his chrome-plated plastic chest.

"What's it like?"

"Hard to explain, but different."

"How's it different?"

The mannequin was completely still for a few moments. Suddenly, he inquired, "You get drunk, right?"

"There have been instances."

"You know how you have to concentrate more to do things, like really think about things to accomplish them when you're wrecked? You think, 'I've gotta stand up slow, so people won't see how wasted I am,' and you do that. Slow, careful. And when you walk, you think, 'I need to balance myself so I don't wobble,' and you do that, thinking about each step, concentrating. And when you finally get to the bar for another, you think about what you're gonna order before you say it—you think of the exact words—so that it doesn't come out all slurred, though it might anyways."

"So it's like you're drunk?" inquired Champ. "In the mannequin?"

"That's not really what I'm saying. My thoughts're clear and regular and there's none of the warmth or tingling or awesomeness that you get when you're wrecked. It's that you have to really concentrate to do things—especially moving around—like you do when you're drunk."

"Okay. I understand what you're saying."

"It's like you're a sober guy stuck in some drunk's body with none of the benefits."

Champ did not think that life inside of a mannequin sounded particularly great.

"I'm getting used to it, though," Eagle said, "and it's a helluva lot better than being a dead guy."

CHAPTER IV
THE FACES OF SERFDOM

Lisanne and Osa departed the hot Nexus Y summer and—through a living window—entered the air-conditioned front lobby of the Corpus Chrome, Incorporated Building. Condensation beaded upon the petite blonde's forehead, and apprehension prickled her insides. Today she would finally be reunited with her resurrected twin sister.

Osa squeezed Lisanne's hand and kissed her forehead. "It's going to go good—I mean well. Don't worry."

"Danke."

The Swedish-Indian American had been full of supportive words and gestures, but it was clear that she was very uneasy about how the three-month-long relationship would be affected by the resurrection of Ellenancy Breutschen. Lisanne had been completely honest when—during their last meal in New Orleans—she had said, "I don't know how this will change our dynamic, or even if it will in any substantial way, but I know that I love you very, very deeply and that you are wonderful." The tall beauty had appreciated the sentiment, but it was clear that she still had some apprehensions.

Shortly after the couple returned from their trip, Osa was assigned four new interaction sessions, and Lisanne was contacted by three major recording artists who wanted to schedule time in her studio. The women tried to see each other as often as they had during the previous months, but it was impossible; they saw each other less, and Ellenancy's resurrection loomed larger.

During this strained period, every act—significant or otherwise—was analyzed and assigned meaning.

On one occasion, Lisanne had forgotten to call Osa and the next day awakened to find three anxious messages from the tall beauty in her vault. The petite blonde was unsure whether her atypical oversight was the result of too many hours in the studio with the congagroove band Aorta Squeeze or because of her preoccupation with Ellenancy's resurrection, but the negligent omission became an incident and a discussion. In their raw relationship, any oversight was portentous and every kindness seemed forced.

Today their purgatory would end.

The women walked in tandem through the Corpus Chrome, Incorporated Building lobby, across a glass-covered pond (in which nine greenish-purple tortoises lazily swam, yawning) and toward the reception desks—three inverted pyramids of gray marble and chrome filigree, behind which sat six good-looking young people who were clothed in sky-blue wool sweaters and matching slacks.

"Everything will work out," Lisanne said to Osa (and to herself).

The tall beauty squeezed some reassurance into her mate's hand.

At the nearest inverted pyramid, a brunette receptionist said, "Guten Tag, Miss Breutschen, and welcome back to Corpus Chrome, Incorporated." The chipper woman flashed teeth, and an Asian man seated beside her smiled, but remained silent.

"Guten Tag," Lisanne said as she and her mate reached the counter.

The receptionist typed silently upon the two hemispheres that were embedded in the desk and—informed by the micropixels of her contact lenses—said to the tall beauty, "You are Miss Osa Karlsson of Brooklyn City."

"That's me." Osa nodded and adjusted the clinging fabric of her sapphire sundress.

With a bifurcate gaze, the receptionist replied, "Welcome to Corpus Chrome, Incorporated," and continued typing once she had uttered the final letter 'd' of her greeting. "I see here that you have entered the lobby thrice, on dates when Miss Breutschen had appointments with our legal department."

"I've only come here twice," corrected Osa.

"There were two ingressions on July sixteenth, though the later—five minutes after the first departure—was to use the bathroom."

"I remember now."

"Today will to be your first trip to the interior, correct?"

"Seems like you already know the answer to that one."

"We do," said the receptionist, flashing her brilliant teeth. "Before you enter the interior lobby, you must be scanned for conventional weapons, swabbed for biological weapons and sent into a nuclear-force detonation chamber in which any nanotech or micro-incendiaries on your person will be isolated and destroyed. Do you have any such devices?"

"No, nothing like that."

"Please fingerprint this agreement," said the smiling brunette as the Asian man slid a sheaf across the inverted-pyramid desk. "It states that you understand and have agreed to subject yourself to our security gauntlet."

Lisanne said to Osa, "I fingerprinted the same exact sheaf."

"You get subjected to all this junk every time?"

"It sounds like a lot of procedures, but it only takes about eight minutes."

The tall beauty looked anxious.

"If you are troubled by the gauntlet," the petite blonde said, "you may wait for me down here. I know how you feel about your privacy."

"No, no. I'm going with you." Osa pressed her thumb, index finger and middle finger to the black glass. "I want to meet her if she's ready, and I want you to know I'm there either way."

"Danke."

The tall beauty nodded, a mixture of apprehension and strength upon her face.

"After you've gone through security," the receptionist said, "you may proceed to Mr. Johnson on floor seventy."

"Danke," said Lisanne.

"You are most welcome. I hope that your reunion is a happy one."

A triangular flap opened in the side of the desk. Out of the glowing hatchway stepped a twelve-centimeter-tall chromium android, its head studded with viewing lenses and speaker-microphone beads. The homunculus raised a tiny flag that read, "Breutschen, L.," and below it, "Karlsson, O."

"Follow the serf," said the receptionist.

* * *

Eight minutes later, the women were led by the homunculus from the detonation chamber to the round interior lobby. There, the little android put the flag into its backpack, waved good-bye to the women, pointed a gun at its left temple, fired and fell on its face. A golden circle rose from its head and began to glow, and from its back sprouted two chromium angel wings, which were embossed with the letters CCI. The serf flapped its divine appendages and rose into the air.

"I want one," Osa said of the homunculus.

"I shall keep that in mind."

"Why? They sell them?"

"I read that CCI is currently developing a model for the private sector."

"I'd like him to clean up after Cyclops," remarked Osa. "Maybe send him for doughnuts."

Suddenly, the serf flew into a living wall, disappearing from view.

The women walked toward an elevator, atop which the names "Breutschen" and "Karlsson" flashed in luminous blue letters. Out of the adjacent lift hobbled three old men, a mannequin (clothed in a red FDNY shirt, a fire helmet, polka-dotted ribbons, jeans and sneakers), and a very good-looking man in his forties with long blonde hair, who wore a shirt that read, THERE ARE BETTER WAYS TO SPEND YOUR TIME THAN READING THIS, above an illustration of an obese man drinking a beer while working on a car engine. The handsome fellow's face and the machine's gelware mask were identical.

Pointing out Osa, the mannequin said, "I'll take one of those."

The old men cackled.

"Dad," admonished the handsome fellow.

"Shhhhh," the mannequin said, "I don't want her to know how old I am."

The son looked at the tall beauty, shaking his head. "Sorry. He's been dead a while."

"What's your name?" the mannequin asked Osa as he strode toward her. Behind him, the aged trio howled until they were seized by syrupy coughing fits.

"Leave me alone," said Osa.

A septuagenarian who had a nose that looked like a russet potato said to the mannequin, "Eagle, you might want to hold off—" and coughed. After clearing his throat, he added, "I think the little one right there's her playmate."

"I've gone down that path before," said the mannequin. "Champ's mother liked to—"

"Dad!" protested the handsome son.

"I like dykes—they're extra tough. And besides, how do they know it's not a woman in here?" The mannequin then rapped its fist upon its chest like an orangutan.

"We know," said Osa.

"What would you do with her if you got her?" asked an old fellow who had artificial black hair and a Star of David tattooed in gold upon the side of his neck.

"I've got equipment and an instruction manual. Illustrated!"

"Bleh," said Osa, repulsed.

"My parts are totally adjustable," added the mannequin.

The doors below the women's flashing names finally parted, and Lisanne pulled her mate toward the conveyance.

"Looks like the little one is in charge," opined the tattooed Jew.

The women entered the elevator, where a demure female voice said, "Welcome, Miss Breutschen and Miss Karlsson."

In the lobby, the fellow with the russet-potato nose was saying to the re-bodied man, "Trust me when I tell you that many women—legions of long-legged ladies—are interested in having illicit relations with a mannequin."

"But did you see her figure? Her rump? That's a soulmate."

The elevator began to close, and a sound like a piccolo flute emerged from the mannequin's mouth slit.

"What the hell was that?" inquired the tattooed Jew.

The doors shut, shielding the women from subsequent comments. As they sat in gelatin seats, pseudopodia embraced them.

Osa guffawed. "That was a first."

The elevator sped like a getaway vehicle toward the seventieth floor.

* * *

Together, the women walked through a living wall and into a brown alcove that was furnished with a buoyed leather couch, a recliner chair, a table and a mote aquarium. Mr. Johnson then stepped through the wall, buttoned his beige tweed suit and joined the couple.

Lisanne stared at the orange polarity curtain that hung on the far side of the room, thinking to herself, 'Ellenancy is alive on the other side of that fabric.' Her pulse raced, and her hands grew cold and damp. The edges of reality darkened, and suddenly, the room wobbled.

"You need to sit down," said Osa, her voice stern, as if she were talking to a misbehaved child.

Lisanne nodded her dizzy head.

Mr. Johnson flapped a paddle-like hand at the couch. "Please, please, please. Sit."

Osa's strong left arm slid across her mate's back and guided her to the suspended sofa, where they sat. The room wavered and stretched.

"I am going to see Ellenancy," said Lisanne, stupid with shock. "I am going to see my sister."

The tall beauty wiped sweat from her mate's forehead and kissed her cheek.

Mr. Johnson pulled a bulb from the nutrient water sphere and handed it to his petite guest, who thumbed the iris and drank.

"Would you care for a softener?" asked the shepherd.

"I just need a moment to collect myself." Lisanne sipped nutrient water and eyed the orange curtain. "How is she doing?"

"Ellenancy's condition has not changed much since you and I last spoke, but I hope and believe that interactions with you will help reorient her."

The word "condition" sounded very ominous to Lisanne.

"How concerned are you about her behavior?" asked Osa.

"At this time, we're not overly concerned. Ellenancy is withdrawn, but she's scored very well on all of the cognitive tests and is intellectually sound. Our primary concern right now is her reluctance to physically manipulate the mannequin unit. She has yet to accept her new body."

"Ellenancy was a very tactile person," said the petite blonde, sipping more water while thinking of a studio session in Stockholm. Ellenancy had played fifteen different instruments by hand while Lisanne processed sounds and built melodies in a computerized mixing vault. "She was a far, far better musician than I, primarily because of her desire to physically command whichever instruments she used."

Mr. Johnson plucked a piece of lint from a diamond-patterned sock and disposed of it. "Her behavior is not unique, but it's less common amongst people who died during the resurrection age, already aware of mannequins. Still," he added, "an intelligent and tactile individual like Ellenancy may take more time to adjust to her new body than would a simpler, less self-aware person."

Lisanne remarked, "I believe we interacted with an example of the latter in your lobby just now."

"That dirty old fireman," clarified Osa.

Mr. Johnson smirked. "That particular individual adjusted very, very quickly."

Lisanne rose to her feet and announced to the shepherd, to her mate and to herself, "I would like to see her now."

"Superb," said Mr. Johnson.

"I know that you need to monitor her behavior," the petite blonde added, "but I would like privacy for the first twenty minutes."

"That is perfectly understandable."

Lisanne straightened the neckline of her green dress, walked toward the polarity curtain and remembered Osa. Halting, she turned around.

Unshed tears glimmered in the tall beauty's eyes.

The petite blonde hastened to her mate and embraced her. "I love you."

"I love you, too."

The women hugged for ten heartbeats and then released each other.

Osa sniffed, nodding. "Go see your sister."

"Ja." Lisanne turned around and strode toward the orange polarity curtain.

The fabric furled out of her way. Beyond lay a sunlit oval room that was covered with sepia wallpaper.

Lisanne stepped inside and saw her sister for the first time in nearly three years. A model 8F chromium mannequin (Petite) with short blonde hair stood at the far window. The silent and unmoving machine was turned away from the visitor and nude; gelware hands and feet contrasted sharply with the chromium body to which they were attached.

A moment after the polarity curtain unfurled, Lisanne addressed the machine. "Ellenancy?"

The mannequin did not reply.

"Ellenancy?"

The re-bodied woman did not turn away from the window.

Lisanne strode toward the nude chromium figure. Clutched in the mannequin's left hand was the generic gelware mask that was supposed to serve as its face.

The petite visitor asked, "Wie geht es Ihnen? Sorry. How are you?" (The shepherd had advised her to speak in English, since it was the primary language spoken by Ellenancy in her later life.)

The machine did not respond.

"Can you hear me?" inquired Lisanne from a distance of four meters.

"No more exams today," announced the re-bodied woman.

"Will you please turn around?"

Atop the inert mannequin, the head swiveled ninety degrees. The face revealed was a concave ebony hollow filled with antennas, smart bolts and pseudopodia. Two scratched lenses glinted within the insectile visage.

Lisanne shuddered. "Do you recognize me?" she asked, trying to stop her hands from shaking.

The machine's bifurcate posture resembled a still photograph of a celebrity who had been ambushed from behind by paparazzi. "Let me focus," said the re-bodied woman as she slid her posterior lenses up two ocular wells. "You're here."

Tears welled in Lisanne's eyes. "Ja, ja, ich—sorry. Yes. I am here." Sniffing, she walked forward.

The mannequin turned bodily, revealing the unit's chrome limbs and torso, gelware hands and feet and pink pubic leaf.

Lisanne hugged the machine that contained her sister.

"The gelatinous parts are the only ones endowed with a sense of touch," said Ellenancy.

The petite blonde withdrew her arms, took one step back and saw her own distended and headless reflection in the mannequin's chrome-plated body.

Whirring, the scratched lenses within the insectile hollow slid forward, rotated and stopped. "The wrinkles around your eyes are more pronounced," said the re-bodied woman. "And your nose and ears are bigger."

Lisanne had always been considered the congenial twin, despite the fact that she was not at all congenial. The blunt remarks were typical of Ellenancy and very, very wonderful things to hear.

"You have aged very little otherwise," added the re-bodied woman.

Lisanne looked at the gelware mask that dangled like a pelt from the mannequin's left hand. "Do you dislike wearing the face?"

Ellenancy reached her free hand toward her sister. A gelware fingertip landed upon Lisanne's forehead, slid down to a blonde eyebrow, glided along the ridge of her nose, swept over a tear-moistened cheek, circled the outermost rim of her left ear, traced back over her jaw and parted her lips. The re-bodied woman withdrew her digit, and a lone strand of saliva hung in the air, connecting the once identical twins until it disappeared.

"I prefer our face," replied the speakers that were sitting at the bottom of the confluence of pseudopodia, antennas and smart bolts.

Lisanne suppressed a shudder. "All re-bodied people are given generic faces until they are deemed capable. Neuro-stitched gelware is very expensive."

The mannequin did not respond to this information.

"You may have your mask cast from my face, though most people choose celebrities or younger, aesthetically-altered versions of themselves."

"But first, CCI must determine whether or not I am worth the investment. Whether I will be a good mannequin."

"Yes," replied Lisanne, firmly. "CCI would like to make sure you are mentally stable before they sculpt personalized gelware for you."

The nude mannequin threw the mask. It smacked against the wall, lingered for a moment and slid toward the floor like an obese inchworm.

"You're angry," said Lisanne, flatly.

"I am. I died, and now I'm this…device…this shiny apparatus with sticky ends." The mannequin hammered a gelware fist upon a chromium thigh.

Lisanne glanced at the polarity curtain, regretting that she had asked for a full twenty minutes of unmonitored interaction.

"Last night I had a dream," Ellenancy said through the inert machine. "The kind of dream that's very vivid and much, much larger than reality. A dream where everything is enhanced and connected and luscious and vibrant.

"We are still children in Berlin.

"Mutti and Vati are still alive and so is Tante Hildie.

"We are in that huge indoor mall, the place where they have all of those great chocolates and chic purses and those very expensive stuffed bears. You and I sneak up to the buffet on the top floor and see a pie that is loaded with nuts and baked pears and dripping with apple syrup, and we steal it. We hide and eat it under a table while Mutti and Vati and Tante Hildie are looking for us, and we can't stop laughing. The flavors, the smells, the joy of our crime, the fear of getting caught… it is all indescribably rich and luxurious.

"And then I woke up, and I was inside this thing. Or, more precisely, I was this thing."

"You are not a 'thing,'" Lisanne refuted, "you are Ellenancy Breutschen—you are my sister."

"Really?"

Ellenancy reached into her insectile face, pinched a pseudopod with her fingertips and yanked it from its housing. Three wires spat blue sparks into the air.

"Can your sister do that?"

Tears streamed from Lisanne's eyes.

Ellenancy threw the plucked device to the ground and again reached into her concave face.

"Nein, nein, du—nein!" shouted Lisanne, clapping her hands to the mannequin's right arm. "Du musst stoppen! Du—"

The mannequin froze in mid-action.

"I cannot move," said Ellenancy, her right hand thrust inside of her face.

Mr. Johnson walked into the room and addressed the re-bodied woman. "A remote computer is monitoring your actions and will do so until you are granted autonomy. It can and will override your control of the unit if you attempt to injure yourself."

The shepherd appraised the inert mannequin for a moment and then turned to Lisanne. "I'm afraid that today's visit is over."

* * *

Nestled within her mate's arms, legs and warmth, Lisanne cried until exhaustion bore her to the world of dreams, wherein she and her sister ran through sunshine as identical twin girls.

Chapter V
Ecumenical Lightning Church of
the Fourteen Rivers

Minister Leonard Durles removed his motorcycle helmet, hung it on the porch stanchion, extricated a brass key from the twelve others within his pocket, inserted it into the front door and twisted the metal. The cylinder admitted three clicks and yielded. He hated that Genet had insisted upon the security device, but after they had been robbed thrice, the thirty-nine-year-old Australian-born religious leader could no longer ignore the threat of thieves. "The ones who took from us aren't part of my circuit," he had said to his wife just before he drove his moped to town to fetch a stainless steel lock for the house they had shared—entrance unbarred—for six years. Even though he had installed the device eleven months ago, the thing still nettled him.

"They aren't part of my circuit," Leonard repeated to the Lord, the lock, himself and the winds that cooled the sweating, grinning, malefic faces of those who would simply take from this world without ever adding anything to it—the enemies of honesty.

The sun-bronzed, red-headed man escaped the sun, the continually glaring gift that He had given Ethiopia, and stepped into his air-conditioned home, a place where the smells of injera and wat warmly embraced him.

Genet, her belly swollen with her second child beneath her white coffee dress, padded on dark bare feet to Leonard and placed a kiss upon his cheek. "I'm pleased you are home," said the twenty-six-year-old Oromo woman; her Cushitic accent highlighted each word in a way that reminded him of how some Indians spoke English. "Would you like a beer?"

"How about you sit down on the couch with Numero Dos, yeah? I can get my own beer."

"But you've been working all day. You must rest."

"I rode 'round on my moped, spoke to some fellas—nothing all that strenuous." Leonard sniffed the air and grinned. "Smells great."

"I'm pleased."

"Is Rahel in the kitchen?"

"She isn't."

The minister frowned. "She's supposed to help you extra on account of Numero Dos. That's the deal, right?"

"She is having dinner with the Norwegian boy. The son of the silver baron."

Leonard was not especially fond of the Scandinavian child, but he did not voice his opinion, since the girl's absence would allow him some private time with his wife. It had been four days since the couple had last made love, and the minister was simmering.

"Let's get you off those swollen feet, yeah?" said Leonard, escorting Genet to the shemma-upholstered air-sofa that was under a buzzing ice-coil. There, the pregnant woman sat upon the yellow cushions and reclined.

The minister gently set his wife's swollen feet upon an air-filled ottoman. "I'll get you a cloth for those and some raspberry tea."

"Thank you. Please turn down and cover the wat."

"After I sneak a taste, I will."

Genet whistled a C-sharp and said, "General news." The mote aquarium that was beyond her feet ran a test pattern.

Leonard entered the kitchen, walked across the tiled floor to the stone island upon which sat four convection spheres, pulled a spoon from the steaming lamb wat, blew upon it, waited, blew upon it, waited, blew upon it, ate, assessed that the stew needed more ground mustard seed (his wife's normally excellent palate was affected by her pregnancy), added the needed powder, sampled it once more, said, "Better," closed the convection sphere, dialed it down to sixty-five degrees Celsius, walked to the refrigerator panel, slid it open, withdrew a bulb of raspberry tea and found a beer, which he uncapped with the bronze crucifix bottle-opener that had been given to him last Christmas by one of the thirteen thousand members of his parachurch. (Some people thought that the gift was sacrilegious, but the minister felt that its giver, a kind old blind woman who was as devout as any person whom he had ever known, put it above dubious appraisal.)

At the sink, he filled a dripless towel with cool water.

"Husband," said Genet from the other room, her voice imbued with concern.

"I only had a taste, so don't go worrying," Leonard defended as he entered the den with a beverage in each hand and the dripless towel over his left arm, as if he were French waiter. "The wat is stellar," he said. (The Lord forgave small fibs that benefited His households.)

Genet pointed at the mote aquarium. "Dead people are talking to reporters."

"That sounds ominous," remarked the minister sardonically.

Leonard sat beside Genet (and Numero Dos), handed his wife the bulb of raspberry tea, set the towel upon her swollen feet and massaged her toes.

The minister glanced at the mote aquarium, the pixels of which were frozen. Upon the stage stood three male mannequins: two Global Senate Army soldiers, clad in green and brown, and a third individual who wore a blue and red British Royal Air Force outfit.

"What're they yapping about?" inquired Leonard, leaning back with his lager.

Genet whistled and said, "Play: Highlight."

The pixels flew through the air, reconfiguring, and the life-sized head of the re-bodied Royal Air Force Chief filled the stage.

> The mannequin's hair was silver and black and surmounted by a beret; his superficial lips were parted, and his expression was neutral.
>
> "I am Air Chief Marshal Sir Gerald B. Thiggs of the Royal Air Force," said the re-bodied man. "I was a pilot in the Chinese-Indian war, and I died on Her Majesty's behalf during the final days of the Nepal conflict.
>
> "I am afraid that I have some quite distressing news.
>
> "Like most of you, I was very critical of Corpus Chrome,

Incorporated's decision to resurrect the serial murderer and rapist Derrick W.R. Dulande. Why they chose such a loathsome man, I do not know.

"I must confess that his assassination did not in any way upset me.

"But let me get to the marrow of the bone.

"I have come here today to state—with tremendous regret, but very little doubt—that Derrick W.R. Dulande's outrageous story of the afterlife is, in fact, true."

The reporters yelled questions at the Air Chief Marshal.

"What?" exclaimed Leonard, his voice freezing the pixels in the mote aquarium. "This is gross negligence, broadcasting this rubbish. Gross negligence!"

"He said more," replied Genet, fear in her dark eyes.

Appalled by the global forum that madmen were given in the year twenty-fifty-eight, the minister said, "Resume play."

Offstage, reporters clamored. The stentorian voice of an unseen moderator ordered, "Hold all questions until after Air Chief Marshal Sir Gerald B. Thiggs has finished."

The media quietened.

Soon, the re-bodied man resumed, "Dulande's preposterous tale of an inverted phantom moon and the giant squid-like beings within its craters, which are our cerebral symbionts, is true. I agonized over whether or not to speak of my experience, but ultimately I decided that it is humanity's right to know.

"I killed other human beings in war.

"I was decorated for these deeds, but they were murders nonetheless. In the domain of souls, the world of the spirit bodies, my soul changed into something permanent, separating it from the rest.

"When I died, I woke up inside the squid-like being Dulande described. I drifted into space, I exploded, and then I flew into the sun, where I contemplated my life for twenty-six years of perdition.

"When I was resurrected, my mind blocked out the memory... but several months afterwards, I recalled what had happened.

"I recalled Hell.

"I convinced myself that the experience must have been a dream—an hallucination of extraordinary vividness—and I dismissed it. But when I heard Derrick W.R. Dulande speak...I could no longer deny my horrifying recollections.

"I ruminated deeply.

"It seemed possible—though very unlikely—that two men who were strangers to one another could have had the exact same hallucination.

"Thereafter, I researched what I could in private. I spoke in clandestine meeting places to some of the cult members who had believed Dulande's tale, but they were imbalanced people of little worth.

"Then I recalled something—a fleeting thirty-year-old memory.

"During the first phase of my transubstantiation—when I drifted from the inverted moon toward the sun—I recalled passing a group of asteroids that were in orbit around what I knew to be Mercury. There were seventeen in total, one of which was the size of a planetoid.

"I should inform you that I have no specific knowledge of the astronomical sciences.

"When I recalled this detail—eighteen days after Dulande's speech—I investigated its veracity. My memory was soon confirmed: Seventeen satellites orbited Mercury at that time, and amongst them was a more sizable aggregation of rock.

"I knew then that my terrible, terrible experience of solar damnation had been real.

"I flew out to Calcutta, where I met Sergeant Katuri Gwatha, and then to Tokyo, where I met Commander Shigero Iwakata. Both of these re-bodied men had killed people and died in wars.

"Each of them had been on medical leave ever since Dulande's speech.

"After I told each soldier my story, he admitted to having had the same exact experience."

The pixels reconfigured to show

the three re-bodied military men standing upon the dais.

The pixels dispersed. Upon the stage was written:

...End Highlight

Minister Leonard Durles cracked his knuckles and shook his head; his tranquil evening alone with Genet had just been sullied by an absurd and malicious madness. Upon the lectern in his mind, he began to compose a sermon for his flock.

"I hope Rahel did not watch that," said Genet.

* * *

On Sunday, the minister (clad in black) sped his electric moped up the dirt road toward the stone church that he had built with the aid of seven other clergymen and thirty Oromos.

Clouds spat water globules that were too obese and erratic to be considered rain upon the earth and Leonard's helmet.

The moped crested a swell that was shaped and colored like Genet's child-filled belly. Beyond the rise, he saw the Ecumenical Lightning Church of the Fourteen Rivers. Minister Leonard Durles looked at the parking lot and wondered why there were so many empty spaces.

Water globules struck the thirsty ground.

The morning beacon atop the holy edifice crackled and shot lightning into the sky.

CHAPTER VI
THE BROKERS OF EXTRALEGAL ACTS

Bald-headed and dressed in a dark gray bodysuit, Alicia Martinez crept inside a copse of oaks and knelt beside a tree. The luminous crescent that was the newly risen moon wove a chiaroscuro through the dark branches around her and lighted the plump and perfect mansion that stood nearby, lording over a finely manicured eastern Connecticut lawn.

Settled, the woman double-tapped her lily and said, "Locate: Carlo Burgacci." Micropixels that were the size of individual rods and cones shone within her left contact lens and displayed an aerial vector map of the surrounding thirty kilometers. Upon it, a red dot advanced down an avenue toward her own green mark. A demure female voice said into her right ear, "Estimated convergence: four minutes." Her quarry then turned a corner.

Policemen whose careers had been terminated by corrupt adversaries, scientists whose work had been suppressed by faceless entities, victims of crimes where the perpetrators went unpunished, disgusted lawyers (such as herself) and other disenfranchised individuals peopled the vast reticulum laid across the globe by the Brokers of Extralegal Acts. The group had assassinated Derrick W.R. Dulande at Alicia's behest, and after she completed this assignment and one other mission (of a 'Peril Level II' rating or greater), her debt to them would be cleared.

The red dot was eighteen blocks from her green mark.

Alicia Martinez looked at the black syringe gun in her right hand and saw that she was shaking. This was the first time that she had been required to enter the field, and she was nervous.

The red dot was two blocks from her current location.

She double-tapped her lily and said, "Hide map." The vector lines disappeared from her left eye.

Alicia activated the cauldron within the plasticore syringe gun, and in her right hand, the tube warmed.

The woman pulled a snug hood over her face, uttered the passphrase "Sammy and Alicia Jr.," paused, and then said, "Sample and match: Environment." Her bodysuit and covered head mirrored the surrounding oaks.

The blue lights of Carlo Burgacci's vehicle spilled upon the lawn, limning fine topiary horses. Alicia went to the edge of the copse and observed.

The wedge-shaped blue vehicle slowed and turned into the dual-niche driveway, where fissures on the tires were coated with fresh foam. Quietly, the car slid past the camouflaged observer, right to left.

Alicia double-tapped her lily and said, "Display: Gunview." Her right contact showed the grass as seen from the telescopic lens embedded in the syringe gun's barrel.

The vehicle stopped. Alicia pointed her weapon at the driver's side window and saw Carlo Burgacci seated behind the steering stick, playing imaginary drums and singing along with music. The plump fellow was alone.

Soon, the song ended, and the fifty-two-year-old man tapped the dashboard. The car's blue headlights turned off.

Alicia glanced at the living wall in front of the mansion and prayed that no person would emerge from the other side. Carlo Burgacci's wife was supposed to be on holiday, but Alicia would not at all be surprised to see some mistress appear. Despite the hidden widow's apprehensions, the group of concentric circles that comprised the entrance did not stir, and the windows along the façade remained dark. Mr. Burgacci was alone with the woman who stalked him.

Beads of sweat ran down Alicia's bald and covered head onto her neck, and for a brief instant, she recognized her journey from courtroom to copse as something absurd. Recalling the happy detour in between these two places that had been her family, the widow pointed her weapon at the man's neck.

The driver's side door retracted into the floor of the vehicle, revealing her target. Instantly and automatically, the weapon fired a miniature syringe. Carlo Burgacci yelled and slapped his hand to his neck as the projectile wormed beneath his skin.

Alicia aimed the cylinder at his arm, and when the gun calculated a high-percentage shot, it spat out another round. She double-tapped her lily and said,

"Full dose." The subcutaneous syringes sprayed serum into his arteries.

Carlo Burgacci fell forward like a bag of potatoes, his forehead smacking the dashboard. The constrictors in the serum caused the man to ball up and clench.

Far calmer than she had expected herself to be, Alicia Martinez strode across the lawn, rolled the huddled man onto the passenger seat, sat inside the vehicle and tapped the placard, which shut the door. The smells of the fellow and his voided bowels filled the car. Covering her mouth and nose, the widow dialed on a deodorizing vent.

Carlo Burgacci unconsciously whimpered and clenched, and a dim cracking sound heralded the conclusion of a weak tooth.

The widow double-tapped her lily, said, "Hide: Gunview," saw clearly with both eyes, punched in the vehicle's security-override code, set the windshield to bugview, checked all nine perspectives for witnesses, saw nobody, and backed out of the driveway, the trembling abductee balled up beside her.

Alicia left the niches and, as quickly as the car's limiters allowed, drove away from the mansion. (In wealthy residential areas like this one, this speed was slightly faster than jogging.)

Five kilometers away, she turned into the parking lot of an abandoned church, pushed her captive to the asphalt, rolled him around to the back of the vehicle, opened up the rear hatch and shoved him inside. The balled-up man was still unconscious, and if his heart rate exceeded a certain tempo (as it would if he regained consciousness inside of a trunk), he would automatically be dosed a second time.

Alicia shut the hatch and sat inside the stolen car, where she put the syringe gun and her sweat-soaked mirror hood into her side-bag, tapped the ice cube icon and said, "Twenty degrees." The air-conditioner blew cool winds upon her dripping face.

* * *

The widow drove toward the compound in eastern Pennsylvania. As she proceeded, she withdrew a self-adhering brunette wig from her side-bag and placed it upon her sticky scalp, where it stuck like a lamprey.

CHAPTER VII
A SLUG AND THE DEMOLISHERS OF HEAVEN

"I would like for the slug to join us."

A sixty-six-year-old Israeli-American who had a long white ponytail and a calm face that was dominated by thick black eyebrows reached into a large bowl of nuts, seeds and dried fruit, which sat upon the green metal table that separated him from Carlo Burgacci. With long fingernails, the serene Semite named Elad withdrew an almond that was the exact same hue as his own linen robes.

The captive's waist and shoulders were restrained by pseudopodia, and his hands were bound in a sphere of dense foam rubber, which lay in his lap like a bowling ball, and his blue cotton suit was scuffed from its rendezvous with the asphalt. Appraising his interrogator, the window (which was crowded with moonlit trees) and the one-way glass, he appeared more irritated than frightened by his predicament.

Carlo Burgacci sneezed and said, "Bless me."

Alicia Martinez and three other shaved pawns—a man, a woman and a person whose gender was currently unclear—watched the interrogation from an observation room behind the one-way glass.

A magnetically buoyed gurney emerged from the living wall behind Carlo Burgacci, pushed by a small man in a white doctor's smock. The lumpy burden upon the plank was concealed by a blue tarp.

Two of the pawns in the observation room glanced at Alicia.

"Have you seen the slug?" the androgyne asked the widow. (The individual's gender was not clarified by his or her vocal timbre.)

"I haven't."

"You may want to leave the room."

"I'll watch," said Alicia.

The small doctor stopped the gurney alongside the captive and twisted the lift dial counterclockwise. Smoothly, the burden sank so that it floated at eye level with Carlo Burgacci.

Elad inquired, "You are Catholic, are you not?"

"Yeah," replied the captive. "And?"

"How do you feel about the comments made by Derrick W.R. Dulande and Air Chief Marshal Sir Gerald B. Thiggs regarding the afterlife?"

"I don't give a shit what those guys said," Carlo Burgacci declared into the cilia-covered sphere that floated in front of his mouth. The crystal cylinder nestled in the verispectragram turned red.

Elad motioned to the truth-descrier. "You care more than you've professed."

Carlo Burgacci looked at the tarp-covered lump upon the gurney. "What the fuck's under there?"

The interrogator ate an almond. "We shall discuss the slug later."

Grimacing, the captive turned away from the gurney. "Smells like shit." The crystal on the verispectragram turned blue.

Elad inquired, "Do you believe that these resurrected men told the truth?"

"I think what they said's crazy."

The crystal on the verispectragram turned magenta. (Alicia recalled that she had received the same exact color when she had spoken of her love for her deceased husband.)

The interrogator plucked a dried apricot from the bowl with his long fingernails. "But some part of you wonders if what they said is true? If, immediately following the death of the body, murderers—whose squid-like souls have acquired permanency through the act of killing another human being—fly from a hollow moon into a solar Hell while all other human souls—unless cryogenically stored—simply evaporate?"

"Who knows what happens when we die? I sure as fuck don't and neither do you."

"Is it correct to characterize your opinion of the afterlife described by Dulande and the soldiers as very, very, very unlikely...but possible?"

"Fine." The verispectragram concurred in blue.

Elad ate the apricot. "And your feelings about th—"

"Hey, enough of this," interrupted Carlo Burgacci. "What do you want? Money?"

"We don't want money."

"Then what?"

"We want your help."

"I have no say in which cauliflowers get pulled from the vault, okay? Those decisions are made by people much higher up than me, on floors of the building I've never even seen."

Elad shook his head. "We're not interested in advocating a specific mind for resurrection."

"So why'd you fucking kidnap me? I'm not that rich. Or handsome."

The interrogator pointed to the large wooden bowl of nuts, seeds and dried fruit upon the table. "I have eaten an entire basin—piece by piece—during the course of one interview. Your compliance will determine how long this session lasts."

Carlo Burgacci contemplated hostile retorts, but instead yielded monosyllabically. "Shoot."

"Were you disheartened by the speeches of Dulande and Sir Thiggs?"

"Not with Dulande. There couldn't be a less trustworthy guy than him, and even though I'm an exec at CCI, I hated that they chose him. I mean, how could Lawrence Cord let the company do that? Put our name on a twisted fuck like that? But when that English guy said the same thing as Dulande, and those two other guys...."

"You were disheartened."

"I spoke to my priest about it. He made me feel better." The crystal turned magenta.

"But the priest did not fully allay your fears?" suggested Elad.

"How could he? Those soldiers were dead. For a lot of years. And they didn't know each other and they all saw the same thing, and nobody else who came back—was resurrected—ever saw anything substantial. That guy Thiggs was a hero and led the attack that ended the war in Nepal. And he seemed competent."

"So the priest was unable to allay your fears."

"Not all the way." The crystal shone blue.

"You work in the health plan bureau of CCI."

"It's a thrilling life. I get abducted regularly."

With his long thumb and index fingernails, Elad picked a sunflower seed from the basin. "Have there been any noteworthy changes in revenue streams since Sir Thiggs and his peers corroborated Dulande's tale?"

"This's public information, the stuff I know. You could search reservoirs or lily vaults."

"Please inform me."

"We're selling a lot more cryonic capsules," Carlo Burgacci said, "and more people are paying in to the post-life preservation plan."

"At a rate in keeping with typical business tides?"

"No. There was a sharp spike in the last four days."

"Since the day of Sir Thiggs's speech?"

"You solved the mystery."

Elad's fingernails sliced the sunflower seed lengthwise, and each half clicked upon the green table. "Do you feel that these occurrences are related?"

"Sure. Though not necessarily because people believe that crazy story." The crystal shone blue.

"If most people don't believe the story," Elad inquired, "why has it affected business?"

"A story like that—coming from the mouths of people who actually died—makes people doubt...makes it harder for them to believe what they believe, 'specially after no other resurrected people saw anything. And just as important, a story like that makes people think about death and maybe how ridiculous their own versions of the afterlife are."

"Please elaborate on that comment."

Carlo Burgacci's eyes dropped to his bound hands. In a quieter voice, he said, "I believe what I was taught and what I feel—I still do—but if I stepped back and looked at it all like a scientist would, I couldn't claim that this story about the squids is any more or less likely than a bunch of halos and wings in Heaven with Jesus, or those forty virgins waiting to service an Arab who did his duty. If you think about it, they all seem like stories that men created to cope with it all."

"To cope with what, specifically?"

"To cope with death."

"Does CCI offer a product that helps humanity cope with death?"

"We do."

Elad leaned forward, his eyes hard and focused. "Do you think that CCI either implanted memories in the resurrected men or somehow coerced them into telling these tales in order to denigrate religious beliefs?"

"No," responded Carlo Burgacci. The crystal shone blue.

"Do you think it's possible that CCI conceived this bleak afterlife?"

"No," said the captive. Again, the crystal shone blue.

"But as a result of Dulande and Sir Thiggs's tales, cryonics business has increased?"

"Yeah, but CCI can't do stuff like that—implant memories." The crystal shone blue.

"How can you be certain? The way in which a mannequin interfaces with a human brain is unknown to all but those who designed it, and is a well-guarded secret. All other competing scientific groups have been…mysteriously…shut down."

"Business has always been good," defended Carlo Burgacci. "There's no reason to do that—make up a story like that just to fuck with people's beliefs. CCI is rich."

"Perhaps Corpus Chrome, Incorporated has bigger ambitions than simply good business. Perhaps CCI intends to become a political group that could one day rival, control or overpower the Global Senate itself."

The captive laughed, explosively. "You spend a lot of time alone, don't you?"

"Do you believe that CCI's agenda is strictly limited to business?"

"I don't know, but I sure don't think they're gonna take over the world or anything."

"I don't 'know' either—this is all speculation—but my group and I are very concerned that CCI, a private organization run by cloaked and inaccessible men such as Lawrence Cord, might one day have unlimited power over the human race because of the life-giving technology it has monopolized."

"This's fucking stupid," barked Carlo Burgacci. "CCI did not create this story to scare people or—or to make us doubt our beliefs." The crystal cylinder turned indigo.

Elad tapped the point of an almond upon the luminous verdict. "You were more certain about that statement one minute ago."

"What's the point here?"

"The hoarding of life-giving technology is tantamount to a monopoly on life itself. Corpus Chrome, Incorporated's privatization of such information and equipment gives them unlimited power and may—in less than a century—lead to both slavery and genocide on a worldwide level." The Israeli American's thick black eyebrows drew together in the center of his head like a bat. "We want CCI's technology made public. This power, this ability to overcome death, is the most important development in the history of the human race. Resurrection is a human achievement that transcends 'business.'"

Frowning, Carlo shook his head. "CCI created the mannequins and should reap the benefits."

Elad sat back in his seat and crunched almonds. "Carlo Burgacci, will you help us bring an end to Corpus Chrome, Incorporated's monopoly?"

"No." The crystal cylinder that was nestled within the miniature white metropolis turned blue.

"Perhaps the slug will prove more persuasive than I," said the interrogator, sliding the verispectragram to the far side of the table.

From behind the one-way glass, Alicia watched the doctor in white lift the blue tarp. Underneath the fabric was a nude man who had been tied down to the gurney rails by his own boneless arms and legs. Artificially elongated optic nerves ran from his grossly swollen purple eyelids to his eyeballs, which floated in a jar of amber fluid that sat upon his stomach. Exposed to light, the mutilated man's pupils narrowed.

Not since the death of her family had Alicia seen anything so repugnant. Her heart hammered.

Carlo Burgacci vomited upon himself, spattering the jar that contained the slug's eyeballs.

Alicia grew dizzy. Sweat ran down her face and nausea twisted her guts, but she did not look away.

"The slug is an example of an uncooperative person," said Elad, sliding the verispectragram in front of the soiled captive. "Carlo Burgacci, will you help us bring an end to Corpus Chrome, Incorporated's monopoly?"

Into the cilia-covered sphere, the captive said, "I—I will. I'll do whatever I can. Yes."

The crystal on the verispectragram shone blue.

Claiming the bowl of legumes, the Israeli American stood up and left the room.

Carlo Burgacci wept.

Upon the gurney, the slug moaned.

Chapter VIII
Within the Brindled Light
of the Glowing Cat

Awake for twenty-eight hours, Alicia Martinez put her fingertips to the façade placard, dialed her code, entered the building, walked through the brownstone atop which her Brooklyn City skyscraper had been built, reached the lobby that was the original building's roof, glanced at the white cockatoos in the coop, ascended to floor number seventeen, strode up the hallway, passed the scruffy neighbor who wandered the hall like a nomad, yawned, pressed her fingerprints, dialed her code and transcended the living wall, entering the apartment wherein her family had been murdered before her eyes. There, the widow strode to the living-room window (beyond which glowed two sunlit buildings), closed the curtain, sat, pulled foam rubber boots from her feet, whistled a C-sharp, said "Loop: sleeping cat," and lay upon the couch. A life-sized Persian feline was sculpted by three hundred thousand pixels upon the stage of the mote aquarium that she had given to her husband on their fifth wedding anniversary.

Exhausted, Alicia pulled a blanket that she had kept since childhood over her clothed body and shut her eyes. The cat's purrs were like velvet upon her aching muscles.

She tried not to think about the slug.

* * *

Twelve hours later and sticky with pungent sweat, Alicia awakened in darkness, lying upon the sofa that had been her bed since the demise of her family. The widow sat up and arched her back, cracking joints, and a terrible taste filled her mouth.

Her nightmare had been a very disturbing elaboration of her waking life, and she was rattled. She looked around her apartment and, by the brindled light of the glowing cat, saw very little. The shadows were impossibly heavy and the sliver of night beyond the closed curtains was a black swatch, excepting two tiny blue rectangles that were windows in the adjacent building. Society was asleep, and Alicia was awake.

She tried not to think about the slug.

The widow rose from the couch, stepped—and nearly tripped—upon her boots and walked over to the wall, her hands out like a blind person's as she reached for the panel. Inside her mind, she saw her husband's and daughter's collapsed skulls, a ruptured squid, Carlo Burgacci waiting for her with a gun, the slug, Elad's eyebrows and the ancient face of Mrs. Dulande. The switch clicked, and ice lights glared, chasing away the images and revealing an empty apartment.

She double-tapped her lily and said, "Search: Chinese restaurant; open now; delivers to home." A moment later, the line began to ring.

* * *

Alicia Martinez sat on the plasticore floor of the kitchen where her family had been murdered and attempted to eat pork egg foo young. The mucoidal meal suggested too many visual horrors to her, and she was unable to eat it.

She tried not to think about the slug.

Twenty minutes later, the widow ate white rice with soy sauce and listened to the messages in her lily vault. Morton Goldman had called to extend an invitation to "catch up" whenever she was so inclined (and also to make sure that she was getting her severance deposits); her mother had called; her father had called ("concerned"); Saul and Werner (her would-be partners in the case against Derrick W.R. Dulande) had called; and a friend from college whom Alicia had outgrown before senior year had called to offer her condolences, months after the fact.

After these transmissions from the world of families, laws, jobs and social lunches was a message from Elad in which the Israeli American said, in a digitally altered voice, "I checked your messages. Be sure to respond to all of the people who have contacted you. Isolation makes people suspicious." Crunching a nut, he ended the connection.

Tomorrow afternoon she would return the calls. To these people she would detail an anecdote of a mild sickness overcome, and perhaps flavor it with a technical difficulty that had plagued her lily. Those who inhabited the world of families, laws, jobs and social lunches were not owed the truth.

She looked at the fortune cookie in the bottom of the bag, and to it said, "Fuck off."

Alone and unable to do otherwise, Alicia Martinez thought about the slug.

The mutilated man was evidence of sadistic psychoses, and was a far fouler deed than killing an already-executed murderer or kidnapping an executive.

Alone and unable to do otherwise, Alicia Martinez thought about the brief exchange that she had overheard immediately after the interrogation.

As the pawns were leaving the observation room, the female had asked the androgyne, "Can Elad really take CCI?"

"He has studied the work of Nicolai Dhanikov."

There had been admiration in the androgyne's voice as he or she uttered the name of the man who had destroyed the Empire State Building.

* * *

The widow tried to distract herself with fiction.

She selected and watched a silly mote aquarium experience about a rocket blasting off from some fake world that was surrounded by gelatin and water. At the end of this idiotic fantasy, she had wept hysterically.

Alicia then put the cat on the stage, shut off the ice lights and lay upon the sofa. Darkness and the purrs of the pixel-sculpted feline were her companions.

The widow dreamt of the Empire State Building and the Corpus Chrome, Incorporated Building. Both buildings were ablaze within the blackened landscape of an abandoned Heaven.

Chapter IX
Guys: A Thesis Statement

"Wait a second."

Champ Sappline sneezed upon the brightlamp-illuminated sidewalk. Sniffling, he righted himself from the constellation that he had just created, locked a nozzle to the canister wherein liquefied garbage crackled, walked to the rear of the truck and turned on the straw. The truck sucked.

"What were you about to say?" Champ asked Candace through his lily.

"I'm happy for you," his ex-wife responded, "but you don't need to give me updates on everyth—"

"But this is major news," defended the garbage man. "It seemed like something you should know. They re-bodied my father. That's big news."

"I'm in Thailand with Alan."

"You guys gypsies?"

"This is only the third trip we've taken since we—" Candace stopped herself abruptly.

"Since what?" In the silence that followed, Champ heard a male voice mumble something. "Are you guys married? Did you get married to Alan and not even tell me?"

"Champ. I'm happy that you have your father again, but I shouldn't be the one you call about significant events in your life at this point."

"Don't make it sound like I'm pestering you all the time. I haven't called you in more than a month. It's just…you know…we were together for so long. Fourteen years. I thought there was a friendship, too. With us."

"When you've moved on with your life—maybe found somebody else—we might learn how to have a friendship."

"Thanks, counselor." Champ unlocked the nozzle and shoved it back into the truck. "'When you no longer want to talk to me…talk to me.' What is that? Existentialism? Buddhism? Seems like you're spending too much time in Asia."

The man on the other end said something unintelligible, his basso voice rumbling like a motorcycle engine.

"I think you should stop calling me for a while," said Candace.

"How long? A couple of months?" Silence filled Champ's ear, and he felt as if he were physically shrinking. "Longer?"

Candace replied, "I suggest that we check in with each other in about a year."

"Let's try two. Eons." The garbage man cut the connection, grumbled and climbed into the vehicle behind the driver.

Mikek surveyed the bugview and accelerated directly in front of a ladybug. The oncoming vehicle veered to avoid hitting the much larger, harder truck.

"I get testy sometimes," explained the driver.

Champ did not respond.

The rolling weapon that Mikek also employed to freight liquefied garbage sped along Fulton Street. The plump fellow dragged on his vapor tube, offered it to the man in the sucker's seat and set the declined cylinder on the dashboard next to the animated picture of his laughing, round-faced wife and two beaming daughters. An airborne riot wagon sped over the truck, its hull thrusters flashing brightly in the skyview octagon.

"You should stop calling her," said Mikek without preamble.

"Thanks for the advice."

"Nothing good ever comes from these calls."

"You on her payroll?"

"You get really, really drunk or you brood, or you do both with profanity. And you play those depressing songs that make people leave the bar. Stop calling her."

"I don't call her that much," defended Champ. "It's been more than a month."

"That's only because you're trying to prove to her that you're independent. If Candace let you, you'd call her all the time."

"We had a lot of good years, and she knows me better than anybody else. We saw the world together."

"Think of your relationship like a hamburger. It was delicious while you ate it, but afterwards.... " Mikek grimaced. "Smelly."

"I might choose not think of it that way."

"As a happily married man, I—whoa, whoa, whoa! Look at that dairy!" Mikek pointed to an octagon that displayed three young women who were emerging from the velvet portal of a dance club, their metallic slips and matching heels glimmering. "The one on the left. Do you see the one on left? That's the living definition of dairy."

Champ watched the chosen woman bump into her friend and giggle. "I suppose you'd hit her with the truck?"

"I'd do a one-eighty on those buttocks."

The garbage truck continued up the avenue, and the image of the stumbling trinity diminished in the rearview octagon.

"As a happily married man," Mikek resumed, "I feel that I have some insights I could share with you—about relationships and women."

"Run them over with a garbage truck?" suggested Champ.

"That's only for pretend. I'd never hurt anybody."

"But your imaginary hospital is filled with gorgeous cripples."

"You gonna practice your comedy that nobody laughs at, or are you gonna learn something from a guy who's got all this?" The driver pointed to the animated picture of his wife and daughters.

"Begin the lecture," said Champ, intending to tune the fellow out.

Mikek cleared his throat and announced, "A man is a tool that a woman uses."

After five seconds of silence, Champ inquired, "That's it?"

"That's the headline," replied Mikek, turning the vehicle north. "A woman wants to move her collection of antique cast-iron sewing machines? She gets a man. She wants the ingredient that turns her egg into a kid? She gets a man. She wants her body kissed all over? She gets a man. Somebody just broke into the house with a gun? Send her a man to see what's the matter."

"I can see why your wife's smiling."

"Let me finish, funny guy. The woman may love the man, she may be kind to the man, she may even be nicer to the man than she is to herself, but the man is a tool that helps her achieve her goals—the primal goals wired into her genes. She wants to have kids, she wants a good home and she wants to be safe.

"And because the woman is so beautiful, the man has no choice but to help her, to be her tool. He never did. That's in his genes—that attraction so strong that he'll accept the woman's goals as his own. He's a sucker. And it's been that way ever since the man was a caveman. Keep the pretty woman safe, make sure she's got enough woolly mammoth meat, roll the rock in front of the cave so the rain doesn't get inside, hold her at night in case a saber-tooth tiger comes along. Serve her. Be her tool. Help that woman have some kids in a safe home.

"If it didn't go that way," Mikek added, "we'd be extinct like those Neandertals. Those men didn't take care of those women—when they were pregnant or whenever—and look how it went for them.

"Not so good."

"Lots of women are supportive of their husbands," opined Champ.

"Of course—and it might seem like those men are in charge—but even still, those men aren't happy unless their wives are happy. And their wives aren't happy unless they're fulfilling those genetic goals or are on their way to fulfilling them.

"There are exceptions, but generally that's what's going on with women and why they bother with us.

"But nowadays—like for the last century—things are starting to get different. Complicated. More intellectual, less primal. If the man gets sick of being the tool—he's not attracted to the woman anymore or his work is more important—there's a divorce. And if the woman thinks the man is not the right tool for her—he won't help her fulfill these goals, or he's already helped her and she's annoyed with him—there's a divorce.

"The woman doesn't need the tool like she used to.

"She can go to the store and get another man—or just do without one. She can pay somebody to move her antique cast-iron sewing machines, she can buy an apartment in a safe building and she can get pregnant on her own.

"How come you think there're so many more lesbians than there used to be? It's because they just don't need us anymore."

"When're men gonna be obsolete?" asked Champ.

"There'll probably be a war around twenty-three hundred."

Mikek steered the vehicle onto a side street. Buildings scrolled up, down, left and right on the bugview.

"I watched a documentary," explained the driver.

Champ withheld a laugh.

Mikek dragged on a vapor tube and set it down. "The point I'm making to you is your wife has a new tool. You should stop calling her."

"I just think we should be friends."

"You're not friends. You're the wrench she threw away."

"Is this—is any of this stuff you're saying—supposed to cheer me up?"

"I'm a man of facts," admitted Mikek.

The truck sped past a sheaf bodega that was surrounded by Bangladeshi men in viridescent suits who sucked upon udon spools and squirted tamarind vials.

"When was the last time you saw your dad?" inquired the driver.

"Last week. The day he got out of CCI." Champ recalled the horde of firemen at the station who had cheered and taken the mannequin into the night. The son of the celebrated fellow had tagged along for a while, but soon, he felt out of place amongst the bonded brethren and departed, unsure whether or not his father would even notice. "He's got a lot of people in his life," added the man in the sucker's seat. "He's a popular guy."

"Sounds like an excuse for not making an effort."

"It's the truth. And we weren't close the first time around."

"But he's alive and you guys have a bond of some kind, 'cause that's how it is with fathers and sons. You can make it better if you want to—you're a grown-up now. A lot better than harassing your ex-wife."

A red light blinked on the dashboard.

"Shit on shit," exclaimed Mikek. "Only people filling a canister this time of night are drunk kids puking and pissing in it."

Surprising both himself and the driver, Champ said, "You're right. I should see him."

* * *

The garbage man sniffed the armpits of the K!RaZee t-shirt that he had snatched from his locker, smelled nothing awful, exited the foam-rubber cab and stepped onto the raised sidewalk, upon which u-shaped vine trees stood in small plots of lavender grass. Yawning, he walked toward a thumping façade, where an animation loop of a wrecking ball that was embossed with a frothy beer mug smashed into a fat man's head (which was made out of bricks).

Seated upon a buoyed stool to the right of the entrance was a hugely muscular Asian doorman, clothed in a maroon suit, who watched a petite girl half Champ's age press her fingertips to the black glass of the identification placard. The device's approval light turned green, and the fleximetal door slid into the ground. Music and the bolstered mirth of inebriation roared through the portal, sending a terrified turkey pigeon into the air. The petite girl tightened her vermillion slip and walked into the establishment.

Champ pulled his long hair behind his ears as he approached the Asian doorman.

"One hundred globals," said the edifice of muscle.

"Really?"

"Are you a policeman or a fireman?"

"No."

"A woman? I've been surprised, but the placard will let me know."

"I'm a man."

"One hundred globals."

"Why so much?"

"Deters losers."

"Seems expensive for a bar. Are the drinks really expensive?"

The Asian man shrugged. "I get mine free," he said, dusting a pectoral muscle as if it were the fender of a valuable car.

Champ sighed, fingered his identification, acknowledged a liability waiver and accepted the debit (from which the Global Senate got their twelve percent). The fleximetal door slid into the ground. Cheers, laughter, polyrhythmic music, malt beer and cinnamon assaulted him.

The garbage man walked inside and winced as the noise overwhelmed his ears.

His pupils gradually adjusted to the dim red and blue lighting of the nightclub, a place seemingly designed to confound the senses.

Cautiously, Champ proceeded. He observed a dance area, which had mote footprints (to aid the uncoordinated) and buoyed dummy partners (both muscular and voluptuous), and, two meters above head level, he saw the floating circular booths that orbited the large establishment. A new song (louder than the last) shook the walls, and a titanic Asian fellow slammed into the garbage man, revealed a (golden-stitch) lion skull chest tattoo and roared.

Champ backed away and accidentally elbowed the young woman who had preceded him into the club. "Sorry about that!"

"Leave me alone!" she replied, reaching into her koala bag for something that would hurt strangers.

The garbage man retreated.

Five girls who were trying to look much older than they were crossed his path, their progress linear and connected, like that of a locomotive. He made eye contact with the caboose and received a frown. A moment later, six jackals in suits whose eyes were agleam with imagined penetrations followed after the quintet.

Champ surveyed the slowly orbiting booths until he descried the mannequin in one that floated on the far side of the establishment. Eagle Sappline wore fireman's neon green and had his arms spread across the bare shoulders of two dark-haired young women. Also at the table were Potato O'Boyd, Bagel Butch, Pedro Cheung and a black couple.

The garbage man plowed through onlookers, dopes and drunkards and eventually reached the shadow of the buoyed booth.

There, Champ titled his head back and yelled, "Dad!"

Potato O'Boyd looked down his russet proboscis, saw nothing and returned his gaze to the re-bodied man, who appeared to be telling an anecdote.

Champ strode beneath the floating booth and shouted, "Potato!" at a volume that hurt his throat.

The oldster looked out, surveying the crowd, as if some long-forgotten memory or spouse had resurfaced to accost him.

"Down here!" yelled the garbage man, waving his arms. "Look down here!"

Potato O'Boyd looked down at Champ and squinted.

"We've only got room for girls up here," said the Irish American.

"It's Champ! It's Eagle's son! I'm Eagle's son."

Potato O'Boyd leaned over to Bagel Butch and said something to him. The Jewish man leaned over the edge and looked down at Champ.

"It's the garbage man," said Bagel Butch, nodding his head.

The Irish American said something to the mannequin, and the re-bodied man responded. Champ circumnavigated a shoving match and returned to his spot beside and below the orbiting booth.

"It's too crowded to use the rope ladder!" yelled the Irish American. "Sorry!"

Champ said, "Okay," and felt melancholy suffuse his blood. His efforts (and one hundred globals) had led to yet another disappointing experience with his father. The garbage man wondered whether he should wait at the bar for a little while or just leave the place altogether.

Leaning out, Bagel Butch pointed to the right. "We'll get you over there when we swing around."

Champ looked in the indicated direction and saw a ramp that he had not earlier noticed. To the Jewish man he said, "Great. Thanks!"

The garbage man hastened to and up the ramp, and as the floating booth glided alongside the platform, he hopped onto its carpeted floor. Looking over, the old men and the black couple waved greetings at the new arrival.

"This is my son," said Eagle, addressing the young raven-haired women who were underneath his arms. "Of...a bitch...brother. This is my son-of-a-bitch brother, Champ."

The swarthy pair smiled and mouthed greetings that were inaudible.

"This one's Gina," informed the mannequin, squeezing the shoulder of the girl on his left, "and this one's Nicole," he said, clasping the one on his right. Both ladies wore yellow and indigo camisoles and matching webwork along their arms and necks.

"They're curious girls," explained Eagle.

"Hello," said Champ, nodding to the women and embarrassed by the envy that he felt. He then took a seat next to the oldsters, across from the mannequin, his dates and the black couple, who were having their own private conversation.

Gina sipped an oily pink and green cocktail.

"How is it?" asked Eagle.

"It's transporting."

"Looks weird. What's in there?"

The woman took another sip, savoring the flavor. "Vodka, infused with lemongrass, lemon peel, star anise and lilac."

"Can I try it?" asked the re-bodied man.

Gina shared a funny grin with Nicole and summarily slid the drink in front of Eagle. The re-bodied man screwed a beaded, dark red thimble onto the tip of his right pinky finger and dipped it into the cocktail. Two tiny air bubbles arose from the extension.

"Tastes like medicine," said Eagle.

"I like it," defended Gina.

A second pair of bubbles floated up from the thimble.

"Like medicine and groin sweat. Hell, that shit's awful."

The woman reclaimed her drink and sipped another kitten's portion. "It's transporting," she reconfirmed.

Eagle wiped his dripping thimble on his neon green FDNY shirt and raised it in the air. "Let me get something good on this."

Potato O'Boyd pushed a glass of Scotch across the table.

The re-bodied man submerged his extension, and two bubbles floated to the surface. "Shit, this's good. Is it the thirty-year?"

"Yessir."

"This shit's expensive."

"At my age," Potato O'Boyd said, "there's no reason to drink anything reasonably priced."

Leaving his left pinky inside the Scotch glass, Eagle looked at Nicole and nodded his head. "It's time."

Excited, the woman shared a glance with her peer and then stuck a magnetic device that was shaped like a hockey puck on the side of the mannequin's head.

"Give it to me!" demanded Eagle.

Nicole squealed, pressing the button that was in the center of the device. An icon that looked like a congregation of psychedelic amoebas blinked thrice.

"Which tweaker is that?" asked Champ.

"Paisley brain," answered Pedro Cheung, cackling drunkenly. "He loves this one."

Eagle removed his pinky from the whiskey, wobbled against Nicole and slumped heavily upon Gina. Laughing, the women helped him sit upright.

The mannequin looked at his son and shouted, "You should be drinking! You need to be drinking!" He activated the menu and typed rapidly.

"Whoa!" exclaimed Bagel Butch, pushing his friend's gelware hand from the screen.

"Don't go hysterical. My son needs—" Eagle cut himself short. "My suntanned brother needs to get wrecked. It's…it's imperative."

"I don't think he needs thirty shots," opined Bagel Butch.

"I don't," agreed Champ. "I've got the morning shift tomorrow."

"Are you a fireman, too?" asked Gina.

"I'm a garbage man."

"Oh." The woman forced a patronizing smile.

Champ said, "Our mother didn't want both of her beloved sons risking their lives as firefighters, and I—unfortunately—lost the coin toss."

"That's right!" yelled Eagle. "What do you wanna drink…hermano?"

"Pick something you want to dip your thimble into and I'll get it for us. My treat."

"The garbage man's a big spender," said Gina.

The mannequin looked at the raven-haired woman, his gelware face neutral, devoid of expression.

"Are you okay?" asked Bagel Butch.

Eagle looked away from Gina and smiled at Champ. "I'd like you to get something with tequila in it. Always liked that flavor. Tastes like spring break."

The garbage man activated the embedded menu and dialed to the screen of tequilas, where he selected one that was more than half the cover charge, fingerprinting his authorization. A half-filled glass soon emerged from an iris in the table.

Eagle played the gelware fingertips of his right hand along Nicole's bare shoulder. "I looked just like Champ before they put me in the robot."

"I hope you dressed better," remarked Gina.

The mannequin withdrew his arms from the women, picked up their oily cocktails and threw them off of the floating booth. "You girls should leave at the next ramp."

"You're kicking us off?" asked Nicole, incredulous.

"I am."

"Gina was just joking."

"Saying mean stuff and calling it a joke doesn't make it nice," remarked Eagle. "I let it go before, but she hit her limit."

"You're seriously kicking us off?" asked Gina.

"I didn't come back from the dead to hang out with stuck-up bitches."

The floating booth stopped. Scowling, the two raven-haired women stood up, squeezed between the table and the men's knees and strode onto the platform.

Gina called back, "Go to hell, you dumb old men."

Bagel Butch replied, "Old-fashioned Hell or that new one with calamari?"

The old firemen laughed, and the black couple chuckled. Champ grinned as the booth floated away from the ramp.

"They should have planks on these booths," stated Eagle. "And that flag with the skull and bones."

"I'd pay extra for those amenities," remarked Potato O'Boyd.

"Anemones?" inquired Pedro Cheung, who was far from sober.

Champ sipped the tequila and pushed it across the table to his father. "Thanks."

Eagle stuck his thimble inside the glass. "I'm glad you came out." Two tiny bubbles rose from his carmine attachment. "Kick the stars, is this shit good."

"Glad you like it."

The re-bodied man leaned in close to his son. "There's a woman in the next one over who's been watching you ever since you got here."

Casually, the garbage man glanced back. Two forty-year-old-women who wore bright cashmere suits looked away from him.

"The one with the pink hair?" asked Champ, hopeful.

"That's her. Why don't you invite her over? I'll take her friend."

* * *

The forty-four-year-old black man who had accompanied the septuagenarians (and, coincidentally, gone to the same elementary school as Champ) waved good-bye to his impressive wife Molly (who had twice eyed the garbage man in a somewhat suggestive manner) and stomped upon the jump pedal. Telescopic legs loaded with combustion relay springs shot the bright red fire wagon into the air above the station. Balconies and windows and billboards and roofs and antennas and float-ads and solar panels fell away, and the sky expanded, its dark canvas flecked with moon-limned clouds that looked like the strokes of hasty painters. Champ looked down and saw the city shrink as if it were a healing laceration.

"This is so much awesomer than in my first life," Eagle said to his son and the pair of forty-year-old Texas businesswomen who sat between the Sapplines on the air bench. (Potato O'Boyd and Bagel Butch were battling the undertow of sleep in the rear of the craft, occasionally admitting snores of defeat.)

"My ears are popping!" Pretty exclaimed to Eagle, clapping her palms to the sides of her head. "It's so fast!"

"It's great, right?" enthused the re-bodied man. "Hop into the sky and zip where you gotta go, and just drag along how much water you need. In my first life, we wasted tons of time stuck in traffic while people were getting burnt up. This's way better."

Eagle leaned forward in his seat and said to the pilot, "Thanks for taking us up. I really wanted Champ to see this."

"My pleasure, Captain Sappline," said Douglas.

Doreen, the handsome admirer with pink hair, leaned her head against Champ's shoulder. "This is beautiful, isn't it?"

"Very."

The multicolored lights of the city were replaced by lunar rays, and the soft, cool luminance made the woman's face look like that of a Grecian statue. Champ brushed pink bangs from two blue eyes that looked upon him with the intensity of floodlights. His heart thumped.

"That's quite a look you're giving me," said the garbage man.

Doreen leaned into him; her lavender cashmere suit was impossibly soft and smelled of lilacs. "You look so handsome when you smile," she said, "like an actor or somebody famous."

Champ had not been complimented so directly in years, and he blushed. The floodlights brightened, enthralling him. If this woman had asked him to get woolly mammoth meat or to move her antique cast-iron sewing machines or to grapple with a knife-wielding intruder, he would have complied. Whether this was a conditioned response or a genetic one or a type of mysterious energy two sibling spirits shared, he did not know, but for three heartbeats, he forgot who he was and where he was, and all he felt was the magnetism of her.

Champ kissed Doreen upon the lips, and she opened her mouth. Warm tongues played behind the fences of teeth. Hands slid across backs.

The craft reached the apex of its launch, paused and began to sink.

Champ's heart rose toward his throat. Doreen's tongue thrust urgently. The fire wagon fell, as did they.

Douglas fingered the lift, and hull thrusters flashed. The craft stopped, jostling the couple apart and eliciting a giggle from each of them.

Eagle leaned forward, a lopsided grimace warping his gelware face. Champ deciphered the expression as a congratulatory wink.

"You two are meant for each other, I can tell," opined the re-bodied man. "Total destiny."

Scarlet and pink, Doreen took Champ's hand and asked, "Do you think... would you ever think about coming out to Texas for a vacation, maybe? A weekend? Something like that?"

The garbage man presumed that the woman had asked him these questions because she did not want to sleep with a man whom she would never again see (and maybe also to find out if he thought that she was worth a trip). Regardless of her reasoning, a seat on a shuttle to Texas was well beyond his budget.

Champ opened his mouth to respond in earnest when Eagle said, "Of course he'll get down to Texas. We're gonna go there soon and visit some friends. Get some hats. Have some rodeos."

"Really?" asked Doreen. "Which area?"

"All around the whole darn thing," replied Eagle. "We'll just swing on by."

Doreen unfastened her pseudopodia, straddled Champ's lap and kissed him like a succubus.

Eagle chirped.

Chapter X
Delayed Reactions

Lisanne hugged Osa, inhaled deeply, and strode past the furled polarity curtain and into the oval room within which her re-bodied sister, clothed in a drooping green robe, sat upon the bed, facing the window. Outside, the rising sun etched the skyscrapers of Brooklyn City and Nexus Y in such a striking manner that the entire view looked false and compressed, like a bas-relief.

With a twisted and anxious heart, the petite blonde addressed her sister's back. "Guten Morgen."

The re-bodied woman said, "Morgen," but did not move at all.

Lisanne had not seen her sister since their troubled reunion last week, and the days between that visit and this one (the first permitted by Corpus Chrome, Incorporated's inner board) had been awful. Mr. Johnson's kind words and Osa's powerful love could not obscure the horrible truth that loomed on the horizon like a diseased moon: If Ellenancy's condition did not improve in the next two weeks, she would be de-bodied, and her brain would once again be a frozen cauliflower.

"Are you still angry?" asked Lisanne, her face reflected in the window beside her sister's generic mask.

"Sometimes."

The petite blonde walked around the bed and stopped beside the chromium machine that held, and was, her sister.

Ellenancy stared outside.

Lisanne said, "Look at me."

"I can see your reflection."

"Use that machine and look at me." Her tone was stern.

The mannequin's head swiveled, stopped and tilted like the skull of a curious bird.

"Are you angry with me, specifically?" asked Lisanne.

"Sometimes."

"Because I authorized your resurrection?"

"It was a selfish thing to do."

The petite blonde wanted to yell at her sister, but feared that such behavior might terminate the visit. Calming herself, she replied, "What should I have said when they called and offered to resurrect you? 'Nein, danke. Nein. I believe Ellenancy would prefer to remain frozen.' Is that what I should have said?"

The mannequin was silent.

"The cryonic plan was your decision," added Lisanne.

"I had hoped for something better. A new flesh body, not this verflucht machine."

"A clone?" inquired Lisanne.

"Yes. A mindless one that could sustain a transplant. Or perhaps one that had its brain euthanized."

"No transplants like that will ever be allowed by the government."

"I suppose…that I was hoping to wake up in a time when such things were possible," said Ellenancy, her head askew.

"It is extraordinarily unlikely that I or anybody you know would still be alive at that time."

The mannequin was silent.

With a gentler voice, Lisanne inquired, "Is it…is it really so terrible inside the mannequin?"

"Yes." Ellenancy faced the window. "When I walk around…it's as if I'm playing a computer game and controlling a character—some other being that is not me, through whom I witness a world that I'm not actually in." She paused for a moment. "It all feels like a dream—a long and antiseptic dream. I know it's real, but it feels imagined."

"But you think. And you feel."

"Distantly."

Lisanne took her sister's left hand and squeezed her gelware fingers. "Do you feel that?"

"After a brief delay and an inaudible click, I am aware of the texture and temperature of your hand. These sensations have been relayed to my brain."

The petite blonde withdrew her hand and sat upon an inflatable stool, currently unable to think of anything else to say.

Ellenancy swiveled her head to face her sister. "I have been listening to files and reading sheaves...doing research to help me make my decision."

A pit opened up in Lisanne's stomach at the thought of her sister simply deciding that she no longer wanted to live. Finding her voice, she asked, "What have you learned?"

"There is a scientific theory that the mind is not the only intelligent part of the human body, but merely the dominant one.

"The theory postulates that our hands and our feet and our arms and our legs have intelligences of their own—not just reflexes, but actual independent thought processes that are separate from the mind.

"When you trip and are about to fall, there is no part of your brain that says, 'I need to pivot, swing my arms and thrust my left leg half a meter to the left.' The body reacts: It applies muscle memory to new stimuli in an intelligent way. The brain is informed during or after the incident, but it did not control or send out the responses."

Lisanne remarked, "I've heard this theory."

"I think it is true," said Ellenancy. "And I think it explains why I hate the machine.

"The satellite intelligences in my natural body were a very large part of my identity. The minds within my fingers, hands, wrists, arms, lips, mouth, tongue, larynx and lungs that enabled me to play violins, oboes, flutes, trumpets, pianos, saxophones, tympani and xylophones are gone, as are the pleasures those satellite intelligences felt in performing these patterns—pleasures that enriched my cerebral existence as well.

"Every re-bodied person lost a lot...but I lost more."

"You were also one of the Sisters Breutschen," responded Lisanne. "You and I produced music that is substantial and will last forever. Our minds produced this music—not our bodies, but our minds."

"You wrote most of our music."

"None of those pieces would sound as they do without your input: They are the result of our minds working together."

The mannequin was silent.

"All of my favorite compositions are the ones that began with your ideas," added Lisanne.

No response emerged from the re-bodied woman.

"Ellenancy?"

"May I hear the music that you wrote while I was dead?"

"I only wrote one piece," said Lisanne. The admission was painful.

The mannequin frowned. "Does my face look sad?"

"Yes."

"Why only one piece?"

"You were the first person who ever encouraged me to write music. Mutti and Vati both wanted me to be a concert pianist, but you were the first person to hear me play something original and say, 'Das mag ich. Sehr gut.' The thought of—" Lisanne looked away from her sister's frowning visage and struggled for a moment against tears. "The thought of writing pieces that you would never get to hear was too sad. I...I just couldn't do it."

Ellenancy stood up from the bed, took one stride, leaned over and hugged her sister.

Lisanne put her arms around the mannequin and squeezed. Within her breast, hope flickered.

"I apologize," said Mr. Johnson, walking into the room, "but I have a meeting in a few minutes and will need to end your visit for today."

The Breutschen sisters withdrew from each other.

Nodding his head in approval, the shepherd asked the re-bodied woman, "Would you like for me to schedule another interaction with your sister?"

Ellenancy looked at Lisanne. "Would you play the piece for me?"

The petite blonde turned to the black man in tweed. "Do you have a room with true-definition spheroid acoustics?"

"Indeed, indeed, indeed."

Lisanne nodded to Ellenancy. "I'll bring it tomorrow."

"You did not load it to a reservoir or a vault?"

"I did not." The mournful dirge had been written immediately after Ellenancy's death, played at her funeral, and—despite the interest of sponsors and reviewers—not once since. Lisanne did not want the piece to ever become a commodity.

"What's it called?" asked Ellenancy.

"'The Dotted Line.'"

* * *

Lisanne and Osa rode in a cab toward The Pinnacle in Central Park. The petite blonde clutched a kernel of hope, but did not indulge in optimism.

At Forty-Second Street, the vehicle was nudged by a ladybug, and the cabbie—a Hasidic man—reciprocated the blow with a swerve that ended in a vengeful bump.

"You're making it worse," chastised Osa. "Stop."

The oncoming traffic orb turned yellow, and the cabbie braked. A stopwall lurched in front of the fender.

Lisanne said, "We are going to listen to 'The Dotted Line.'"

"We are?" asked Osa, excited by the prospect of finally hearing the secreted piece.

"Ellenancy and I, not us." The petite blonde instantly regretted her choice of words. "I'm sorry: I didn't mean to say it like that."

Osa nodded her head. "I know you didn't mean to."

CHAPTER XI
ORIENTAL LAPDOG

A face emerged from the wall and said, "Autumn's sleeping over—you need to clean up this room."

To his father's disembodied visage, Snapdragon responded, "Last time she was here, she got angry that I put the plant-eating dinosaurs with the meat-eating ones. I don't wanna get anything wrong."

"We don't want her to go home and tell Mrs. Tannstein that our place is messy, do we?"

"She's a tattler," said Snapdragon, sighing.

"You'll get ice cream if you make it look clean."

"With the peanut elephants?"

"With peanut elephants," confirmed his father. "But don't tell Mommy."

"Deal."

Below the man's round face, a broom clutched by a disembodied hand emerged from the wall.

"Use this."

Snapdragon took the broom from his father and swept his spongy dinosaurs into a pile, where they clutched and slapped and squawked and roared and played musical instruments. The Asian boy then picked out his favorite (a pterodactyl with a bass guitar), shoved it into the center pocket of his bumper overalls and swept the Jurassic period under his bed. As long as there was room underneath his mattress, he was a capable cleaner.

* * *

After a vegan meal (Autumn did not eat meat and became sick if she even smelled it), the two children went into the den, where Snapdragon sat on the air bench and casually placed his left hand atop a spaghetti stain that his pants had somehow acquired during dinner. Clothed in a black cotton one-piece, the Jewish girl sat upon her regular and special legs as if she were going to make a cobra come out of a basket with a flute.

"What do you wanna watch?" asked the boy. "My parents said we could have the m.a. until twenty-three."

"What are my choices?"

"There's stuff with robots. There's stuff with monsters. There's stuff with robot monsters."

"Are there some more sophisticated options?" asked Autumn.

"Dinosaurs?"

"Things with cultural significance."

"There's smart stuff. Is that what you watch at home?"

"We don't have a mote aquarium."

"Are you poor?" Snapdragon ruminated for a moment. "We have an old one you could borrow."

"I told you this before," the girl said impatiently, "my parents don't want one in the house. They feel it would be a distraction."

"From what?"

"From my academic pursuits and my yoga classes. I also write poems."

"If you don't wanna watch m.a., we can build a fort."

Snapdragon imagined himself and Autumn hidden within a castle like the ones that he built with the dining room chairs, arranged in a rectangle, draped with blankets, surrounded by a barbican of pillows upon which he set fearsome guardian beasts that vaguely resembled the stuffed bears and penguins and otters with which he slept every night. Within this safe environment, secreted from the eyes of adults and the judgments of a kingdom that did not understand his puberty, the Asian prince would be able to kiss the Jewish princess (or at least lick her hands).

"I am interested in watching a mote aquarium experience," declared Autumn. "I should learn about popular culture, which has anthropological value."

Snapdragon returned to his original agendum. "Robots?"

The girl seemed to be no more intrigued by this idea in its recapitulation. Looking at her host, she suggested, "Perhaps we should watch something about China?"

"I'm American," defended Snapdragon.

"I know. I just think that it would be nice to watch something about your heritage, since I'm a guest in your home."

"Oh. Okay."

Snapdragon whistled a C-sharp and said, "Turn on." Myriad luminous pixels sprayed from the tube onto the stage. "Don't touch it," he warned his guest. "I once broke it like that."

The comet of luminous motes sped to all eight corners of the aquarium.

Snapdragon whistled and said, "Search reservoir: China."

Rendered upon the stage in three-dimensional characters was the following:

There are 92,765,017 m.a. experiences related to China.
Review Options or Refine Search?

Snapdragon looked at Autumn and inquired, "What do you want to see about China? I hear their kung fu fights are good."

"Gender relationships and small dogs are subjects that interest me."

The Asian boy sighed through his nostrils. "I know you like little doggies." (He had been exposed to the girl's irritating pet on several occasions: The tiny beast barked constantly, perhaps angry that its bulging eyes and elastic tongue did not fit inside of its evil head.) "Refine search."

Upon the stage were the words:

Refine Search…

Snapdragon prompted his guest with a nod.

Autumn said, "China; gender relationships; small dogs."

The following words were rendered upon the stage:

Oriental Lapdog
Length: 239 minutes
Audience: Adult

"That looks like a good choice," said the girl.

Snapdragon did not agree (the experience was very, very long and intended for adults), but he withheld his contrary opinions since he wanted his guest to have a good time. He whistled and said, "Play."

The luminous pixels rendered

> *a cliff edge upon which sat a goateed Chinese man who wore a crimson robe and a round hat. He looked at the turquoise waters below his dangling feet.*

Within the ocean were the words:

> *Li Wai Fung presents—*

"Skip credits," said Snapdragon, who wanted to have time to build a fort.

The motes rendered

> *a jade castle. The edifice was as large as a continent and comprised of ten thousand and seventy-two towers, each of which had nine hundred amethyst windows. Atop the merlons, spires, parapets and walls were ten million purpureal banners, which were pulled east by the western wind and then north by the southern wind. The fabric snapped with each new gust. Drums thudded, and weird Oriental instruments twanged. Horses, newly shod and dressed in brilliant steel, trotted through the courtyards. Warriors, dressed in armor, stood upon the barbican.*

(The sight of the warriors and their weapons gave Snapdragon hope.)

Snow fell upon the eastern half of the castle. The flags on that side grew heavy with moisture and were darker than those in the west.

At the very top of the easternmost tower was an amethyst window that was brighter than any other. In the luminous pane sat the silhouette of a woman whose head was surmounted by a stack of equilateral triangles. A weird flute played three ugly notes.

Inside the tower sat the Chinese princess. She was clothed in a golden gown, which was fastened to her with purpureal ribbons. Two smiling men who wore pink makeup adjusted the triangles of hair that were atop her head.

"She's beautiful," said Autumn, her voice freezing the pixels in the mote aquarium.

The woman reminded Snapdragon of his Aunt Sally. "She's okay. Resume play."

The princess looked around her room. Its walls were covered with white and blue silk that had been sewn into scalloped folds to resemble a waterfall. The rug was dark blue, like a pond, and the ceiling was light blue, like the sky. In the corner, a little blind girl played a weird flute, and an armless old man yodeled while twanging a broken lute with his toes.

The smiling men who wore pink makeup asked the princess, "Do you like your hair?"

"It's in English?" asked Autumn, her voice freezing the pixels in the mote aquarium.

"They change the mouths with computers so you can understand it." Scratching his armpit, Snapdragon said, "Resume play."

"These are very fine triangles," said the princess. "But what does it matter? Only the king who never smiles, my father, shall see them. Only he shall enjoy the beauty of such artfully-arranged hair."

The smiling men giggled and said, "The king who never smiles has a surprise for you!"

"Has he finally found a worthy suitor?" asked the princess, suddenly hopeful.

The smiling men did not answer, but instead giggled and minced about on the long toes of their bare feet. In the corner, the blind girl played five ugly notes, and the old man yodeled.

The motes dispersed and rendered

a gold hallway. The princess entered this place and sat upon a bier that was made of jade. Four fat men who wore bloodstained diapers raised the royal platform and carried it forward. The smiling men followed, prancing.

The motes dispersed and rendered

a white chamber. Its walls, floor and ceiling were covered with Chinese ideograms that were nearly the same shade of white as the surface upon which they had been painted. The fat men with bloodstained diapers carried the princess's bier through this chamber. Following behind them, the two smiling men looked at one of the myriad ideograms. The isolated ideogram was itself comprised of thousands of tiny ideograms.

The motes dispersed and rendered

a chamber that was peopled by five hundred armored swordsmen. The fat men with bloodstained diapers carried the princess's bier into this room and down the aisle. Each swordsman cut his arm when the princess passed. Blood dripped onto the marble, echoing throughout the room. The smiling men pranced behind the bier.

The motes dispersed and became

the royal antechamber. The fat men with bloodstained diapers carried the princess's bier across this room. A very tall man guarded the next door. His sword was huge and had twenty-nine tempered-steel blades.

('I hope he uses that in a fight,' mouthed Snapdragon silently.)

The very tall man raised his weapon. Green brazier light played upon the straight, curved, forked, corkscrewed and serrated blades. The very tall man knelt before the bier and said, "The king who never smiles is ready to see the princess." He pricked himself with the polybladed sword and was cut twenty-nine times. Each of his wounds dripped blood onto the marble floor.

Two stone doors opened. The fat men with bloodstained diapers carried the bier forward, their feet splashing in the tall man's blood. Behind the bier, the smiling men pranced.

The motes dispersed and became

a vast enclosure. Clouds hung beneath the ceiling, and the far end of the room was not visible. The fat men with bloodstained diapers carried the princess's bier into the room, making bloody footprints upon the carpet, atop hundreds of similarly shaped brown stains. Behind the bier, the smiling men pranced.

Snapdragon and Autumn watched the princess and her retinue traverse the chamber for eighteen minutes. (The Asian boy spent most of this time pondering forts and peanut elephants.)

The princess raised a spyglass to her eye, aimed it and said, "I see my father." "What is the king who never smiles doing?" asked the smiling men. "He is painting upon a solitary rice grain." "What image is he painting upon the rice grain?" The princess put a special attachment upon the spyglass, peered through and said, "I must hold the spyglass very still in order to see such a small canvas."

Snapdragon and Autumn watched the Chinese woman adjust her telescope for four minutes.

"I see his art!" exclaimed the princess. "What is the subject matter?" inquired the smiling men. "My father is painting an image of us approaching his throne. He is currently detailing my magnified right eye!" "Wonderful!" exclaimed the smiling men.

The princess waved to her father. "Did the king who never smiles return your salutation?" asked the smiling men. "No. That would have required him to put down his paintbrush and rice grain." "He is devoted to his art," responded the smiling men. The princess announced, "We shall lunch upon this hillock."

The fat men with bloodstained diapers set the bier upon the hillock.

The eleven-year-olds watched the princess eat a bowl of rice for twenty-eight minutes, during which time, the royal personage commented upon the unique character of each and every grain. (Snapdragon prayed for the violent return of the man with the polybladed sword.)

The fat men with bloodstained diapers carried the princess's bier across a bridge. Below them, the smiling men danced across the water on the tips of their long toes.
The fat men with bloodstained diapers carried the princess's bier across seven hills and into a forest that was filled with domestic black bears. One of the beasts approached the bier and roared. Its teeth had been pulled out and replaced with jade fangs.

"That's very cruel," said Autumn, her voice freezing the pixels in the mote aquarium. "Resume play."

> *"That is beautiful," the princess said of the bear's jade teeth.*
> *The bier was borne out of the forest and to the tallest mountain within the royal chamber. Prancing behind them were the smiling men.*

Snapdragon and Autumn watched the fat eunuchs and the smiling men struggle up the snow-covered mountain for nineteen minutes.

> *The princess grew excited and pointed. "There he is!" said she. "The king who never smiles, my father."*
> *Seated upon a throne that had been carved from the mountaintop was a strong old man with very long eyebrows. He wore turquoise robes, green ribbons and a jade crown upon his head. The fat men with bloodstained diapers, the smiling men and the princess were filled with awe.*
> *The king who never smiles looked at his daughter and said with a voice like thunder, "You are nearly a woman." The princess became nervous. "I have found a suitor," said the king who never smiles. The princess's eyes widened with joy. The king who never smiles pointed to a coffin that was made out of jade and silver.*
> *The princess asked, "May I open it and look upon him?"*
> *"You may not," boomed the king who never smiles. The princess was saddened by this announcement, but did not question her father. "Before you are allowed to look upon him, you must complete the Ritual of the Lapdog," declared the king who never smiles. "I do not know how to perform this ritual," said the princess.*
> *The king who never smiles pointed to a small ivory box that lay beside his feet. "Come hither," said he. The fat men with*

bloodstained diapers lowered the bier, and the princess walked
toward the peak. Stones and ice poked her feet through her silk
slippers. Pained, she cried out.

"Do not make animal noises," admonished the king who
never smiles. "Common people may yell or grunt without
purpose, but everything that a royal does is important and will
be remembered."

The princess withheld her cries as she trod upon the sharp
terrain. Soon, she reached the ivory box, knelt and opened the
lid. A small white dog with large eyes, a wagging tongue and a
pushed-in face looked up at her and barked twice.

"I love him!" said Autumn, her voice freezing the pixels in the mote aquarium. "I want to look at him."

Snapdragon stood up and helped his guest to her feet. The knee joint in the girl's polymer leg clicked loudly, but the boy pretended not to notice.

"I don't need help," Autumn stated, "but thank you."

Together, the children walked to the frozen lapdog. Shards of light were captured in the animal's bulging eyes, and a leonine mane sprouted from its neck; surrounding its paws were puffy boots of brindled fur. A lone bead of moisture stood upon its black nose.

The eleven-year-olds viewed the little beast from all sides and, after a second orbit, returned to the air bench. "Resume play," said the girl, pleased with her inspection.

The princess looked from the lapdog to the king who never smiles
and awaited an explanation. Instead of speaking, the king who
never smiles peeled a tangerine.

For eleven minutes, Snapdragon and Autumn watched the patriarch pull skin from the fruit, withdraw its seeds with sharp ivory chopsticks and arrange the isolated segments upon a stone plate.

"The Ritual of the Lapdog," the king who never smiles said, "is how I determined that your mother should be my queen." The lord ate a tangerine segment. "The lapdog is to be the intermediary between you and your suitor. While you are performing the Ritual of the Lapdog, you and your suitor may not look upon each other, nor may you touch each other. The cloud of lust is created by the exchange of such gazes and sensations, and thus, they are forbidden. You, my daughter, will speak to the lapdog as if it were your suitor, and the suitor shall speak to the lapdog as if it were the princess.

"After three years of canine proxy, I will examine the lapdog and determine, from its health and humor, whether you two are well matched."

The king who never smiles arose from his throne, and his supernatural shadow darkened the entire mountainside. And the lord said, "Follow the terms of the ritual without deviation. If you should look upon each other once or touch each other once, the ritual is nullified."

"Thank you," said the princess.

The king who never smiles sat upon his throne and reclaimed his supernatural shadow. "You may take the lapdog," said he. "I will have the coffin with the suitor delivered to your tower so that the two of you may begin the ritual. Leave me now."

The princess bowed, cradled the lapdog in her arms and boarded the bier. Quietly, the men with bloodstained diapers carried her down the mountain. A cloud concealed the procession, and hidden within it, the princess cried.

Snapdragon rose from his seat and walked to the bathroom. On his return trip, he detoured into the kitchen, ate three scoops of peanut elephant ice cream, drank a cup of chocolate milk, burped and washed his hands.

"What'd I miss?" the boy asked his guest, his voice freezing the pixels in the mote aquarium.

"The princess and her suitor are about to have their first dinner in the banquet hall."

"No fighting or anything good?"

"It's not that kind of a story."

Yawning, Snapdragon said, "Resume play."

Platters filled with roasted meats, golden snow peas, purple lobsters and sesame lo mein covered the banquet table. The princess sat in a jade throne, where she was separated from the unseen suitor by a rice-paper wall. Her lapdog was at the far end of the table, nestled in an opalescent pillow.

To the canine proxy, the princess said, "Please tell the suitor that I am pleased to finally share a room with him." The animal looked away from the princess and toward the man behind the rice-paper screen.

"Please inform the princess," the unseen suitor responded, "that I am very impressed by the food and the banquet hall." The lapdog looked at the princess.

The princess said, "Please tell the suitor that his voice has a pleasing cadence." The lapdog looked at the unseen suitor.

The unseen suitor responded, "Please inform the princess—

Snapdragon fell asleep.

* * *

The boy awakened.

The princess was seated in the rear of a barge, which men with bloodstained diapers rowed across an indoor lake. To her left was a rice-paper screen, behind which sat the unseen suitor. In a tiny white dinghy tethered to the back of the vessel sat the lapdog, trembling and skinny.

"Please inform the princess that we should withdraw the phalanx!" the unseen suitor barked at the lapdog. The animal in the dinghy turned its anxious face toward the princess.

"Please tell the suitor that only a person with peasant blood in his veins would yield the western towers so easily," responded the princess, her words like icicles. The shaking animal gnawed fur on its haunches and coughed.

"Please inform the princess that the western towers have been in disrepair for six centuries and—"

"Please tell the suitor that such information is irrelevant!" The bewildered lapdog did not know where to look.

"Please inform the princess that if she bequeaths the long-neglected western towers, her kingdom will grow rather than be diminished by warfare!"

The lapdog nervously chewed its haunches and whimpered.

"Please tell the cowardly suitor that—"

Snapdragon fell asleep.

* * *

The boy awakened from a dream in which the mote aquarium experience had concluded with a spectacular robot battle. Looking at the stage, he saw the princess (who was currently sitting sidesaddle upon a white horse) and silently mouthed the word "Crap."

The smiling men carried a rice-paper screen alongside the horseback princess. Sitting on the back of a donkey that walked two meters ahead of the princess and the unseen suitor was the lapdog, which was now calm and plump.

"Please ask the suitor for his thoughts upon the speech that I have written for the people of the western towers." The lapdog swiveled its fat head toward the unseen suitor.

"Please inform the princess that her speech is a masterful weaving of philosophic and patriotic threads, and that her verse is more musical than a ghost-face's sonnet."

226

"The speech was beautiful," Autumn informed Snapdragon, her voice freezing the pixels.

"Uh-huh," the boy replied in the middle of a yawn. "Resume play." The motes stirred, and once again, the weary host fell asleep.

* * *

Snapdragon awakened from a kissing dream. On the mote aquarium stage, the princess stood directly before her father, who was seated in his throne that was the mountaintop.

"Crap," muttered the boy, freezing the pixels. "Resume play."

> *The rice-paper screen that concealed the unseen suitor was on the mountain beside the princess. Above them, the king who never smiles looked down and said, "It has been three years since you began the Ritual of the Lapdog." The lord leaned over and lifted the ivory box.*

For sixteen minutes, Snapdragon and Autumn watched the king who never smiles examine the lapdog's tongue, teeth, gums, lips, beard, tear ducts, snout, spine, follicles, toe nails and tail. The patriarch shaved a rectangle of fur from the animal's haunches, revealing skin that bore the scars of nibbling.

> *The king who never smiles addressed the princess and the unseen suitor, "The canine proxy evinces fourteen months of hostility between you. Was it so?"*
>
> *"It was so," said the princess and the unseen suitor.*
>
> *"The canine proxy evinces twenty-two months of harmony between you. Is it so?"*
>
> *"It is so," said the princess and the unseen suitor.*
>
> *"It was this way between the queen and myself. The joining of two willful spirits is a very difficult enterprise."*

227

The king who never smiles set the lapdog upon the ground, looked upon his daughter and said, "Princess." "Yes, my father?" "Upon a grain of rice, paint the image of the suitor as you imagine him to be." "I shall." The princess then painted an image of the unseen suitor.

"Suitor." "Yes, my king?" "Upon a grain of rice, paint the image of the princess as you imagine her to be." "I shall." The king who never smiles and the princess waited while the unseen suitor painted.

And then the lord said to them both, "Forever keep this portrait that you have painted, for it is the true form of your partner."

The king who never smiles rose from his throne that was the mountaintop. He then willed his supernatural shadow to go east, and it did. "Ladymen," said the king who never smiles to smiling men. "Yes?" replied they. "Remove the rice-paper screen so that the princess and the suitor may finally look upon each other." The screen was removed.

The princess and the suitor then saw each other for the first time.

The suitor was thin and tall and had big ears. He looked unlike the handsome man whom the princess had painted upon the grain of rice, yet she exclaimed, "You look just like the picture that I painted!" The princess wept with joy, unable to see that he was not the handsome man of her imaginings.

"And you look just like the picture that I painted!" exclaimed the suitor, unable to see the discrepancies between the sizable princess and the petite woman of his imaginings.

The king who never smiles said, "You are now wed."

The princess kissed her suitor, who was now the prince.

And on that day, the king who never smiles became the king who smiled once.

Chapter XII
Triumphant

Champ helped Doreen into a cab, kissed her deeply, withdrew, said, "I'll see you in Texas," and shut the door. The sensual, uniformly pink-haired businesswoman waved good-bye through the cab's rear window and was gone.

For two days and nights, Champ and Doreen had enjoyed each other's company in a largely physical manner: kissing, nibbling, biting, tasting, engulfing, thrusting, exploding, melting and embracing. Their potential as a couple did not transcend the bedroom, drinks and comedy sheaves, and early on, they had both acknowledged and accepted this limitation.

Sucking basil udon, the garbage man walked south on a raised sidewalk, glanced at the stone hotel from which he had recently emerged and nodded a salutation.

Champ felt like a champion.

During the forty-eight hedonistic hours that he had spent with the lively Texan, he had reclaimed himself. Champ Sappline was no longer the bitter half of a divorced couple, but a handsome and funny stud. His pelvic, thigh, gluteal and abdominal muscles were sore in a fantastic way.

Champ wondered at the power of flesh over the mind, but the brief contemplation was superseded by the image of Doreen astride him and the feel of her heavy breasts in his welcoming hands.

* * *

After discarding the empty spool, the garbage man walked between two upraised stopwalls and double-tapped his lily. "Connect to Dad."

"How was she?" asked his father.

Champ detailed several sexual highlights.

Eagle chirped.

Climbing the steps to R.J. the Third's apartment, the garbage man was ambushed by fifth-floor hostiles. The quartet shoved him against a wall and slapped his face seven times before he was able to carry his red cheeks to safety.

* * *

Late the next afternoon, Champ, whose face was still swollen from the assault, and R.J. the Third, clothed in silver, ascended the stairs. The pair stopped upon the fifth-floor landing.

"This floor is peopled by sneaky cowards!" announced the popinjay. "I put it to you that you have not one bravo courageous enough to approach me or my handsome companion in open, fair combat." He paused for two seconds. "Here I stand, unopposed. Thou art bested!"

"Assholes!" Champ added for flavor.

Three fleximetal doors slid into the ground. From darkened apartments emerged seven enemies: Five younger men in boxer shorts and slippers, and two elders in suits. The septet advanced, wielding open hands with which they intended to administer shoves or slaps or both types of violence.

Heavy metal music blared.

Champ, R.J. the Third and the shocked fifth-floor adversaries looked to the hall window, beyond which rose a red fire wagon. Upon the platform of the levitating vehicle stood the re-bodied man, Captain Eagle Sappline, holding two glinting nozzles as if they were six-shooters. The music that poured through the open window grew louder.

Riffs prophesied doom.

"For the glory of floor six!" yelled Champ and R.J. the Third, racing to the stairs.

"Eat it!" advised Eagle, his voice amplified by speakers. White foam splattered surprised faces, filled open mouths and knocked adversaries to the ground.

"You're pitiful!" goaded the mannequin.

Champ and R.J. the Third reached the sixth floor.

"Thanks," the garbage man said via his lily to his father.

"They deserved it," replied Eagle. "I'd like to hang out, but I better have Douglas take me back—this is a total violation, doing something like this with a wagon."

"I'm sure," replied Champ.

R.J. the Third typed in his code, and the fleximetal door sank.

Eagle said, "See you on Friday at Billiardhaus."

"You bet."

Champ entered the apartment, went to the common room and waved through the window to Eagle, who was standing at attention upon the fire wagon's platform. The re-bodied man saluted his son and was carried off.

Two slovenly sixth-floor shut-ins and the herpetology student patted the garbage man on the back.

"That was a magnificent plan, Mr. Sappline," said R.J. the Third. "Accolades and libations shall not be withheld!" Wedged beneath the sofa for fifteen hours, Architect shifted some tonnage and offered a meow of approbation.

* * *

In the annals of the intra-building war, this perfectly coordinated attack was recorded as an undisputed victory for floor six.

Chapter XIII
It Needs Work

Lisanne, dressed in a sleeveless amber suit, and Ellenancy, covered by a maroon robe and slippers, entered an elevator within the Corpus Chrome, Incorporated Building. Joining them, Mr. Johnson put his fingertips to a placard and said, "Floor eighty-five."

The metal door slid shut and presented a reflection of the mismatched identical twins. Within the mirror image, the mannequin's chrome plating hosted myriad warped reflections.

The elevator rose, silent and fluid.

"How many floors are in this building?" asked Lisanne.

"One hundred and fifty."

Ellenancy opined, "The view from the roof must be lovely."

Pleased to hear a positive sentiment emerge from her sister, Lisanne asked Mr. Johnson, "May we go to the top?"

"The elevators don't go past floor one hundred and twenty."

"How do people access the top thirty floors?" inquired the petite blonde, perplexed.

"I don't know." The shepherd grinned. "That's one of the mysteries of this place."

"What is up there?"

"Another mystery." Mr. Johnson chuckled.

The elevator door slid wide, and the exiting trio entered a hall that had brown carpeting upon its floor, walls and ceiling.

"The audio room is this way," said shepherd, motioning with a paddle-like hand for the sisters to precede him.

The mannequin balked.

"The rug—" Ellenancy slid her right slipper across the two-centimeter-tall fibers as if it were a razor upon coarse skin. "I'm afraid that I might fall over."

"Take off your slippers and use the gelware on your soles," recommended the shepherd. "That should make it a bit easier for you to get a sense of things."

The re-bodied woman stepped out of her slippers, set her bare gelware feet upon the carpet and wobbled. Adjusting her knees, she balanced herself.

Lisanne picked up the discarded slippers and put an arm around Ellenancy's back. "In Ordnung?"

"Ja."

The siblings followed the shepherd.

After her twentieth stride, Ellenancy paused and informed her sister, "I can do this on my own."

Lisanne withdrew her supportive arm, and walked up the carpeted hall alongside the mannequin.

* * *

Seated upon a plush divan in the middle of a brown and gold room that was embedded with seventy-two perfectly calibrated speakers, the Sisters Breutschen listened to the sequentialist composition entitled "The Dotted Line." The music was a window, and the anguish that Lisanne had felt when she lost her sister, her best friend and her creative partner to pancreatic cancer was quite visible through its sonic pane. It was a good piece, but the petite blonde loathed listening to it.

The resurrected object of the dirge remained still, silent and inscrutable as she heard the composition.

Four minutes after the piano's final note had dissipated, Ellenancy said simply, "I would like to hear it again."

Lisanne whistled a C-sharp and said, "Play: 'The Dotted Line.'"

The piece began for a second time, and Lisanne glanced at her sister's face, which was set in a neutral expression. As with all works of pure sequentialism (the compositional form that the Sisters Breutschen had originated), "The Dotted Line" was linear music with no concurrent harmonies. A solitary flute played a melody, a lone woman sang inversions of the melody, tympani suggested a theme, a trumpet rebuked the theme—but no two notes ever rang simultaneously. This was the only sequentialist piece that Lisanne had written without Ellenancy's input, and the grief-stricken woman had interspersed several meaningful gaps of pure silence amongst the lonely melodies.

The music ended. Two minutes after the last overtone had dissipated, Ellenancy said, "I would like to hear it again."

Lisanne was anxious to know her sister's thoughts on the funereal composition, but she did not inquire after them: Ellenancy would speak when she had drawn her conclusions. The petite blonde whistled and said, "Play: 'The Dotted Line.'"

After the siblings had listened to the seventeen-minute composition for the fifth time, Ellenancy said, "I know that this piece is very meaningful to you, but I have several ideas that would improve it."

Stunned by the comment, Lisanne said nothing.

The mannequin swiveled her head toward her sister and widened her irises. "The violin and mandolin sections in the middle—the ones that recall 'The Line That Connected His Eyes to the Mountaintops'—should modulate away from each other, not together as you currently have them."

Lisanne had never been so happy to receive criticism in her entire life. Her eyes glimmering with joyful tears, she said, "I agree. I was never fully satisfied with that part."

"I have some melodies in mind already. When you come tomorrow, please bring a violin and a mandolin."

* * *

Tears were pouring from Lisanne's eyes as she left the Corpus Chrome, Incorporated Building and double-tapped her lily. "Connect to Osa," she said, walking toward the street to hail a watery cab with her blurry hand.

"How are you?" asked Osa, her voice warm with concern.

"Great. I'm great." Lisanne sniffed and wiped her eyes. "Will you meet me at Tildman's instead of Bo-Bo Thai?"

"What's Tildman's?"

"It's a classical instrument store near Lincoln Center."

"Definitely! When?"

A hungry cab nudged past a box van and two ladybugs, veered around a plasticore canister and bumped into the meter-high curb just beyond Lisanne's toes. "I shall be there in twenty minutes."

"I'll leave now. I can't wait to hear what happened. I love you."

"I love you." The petite blonde sat in the back of the cab and was gripped by pseudopodia.

* * *

"This one looks really nice," opined Osa, pointing to a lacquered wooden instrument that was held by micron wire inside the store's central display cylinder.

"That's a viola. Ellenancy wants a violin."

"Oh."

Osa looked a little embarrassed.

Lisanne took her mate's hand, squeezed and said, "They look similar," hoping that the remark did not sound condescending.

The tall beauty did not make any more suggestions.

* * *

The next morning, the petite blonde carried an inflated coddle bag that contained a violin, a bow, and a mandolin through the security gauntlet in the Corpus Chrome, Incorporated Building.

When Lisanne shook hands with Mr. Johnson, he was wearing an olive tweed suit and the brightest smile that she had ever seen upon his face.

"She asked for sheaves," the shepherd enthused, "yesterday, right after you left."

"What is she watching?"

"She isn't watching anything," said Mr. Johnson, his smile brightening further.

"She pulled up piano screens and has been playing etudes, working on her dexterity."

"That is terrific news!"

"Indeed, indeed, indeed."

* * *

Lisanne walked past the furled polarity curtain and into the oval room within which dwelled Ellenancy.

"Guten Morgen," the gift-bearing guest said to her sister. "How are you?"

"Terrible," said the re-bodied woman from her chair across the room. Her lenses were focused on two sheaves, which were laid in tandem upon a desk to simulate a piano keyboard. "Everything I play sounds like Abfall, verfluchter Abfall."

The re-bodied woman fingered a melody from "The Line That Bisects a Marriage and Unites the Fingertips of Lovers." Her articulation of the long phrase was stilted and slow, and contained twelve wrong notes.

"If you say that this sounds good," Ellenancy warned, "I'll throw something at you."

"Perhaps you should try the melody at fifty-six beats per minute," suggested Lisanne.

"It sounds bad enough at this speed—I cannot slow it down more."

"Then you should play another melody." Lisanne pondered some possibilities, sat upon a stool and put the coddle bag on the floor. "Try the second departure from 'The Line That is Scratched in the Margin of a Holy Text as an Act of Desecration.'"

"That is not a challenging passage."

"Precisely."

Ellenancy fingered the slow simple melody, misplaying six of its eighteen notes. "Abfall," muttered the re-bodied woman. A moment later, she attempted the phrase a second time and did no better.

"This melody is a good one for you to practice," stated Lisanne. "You must reorient yourself with simple material—as did Irena after her car accident."

"Scheiß." The mannequin eyed her sister, and looked down at the coddle bag within which the instruments were suspended. "Did you bring the violin and mandolin that I requested?"

"I did," said Lisanne.

"May I have them?"

"I think you should continue to work with the touch-screens for now."

"Don't patronize me," warned Ellenancy.

"I am your older sister."

"By eighteen minutes."

"I gained two and a half years of seniority while you were away."

"Scheiß."

"Practice."

Lisanne watched the mannequin misplay the simple melody for two hours.

"That did not sound wretched," said Ellenancy, after her first correct articulation of the phrase.

"See if you can play it consistently."

The mannequin played the melody correctly three times in a row.

"Increase the tempo to ninety beats per minute," said Lisanne.

Ellenancy activated the metronome, and a green light blinked, clicking as it demarcated time. When she played the eighteen-note melody at this increased tempo, new errors occurred.

"Slow it down to eighty-two."

* * *

The sun ascended, perambulated across the vault and descended; office buildings ingested, digested and expelled employees; sick people in the geriatric wards of hospitals awakened to another day of agony, suffered, and returned to the domain of slumber, wherein they dreamt of painless halcyons; a dog named Gnaw roused, watched a door, growled, ate a meal, returned to its post, barked, chewed upon a bone and imagined juicy shins; people were divorced and people were married, and twelve unhappy newlyweds endeavored both acts in quick succession.

A petite blonde woman who was filled with hope cancelled her plans with her mate and instructed her re-bodied sibling.

For many hours, the Sisters Breutschen saw only the invisible path of those eighteen notes.

* * *

At twenty-two forty-five, Mr. Johnson entered the room, yawned and informed the women that their visit must be concluded.

"I'm not tired," protested Ellenancy.

"You need to relax your mind and sleep, just like any other person," stated the shepherd. "Don't try to do too much too quickly."

A frown creased the mannequin's visage.

"I'll be back tomorrow," said Lisanne, realizing that she would need to postpone the studio session that she had scheduled with the shriekpunk band Plague Injection.

"Will you leave the instruments here?" asked Ellenancy.

"You will play them all night if I do." Lisanne picked up the coddle bag. "The shepherd said that you need to rest."

The mannequin's frown became an exaggerated, childish pout.

"You will get to play them soon." The petite blonde kissed her sister's cheek and added, "I know that you are dissatisfied with your abilities, but you have improved significantly since this morning."

"Indeed, indeed, indeed. You'll be playing 'The Line That Bisects a Marriage and Unites the Fingertips of Lovers' within a week."

The Sisters Breutschen looked at the shepherd.

Mr. Johnson grinned, admitting for the first time, "I'm a fan."

* * *

Inhaling the filtered summer air of Nexus Y, Lisanne suddenly realized that she had not eaten a meal since the previous day. She searched her lily vault for a nearby Nippon stand, located one, leaned against its bamboo counter and ate three bonito-flake rice balls in as many minutes.

The woman took a cab back to her apartment building, ascended, showered, pulled on pajamas and sat on the sofa. There, she let the air out of the coddle bag and withdrew the mandolin. The melody that she had heard four hundred and ninety-four times that day was the only one that she could hear, and so she played it.

A shadow fell across her bare feet.

Lisanne looked up. Standing before her was Osa, dressed in a violescent sari and raised clogs. The tall beauty held a bottle of champagne in her right hand, and a shopping bag that was laden with odiferous curries in her left.

"You don't look real happy to see me," said Osa.

"I was not expecting you."

"That's how surprises work." The tall beauty glanced at the mandolin and asked, "Are you working? Should I go?"

Lisanne pondered the question for a moment.

"Fine."

Osa put the food upon the coffee table and, without another word, stormed out of the room and through the door.

Alone in her apartment, Lisanne fingered a melody on her mandolin, contemplating the meaningful moments of silence in both "The Dotted Line" and her brief conversation with her mate.

Chapter XIV
Blood Pudding

Pudding Rodensby sat down, put his varicose right hand upon the controls of his buoyed chair, glided past his collection of antique firearms and floated toward the lacquered front door, where his surgically dwarfed white-haired English mastiff currently stood growling. The old man had acquired the dog when it was a similar-sized (but brown) puppy thirty-one years ago, and he knew that the little beast only made noise when it had a reason for so doing.

Ascot yowled. Pudding wondered at the cause of the hound's midnight perturbation, and hypothesized that the noisy couple who had moved in up the hall were having another row.

The dog woofed thrice, and a chill climbed the flaccid skin that covered its master's back: The old Englishman fully comprehended the gravity of a triple bark.

Wary, Pudding stood from his chair, adjusted his woolen pajamas and strode toward the automated hinge door. The tiny sentinel interposed its body between the oldster and the portal, barking thrice as a reminder.

Pudding smelled smoke. Suddenly, a fire alarm bleated in the hallway outside.

"Jasmine," Pudding called to his wife.

"Occupied," his spouse replied from the study. (Pudding received this response from Jasmine whenever he contacted her and she was on the telephone with a friend or reading a mystery novel with a conclusion that she could not foresee, which was a rare occurrence.)

Ascot woofed thrice.

"Was that a triple bark?" his wife inquired from the other room.

"It was. It seems that there is some sort of fire."

"Really?"

Pudding looked through the eyehole, and the white fire outside made him squint. "Flames are apparent."

Jasmine walked from the study, clothed in a green summer dress and padded socks, her upright posture resistant to the curvilinear solicitations of time. Clutched in the retired English professor's right hand was a book entitled *The Weird Demise of the Man Who Scratched His Back with His Toes.* "I hear alarms," said the woman.

"Yes. They started up just a little while back."

"Is it outside our door? This conflagration?"

Pudding motioned for his wife to look for herself.

Jasmine walked to the door and peered through the eyehole. "That is bothersome." Shaking her head, the woman stepped away from the portal.

"I suppose it would be a poor idea to open up the door and look for an avenue of escape?"

"Our apartment is hyper-oxygenated and contains a rather impressive amount of wood," responded Jasmine.

The dog barked thrice.

"Ascot is taking this seriously," said Pudding.

"I suggest we—"

A loud crack precluded the woman's statement. The front door bulged, and the little mastiff voiced two foreboding triple barks.

"To the balcony!"

The ninety-one-year-old man flung a varicose arm around the back of his eighty-three-year-old wife and walked her across an Oriental rug, through the sitting room, down to the sunken den, up to the hallway of familial crests, past antique weapons and toward French doors that led out onto the balcony. Ascot trailed behind the aged couple, interposing itself between its masters and danger.

Through the exterior windows, Pudding saw a red fire wagon fly past, its lights glaring. "This all seems rather significant."

"It does."

Pudding heard the front door groan and crack.

"My goodness," said Jasmine.

A cloth bookmark fell from the woman's novel as the couple neared the French doors. Alarms rang, and Ascot scolded its charges in order to hasten their departure.

Suddenly, the lights went out. The fire alarm stopped, and unseen flames crackled.

"My goodness," said Jasmine.

Pudding fingered the release placard, but the French doors did not open.

"The power is down," said the woman.

"I am well aware of that," responded the Englishman, gesturing at the darkness. "And this is no time for redundancies." He fingered the placard once again, but the doors did not respond. "Damn."

"The placard is electric," Jasmine said, "and so the doors must be opened manually."

"I see your point." Pudding had no idea how to accomplish this task and thus began ruminations.

Ascot unleashed three triple barks.

"I've never heard that amount before," remarked the Englishman.

"Nor I."

"I'll get a firearm—for the purpose of blasting open the door!"

Jasmine was irked. "You told me that none of your guns were functional."

"Without bullets, that is indeed the case!"

Pudding hastened back toward the heart of the apartment, and Ascot barked at its master, making a very small obstacle of itself. The Englishman stepped over the dog, entered the armory (Jasmine's name for the firearm showroom) and was struck by the light and heat of the fire that consumed the reception area, which was only twenty meters off.

Suddenly sweating, the old man strode toward the World War II display case, swung its door wide, snatched a Luger semi-automatic pistol, opened a hidden drawer and withdrew a fully loaded ammunition clip that he then slid into the weapon's stock. Emboldened by the hyper-oxygenated air, fire consumed the lacquered wainscoting and floorboards on the far side of the room. The dog chastised its master.

Man and hound soon sped away from the conflagration.

"I found the manual release lever," Jasmine said when her husband returned.

"Swift work," remarked Pudding, pleased that there was a point of egress, but also disappointed that he no longer had a reason to fire the gun.

The woman opened the French doors.

"Ladies first," said the Englishman, gesturing outside.

Jasmine exited the hot hall, followed by Pudding and Ascot.

"Oh, dear," said the woman.

Smoke and flames filled the night. The burning skyscraper in which the Englishman and his wife lived was reflected in the dark windows of the surrounding buildings.

"This is exactly why I didn't want an apartment on the forty-first floor," remarked Jasmine.

Pudding did not respond to her statement.

An explosion shook the building. Frightened, Ascot retreated into the apartment.

"Come back here!" Pudding yelled at his hound. "Ascot! Come hither! Come!" Tears welled in the oldster's eyes, and in that moment, he could no longer deny the perils that he and his wife currently faced.

Jasmine embraced her husband like an animate skeleton, patting his back with long phalanges. "He has fetched my placeholder," said the woman.

Pudding pulled away from his wife, wiped tears from his eyes, looked at the ground and saw Ascot, who was seated by his right foot. Dangling from the little hound's mouth was the recovered bookmark.

Filled with pride, the Englishman said, "This is why—for over two hundred and fifty years—the Rodensbys have accepted no other dog."

Pudding patted Ascot upon the head, and during this reunion, Jasmine shut the French doors. All around, hot winds aggravated smoke and sparks.

"It's like an oven out here." The Englishman wiped sweat from his forehead, walked to the balcony edge, gripped the warm rail, looked toward the ground and coughed. "I can't see past floor twenty-five."

"I presume the fire started in that restaurant." (Pudding knew what her next remark was going to be.) "This is precisely why I argued against

243

commercial enterprises in our building." (The Englishman's assumption had been correct.)

Pudding saw a fire wagon emerge from the opaque strata of smoke. The craft ascended, blasted reverse thrusters and halted outside a balcony that was one flight below and eleven apartments north of the Rodensbys.

Scheming, the Englishman walked to his telescope (purchased at a discount through his astronomy club), swiveled it with his free hand and observed the fire wagon. The fleximetal door in the side of the suspended craft slid down, and a fireman who clutched a forge-ax and wore a neon-green watersuit leapt onto the balcony. There, he activated his reflector-spotlights, and looked like a bright alien.

Pudding wiped soot from the telescope lens and gazed again.

The fireman lit his forge-ax, swung the glowing steel into French doors and plunged into the apartment. Flames like windblown curtains reached out at the night. Nozzles upon the side of the fire wagon spat foam into the bright fury.

"One fellow has entered," Pudding informed Jasmine. Standing upright, he gathered hot air into his lungs and yelled out, "Help us! Over here!"

The Englishman leaned down and peered through the telescope. Five more firemen in neon-green watersuits leaped from the open craft onto the nether balcony and raced toward the opening. Flames lashed the foremost man's water-filled armor, and steam hissed from his shoulder pipes. The quintet adjusted their temperature settings and—surrounded by frigid waters and ice chips—raced into the flames.

A window shattered behind the Englishman, and he turned around. A cocker spaniel, dripping fire, ran in circles on the adjacent balcony. Saddened by the sight, the oldster looked away.

Somewhere in the smoke below, two people shrieked the word "Help!" over and over, until they were abruptly silenced.

A person wrapped in burning blankets fell from an upper story into the strata of black smoke below.

"Over here!" Pudding yelled to the fire wagon that floated eleven apartments north of his own and one flight down. "We're definitely ready for a rescue!"

"They're retrieving the Walters," said Jasmine. "They're a priority,"

Confused, the Englishman looked at his well-informed wife. "A priority? Why? Because they're younger?"

"Yes. And because there are five of them."

Pudding snorted, "That's not fair."

"But it's not unfair," replied Jasmine. (The sterling woman had an unflagging sense of propriety.)

Nettled by jealousy, the Englishman leaned to the telescope and looked at the fire wagon's windshield. A person with weird eyes emerged from the rear compartment of the craft, sat in the driver's seat and manipulated the dashboard. Three mesh spheres sprouted from the top of the vehicle and began to whirr, sucking black smoke from the air.

"He should rescue us while his men are locating the Walters," said Pudding. "We are quite ready to go."

"We're not a priority."

The Englishman put his right hand to the side of his mouth and shouted, "Hello! Please retrieve us! These flames are hasty!" He looked through his telescope to gauge the efficacy of his solicitations and was unimpressed. "That yob is not responding."

"We're not a priority," repeated Jasmine. "He can't abandon the firemen who're—what're you doing!?!"

Pudding pulled upon the Luger's toggle joint. Metal dug into his thumb and index finger, but eventually, he mastered the Axis device. At the exact moment that his wife yelled "Don't!" he fired a bullet directly over the fire wagon. The booming report echoed in all directions.

Lowering the gun, the Englishman peered through his telescope. The fellow with the weird eyes stared at him from behind the craft's windshield.

"That roused his interest."

Resolved, Pudding stood upright and pointed the barrel of the gun directly at the man with the weird eyes.

"No!" yelled Jasmine.

The fire wagon's exterior speakers crackled, and a voice said, "Don't go hysterical. I'm not a driver, but I'll try and get you."

The craft tilted toward the Rodensbys, and its rear thrusters flashed.

Stunned by the turn of events, Jasmine said to her husband, "You saved us."

Pride expanded within Pudding like an atomic explosion, and as he put his right arm around Jasmine, he said, "I did."

The woman scooped Ascot from the ground and kissed Pudding's left cheek. "Thank you."

"It was for love and honor."

The fire wagon sped toward the English couple.

Ascot unleashed three triple barks, and a chill ran down Pudding's spine.

"He is approaching rather rapidly," remarked Jasmine.

"Run!' yelled the amplified voice. "I've lost control!"

Pudding cried out, "Oh my—"

The fire wagon slammed into the balcony. Stone, a potted plant, the railing, the telescope, the miniature mastiff, the Englishman's left side and most of his wife were crushed between the front of the craft and the building. Cracked ribs stabbed Pudding's pounding ninety-one-year-old heart.

CHAPTER XV
ROTTEN MANGOES AND EXCRETA DELETED

Champ returned the dissolvent nozzle to its holster on the garbage truck. "I feel a little weird about it," he said to the sexy pink-haired Texan who had unexpectedly called him during his night shift.

"Why?"

"You bought me a shuttle ticket to Houston so that I could visit you. And I'm using the word 'visit' as a euphemism."

"I have more money than you do, and I want to have fun on my birthday." In a sultry voice, Doreen added, "You'll get to pay me back for the ticket. Repeatedly."

Prompted by the breathy utterance of the lascivious adverb, Champ's phallus swelled inside his orange suit. "The terms of your deal are understood."

"Champ!" Mikek shouted from the driver's seat.

"I'll get you a gift, though," the garbage man said into his lily. "If I'm coming out on your birthday, I need to do that. I have some ideas."

A husky laugh reverberated in his ear, followed by a request for the kind of birthday gift that Doreen wanted forcefully given to her.

"I've gotta go," said Champ, adjusting his uniform's crotch netting. "See you next month."

"Looking forward to it." Doreen audibly wet her lips.

The garbage man double-tapped his lily, walked toward the backseat door and twisted the handle.

Mikek said, "Champ...look," and pointed to the sky.

Champ glanced north and saw a thick pillar of firelit smoke. Horripilations beaded his skin. "What's burning?" he asked.

"A high-rise on the Upper East Side."

"Excuse me." Champ walked away from the vehicle and double-tapped his lily. "Connect to Eagle."

Heavy metal music wailed in the garbage man's right ear. At the end of a tortured guitar solo, Eagle's prerecorded voice said, "I'm busy right now. Leave your info. Stats if female." Two beeps followed the outgoing message.

"Dad, this is Champ. Just heard about the fire and I want to make sure that you're okay. Give me a call whenever you get this."

The garbage man double-tapped his lily and entered the back of the vehicle.

"Nothing?" asked Mikek.

"Nothing."

Champ slammed his door, withdrew a postcard-sized picscreen from his pocket, smoothed out its wrinkles and clicked its input bead. "Search: News; Nexus Y; fire on the Upper East Side."

He waited for two seconds.

Upon the wrinkled picscreen shone a scintillating tower of flame, around which fire wagons swooped like lightning bugs. Little dark bits that were furniture, trees and people fell from the crumbling balconies and slammed upon the growing heap of unidentifiable detritus at ground level.

The lily in Champ's ear linked to the audio, and a reporter's voice commented, "—that the fire seems to have originated in the restaurant on the twenty-fifth floor when an—"

Champ double-tapped and said, "Search: Nexus Y; fire on the Upper East Side; fireman; casualties." Holding his breath, he stared at the wrinkled picscreen, which showed men combating the malefic element.

A demure female voice said, "No information released."

Mikek turned around in his seat. "Anything?"

"Nothing."

"Let me drop you off. I can get the other canisters by myself."

"Thanks," Champ said, "but I think I better keep busy. I don't want to go home and just...." He exhaled heavily and shook his head. "I want to finish out the shift."

"I understand." Mikek turned around, primed the engine and thumbed the accelerator. The plump and hairy man drove the vehicle south, toward Asiatown.

* * *

At the next canister, while duck skeletons, firecrackers, bok choy, fried rice and Jesuit pamphlets were dissolving, Champ called Eagle. Again, the garbage man reached a message vault rather than his father.

The truck sucked soup until it gurgled, and Champ replaced the nozzle. Numb with preoccupation, he climbed into the vehicle.

Mikek drove south.

* * *

The garbage man shoved the dissolvent nozzle into a full canister, locked the valve and switched on the juice. Shoes, dolls, a leather jacket, three turkey pigeons and eighty-nine udon spools hissed as they were rendered into homogeneous soup. Again, Champ called his father.

Nobody answered.

* * *

The garbage truck sped past the Corpus Chrome, Incorporated Building and into the Wall Street area. Mikek pointed out two women who wore tight viridescent slips and high-heeled sneakers. Out of respect for Eagle, the driver did not speak of running them over, but said only, "The truck likes them."

The vehicle slid into a parking niche alongside a full canister.

Champ looked at the wrinkled picscreen, which showed the charcoal edifice that had once been the Upper East Side high-rise. Black smoke billowed from hundreds of windows.

"Looks like they put it out," said the man in the sucker's seat.

"Good."

Champ called his father for the fourth time that evening, his heart pounding as he waited. When the prerecorded message began, he cut the connection and said, "Connect to Firehouse Eighty-One, front desk."

A man with a heavy New York accent said, "All personnel are currently unavailable. Leave a message after th—"

Champ cut the connection, climbed out of his seat, yanked the dissolvent nozzle from the truck and slammed it into the top of the canister. Frustrated and frightened, he kicked the steel barrel and yelled, "Goddammit!" His vision blurred as he assaulted the receptacle, repeatedly, with his right boot. "Godfuckingdammit!"

* * *

Twenty-five minutes later, Mikek drove Champ to Eagle's Midtown firehouse. All of the lights in the building were off, and the parking garage was empty. The station was bereft.

* * *

The driver attempted to go to the Upper East Side, but upraised stopwalls and unhappy police officers barred the way. "Goddammit," said Champ, from within the sucker's seat.

* * *

Wearing jeans, flip-flops and a plaid t-shirt, Mikek walked from the bar to the table at which drooped the blonde man in orange.

"Get anything from those other guys?" the driver asked as he plopped himself upon a stool.

"No. None of them picked up." Champ had called Potato O'Boyd, Bagel Butch, Pedro Cheung and Douglas.

"He'll be okay." Mikek put a thermomug of hops-heavy Belgian ale in front of Champ. "On me."

"Thanks." The garbage man raised the beer to his lips.

His lily beeped, startling him, and the demure female voice announced, "Incoming call: R.J. the Third."

"Shit," said Champ, disappointed. Double-tapping his lily, he answered, "Yeah?"

"You need to come home right now." R.J. the Third's voice was atypically subdued.

"I'm waiting to hear—"

"Silence! Come. Home. Right. Now! Do not accept any other calls on your lily until I have briefed you."

"I have more pressing concerns than the building war right n—"

"This is another matter altogether!" yelled R.J. the Third. "Make haste and trust nobody. Goodbye!"

"Wait!"

The connection died.

"I've got to go," Champ said to Mikek.

The driver looked up from his beer. "You hear something about your father?"

"I'm not sure."

"Let me know what's goin' on whenever you find out, okay? I'm very—" A young black woman wearing a white silken camisole, frill shorts and padded slippers walked past Mikek. "—concerned."

* * *

Clothed in odiferous orange, Champ fingered his identification into the Antique Conditions placard. He entered the building and climbed the stairs, his eyes vigilantly surveying the area for signs of fifth-floor hostiles. The building was eerily quiet, excepting some old steps with creaky dispositions. Behind an anonymous door, a dog growled an almost chromatic melody.

The garbage man reached the fifth-floor landing, stepped carefully over heaps of eggshells, surveyed the enemy's hall and hastened up to safety.

Outside R.J. the Third's apartment, Champ fingered the placard and dialed his code. The door slid into the ground, revealing the black-haired, bug-eyed man in silver who stood in the hallway, his mouth and pierced nose covered by an air filter and a migraine pen aimed at his tenant's face.

"Put that thing d—"

"Enter slowly," R.J. the Third directed, "and like a mongoose. Enter slowly and like a mongoose."

The garbage man strode into the apartment, his gait unaltered. "Have you heard something about—"

"Acolyte!"

The herpetology student leapt from her closet and fingered the placard, sealing the apartment. Clutched in the woman's right hand was a canister of hangover gas, and covering her mouth and nostrils was an air filter.

Champ said, "What the hell's g—"

"Silence!" demanded R.J. the Third, his voice an uncommonly loud whisper.

"Tell me what's g—"

"Follow me!"

The popinjay strode forward as if he were showing a military troop the proper way to march.

"¡Vas, rey de basura!" ordered the herpetology student. "¡Gringo estupido!"

"That didn't sound complimentary."

"¡Vas!"

The Spaniard stamped upon Champ's shadow as if the act might somehow bruise his physical being. (A person on the fifth floor punched the ceiling in reply.)

Champ followed R.J. the Third past the animated posters, across the silver rug and toward the bathroom door. The toilet icon had its lid raised, and the fleximetal plank slid into the ground. One by one, the trio entered the rose enclosure, where Architect sat upon the throne like the top half of a globe.

R.J. the Third kicked the bathmat aside and pulled the rope handle, opening the trapdoor that led to the purloined fifth-floor kitchen.

Champ asked, "Is my f—"

"Go!" ordered R.J. the Third. "Time is not unlimited!"

"¡A bajo—tu vas!" the herpetology student advised from behind her air filter, pointing to the open trapdoor.

Champ applied himself to the rope ladder, and R.J. the Third slammed the hatch shut. Darkness blinded the garbage man like a black hood pulled over his head as he descended. The sole of his right boot pressed upon the wooden floor, followed by its sibling. For reasons unknown, the weight-activated amber lights did not illuminate.

The room was opaque.

"Hello?" Champ ventured into the darkness.

A tiny stitch of blue lightning flickered at head level.

"Champ?" inquired a man whose voice was weirdly reverberant.

The garbage man smelled plastic, chrome and charcoal.

"Dad?"

"Yeah."

Relief flooded Champ's body like an intravenous salve.

Ponderous footfalls thudded within the purloined kitchen, and soon, gelware hands gripped the garbage man's shoulders, slid across his back and pulled him to a plastic chest, embracing him.

Champ hugged Eagle. The odors of charcoal, molten metal and burnt rubber filled his nostrils, reminding him of how the city had smelled right after the Empire State Building had been destroyed. "I was scared," he said to his father.

"I saw your calls. But I was worried it might be them, pirating your line or something."

Champ withdrew from his father. "What're you talking about? And why are you down here in the dark?"

Eagle did not respond to the question. Champ heard a buzz and a dim sine wave. Blue lightning flickered, larger than before, closer.

"Dad?"

"I fucked up." The sine wave stopped.

"What happened?"

"You saw the fire, right? You know how it started?"

"I'm more interested in what's going on with you right now. Why you're sitting down here in the dark, smelling like a cookout."

"I need to tell you about the fire—so you'll understand," stated Eagle.

"Okay. Tell me what happened."

"That skyscraper…it had these three huge garbage chutes that ran all the way up and down it, into storage tanks where they dissolve the trash for—well, I guess I don't need to tell you about garbage."

"I'm an expert."

"Right. Well, the tank where they keep frying oil in the restaurant had been leaking for weeks—maybe months—right into the chutes, and one of the chutes was clogged with trash from the twentieth floor on down. So all the garbage in there was soaked through with frying oil—it was like a two-hundred-foot wick, ready to go. When it caught—maybe a cigar or a candle started it, could've been anything—it went quick and was very, very hot. Melted the sprinkler nozzles before they could do anything, and those heads are made of tempered steel. Five floors were gone in a couple of minutes."

The mannequin buzzed.

"Dad? Can we—"

"And the way they make buildings now," Eagle resumed, "lighter, with all that ventilation, there's so much oxygen, so many places for the fire to go. Fuck. It was crazy."

"Are you okay?"

No response came from the re-bodied man.

Champ asked, "Can I turn on the—"

"I killed four people."

Stunned by the admission, the garbage man waited in silence for more information.

Tiny blue lightning flickered.

"All of the wagons were scrambled to the fire," Eagle continued, "every single wagon in Nexus Y. We didn't have enough manpower at the stations to fully outfit them all, so lots of the wagons had skeleton crews, some just a couple of guys.

"The computer prioritized assignments for us. We were there to do rescues rather than fight the fire, 'cause a fucking hurricane couldn't've put that thing out. I was in charge of six guys, including Douglas—he's that black guy you knew from elementary school."

"I know who he is."

"We went to the fortieth floor to pick up a family. The Walters. The guys went in. I updated Central and fought the fire with long-distance hoses, like I've been doing since I've been back. I turned the air filters on—they suck the smoke out of the air and are really, really strong." Something crackled within the mannequin.

"Dad, can I please turn on a—"

"There was this old guy," interrupted Eagle. "On a balcony on the floor above me, and he shot a gun to get my attention. His apartment was goin' up fast, and the one next to him was already gone. He wanted me to come and get him and his wife, and he threatened me with the gun, which was stupid since the windshield's bulletproof, but probably he didn't know.

"I knew if I waited for my guys to get back, those two old folks weren't gonna make it.

"The fire was right behind them.

"I've only driven a fire wagon—the flying kind—twice, and it was just for joy-riding, but it didn't seem real hard. So I thought I could pick up the old couple and get back before my crew got the Walters' out.

"I tapped the thruster and flew at them, but something was wrong. I yelled for them to get out of the way as soon as I realized that I still had the air filters on, 'cause the suction on those things fucks up how it flies.

"The thing was totally out of control.

"I closed my irises and slammed into them. Killed them both. I heard the man scream and a dog bark.

"The wagon plowed into their apartment. I opened the door and was in some burning room with old guns and stuff. I tried to get to my guys up the hall, but just burnt the mannequin. The fire was everywhere.

"As I was stuck there, Douglas and one of the Walters' kids—a boy of thirteen— got to the balcony where I was supposed to be. The balcony collapsed and they fell to their deaths.

"The other firemen at the Walters's called for a pick-up and got out alive with the rest of the family.

"They picked me up after, but none of the guys seemed happy to see me. They were all thinking the same thing—I could see it on their faces. They were thinking, 'This dumb robot killed four people.'"

"You didn't kill anybody," Champ argued, "you were just trying to save those—"

"It was against procedure to go after them. And I can barely drive that thing anyways. It was a stupid thing to do. I was stupid."

"You were trying to save lives. It's not your fault."

"It sure as hell is. I didn't follow procedure and four people died." The mannequin buzzed, and a sine wave beeped intermittently like code.

"It was an accident and your intentions were good. People will understand."

"They might or they might not," replied Eagle. "But no matter what, this— what I did tonight—was a major violation of the contract I made with CCI. I disobeyed a top regulation, and four people are dead because of it."

A new fear blossomed within Champ as he reached over, tapped the light switch and saw his father. The unclothed mannequin stood unevenly on warped legs, blackened and covered with soot, and the gelware mask that had been cast from his son's face was covered with blisters. His scorched hands resembled fried chicken wings.

"Does it hurt?" asked Champ.

"They called me."

"CCI?"

"Yeah." A blue spark flickered within the mannequin's mouth slit.

"What...what did they say?"

"I need to report to the main building. They gave me two hours."

Champ's throat dried up. "When was this?" he asked weakly.

"A while ago," said Eagle. "More than two hours."

"What're they gonna do?" asked the garbage man, his heart hammering. "Did they say what they were gonna do?"

"Look at me...and think about what I did." The re-bodied man turned his blistered face away from his son. "Do I really need to say it?"

In a quiet voice that might have issued from the mouth of a five-year-old boy, Champ asked, "They're gonna take the mannequin back?"

Eagle did not respond. The sine wave stopped, and a spark crackled in his mouth slit.

"Dad?"

Champ put his hand on the mannequin's shoulder.

"Dad? Can you—"

"I came to say good-bye," said Eagle.

"No."

With his buzzing voice, the re-bodied man said, "Son. Look at me."

Champ appraised his damaged father.

"I don't have a whole lot of choices," remarked Eagle. "Any choice, really—this machine is completely fu—" He stopped in mid-sentence.

"Dad?"

The mannequin straightened like a soldier at attention.

"What're you doing?" asked Champ.

Arms stiff at his sides, the mannequin dropped to his knees. A hissing noise sounded from within the sooty head.

"R.J.!" yelled Champ. "Get down here right now!"

The popinjay descended the rope ladder like a pale arachnid.

Exhaust vents opened in the back of the mannequin's head, admitting bright white gouts of vapor. Frost covered the machine's blistered face, burnt hair and singed cranium.

"No!" yelled Champ, horrified.

The icy skull retracted like a turtle's head into the torso. Two bulbs rose from nascent openings in the mannequin's shoulders, locked into place and illuminated, alternately flashing yellow and red. Suddenly, the skirls of disharmonic piccolo flutes filled the room.

Regressed to helpless infancy, Champ stared.

R.J. the Third put an arm on the garbage man's shoulder. "I'm sorry."

"They froze him. Those goddamn CCI assholes froze him. All he was trying to do was help some old people."

Staring at the kneeling, headless mannequin, Champ was flooded by a deluge of unhappy memories: his father's funeral, the weird men whom his mother had invited into his home when he was a boy, the negative opinions of comedy club managers about his stand-up routine, the empty people with whom he had worked in finance whose lives were decimal points, the caustic remarks that had tarnished the latter years of his marriage with Candace, her adultery, the derisive gazes that he regularly received because of his occupation, and the stolen kitchen under a toilet that was the only room that he could afford. These were defeats that he had accepted.

"I won't lose him," declared Champ, resolved to win at least one battle in his life. "I won't let those assholes do this to him."

"I do not mean to be confrontational," R.J. the Third responded, "but it appears that they have indeed already done it."

"But they don't have him yet." Champ ruminated for a moment. "You know people who're good with electronics, right?"

"I know many such individuals. The people in my fan club are amongst the smartest—"

"Do you think any of them could open him up, find whatever wireless controllers are in there and rip them out?"

"I know a Frenchman named Sagesse who extricates stolen merchandise from the Net. He is very familiar with—"

"Good," said Champ. "Call that guy. Where is he?"

"He dwells in a place that is humanity's greatest shame and most odious mistake." R.J. the Third shook his head mournfully. "I speak of New Queens: the cancer of planet Earth." (In the bathroom above, Architect mewled.)

"Tell him we're coming over."

"I am loath to go there, but for two such valuable allies of floor six, I shall."

Champ envisioned himself and R.J. the Third awkwardly loading the locked-down mannequin into a cab. Into his lily, he said, "Connect to Mikek."

"Have you heard about your father?" inquired the driver, his voice slurred by beer and fatigue.

"Take an ethanol pill, suck a vapor tube, get the truck and meet me in front of my place as quickly as you can," ordered Champ. "It's important."

"Get the garbage truck? Now? Tonight?"

"Please, Mikek."

"Shit on shit."

"Was that a yes?"

"An angry one."

* * *

Champ and R.J. the Third positioned their boots at the edge of the trapdoor and hoisted the rope ladder that they had tied to the kneeling mannequin. The machine—lighter than a man of comparable size—rose steadily. Epaulette bulbs and piccolo flutes soon turned the bathroom into a claustrophobic dance club.

"¡La cabeza! Dondes?"

"His head retracted into his torso," R.J. the Third informed the woman. "Nothing to worry about."

"Do you guys have a tarp or something—like for moving furniture?" asked Champ. "We shouldn't take him outside like this."

"I get," said the herpetology student.

The garbage man leaned over, untied the rope and curled his hands behind the knees of the inert mannequin while the popinjay secured the machine's shoulders. Together, they carried the blackened body through the apartment and to the front hallway, where they set it down as if it were a recliner chair that had been wounded in battle.

The herpetology student emerged from her hall closet and threw a plaid tarp over the kneeling mannequin. Champ tucked the fabric around the L-shaped machine, and R.J. the Third bound it with twine. The lights were obscured by the woolen tarp, as were the dissonant flutes.

"He now look like a furniture," commented the woman.

Champ eyed R.J. the Third. "Let's get him downstairs."

"Has your peer arrived?" inquired the popinjay. "Your brother in rubbish?"

"He'll be here soon. And I'd rather have my dad downstairs, ready to go."

Champ grabbed the bundled mannequin's knees with his sooty hands while R.J. the Third clasped the machine's shoulders. The herpetology student fingered the placard, and the fleximetal door slid into the ground.

Quietly, the bearers hastened from the apartment, reached the stairwell and—in tandem—began their descent.

"Do you recall seeing eggshells piled upon the fifth-floor landing earlier this evening?" asked R.J. the Third in a whisper.

Champ's right foot caused an antique step to creak. "They were there."

"Then the absence of such detritus would evince recent activity by our adversaries?"

A stuffed cabbage smacked the side of the garbage man's head.

"Jesus Christ!" shouted Champ. Cold raisins, ground meat and wilted leaves clogged his right ear and clung to his neck.

Undaunted, the sixth-floor residents continued their descent to the landing, where they saw two twenty-one-year-old hostiles in the abutting hall. Each enemy wore a kitchen apron and held a bucket that was filled with stuffed cabbages and rotten fruit. The tall skinny Indian who stood on the right reached his rubber-gloved right hand into his stockpile and divined a moldy mango, which dripped clear serum.

Flies buzzed encouragement.

"Not tonight," warned Champ. "We need to take this chair downst—"

The Indian flung the mango, and it impacted the wrapped mannequin, erupting in a welter of orange pulp, clear fluid, moldy clumps and hoary fur.

Furious, Champ set his half of the burden down and ran directly at his foe.

"Class III, Class III!" shouted the frightened Indian, dropping the noisome bucket and raising his open hands. "Shoving and slapping, shoving and slapping only!"

Champ swung a hard fist at his foe's jaw, and the cracking impact burned his knuckles. The Indian's head jerked to the side, and his dark eyes turned white. Unconscious, he fell face-first upon his own shadow.

The other adversary retreated to safety.

Rejoined, the sixth-floor warriors carried their wrapped burden down the stairwell. They were not again molested.

"That interaction shall put us in Class IV," R.J. the Third observed when they reached the ground floor.

At that moment, Champ was not especially interested in the rules of intra-building warfare.

The pair bore the mannequin outside and placed it upon the sidewalk. Dim and artificial light illuminated the drear avenue.

The garbage man double-tapped his lily. "Connect to Mikek."

A moment later, the driver said, "I'm five blocks away."

"Open up the containment tank."

"It's full of soap. Tonight's scrub-down."

"Dump it," ordered Champ.

"In the street?"

"Yeah. Be discreet."

"If we get caught, I'm gonna say you made me do this—had a migraine pen pointed at me the whole time."

"No problem."

Champ did not know if the tank's meter-thick polymer walls would block the signals that the mannequin both sent and received, but he intended to do all that he could to prevent wireless communications between the machine and its makers. Suddenly paranoid, he looked up and down the street for Corpus Chrome, Incorporated officials. All that he saw was a tangled young couple who were busy inhaling each other several blocks away.

"I, too, believe that the tank will block the signals," said R.J. the Third, who then paused to appraise his comrade. "I didn't know you were intelligent."

The orange and green garbage truck turned onto the empty street, its headlights blazing across weathered façades and illuminating the kissing couple. A nozzle extruded from the side of the vehicle and sprayed suds.

"You goddamn idiot!" shouted the young man as he and his mate scrambled away from the squirting vehicle, their legs dripping with foamy excreta.

The girl then launched more obscenities than could fit inside a jumbo-sized crossword puzzle.

Remorselessly, the garbage truck sped away from the dampened pair, roared up the avenue and stopped beside Champ, R.J. the Third and the kneeling mannequin. The metal flap to the containment tank swung wide.

Carefully, the sixth-floor warriors loaded the machine into the sudsy metal coffin and shut the door.

Of the peed-upon couple, Mikek said only, "It's rude to kiss in public."

Chapter XVI
We Walked Upon Harp Strings

With nimble gelware fingers, Ellenancy removed an errant blonde hair from the lapel of her beige silk suit and pointed the follicle at the oval room's picture window. "How many people died in the fire last night?"

Beyond the glass, funereal smoke tainted the sky.

"Three hundred and twenty-one are presumed dead," said Lisanne.

The re-bodied woman dropped the hair. As it fell, she dexterously plucked a melancholic melody from the lute in her lap, a phrase that was an excerpt from a piece entitled "The Line That Defines the Boundary Between Compromise and Defeat."

"That was well-played."

"Danke. I will be able to play the entire piece correctly on Saturday."

"I agree."

During the last two weeks, the twins had spent nearly every waking moment rehearsing for their upcoming reunion performance at the Perfect Pitch Auditorium in Lincoln Center. Ellenancy's prowess with her new body and her ability to play assorted instruments had improved daily, at a rate that Mr. Johnson described as "quite extraordinary," and the re-bodied woman no longer spoke of relinquishing the mannequin. The siblings rarely discussed things other than music, and when Lisanne had mentioned Osa, Ellenancy had remarked, "If you are still seeing her when I'm granted autonomy, I'll be happy to meet her."

The petite blonde had seen her tall mate thrice in the last fourteen days, and these visits were strained, tired evenings from which neither woman had derived much pleasure. Their patient lovemaking had been corralled into smaller, hastier experiences, during which Lisanne's thoughts flitted about as erratically as a bat's shadow.

Osa had noticed the change.

During the fire the previous night, the tall beauty had called from her Brooklyn City apartment and declared, "I'll be at your place tomorrow. We need to talk."

The woman hung up, and the petite blonde had slept for three twisting, anxious hours before she finally gave up, drank her morning quadruple espresso and wearily returned to the Corpus Chrome, Incorporated Building.

The Sisters Breutschen reviewed their alterations to "The Dotted Line," discussed (and dismissed) a radical modulation, and changed the instrumentation in the coda from bassoon and piano to violin and piano (partially because Lisanne now needed to play all of the wind instruments). Concurrent with these discussions, Ellenancy played scales, melodies and etudes upon a violin, two lutes, a viola and a harp. Lisanne helped to remedy errors.

Outside their window, the sun walked across the welkin, its ramble a clandestine act that was hidden behind an inky veil of smoke.

The conversation with Osa drew nearer, and Lisanne's preoccupation with it grew. She did not know what the result of the talk would be, but she hoped and believed that their problems could be fixed if they were both patient and thoughtful.

At twenty-one fifteen, the petite blonde left the Corpus Chrome, Incorporated Building.

Her mind was a pretzel.

* * *

Lisanne pondered the coming conversation as she rode into Central Park, departed the cab, walked through the living wall into her building's mustard lobby, strode past the gelbench upon which (nearly five months earlier) Osa had waited for her with an apology, entered the elevator that knew her name, rose past the floors that had witnessed the couple's first kiss, saw her own reflection, frowned at the circles that were under her eyes (and the brown sleeveless dress that she was wearing), exited, walked south upon the one hundred sixty-eighth floor, stepped through the living wall and entered her apartment.

Crackling nanobuilders healed the wound of her ingress.

A charged spectral element that Lisanne could not properly define informed her of Osa's presence in another room.

The petite blonde tapped an up arrow, set her clutch inside the extruding drawer, pressed the close button, and walked past the parlor hall, through the den (where the women had watched both great and terrible mote aquarium experiences), up the ramp and into the dining area, where she had shared her first morning coffee with the woman whom she loved.

Seated upon a buoyed chair at the marble table was Osa. A glass of wine that matched her burgundy dress stood beside her folded hands.

Lisanne said, "Guten Nacht."

"Hi."

"Sorry I'm late."

No lectures about tardiness spilled from the tall beauty's mouth.

The petite blonde walked over and kissed her mate upon the lips, but was dryly received.

"I didn't know what you'd want to drink," said Osa.

"I shall get myself a water."

Lisanne walked out of the room, towards the wall unit in the kitchen; her nerves were taut.

"How's your sister doing?"

"She is adjusting very well to the machine."

"That's good," said Osa, the timbre of her voice both contradicting and confirming this sentiment.

Lisanne tapped the water bottle icon, and the bottom of a crystal container extruded from the wall. Claiming the vessel, she returned to the dining room, where her mate sat staring at her wine glass as if it were a cauldron.

"I'm nervous," said the petite blonde.

Osa nodded in agreement, but did not look up.

Lisanne sat across the table from her mate, thumbed the bottle's iris and moistened her parched throat.

"I'm not happy," said Osa.

"I know."

"Thanks for noticing."

"I'm not happy that I've made you unhappy. I didn't sleep well after we spoke last night."

Osa drank a sip of wine and set the glass down. "I know this is gonna sound selfish, but…is this how things're going to be? Now that she's back?"

"I honestly do not know," admitted Lisanne. "She and I are preparing for the Saturday performance, and have begun a new composition. And she is still adjusting to the machine."

"I know, I know, but after this passes—after you do this show and she is okay and out of CCI—how do you think things will be? With her and with us?"

The petite blonde would not varnish the truth. As her first husband Garren had said during their final conversation as a married couple, "It is better to assess the malignancy of a tumor than to push it deeper down."

Looking at her mate, Lisanne said, "A major person has returned to my life and I am writing music again. I very much want to be with you, but things cannot continue exactly as they were before. My life has changed."

Osa nodded. "I'm happy that you have her again, and that you're writing new music—really—but I'm not sure where that leaves us. We had something that was intense and worked, and now it seems like I'm gonna get about half as much of your time and attention, if even that much. And if these last few weeks are any indication, you'll be preoccupied during a lot of the time we do share."

"I had several serious relationships—and two marriages—during Ellenancy's first life," defended Lisanne.

"But Garren and Robert saw how available you were from the start. They knew what role Ellenancy had in your life and accepted it."

"And you cannot accept it? That is beyond your capabilities?"

"Talk to me like that again and I'll throw you across the fucking room."

Fear tingled Lisanne's skin like static electricity: Osa had spoken of the physical fights that she had gotten into with Georgia (the shriekpunk singer), as well as with her Cuban mate in college. Violence was suddenly very possible.

Osa looked down at her wine and shook her head. "I hit a student yesterday," she admitted, shattering her crimson reflection with a fingertip. "I've never done that to a kid before. Never even come close."

Lisanne waited for an explanation, hoping that her face did not betray her alarm.

"I haven't been sleeping very good," the tall beauty continued, "and last week, Autumn made some comment about how tired I looked and asked if it had something to do with you. I ignored her, but she started talking about you—she listened to some articles after your visit—and I pulled her into the hall. She told me not to grab her, and before I could stop myself, I slapped her across the face.

"I went home.

"I typed a formal apology to her parents, but they took her out of my I.S. anyways, which I don't blame them for doing."

"I'm sorry to hear that," said Lisanne. "I know that she was your favorite."

"That's when I knew…I knew I couldn't just wait and see how things went with us. I tried to be patient, but my behavior—my body—told me I needed answers. I know how huge all this is for you, but I just can't wait around in limbo and hope. I need assurances. I need to feel significant in this relationship…or I need closure."

Lisanne took Osa's left hand and said, "I love you."

"That's not what I'm asking for. If I thought you didn't love me or if I didn't love you, we wouldn't be having this conversation at all. Your sister coming back—it's like…it's like all of a sudden you have a child and a best friend and a job that you didn't have when we started. It's taken you away, physically and emotionally. And completely." The tall beauty withdrew her long sepia hand and added, "And maybe you don't realize this, but it's very fucking hurtful that you haven't introduced me to her yet."

"I'm sorry that your—"

"Why haven't you introduced us?" Osa asked with pain in the corners of her eyes. "Is she not interested in me at all?"

"She said that she will meet you when she's granted autonomy."

"I'm glad she's so fucking enthusiastic."

"I wasn't aware that you—"

"You're right. You're not aware. You're aware of what Ellenancy needs, and how well she can play goddamn scales on a lute, but I'm crying every night and you're not aware." Osa stood from the table. "I think this talk's over. I got my answers."

"Please sit down," said Lisanne, reaching for her mate.

Osa batted her hand away. "Don't touch me."

"Please sit down. Please. We're in the middle of a discussion."

"You are—not me. I knew it was gonna go like this, from the moment you got that call in New Orleans. She's too big, and I'm just some Brooklyn City teacher you think's pretty who you like to play with. In two months, you'll have some other woman—or man—for a pet."

"That isn't the case. I love y—"

Osa turned away and thundered across the room.

Mind and cheeks burning, Lisanne hastened after the woman in burgundy. "Bitte, stoppen Sie—stop! Osa, stop!"

The tall beauty paused beside the couch and turned around. "What?"

"You have blamed me for everything, but you are making this happen, too. I should have been more considerate of your feelings—yes—but you are not without fault. You said that you knew we were doomed since New Orleans, and to me, it was very apparent that you felt that way. You never gave us a chance to change."

Eyes filled with fire, Osa took a menacing step toward her mate. "I wasn't gonna say this, but fine. Fine! The last time I was here—after we went to bed—I woke up in the middle of the night and was really upset about what was going on with us, and I started to cry. I couldn't stop, I felt so goddamn awful. And you heard me—I know you did because you breathe different when you're asleep—so the whole time I knew you were awake. Your lover, your mate, your friend is crying beside you for an hour, and you act like you're asleep! I'm crying about us—about you—and you just lie there and fucking ignore me!"

Osa slapped Lisanne.

The room wobbled all around the petite blonde, and she stumbled backwards, toppling onto the couch, her right cheek aflame and her vision blurred.

"That's when I knew for sure how things were!" yelled the tall beauty. "And if you deny it, I'll fucking choke you!"

Ashamed of her own actions on the aforementioned evening and stunned by the violence, Lisanne said nothing.

"Send my shit with a messenger service—I don't ever want to see you again," said the tall beauty, tears running down her face.

Osa turned from her mate, strode up the hall, and passed through the living wall.

Crackling nanobuilders removed her silhouette.

Bright pains pricked Lisanne's struck cheek, and her stomach roiled as if filled with coffee grounds. The hollow dizziness that was a combination of anger, regret, relief and grief was familiar to her from her other breakups, although it was somehow rawer and sadder in this instance. It was painfully clear to her that she and the tall beauty would have lasted as a couple for a very long time had her sister's mind remained in cryonic storage.

This contemplation made her weep openly.

The woman sat with her hollow dizziness for two slow hours before she stood, walked to the bathroom, and took a long hot shower.

* * *

Clothed in a cashmere robe and refreshed, Lisanne walked to the dining room table and drank the glass of wine that Osa had earlier poured. As the floral fluid traveled down her esophagus, she thought of a name for the new composition that she had been working on with her sister.

Into her lily vault recorder, the petite blonde said, "'The Line That is Central to the Soul and Stronger Than All Radiating Spokes.'"

CHAPTER XVII
SATURDAY, AUGUST 31, 2058

A raindrop fell from the clouds, passed its reflection in a turkey pigeon's eye, struck the windshield of an airborne fire wagon, dripped from the vehicle, sped past the one hundred and fifty floors that comprised the Corpus Chrome, Incorporated Building, struck the brunette wig affixed to the shaved scalp of an anonymous female pawn, slid through follicles to the woman's nape and descended the bumps of a protuberant spine to the small of her back.

Today, Alicia Martinez would pay off her debt to the Brokers of Extralegal Acts.

The widow watched the flying craft speed toward the ceremony that was being held in northern Nexus Y for the twenty-seven firemen and eleven police officers who had perished in the burning high-rise on Wednesday.

Shortly after the fire, the ponytailed sixty-six-year-old Israeli American had called a meeting at the Pennsylvania compound. Elad had explained to the gathered pawns, "We will raid the Corpus Chrome, Incorporated Building on Saturday. Because of the funerals that afternoon, an unprecedented number of officers will have the day off and there are not likely to be any airborne riot wagon patrols, which are our primary concern for obvious reasons. The day will be cloudy, which also gives us a great advantage.

"It is our organization's hope that not one person will be killed during this raid…but if CCI employs violent force, so shall we.

"Either way, on Saturday, the thirty-first of August, we will emancipate the resurrection technologies from the bonds of business."

A drop of rain spattered upon the tip of Alicia Martinez's nose as she leaned against a U-shaped tree that grew in the park across the street from the Corpus Chrome, Incorporated Building.

The widow double-tapped her lily and said, "Telephoto: five hundred." In her left eye, the image dimmed, flashed and displayed glaring glass.

She double-tapped her lily. "Telephoto; five hundred; polarize." The glaring glass disappeared, and she saw into the lobby. Seated behind three inverted-pyramid marble desks at the rear of the lobby were six ethnically varied receptionists who wore sky-blue wool sweaters and slacks. To their right, a little chromium homunculus escorted a tall man toward a living wall, beyond which lay the impenetrable security gauntlet.

The Asian and Indian receptionists were talking.

Alicia double-tapped her lily. "Telephoto: two thousand; image auto-stabilize; read lips; convert to audio."

She waited for the remote computer to process all of her commands. Two seconds later, the mouth of the male Asian receptionist shone diaphanously in her left eye.

A dry voice that was the remote computer's default male timbre said in Alicia's lily, "—don't think so. She said that she wanted to get a cat, but I'm allergic to cats. And then she said that I was giving her an ultimatum. And I said if she already had a cat, and I told her to get rid of it, that would be an ultimatum, but her not buying a cat when—" The Asian man's mouth stopped, and the computer voice halted.

A moment later, the receptionist resumed his complaint, "She says she doesn't want one of those hypoallergenics. She says they're not natural and she wants natural, though she didn't have any problem getting those tissue implants in her—"

Alicia double-tapped her lily, said, "Natural view," and saw clearly from both eyes.

Heralds of a greater precipitation spattered upon her wig, a turkey pigeon's beak, a garbage canister, a discarded mandolin string and an empty cylinder of peanut elephants.

Upon her lily, Elad said, "Contact in two minutes."

Alicia looked up. The white sky was littered with dirty gray rags that were swollen rain clouds. From the aggregate of lazing tufts emerged a lone stratocumulus that moved with the deliberateness of a shark.

The widow looked back to the lobby, double-tapped her lily and said, "Telephoto: one thousand." The Asian receptionist, oblivious of the coming storm, spoke to the woman who was seated beside him. Suddenly, the pair laughed.

Alicia resented their mirth.

In her ear, Elad said, "Contact in one minute."

A woman with a saccharine brogue said, "Unless you have priority information, leave the line open."

In the lobby, a guest was escorted through the living wall into the security gauntlet. Two drops of rain spattered upon Alicia's wig, and underneath the porous adherent, her bare scalp sweated.

A heavy shadow slid across the traffic.

Alicia looked up. Overhead, the tip of the dark stratocumulus touched the top of the CCI Building. The widow could not see the vehicles that were hidden within the artificially generated cloud, but she knew that they were there.

The lily in her ear was silent.

Rain poked her shoulders.

Alicia surveyed the lobby and the abutting areas, but saw nothing that concerned her. Again, she looked up. The top thirty floors of the Corpus Chrome, Incorporated Building were concealed by the dark gray stratocumulus.

The widow felt a terrible dread.

Something crackled.

White explosions flashed within the dark gray mass. A piece of molten steel plummeted one hundred and twenty stories and impaled the trunk of a parked car.

Two more explosions illuminated the stratocumulus. Green fluid dripped down the side of the chromium edifice like blood.

Alicia surveyed the receptionists in the lobby. All six of them remained oblivious of the violence above.

Again, the widow returned her attention to the unnatural cloud.

Thirty pinpricks of yellow light crackled within the stratocumulus, and six large red flashes replied to the barrage. Suddenly, an object that glinted and weirdly wriggled dropped from the cloud.

Alicia double-tapped her lily, said, "Telephoto: two thousand; auto-stabilize," and turned her gaze to the plummeting thing. The lens dimmed for a moment and then brightened.

"My god," said the woman when she saw the thing that fell.

In her left lens shone the magnified image of a headless quadrupedal black and chrome robotic construct that had eight arms, six of which terminated with revolving-barrel machine guns. Sparks and smoke trailed from a gaping wound in the machine's chest.

Seven of her peers (pawns in purloined military gear) plummeted from the cloud. Their smoking heads resembled burnt matches.

The falling robotic construct crushed a parked car that was less than half its size, and nearby, the septet turned into red paste. Pedestrians fled the area.

Alicia looked into the lobby. People with white worried eyes emerged from the living wall, hastened past the inverted-pyramid desks and exited the building.

The widow double-tapped her lily. "Open line: they are evacuating the building."

Twenty pinpricks of light crackled within the cloud, and four red bursts replied. Somebody yelled half of a word on the open line and was silent thereafter.

The intensity of the rainfall increased.

Wet clothing clung to Alicia's chafed skin. The woman had lost her appetite and more than twenty pounds since the night that she had seen the slug, and the dreadful thing that haunted her mirrors was a bald, emaciated creature that had loose teeth.

Something exploded within the stratocumulus. The gaunt widow looked up.

From the cloud fell a ten-limbed black and chrome robotic construct, which was orbited by three brilliant fire spheres. Two blue thrusters in the machine's underside flashed, hissing, and sped it back to the obscure battle.

Shortly after the metallic aggressor had returned to the stratocumulus, four men with heads like burnt matches fell from the sky and painted the pavement with their insides.

A deep explosion resounded, and hasty evacuees yelled.

One of Elad's purloined military vehicles fell from the artificial cloud, three sundered thrusters trailing behind it like the cans from a newlyweds' bumper. At street level, evacuees ran away from the plummeting craft's shadow toward the park where Alicia safely observed the conflict.

"Run, Mrs. Albren, run!" shouted a neatly bearded black man in tweed to a thin old woman who had once been beautiful.

The vehicle smashed into the ground behind them and exploded. A spinning piece of metal shot from the wreckage and took the black man's right arm from his shoulder. Groaning, he fell to his knees and clutched the wound with his remaining hand.

Crimson ribbons drained between his fingers.

"Mr. Johnson!" screamed the thin old woman, hysterical.

"Go. Get out of—" were the last words that the man in tweed uttered before he fell to the ground and spilled his red life upon the pavement.

Alicia Martinez stomped upon the spirit of compassion that threatened to make her useless.

"We're almost in," announced the Irishwoman on the open line.

Frightened people careened from the building, shouting and coughing and yelling. The Asian receptionist saw Alicia and said, "Run! Can't you see what's happening!"

"My husband's inside."

"Uh…he'll come out," said the fellow, who then continued his beeline.

Men, women and mannequins hastened from the besieged skyscraper.

Alicia double-tapped her lily and said, "Open line: full evacuation in progress."

A wind blew, and the rain fell aslant. Wet cloth rubbed upon the sharp points that were Alicia's shoulders, elbows, hips and knees. Suddenly, she began to shiver.

The gaunt widow double-tapped her lily and said, "Remote view: vanguard." Her right eye received a visual transmission from a pawn who was seated within one of the stolen military vehicles.

The man undid his pseudopodia, stood up, checked his razor gun, surveyed nine armored pawns, listened to what a red-headed woman said, nodded in affirmation, filed in line behind his peers, ran up a gangway, stepped over six corpses whose heads had been charred, strode through a nascent hole, splashed past a viridescent waterfall, scrambled down a rope ladder, landed upon his feet, pivoted and surveyed an enormous teal enclosure that accounted for fifteen floors of the building.

Spherical lights illuminated the green fluid that leaked from the broken hoses and cracked chromium vats in the high ceiling, and drifting about the room were three dozen kidney-shaped chrome objects, each far larger than a truck.

None of what Alicia saw through the man's contact lens made any sense.

"What the hell am I looking at?" somebody inquired on the lily's open line.

The pawn zoomed his lens at a wobbling chrome kidney. Green fluid dripped from a crack in its side.

The Irishwoman said, "We need to get these to—"

A black and chrome robotic construct dropped from the ceiling and landed upon the floor, fire spheres orbiting its sixteen arms. Somebody yelled.

Pawns sprayed the construct with lava bolts. The defender flung flaming orbs at six pawns and instantaneously blackened their heads.

An anonymous pawn said, "It's gonna ki—"

A missile sped into the enclosure.

The man through whom Alicia saw the scene raised his hands in front of his face. Somebody yelled, "Don't!"

A thunderous explosion shook the building, and the image in Alicia's eye went white. People screamed. Detritus, eleven burning pawns and two molten robotic constructs fell from the cloud and impacted the pavement.

At that moment, Alicia knew for certain that the Corpus Chrome, Incorporated Building was going to be obliterated.

The remaining evacuees bolted from the building as quickly as they could. Amongst them, she recognized three lawyers from the firm where she had once worked, including Morton Goldman. Alicia hid her face from her old mentor, who fled, panicked and bleeding.

The stratocumulus lifted from the cylindrical edifice, revealing stories that bled green blood and exhaled black smoke through gaping holes. A few specks that were people clung to riven steel.

Two sizzling missiles emerged from the artificial cloud and sped into the building. Thunder boomed. Windows spat scintillating glass, and boils erupted upon the chromium façade like a disease. A giant chrome kidney arced from the structure, plummeted one hundred and forty stories and flattened a box truck.

Alicia looked at the lobby and saw that it was empty. Beside one of the inverted-pyramid desks laid a dead elderly man, his hands clutched to his failed heart.

The gaunt widow double-tapped her lily. "The lobby is clear."

She knew what would happen next.

Nine missiles shot into the Corpus Chrome, Incorporated Building's open, smoking wounds. White fire overpowered retinas, and the world shook. Warts and pustules ran up and down the façade.

The gaunt widow in gray tasted ash, charcoal and tears.

Suddenly, Alicia Martinez no longer knew who she was.

A sooty man crawled across the pavement, moaning the name "Samantha" until he found a prostrated plump woman whose chest had been impaled by a girder. The crawler touched his dead wife's face with a trembling index finger.

Alicia Martinez did not know who she was, but she knew what she could not be.

She double-tapped her lily and said, "Connect to a police reservoir."

The gaunt widow recorded a message in which she detailed what she knew of the Brokers of Extralegal Acts. She was aware that all of the names that she had been given were false and that the compound was expendable, but she hoped that some of the information that she related would prove useful.

After she finished her account, Alicia wiped her eyes and walked over to the crawling man. To him, she said, "I used to have a daughter and a husband."

The fellow looked up.

"I'm sorry," said the gaunt widow, stupidly.

The crawler's eyes were terrible.

Alicia Martinez turned away from the bereft man, strode into the lobby of the Corpus Chrome, Incorporated Building, sat behind an inverted-pyramid desk, looked up at the marble ceiling and waited for one hundred and fifty stories to crush her into something less reprehensible than what she currently was.

Angry thunder was the last sound that she ever heard.

CHAPTER XVIII
CRACKED HEADS

Alone in his padded sleeping quarters, Gregil looked across seven hundred empty kilometers at a small blue, green and brown planet. His exhalation fogged a portion of the window, covering a cataract of inclement weather, a continent and an ocean. He then clarified the blurry world by wiping the glass with his fist.

An alarm lanced his equipoise. Yellow and red emergency lights glared, stinging his dilated eyes.

The strong American Russian turned away from Earth, plugged an acorn into his ear, pulled on pants and—without a shirt or shoes—ran through the living wall of his chamber, down a foam-rubber ramp, through a second living wall and onto a corrugated plastic catwalk that threaded the circumference of the space station. Yellow and red lights flashed all around the rim.

Running in half-gravity, Gregil clicked the stem of his acorn and asked, "What's the situation?"

"The CCI building is under attack," replied Karie.

"Under attack?" Gregil was shocked by the information. The corrugated plastic bit into the soles of his feet, but he did not slacken the pace of his beeline.

"Yes. Under attack."

"I'm almost there."

The American Russian slipped on his own blood, caught the railing, righted himself and continued forward.

Six pounding heartbeats later, Gregil plunged through a living wall and entered the satellite's hemi-cylindrical command room. There, he surveyed the manual control panels. All of the microphones and typing hemispheres had retracted inside the inverted-pyramid consoles (where they were inaccessible), and the word

"OVERRIDE" sat upon twelve screens and floated upon ten stages.

"Oh, God," said Karie, listening to her lily with tears in her eyes. "The building's collapsing."

The shirtless man surveyed the command room. Upon the stage of the Transmissions Monitor floated a list of recent activity.

> *Emergency Override in Progress…*
> *Lunar Diamond Vault: Locked*
> *Lunar Diamond Vault: Unlocked*
> *8.31.58 Payments: Transferred*
> *8.31.58 Payments: Withheld*
> *Emergency Mannequin Shutdown: Enabled.*
> *Emergency Mannequin Activation: Enabled.*

Gregil was horrified.

"We've got to stop this from happening!" cried the American Russian. "Those signals can't go out at the same time!"

Karie's voice was almost inaudible. "They did."

* * *

Sarah walked onto the rear deck of the northern California home that she shared with William, her resurrected mate. The silver-haired woman had divorced her second husband the moment that she found out her first spouse was going to be re-bodied, and she had not once doubted the wisdom of her decision. Fortunately for her, the discarded mate was a congenial guy who harbored no ill will towards her or the resurrected poet who was his predecessor and successor.

In his first life, William had longed for a view of the Pacific Ocean (because of his years in the Coast Guard and the month-long pleasure cruise during which he and Sarah had conceived their first child), and this isolated coastal dwelling—in another century, a place where the keepers of the nearby lighthouse had lived— had come on the market at exactly the right time.

The silver-haired woman set her coffee upon the table beside her rocking chair, adjusted her woolen robe and sat down. "The breeze is nice."

William raised his gelware face to the wind, his gray hair blowing behind him, long and leonine. "I can feel it," he said.

Looking at the coffee, the re-boded man screwed a dark red thimble onto the tip of his pinky and lowered the extrusion toward the steaming beverage.

"It's still too hot," Sarah informed her husband.

William put his thimble into the coffee and yanked it out. "Ouch. You're right." He shook his hand back and forth to cool the carmine attachment's taste-, touch-, and smell-sensitive flesh.

Sarah blew upon the coffee for a few moments, took a sip and set it down. William dipped his thimble.

"I'd like to go to the lighthouse today," said the re-bodied man. "Work on the poem."

"That sounds like a wonderful plan." The silver-haired woman liked how her husband always referred to his current work as "the poem" as if the hundreds of pieces that he had written were all part of one continuous tapestry. Sipping coffee, she looked at the sunlit waves beyond the balustrade.

William said, "The sound of the ocean helps me to—" and stopped abruptly.

Sarah set the coffee upon the table. "William?"

The re-bodied man stood up like a soldier at attention and then dropped to his knees; flashing lights burned through the shoulders of his white linen shirt.

Frightened and confused, Sarah rose from her seat.

The sound of three dissonant piccolo flutes emerged from the mannequin's mouth slit.

"William," inquired the silver-haired woman, anxiously. "Can you hear me in there?" She touched his right cheek.

The gelware felt like ice.

Sarah double-tapped her lily. "Connect to CCI! Emergency!"

Frost covered the right side of the mannequin's face, and the other half blistered with heat.

Sarah's vision began to narrow.

A vertical fissure cleft the mannequin's face, and the top of its head cracked open. Green steam flung frozen shards and boiled clumps of brain matter into the air.

* * *

Po Li and his re-bodied brother walked out of Yeehaw!!! (a strip club that featured robust American women [many of whom had Australian accents, for some reason]) and onto the top level of Hong Kong's nine-tiered sidewalk. The Chinese man was drunk, and therefore certain that the redheaded girl who had taken all of his money thought that he was better than all the other guys in the establishment. Jennifer Smith from Iowa Town, Oklahoma had said that she liked Po Li, and he fully believed her.

Outside, the glowing night was damp and warm.

The brothers walked forward, and people stared at the mannequin, which always attracted attention. If Po Li were honest with himself (which was rarely the case), he would admit that he preferred the high-profile companionship of his mechanical sibling to that of the original corporeal version (who was only a Nobel prize-winning scientist).

The resurrected man stopped.

"Mat ye?" asked Po Li.

Suddenly, the mannequin stood at attention and dropped to his knees.

"Mat ye?" repeated the drunk fellow, perturbed and swatting his brother's left arm.

Flashing lights burned through the shoulders of the machine's silk shirt.

"Nei bin baak ma?" inquired Po Li, perplexed by the anomalous occurrence.

The skirl of three dissonant piccolo flutes emerged from the re-bodied man's mouth slit. His drunk brother looked around, embarrassed and confused.

People were watching.

Po Li tried to force the epaulette lights back into the machine, but the belligerent bulbs refused to be submerged. Spectators gathered around to observe the malfunctioning mannequin.

"Zi, ting, ting!" the drunk yelled at the embarrassing machine, which continually flashed and ululated.

A pretty Japanese girl with blonde hair giggled.

Po Li slapped the mannequin, and the palm of his right hand stuck to its cheek. The other side of the mannequin's face soon blistered with heat.

People withdrew from the skirling cynosure until one onlooker suggested to the others that the machine might explode, at which point, everybody ran away.

Po Li's right hand filled with ice.

The mannequin's head cracked in half, and the drunk yelled. A geyser of green steam sprayed cooked and frozen brain matter into the air.

Po Li tore his hand loose and ran.

Upon the mannequin's cleft face were three fingertips and a frozen palm.

* * *

The re-bodied rabbi in black hurried up a moonlit Baghdad street toward the synagogue that she had erected in her first life. An Arabic fabric merchant named Asri walked beside her, his palms pressed together and his head tilted forward respectfully. As he matched the woman's long fast strides, he ruminated upon why Jews were always in such a hurry. Perhaps they were compelled to make up for the days that they squandered observing Shabbat (which had ended about two hours ago), or perhaps they feared that moving slowly would give their myriad enemies an easy shot. Or maybe, since Jews did not have a proper afterlife, they just wanted to do as much as they could before it all ended.

Asri did not voice his theories.

The re-bodied rabbi led the merchant inside the synagogue, through the atrium and up the central aisle. At the front pew, she stopped and pointed. Asri leaned down, inspected the torn cushion, pursed his lips, reviewed his mental catalogue and told the holy woman that he had the needed material and would presently return.

The merchant hastened from the synagogue, strode up the tiled street, entered his shop, climbed to the second floor, pulled two meters of cloth from a hanging spool, cut and bundled the fabric, grabbed his kit of assorted mini-stitch sewing machines and returned whence he came.

When he put his hand to the atrium door, he heard an unpleasant noise that sounded like three flutes having an argument.

Asri entered the building and looked up the aisle.

The mannequin was upon its knees before the lectern, skirling and flashing. Green steam rose from its cracked head and the brain-spattered parchment of an ancient Torah.

* * *

Three noteworthy Royal Air Force men sat in the cockpit of a decommissioned warplane that Air Chief Marshal Sir Gerald B. Thiggs guided toward the sunlit Andes Mountains.

"Let us have an up-close look at those peaks, shall we?" Captain Potsley suggested to the re-bodied pilot. "It is a wonderful thing, this old craft."

"Fantastically wonderful," confirmed Officer James.

"She can still carry us to the tops of the Lord's grandest works," Chaplain Smithson remarked, and affectionately hammered a fist against the steely wall of the cockpit.

A white mountain peak filled the windshield.

"Sir Thiggs?" inquired Captain Potsley, looking over at the pilot.

The re-bodied man dropped to his knees. Flashing lights superseded his golden epaulettes, and three discordant notes skirled as the plane raced toward the mountain.

The top of the mannequin's head cracked open, admitting a geyser of green steam and clumps of brain matter, which were either cooked or frozen.

Englishmen hastened for the controls.

In a fraction of a second, the mountain turned the cockpit into a two-dimensional object.

* * *

Rita May heard an eerie skirl that was not the sound of wind blowing through cracks in the walls. Abandoning a swollen cow, she walked outside the barn and saw her re-bodied father fall off a horse for the first time in his entire life.

Chapter XIX
The Dotted Line (Connected)

Ellenancy played an ascending melody on her violin.

When the final pitch died, Lisanne struck a low note upon the lacquered grand piano at which she was seated. (The timbral shift reminded her of the first time she had visited America.)

The mannequin played a conjunct refrain on her violin.

When the final pitch died, the petite blonde struck a low note, played it again and sustained it for five seconds. (She remembered a dead deer that she had watched decay in her parents' backyard throughout the summer of twenty-thirty-one.)

Ellenancy played a sad scale on her violin and then muted her instrument; Lisanne struck twice in response. The last piano note resounded portentously in the harp of the grand piano, traveled about the lavender and gold interior of the Perfect Pitch Auditorium and died. "The Dotted Line (Connected)" ended.

Eighteen hundred and forty people warmly applauded the women and the piece, which was the first one that the Sisters Breutschen had played in front of an audience in over four years. The word "Brava!" leapt from many mouths.

Wearing identical faces and emerald dresses, Lisanne and Ellenancy stood from their upholstered mahogany divans, walked in front of the twelve instruments that were positioned about the hemicircular stage and bowed.

Waves of appreciation rippled through the audience, and ebullient people rose to their feet.

The sisters stood upright.

Lisanne surveyed the crowd for one specific person, but instead saw friends, peers, critics and strangers who slapped their hands together and shouted accolades. Looking to the rear of the auditorium, she descried a tall raven-haired woman in the shadow of the mezzanine. Her heart leapt at the sight, and all around her, applause swelled. The auditorium lights then brightened, chasing the shadows from the huge room. Underneath the mezzanine stood a tall stranger who was not her former mate from Brooklyn City.

Tears sparkled in Lisanne's eyes.

Ellenancy took her sister's left hand, and the Sisters Breutschen bowed a second time. The word "Brava!" burst like popcorn throughout the appreciative crowd.

The siblings stood upright.

Ellenancy turned her gelware face to Lisanne and smiled. "Thank you for making me do this," said the re-bodied woman. "Danke. Danke."

Lisanne nodded and tried to reply, but instead began to sob, thinking of how much she wanted to share this moment with Osa.

The Sisters Breutschen hugged each other for a warm minute, parted and faced the audience. Dewy eyes sparkled throughout the auditorium like a sympathetic constellation.

Lisanne stepped over her sadness, wiped tears from her cheeks and raised the palms of her hands, asking the audience for silence.

The applause diminished. Soon, the crowd replaced their buttocks in the auditorium's padded velvet seats and focused three thousand six hundred and eighty smiling eyes on the petite blonde.

"Danke, danke, danke," Lisanne said to the rapt assemblage as her sister enthusiastically squeezed her hand. "Ellenancy and I are very—"

Yellow and red lights flashed within the auditorium. Lisanne looked to the ceiling and the emergency exits, but descried nothing. Lowering her gaze, she saw that thousands of eyes had shifted from her to the person who stood directly beside her. People pointed fingers.

The discordant sound of three piccolo flutes startled Lisanne as she turned to Ellenancy, who was upon her knees, lights flashing red and yellow atop her shoulders.

Stunned, the petite blonde struggled to regain her voice. "What is happening? Can you hear me?"

The right side of the mannequin's face was covered with frost, and the left side was blistered with heat.

"Ellenancy…?"

The discordant flutes screeched like a teakettle. A vertical line cracked the middle of the mannequin's face in half.

"Nein, nein, *nein!*" shouted Lisanne.

The top of the mannequin's head split open, and a geyser of green steam shot frozen and boiled gray matter into the air.

People shouted.

Lisanne was numb.

The machine toppled forward, yanking the petite blonde from the stage by the hand. People screamed.

The floor of the empty orchestra pit concussed the side of Lisanne's skull, and the terrible world went dark.

Chapter XX
The Garbage Men

"I cannot believe that I am in New Queens on a Saturday afternoon!" R.J. the Third complained to Champ as they walked up the cracked, neglected and noisome street. "I would not be surprised to learn that Architect is protesting my presence here by brutally knocking his head against a pillow. A firm pillow."

"It's that one, right?" asked the garbage man, pointing to a huge gray and blue building that looked like it belonged in a post-apocalyptic world where the only available protein was human flesh. (The only other time that he had seen the edifice was during the clandestine mannequin dropoff, which had occurred four nights earlier.)

"Yes, that is his lair."

The garbage man, clothed in jeans and a t-shirt that read The messiah is here. Right here., and the popinjay, clad in silver, strode toward the building, upon which swatches of peeled paint hung like the cracked tongues of sick canines.

"Sagesse couldn't fix it up a little?" inquired Champ. "Looks like a holocaust."

"You are a fool, Champ Sappline!" R.J. the Third pointed to the edifice and stated, "This abraded shell…this foreboding façade…this dilapidated husk—yes, that is the most apt description—this dilapidated husk in the middle of the most wretched place on planet Earth—I speak of New Queens—"

"Figured."

"—this dilapidated husk is engineered to disguise the illicit honeycomb within." The popinjay scratched his short black hair, fingered the trio of rings on his big nose and spat.

Walking east, the duo avoided gum, cans, milk cartons that had green fur, chicken bones, toilet paper, towels, tampons, a towel that looked as if it had been used as a tampon, urine-filled paint buckets, a cabbage that resembled a rotten head, a defunct exercise bike, half of a sneaker, a flat basketball and a dead turkey pigeon that had been blinded by bleach.

"New Queens is in dire need of some fine garbage purveyors such as yourself," observed R.J. the Third.

"They shouldn't've pissed off the union."

Champ's lily beeped, and a demure female voice said, "Incoming call: Potato O'Boyd." This was the third time that the old Irish American had beeped in the last twenty minutes, but the garbage man refused to answer. He had not spoken to any of his father's friends since the night of the fire and was wary of revealing the location of the mannequin to anybody: Corpus Chrome, Incorporated had called nine times, and their most recent message intimated that their next action was an in-person visit, which would be supervised by police officers.

At the concrete stoop of Sagesse's building, the duo climbed the steps to a rusty hinged door. The air smelled vaguely of semen.

Champ asked, "Does he know that we're—" but stopped his inquiry when the door slid ajar. The points of two chopsticks emerged from the centimeter-wide opening and snapped together like the mouth of an alligator.

"Payment," said a girl from inside the building.

The chopsticks reopened.

"Let me see my dad first."

The chopsticks retracted, and the door slid shut.

"Hey!" objected Champ.

R.J. the Third eyed the garbage man and said, "I think you shall have to pay him first."

"What if he broke my dad? I'm not gonna pay that guy if he screwed him up."

"Whether or not his enterprise was successful, Sagesse did many hours of labor at your behest. His compensation, therefore—"

"That's a bunch of crap," said Champ, withdrawing the money card into which he had transferred all of his savings.

The door slid ajar, and the two chopsticks returned, clicking thrice. Sighing through his nose, the garbage man decided that he would pay, but that if he was unsatisfied with the Frenchman's work, he would take the card back one way or another.

"Fine."

Champ extended the green plasticore rectangle and had it snatched from his fingers by snapping chopsticks.

The door shut, remained closed for ten seconds and opened wide, revealing Sagesse, a large black French fellow who had tiger-striped dreadlocks. Securing a belt around his bright red Japanese robe, he said, "Enter."

Champ and R.J. the Third walked into the anteroom, and a Japanese girl in a cheetah bikini manually shut the door behind them.

"Follow."

Sagesse walked across the varnished hardwood floor into a hallway, quiet as a feline, and the pair from Nexus Y followed.

"Were you able to get him offline?" Champ asked the tiger-striped dreadlocks that hung down between the large man's shoulder blades.

No response issued from the mouth within the ropy hair.

Champ's lily beeped, and the demure female voice said, "Incoming call: Butch Goldberg." Again, the garbage man let the caller go to his reservoir.

Walking along the hallway, the trio passed a framed animated poster for *The First and Final Rocket*, upon which Honcles the homunculus fought the mechanical bird on the titular vehicle's windshield, observed from behind the cracked glass by the black scientist, Arthur, and his white-haired father. For reasons that were most certainly related to his own shortcomings, the image from R.J. the Third's (self-proclaimed) meisterwerk filled Champ with a deep melancholy.

"Would you like for me to put my signature upon this fine artifact?" the popinjay asked the tiger-striped tendrils.

"No."

"I appreciate that you wish to keep it in mint condition."

Sagesse walked through exposed bricks that were actually a hidden (and perfectly sculpted) living wall. The duo from Nexus Y transcended, and behind them, nanobuilders crackled.

Champ smelled copper, filaments, smoke, oil, rubber, acids and molten plastic while his eyes adjusted to the dim blue lighting of a cavernous enclosure that had once been a brewery. The far wall was a honeycomb of plasticore storage units, which could be accessed by skiffs, catwalks and ladders. In the illuminated cubicles, the garbage man saw six foam-rubber cars, twenty mote aquariums, eight bubble mopeds, a gold-plated lion skeleton, an airborne riot wagon, a famous painting of fat women, a pile of guns, a bisexual humpball and several hundred plastic crates that were decorated with Japanese flags.

"Where's my dad?" asked Champ, firmly.

Sagesse walked toward the honeycomb. "Follow."

Irked, the garbage man strode behind the French fellow and the popinjay. The foam floor absorbed the sounds of their footfalls.

R.J. the Third said to Sagesse, "A katana—a samurai sword—would wonderfully complement those robes that you have on."

No comment emerged from the pile of tiger-striped dreadlocks.

Champ's lily beeped, and the demure female voice said, "Incoming call: Mikek Ghentz." The garbage man could not remember the last time that he had received five calls in an hour, and at that moment realized that something must be wrong. Double-tapping his lily, he answered, "Yeah?"

"Are you watching the news?"

"Never."

"Is your father okay?"

"I'm at…the place…right now. This is the first appointment I could get with the guy."

"They blew up CCI," said Mikek. "Did you know? About an hour ago."

"What? Who did?"

"Terrorists. They destroyed it. And then all of the mannequins…their heads…." The driver hesitated. "Their heads exploded."

Fear seized Champ as he followed Sagesse and R.J. the Third onto the railed skiff. The French fellow twisted the lift dial clockwise, and suddenly, the warehouse floor dropped away.

"They're calling it genocide," said Mikek.

Dizzied by the news, Champ gripped the rail to remain upright.

The driver gently inquired, "Is your dad…have you seen if he…if he…?"

"I'll call you," the garbage man said and then cut the connection.

Rising, the magnetically buoyed skiff passed the Japanese-flag-decorated crates, two bubble mopeds and a stack of mote aquariums, each of which had a dent in the same place (the top right corner) as did the unit that R.J. the Third possessed. Sagesse then twisted the dial counterclockwise, stopping the platform in front of a darkened cubicle.

Sweat glazed Champ's face, and his chest thudded.

The French fellow whistled a C-sharp and said, "Ampoule."

An orb in the ceiling of the enclosure illuminated. Pure white light glinted upon myriad crisscrossed wires, an almost visually incomprehensible metallic tangle.

Squeezing the skiff rail with both hands, Champ surveyed the chaos. A fire-blackened chromium torso and a matching left arm were suspended in the metal latticework as if caught in a spider web and a pair of disembodied legs knelt in the left corner, proffering more wires. Against the right wall were an acid-filled bucket that was labeled "Bugs, Transmitters & Receivers" and a table with a score of microsurgical tools, in the center of which sat the mannequin's head.

The skull was intact.

Relieved, Champ relaxed his grip upon the balustrade and exhaled trapped air.

Sagesse pointed to Eagle's head. "Offline."

"Did I not tell you that Sagesse was the master of extrications?" R.J. the Third said, in an effort to win himself a few accolades.

"Yeah. But…but my dad's a mess." Champ gestured at the chaotic room that was his father.

Sagesse shrugged.

"The brain's still frozen, right?" asked the garbage man.

The French fellow nodded an affirmation, his dreadlocks stirring like the trunks of huddled elephants. "Oui."

"Can you put him back together?"

"Two thousand sixty."

"Globals?" asked Champ, surprised by the low price.

"Year."

"You can't fix him until twenty-sixty? No way. You've gotta be joking."

The French fellow refuted this statement with a shake of his head, his dreadlocks stirring like the fronds of rainforest trees.

"Sagesse is not inclined toward japery," informed R.J. the Third.

Champ was furious. "This is fucking unbelievable."

"Believe," said Sagesse.

The garbage man shouted, "That's it!" and clenched his right fist.

R.J. the Third clapped a hand to Champ's shoulder and said, "Before you launch that fist of yours, I would like to remind you that Sagesse is the man who dismantled your father and, very likely, the best—if not only!—man who can rebuild him. Perhaps also ponder that Sagesse is far, far larger than you and a Negro."

Champ stuffed down his anger and asked the French fellow, "Can you maintain the liquid nitrogen until then? For a year and half?"

"Of course."

"Fine."

Sagesse whistled a C-sharp and said, "Arret."

Darkness enshrouded the metal abstraction.

Epilogue I
The Limitations of Flesh

Summer, A.D. 2059 (One year later)

A lithe black woman who was dressed in a knee-length corduroy shirt that had bursts of white wool around its collar and sleeves took Miss Karlsson's hand and kissed her on the mouth. Snapdragon stood at a nearby drinking spigot, taller and thinner than he had been a year ago, watching the two beautiful giants.

The stranger pulled away from the instructor, glanced at the gawking twelve-year-old and said with her purple-painted lips, "Hello there."

"Um…h-hello."

"You must be Snapdragon. I've heard a lot about you."

"I didn't do it!" defended the Asian boy, who then ran down the hall, past myriad cubbies, through a living wall and across tuffgrass, toward the yellow foam-rubber car within which sat his father, eating cinnamon-flavored peanut elephants. In the back of the vehicle sat Autumn, shaking her head and mouthing something that might have been "You are great!" but wound up being "You are late," when she repeated it to him ten seconds later.

Snapdragon hugged and kissed his father, but was careful to call him "Dad," rather than "Daddy," in front of his female friend.

"Sleepovers are the best," the boy said to the Jewish girl. "It makes everything much funner."

"More fun."

"We agree."

* * *

Sitting on the bed beside Snapdragon, Autumn separated the herbivorous dinosaurs from the carnivorous ones and said (not for the first time), "These shouldn't go together."

"Maybe they can teach each other? The meat-lovers can show the other ones what they're missing."

The girl did not seem to care for this idea. Methodically, she divided the dinosaurs by their culinary inclinations and then sorted them by size and estimated intellectual capacity. The boy watched, enjoying the way his guest pursed her lips when she ruminated.

"Snapdragon?" inquired Autumn, her eyes focused upon the spiky terminus of a stegosaurus tail.

"That one's Roger. I changed his name from Peter, which's what it said on the box."

"Do you like Elizabeth?"

"My stuffed penguin? Of course. She's best friends with Alfred the puffin."

"I'm talking about the girl in our interaction session," clarified Autumn.

"Liz Cheung?"

"Yes. Her."

"She's okay," said the boy, shrugging. "She wants to hang out."

Autumn gauged Snapdragon for a moment and then turned her gaze to a tyrannosaurus rex that held a flute in its tiny arms. "Do you think she's pretty?"

"For a tyrannosaurus."

"Not that. Elizabeth. Do you think she's pretty?"

"She's okay."

Autumn fixed her brown dress, folding her real and special legs beneath its hem. "She was wearing shorts at Ezekiel's birthday party."

"Ezekiel's hamster is incredible."

"I think she likes you," said Autumn, scrutinizing the shell of an anklyosaurus who wore sunglasses. "A lot of girls look at you now."

"Because I got taller. They can see me better."

"They think you're cute," said Autumn, her cheeks turning scarlet.

This information made Snapdragon nervous. "Um…wanna watch m.a.?"

"I would enjoy watching something that's both topical and educational."

"As long as there're some robots."

* * *

The twelve-year-olds went into the den and sat upon the air bench, their shoulders and legs touching. (Snapdragon was glad that his new jeans and King Monster t-shirt did not have any stains upon them.)

Once the test pattern finished, the boy whistled a C-sharp and said, "Search reservoir: Topical; educational; robots."

Rendered upon the stage in three-dimensional letters was the following:

Top Recommendation for Search: Topical/Educational/Robots…
Speech given by Steven Cord on the night of August 31, 2059,
at the Corpus Chrome, Incorporated Memorial.

"It's some dumb guy talking," said Snapdragon.

"I would like to watch that speech."

"It's gonna be boring. Crazy boring."

"We can watch something that's more exciting afterwards."

"Deal." Snapdragon whistled a C-sharp and said, "Play."

Rendered upon the stage by three hundred thousand flying pixels was

a kidney-shaped chrome dais. The platform was the size of a full city block, and its perimeter was decorated with thousands of disembodied mannequin hands. The upraised appendages clutched spheres of blue light that illuminated the myriad spectators who surrounded the memorial.

Seated alone upon the raised platform was a weirdly shaped person.

The pixels dispersed and then rendered

the misshapen individual on the dais. The fifty-six-year-old man was clothed in a chrome-thread suit and lying on his back atop a buoyed divan. His face was covered with burns, his scalp was blistered and he lacked his left arm and leg. In the socket beside his blue right eye was something that resembled a prune. Tubes connected him to buoyed cylinders that contained fluid, tissue, oxygen, lungs and intestines.

The weirdly shaped man said, "Lawrence Cord never felt the need to explain himself or his company to the public, but I do feel the need to defend his legacy on this day of remembrance, one year after the tragedy."

"I remember when that happened," said Snapdragon, his voice freezing the pixels in the mote aquarium. "Smelled like lighter fluid for a week. Resume play."

"My name is Steven Lawrence Cord.

"The founder and president of Corpus Chrome, Incorporated, Lawrence Robert Cord, was my father."

All around the dais, the spectators were silent.

The misshapen man continued, "Before the dedication, I would like to clarify a few things about the tragedy and also about Corpus Chrome, Inc. I have released several statements to the media, but because of my injuries on August thirty-first, I have been physically incapable of speaking until now.

"False accusations persist, and I intend to dispel those."

The lungs in the pulmonary cylinders expanded.

"During the final explosion that destroyed the building, there was a millisecond during which the blast that killed my father, his partners and many others disconnected several computers

that should have been connected, and fused together other circuits that were never meant to be fused. As a result, a fully loaded emergency signal was sent to our space station, and this signal included an override command.

"Our lunar diamond vaults were sent contradictory 'lock' and 'unlock' signals. The security system was overloaded and defaulted to release. The rooms depressurized, and diamonds valued at over ninety trillion dollars were sucked into the vacuum of space.

"On Earth, the mannequins received two contradictory signals: 'freeze the brain' for cryogenic storage, and 'heat the brain' to bring it out of stasis. The simultaneous application of these two temperatures destroyed the minds within.

"That is what happened.

"I miss my father dearly…but I am glad that he was not alive to witness this genocide. It would have…" Steven Cord shut his mismatched eyes, wheezed and leaned forward. In two of the cylinders, amber fluid effervesced.

"He's sick," said Snapdragon, his voice freezing the pixels in the mote aquarium.

"He's dying. Those machines are keeping him alive."

"Oh," said the boy. "Resume play."

The misshapen man shuddered, raised his head, shifted in his divan and resumed his speech. "During the past year, Global Senate scientists have dissected the mannequins and the two giant kidneys that survived the blast, yet they have not reached a consensus as to how these machines functioned.

"I will explain how the mannequins and the kidneys functioned to the best of my abilities, but I am not a scientist. The people who created these devices are dead or have chosen to remain anonymous, for obvious reasons.

"I should mention that the reason we at Corpus Chrome, Inc.

secreted our technology was because we needed a tremendous amount of capital to achieve our goals, and we did not want competition in the marketplace to slow our progress.

"At this point in time, there is no need for secrecy."

Steven Cord paused, and beside him, two cylinders rotated.

He said, "The kidneys were schools.

"Inside each school was a solution filled with quadrillions upon quadrillions of microbacteria, and two hundred human minds that Corpus Chrome, Inc. had purchased from families or received as donations. These minds—the scientists called them playgrounds—were dead except for one small area that lacked one specific chemical— perhaps glucose or oxygen, or a neurotransmitter like glutamate or GABA.

"The microbacteria that learned to make or deliver the needed chemical to this part of the brain were allowed to reproduce. The others were destroyed.

"The trained microbacteria were culled from each of the schools, and then combined in a solution of hyperconcentrated fuel sources. This microbacterial colony could create and supply all the material that a brain needed to function for a century, if not longer. Communications betw—"

Steven Cord wheezed, and his lungs deflated in a nearby cylinder. Pained, he closed his eyes.

Murmurs rippled through the offstage crowd.

A stocky Thai woman in a sky-blue wool suit who was an attendant ran to the cylinders and twisted two dials. The lungs inflated, and Steven Cord's eyes flickered open.

"Thank you," said the misshapen man.

The Thai attendant nodded, adjusted three blood filters, sponged sweat from her patient's blistered face and departed.

Trembling, Steven Cord faced the crowd. "Communications between a living brain and a mannequin unit were achieved through the quadrillions of two-way nanosatellites that we installed throughout the cerebral tissue.

"*Motor commands from the brain were carried by microbacteria to the nanosatellites, and the nanosatellites converted these commands into ultrasonic frequencies that activated mechanisms throughout the mannequin unit.*

"*At the same time, sensory data gathered by lenses, microphones and gelware were converted into ultrasonic frequencies, relayed into the nanosatellites and taken by microbacteria throughout the brain, where they were chemically translated into thought and sensation.*

"*That was how Corpus Chrome, Inc. resurrected the dead.*"

Bubbles gurgled in the cylinders behind Steven Cord. His blue eye and glistening prune surveyed the crowd.

"*I would like to take a moment to tell you about my father.*

"*Lawrence Robert Cord was born in North Carolina in nineteen-seventy-eight. When he was nine years old, his youngest sister died of pneumonia.*

"*Shortly thereafter, Lawrence Cord's father was diagnosed with stomach cancer. The man died a slow and painful death over the course of three years.*

"*When Lawrence Cord was twenty, his mother was diagnosed with a very aggressive case of macular degeneration and went blind. He dropped out of college to care for her, taking a job at a local pharmacy.*

"*While at the pharmacy, Lawrence Cord met a woman named Allison Warton and fell in love with her. She helped him with his responsibilities at home, and supported him financially as well.*

"*Three years into their relationship, a pulmonary embolism unexpectedly killed Lawrence Cord's mother. After the funeral, the couple left North Carolina and never returned.*

"*Lawrence Cord and Allison Warton were married. Allison encouraged my father to finish his bioengineering degree, and she financially supported him while he did so.*

"She became pregnant. The pregnancy was an accident, but they decided to have the child. She died when she was in labor, but I lived.

"My father never remarried."

Steven Cord paused as his lungs sucked air from an oxygen cylinder.

"Lawrence Cord was a religious man.

"When I was a boy, he took me to church every week. We said grace before every meal, and when I was older, we discussed scripture.

"Lawrence Cord's devoutness perplexed many of his scientific peers, but even they recognized that it was his faith in God that had helped him survive the many terrible tragedies of his early life.

"His scientific knowledge and his spiritual views defined him, and are the reasons that Corpus Chrome, Inc. came into existence.

"He did not often explain himself to people, but he once articulated his views to his minister, who had questioned the ethics of this enterprise.

"My father said, 'God gave us the ability to reproduce so that we could grow as a race and become smarter, but he also gave us flawed bodies so that we wouldn't be content. He gave us bodies that got pneumonia, bodies that got cancer and bodies that could not endure the cold. He gave us bodies that functioned optimally for only a small portion of our lives.

"He gave us bodies that died.

"'Look at our arts—at the fantastical fictions we produce as a species. Our towering giants, fountains of youth, invulnerable superheroes, immortal vampires, shape-shifting werewolves and indestructible robots are all rooted in the same exact thing: We are dissatisfied with our mortal bodies.

"'I feel that we can and should do more for ourselves than just accept that life ends when a disease comes along or when

our ninety-year battery runs out. I believe God gave us the intellectual tools to build something better.

"'If we can engineer it, why not have a branch of humanity that removes itself from the continuous cycle of birth, growth, procreation, decline and death?

"'What could a man who lived for two hundred years conceive of? Or a woman who lived for two thousand years on a distant planet?

"'What if people could design their own bodies, and each person lived in a different, unique body that was a true expression of his or her inner self?

"'The mannequin is just the beginning—a starting point for all of us.'"

Steven Cord surveyed the crowd of thousands and said, "That was his dream.

"That was my father.

"That was Corpus Chrome, Incorporated."

The pixels dispersed and rearranged to show

an aerial view of the kidney-shaped chrome platform. The blue bulbs that were held in the disembodied mannequin hands changed to an amber hue and pulsated, imitating candlelight.

Steven Cord said, "The Corpus Chrome, Incorporated Memorial is dedicated to all of the innocent people who were killed here on August thirty-first, two thousand fifty-eight or in connection with this tragedy."

The pixels dispersed.

"That was depressing," said Snapdragon. "Can we watch some robots pound each other?"

The Jewish girl fixed her brown dress and turned to face the Asian boy. "I'd be very interested in watching something with robots."

Snapdragon smiled, and suddenly, Autumn kissed him on the mouth. Her soft palms held his cheeks, and his body sang.

The boy wished that the kiss would never end, but they had to breathe, and so it did.

EPILOGUE II
NEW COMPOSITIONS

AUTUMN, 2059

The foam-rubber cab drifted alongside the curb that delineated the western edge of Prospect Park.

"Stop here," said Lisanne, who was embraced by pseudopodia in the back seat of the vehicle.

The cab halted.

Brushing long hair from her eyes, the petite blonde looked through the window at the tuffgrass field, where children who were wrapped in baggy blue uniforms ran, smiled and shouted. Standing like a gorgeous giant amongst the maelstrom of boys and girls was the tall beauty of Swedish and Indian descent whom she had not seen in more than a year.

The sight of Osa both gladdened and pained Lisanne.

"Do you need assistance getting out?" inquired the cab driver, an amiable Iranian man who smelled of cloves.

Lisanne said, "I would like to sit here for a moment. You may keep the meter running." She wanted to calm herself before she approached her former mate.

"Sit as long as you like."

The Iranian man turned forward, double-tapped his lily and spoke Arabic. Near his right knee, the meter quantified time monetarily.

Lisanne looked through the side window once more. Thirty meters away, Osa walked to a fallen child, knelt beside the boy, said something to him, listened to him, stood up, helped him to his feet and guided him back to the tumult of limbs and laughter. The tall beauty drank water from a clear bulb, its fluid sparkling like a hidden sun revealed.

On August thirty-first, twenty-fifty-eight, Lisanne had awoken with a concussion and a fractured skull in a Nexus Y hospital. She did not speak to anybody for forty hours and had refused all visitors. Her thoughts had been alternately detached and morbid.

Osa had left a message in which she extended her condolences and proffered her company. Lisanne had listened to the recording many, many times during her hospitalization. She desperately wanted to weep upon the tall beauty's shoulder and hear her words of comfort and hold her tightly beneath a heavy blanket, but she neither accepted the offer nor returned the call. The petite blonde's terrible despair was not something that she could share with the woman whom she had neglected.

In the bleak, hopeless period that followed her release from the hospital, Lisanne had gone to Berlin to stay with her first husband Garren, his wife Sofia and their two boys Owen and Karl, both of whom were superb young athletes. She attended the boys' sporting events, ate fine meals, went to the opera and shopped, rarely discussing the sibling whose blasted remains she had privately buried. Lisanne had tried to forget her sister's second life, which was little more than a brief, difficult and occasionally nightmarish epilogue.

After five weeks, the petite blonde left Germany and went to a mountain chateau in the Russian Timan Ridge that was owned and inhabited by the librettist Petr and his choreographer mate Wyl, both of whom she had worked with prior to developing sequentialism with her sister. This activity-filled sojourn (like the one in Berlin) included important people from her past and helped her reclaim her identity, though still, her thoughts were morbid.

After two months abroad, Lisanne returned to Nexus Y.

She felt better than she had when she left, but there was an emptiness that pulled at her like an undertow. The thought of building a deep attachment to another temporary person filled her with an awful melancholy.

It was then that Lisanne decided to have a child.

The doctors took an egg from her. She wanted a girl, but would still love a boy and so did not opt for sperm selection.

When the doctors called to tell her that the fertilization had succeeded, she had wept. Later that same day, she began a new musical work that was very different from her sparse sequentialist compositions—a lush and joyous double symphony. The music had poured out of her.

Seated in the rear of the cab, Lisanne clicked the release button. Pseudopodia retracted from her pregnant belly.

The car door opened, and a cool autumn wind stirred the petite blonde's bright yellow sundress.

Double-tapping his lily, the Iranian cab driver turned around. "Don't strain yourself! I'll help!"

The man leapt from his seat and raced to her side, as if she were filled with nitroglycerin rather than a human child. "My wife delivered last year," he explained as he helped her to her feet.

"Danke."

The cabbie nodded and climbed inside his vehicle. "Should I wait for you?"

"Please do."

On aching arches that were supported by foam slippers, the seven-months-pregnant woman strode across the tuffgrass, toward the flock of children and the person who towered above them. As she walked, there was a brief independent motion within her abdomen.

The skinny black boy named Pinto pointed. "It's Miss Boychin!"

Osa turned around and saw Lisanne.

Their eyes met.

The tall beauty's gaze was a universe.

Clearing her throat, the petite blonde said, "Guten Tag."

"Um...hi," replied Osa, stunned. Her dark eyes glanced at the petite woman's swollen belly and widened. "Wow."

The women hugged, mindful of Lisanne's aquatic hump.

They parted, and looked at each other for a silent moment.

"This's a surprise," said the tall beauty. "Um...a shock, actually." A long index finger pointed at the occupied belly. "I don't imagine that's from drinking too much beer."

"It is not."

"I never knew you wanted a kid."

"I did not want one until recently," said Lisanne.

"Was it…um…intentional?"

"A Petri dish was involved."

"Oh." Osa ruminated for a moment. "I have no idea what I'm supposed to say right now. It's nice to see you, but it's been a year and you ambushed me. And you're pregnant."

Lisanne looked directly into Osa's dark eyes and said, "I want to apologize for not returning your call last year, when I was in the hospital. I appreciated your offer, but I felt that I could not see you…considering what had happened between us. Accepting your support…nein…I didn't think it was the right thing to do."

"I wanted to help you—be there—but I knew why you didn't get back to me." The tall beauty nodded her head and then lowered her gaze. "I'm sorry I hit you, I was just…I was really, really upset with what was going on with us. I was a fucking mess."

"And I am sorry that I neglected you the moment that my sister came back into my life. You are the only person who ever mattered to me as much as she did."

Osa clenched her jaw, and her eyes sparkled. "Don't say things like that." After a moment of interior warfare, she said, "I'm seeing someone. And it's serious."

Lisanne had assumed that this would be the case. "What is her name?"

"Nadine."

"I hope that you two are happy."

There was an awkward silence, during which the former mates were unable to look directly at each other. A child fell upon the tuffgrass, laughing, and small life stirred within the pregnant woman's belly.

"I wrote several new pieces." Lisanne reached into her clutch, withdrew two loaded tickets and proffered them with a shaking hand. "These are for the premiere. You may bring Nadine if you wish."

Osa took the tickets. "I don't know if…if that's such a good idea. But thanks." She wiped tears from her eyes with the back of her hand. "I'm glad to see you're okay. Really glad."

"Danke."

Osa sniffed, and asked, "Is it a girl?"

"Two girls."

Epilogue III
Manifestation of the Fuzzy Gray Entity

Winter, 2060

It was a fuzzy gray entity.

A familiar voice said, "His fingers just moved. There—on his right hand. That one and that one. Did you see them?"

"I, too, saw his digits display motility!" enthused a loud tenor voice.

"Fruit," said a third voice.

A spheroid covered with coarse hair pressed against an appendage of the fuzzy gray entity. This object had weight, but was not heavy. The fuzzy gray entity grasped the hirsute spheroid.

"He crushed it—spectacularly so!" exclaimed the loud tenor voice.

"Can you hear me?" said the familiar voice.

The fuzzy gray entity realized that it was a he and that he was Eagle Sappline. He tried to raise his eyelids, but instead opened two irises. The face immediately before him looked like his own, albeit thinner and a few years older.

"It's me," said the doppelganger. "I'm Champ. Your son."

Suddenly, Eagle Sappline remembered his resurrection and subsequent death.

"Guess I'm on again," said the re-bodied man, seeing that he was seated in a chair in a cubicle within a big warehouse. Beside his parka-wrapped progeny stood R.J. the Third, clothed in silver wool, and a large black man who had a heavy overcoat and tiger-striped dreadlocks. The cold trio exhaled steam.

"What happened?" inquired Eagle. "I thought CCI was gonna take back the robot."

"R.J. the Third and I snuck you over here, and Sagesse took out your wireless transmitters and receivers."

"Sagesse is the big black guy with stupid hair?"

"Yep."

Eagle swiveled his head to Sagesse. "Thanks."

The black man nodded his head.

"Are they still looking for me?" the re-bodied man asked his son. "CCI?"

"CCI's out of business."

Eagle chirped.

Sagesse looked at Champ.

"He's laughing," explained the garbage man.

"What happened to them?" asked Eagle. "Robot revolt or something?"

Champ, R.J. the Third and Sagesse exchanged glances that seemed rather grave.

"And where the hell am I? Is this Nexus Y?"

"No," the popinjay answered, "I am afraid that you are in New Queens." The fellow turned his shameful face to the ground. "We had…no other options…but to bring you…here."

Champ knelt beside the wooden armchair in which Eagle was seated and asked, "How do you feel?"

"Pretty good, I guess. Robot regular."

R.J. the Third took a step toward the mannequin and leaned in close. "I have a question for you, Mr. Sappline." The popinjay raised a finger into the air. "During the sixteen-month period of your second death, do you recall waking up in a cephalopod-like body inside a crater within a hollow moon, and summarily floating into the sun for some rather unhappy contemplations?"

Annoyed, Champ faced R.J. the Third. "CCI made that shit up—the Global Senate found the scripts for Dulande's speech and that English pilot's in a CCI vault."

"Or!" exclaimed the popinjay. "Or the Global Senate fabricated the evidence to further discredit CCI after financing its destruction!"

"You spend too much time talking to those paranoid idiots in your fan club." The garbage man turned his head and said, "No offense" to the big black French fellow who was a member.

Sagesse was uninterested in both the insult and the apology.

Eagle pondered the interim between his shutdown in the annexed fifth-floor kitchen and his re-resurrection a few minutes ago. "I don't remember anything like that with squids or whatever."

"And what exactly do you recall, hmmm?" inquired R.J. the Third, as if he were a lawyer from an old movie.

"Nothing," replied the re-bodied man. "Dying—both times it happened—was like going to sleep, but without the going to the bathroom or the dreams to break things up and show you time's passing."

"See?" Champ said to R.J. the Third.

"This proves nothing!" The popinjay stepped back and scratched his short black hair. "It took some of the other infernally-damned gentlemen weeks—or months!—to recall the trauma of solar Hell, so perhaps—"

"Shut up," barked Champ.

Pouting, R.J. the Third folded his arms.

Eagle surveyed his legs, arms and torso and saw that the chrome-plating had been covered over with flesh-colored foam latex and a tasteful amount of artificial hair. "You guys fixed me up."

"Yeah," said Champ. "I wanted you to blend in a little better—so you could do what you wanted without attracting too much attention."

"This looks realer than that chrome," remarked Eagle. "Why didn't those idiots do it like this in the first place?"

"It seems that CCI had some agenda with wanting the mannequins to stand out so that people would start to get used to the idea of alternative bodies."

"Got it," said the re-boded man, uninterested in an explanation of that explanation. "Anything fun coming up? Parties or Super Bowls?"

A big grin illuminated Champ's face. "I'm getting married."

"Great!"

Eagle willed a smile to his face. The gears, antennae and pseudopodia beneath his eyes whirred, and as his mask crinkled, he felt a very faint tickling sensation.

"I can't feel my face too good."

"The gelware mask was totally ruined in the fire," Champ said, "so the makeup artist who redid your body sculpted this one for you. It isn't touch-sensitive like the other, but it looks real and'll help you blend in."

Eagle did not suppose that he had any other facial options and so said, "Great. Thanks."

"Sure. Can you feel your hands? Sagesse took the gelware from your feet and rebuilt them."

Eagle looked at his right hand, which contained a crushed kiwi, and wriggled his digits. The gelware index, middle and ring fingers relayed the cool, wet and coarse textures of the fruit, but his thumb and pinky were numb (though motile). Activating his other hand, he assessed the sensitivity of his remaining digits.

"Six out of ten," announced the re-bodied man.

"Sixty percent," said Sagesse.

"That was his guarantee," R.J. the Third commented to Champ.

"So who're you marrying?" asked Eagle. "That Texan with the pink hair?"

"Nope."

"That snaky girl you live with who goes around with no shirt?" The re-bodied man recalled the sizable serpent tattoo that covered the woman's torso. "She's a wild one, you can tell. Nothing's off-limits with a girl like that. Total buffet."

"Not her," responded Champ.

Eagle ruminated for a moment and thought of something horrible. "It better not be that lousy ex-wife who cheated on you. I'll get in the way of that disaster."

"It's not her. It's Douglas's wife—his widow. Her name's Molly."

Guilt assailed the re-resurrected man. "But...but I killed her husband in that fire."

"We don't look at it that way. Nobody does. You and Douglas were firemen—that's a dangerous job. You were both trying to save lives and an accident happened. You got a posthumous award for bravery, and so did he."

Although Eagle still felt responsible for Douglas's death, he was pleased to hear that his peers did not hate him. "How'd you two get together?"

"Molly saw me in the pool hall where the firemen go—I'm still on the team with Potato and Butch—they say 'hi,' by the way, though most people think you died permanently—and she remembered me from those nights we all went out. She came over and started talking to me, and we just got along great."

Eagle pondered Douglas's wife and recalled that she was friendly, pretty and laid-back, even though she seemed like an intellectual. "Molly seemed real nice. And two hundred and ninety-nine times out of three hundred, black girls are good in bed."

Sagesse did not seem thrilled by this comment.

"She's a great companion," remarked Champ.

"Does she live with you under the toilet? There enough room for two down there?"

"She's got her own place, a nice one, and she owns a nightclub, too. She lets me do standup comedy there on Tuesdays."

"Sounds like you made a damn good choice."

"I think so."

"It's a good thing you're handsome."

"It gives me options."

Eagle saw an antique gas motorcycle inside the cubicle on the opposite wall and pointed to it. "My dad had one of those when I was a kid, same exact model." The re-bodied man recalled his father and a Mexican woman whose name he did not know seated upon the motorcycle. "The sound of that engine used to scare the hell out of me—like an angry dog or a pissed-off lion or something. I always thought it was gonna explode, which really cracked him up…" He stared at the artifact for a moment and added, "It's not as big as I remember."

Eagle flung the mashed kiwi into the warehouse. "I want to go over there and look at it. This thing ready to go? The robot?"

"Yes, but take it slow," cautioned Champ.

The re-bodied man willed his shoulders forward, and the mannequin leaned forward; he willed his hands to the armrests, and the mannequin's hands gripped the armrests; he willed his bent arms and legs to straighten, and the mannequin's arms and legs straightened.

The re-resurrected man rose from his wooden seat.

"Seems like the robot's working," commented Eagle.

Champ's eyes widened in terror. "No!"

Eagle's vision blurred. The warehouse around him wobbled and turned green.

Champ turned to the black man and yelled, "Help him!"

"Merde."

Sagesse hastened forward, trailing his tiger-striped dreadlocks.

Eagle touched his face, and the prosthetic mask crinkled. He withdrew his hands and saw that his fingertips were covered with green fluid.

"What the hell is—"

Eagle was a fuzzy gray entity…

…and then he was not.

Epilogue IV
Dedicated to My Mother

Winter, 2089 (twenty-nine years later)

The Breutschen sisters (dressed in iridescent black contour suits) and their husbands (clothed in dapper gray tuxedos) listened to the final notes resound within the lavender and gold Perfect Pitch Auditorium. Music dwindled and died, and soon, the orchestra was still. After five seconds of silence, the words "Thank you for attending the Lisanne Breutschen Retrospective" floated up from the outstretched arms of the conductor and sped toward Nancy's face. Her twin Ellen took and squeezed her hand.

The audience stood, applauding the performers and the deceased composer.

Upon the stage, a Canadian maestro of incomparable skill motioned to Lisanne Breutschen's daughters and said, "Please join me."

A new surge of enthusiasm rippled through the crowd.

Nancy shook her head and said, "Thank you, Maestro, but no. This applause is for you, the musicians and my mother."

The conductor nodded his head respectfully, turned back to the appreciative audience and bowed.

"You two should go up there," suggested Nancy's husband. "They'd like to see you."

"This is a retrospective of our mother's work: The audience should contemplate her life and her absence."

"But they want to see you both—you're a part of her."

Irked, Nancy said, "We didn't make this music."

"You're wrong about that," said someone in the row behind the twin sisters.

The siblings turned around and saw a tall, sixty-year-old woman who had wrinkled sepia skin, silver hair and large dark eyes. "You two are the reason these pieces exist," said the stranger.

"Did you know our mother?" asked Nancy.

The tall woman nodded. "We were close for a little while."

The applause dwindled, and upon Nancy's contact lenses, the words "Please Exit the Auditorium" sped intrusively towards her face, chased by the announcement, "The Gala Room is Now Open!" Triple-blinking to turn off the micropixels, she asked the stranger, "Are you Osa Karlsson?"

The tall woman was startled by the inquiry. "Um…yes. I am. She told you about me?"

"Yes."

Lisanne had spoken of Osa Karlsson when her daughters had asked her what it meant to be in love.

"She spoke very highly of you," added Ellen.

"That's nice to hear," said Osa. "I didn't know if she ever—" Her voice dropped out, and she turned her head away from the twin siblings. Without another word, the tall woman in black walked to the aisle and left the auditorium.

Nancy remarked, "She must have been a very beautiful woman."

* * *

At the end of a memorial reception that was filled with melancholic and beautiful toasts to the deceased composer, Nancy and her husband parted from Ellen and her spouse and took an air carriage to the airport, where they boarded a shuttle bound for Berlin.

* * *

Two brindled French bulldogs that were named Gunther and Harry tumbled with flopping tongues and bulging eyeballs toward the humans. Nancy and her husband dropped to their knees and, for twenty minutes, played with the maniacal canines.

The couple withstood the application of much slobber.

Soon, the petite blonde grew hungry (she had not eaten at the reception) and turned the den into a kitchen. Into the victualizer, she said, "Build: bite-sized boneless whole geese; herbs; hot. Build: bite-sized potatoes; butter; sour cream; chives; hot. Build: haricot verts; peach segments; roasted almonds; truffle oil; warm." A green light on the marble wall-panel blinked, and the woman turned to her husband. "Is there something else you would enjoy?"

"That sounds good."

Nancy tapped the blinking light, and the victualizer hummed a melody as it assembled the described foods with a ninety-eight percent waste-free protein-vitamin-fiber compound. Thirty-two seconds later, a glass platter emerged from the wall, bearing twenty miniature geese, ten tiny baked potatoes and forty haricot verts. Silver toothpicks jutted from a pincushion in the center of the dish.

The couple pierced, raised, chewed and swallowed the bite-sized whole potatoes, haricot verts and boneless geese. As they ate, they listened to broadcasts from the peace summit between the Global Senate and the Greater Free Republics, yet were not hopeful that the sleep wars in Asia, Africa and the Americas would end in the near future. For twenty minutes, the couple discussed the paintings that Nancy's gallery had recently acquired, and for half that amount of time, they talked about the underground buildings that her husband was currently designing for a firm in Beijing.

After he swallowed the last miniature boneless goose, the architect said, "I'd love to watch something in the mote environment for a little while."

"We should finish that experience we started last weekend," suggested Nancy.

"The one with the resurrected fireman and that garbage man?"

"Yes. I'm curious to see what happens to them."

"It's pretty funny," her husband said, "and those guys are really stupid."

"They aren't stupid. And I believe Barry Watts won an award for his performance."

"Which one's he?"

"The one who plays Champ."

"The garbage man?" Her husband shrugged, unimpressed. "He's mediocre."

"He is a very handsome mediocre."

Epilogue V

The Very Final Act from the Mote Environment Experience entitled,

The 75% True Story of Champ and Eagle Sappline (The Zenith Achievement in the History of the Arts by R.J. the Third)

Clothed in blue flannel sleepwear, Nancy and her husband walked through a living wall and into the mote environment, the walls of which were black and filled with billions of micromagnetic processors.

"Do you want to sit in the center again?" asked the petite blonde, hoping for an unexpected answer.

"Yeah. I like being right in it, feeling it all around me as if I'm actually there."

Nancy thought that sitting in the center of a mote environment was a bit taxing (one had to regularly pivot), but said, "Okay," because it mattered more to her husband than it did to her.

The couple walked to the middle of the room, where the architect whistled a C-sharp and said, "Divan; two people." An iris in the floor opened up, and the requested furniture inflated.

Husband and wife sat upon the trapped air and leaned against each other.

With concern in his gentle brown eyes, the man looked at his wife and asked, "Are you okay with today? The retrospective and everything...?"

Nancy had maintained her composure throughout the evening, excepting when the orchestra had played "The Overlapping Joys." "It is sad," she remarked, "but it has been three years. And it is wonderful that her music is appreciated by so many people…that she continues to have a presence and an impact even though she is gone."

Her husband smiled, squeezed her with strong arms and kissed her on the lips. For ten heartbeats, they held each other.

Wiping her eyes, Nancy sat upright and whistled a C-sharp. "Resume play: *The 75% True Story of Champ and Eagle Sappline.*"

The nozzles of the mote environment sprayed billions of pixels into the room and rendered (through expert foreshortening and forced perspective)

a gigantic compartment-style warehouse

that was far larger than the entire apartment building within which Nancy and her husband lived.

A meter away from the couple—but rendered smaller-than-life to create the illusion of a much greater distance—the actors who played

> *Champ Sappline, clothed in a parka, and Sagesse, wrapped in a red Japanese robe, grabbed the arms of the teetering mannequin. Green fluid dripped from the machine's eyelids and lips.*
>
> *"What the fuck just happened!?!" the garbage man yelled at Sagesse.*
>
> *The French fellow tore off the mannequin's mask. Green fluid bathed the mandibles within its concave face, and steam rose toward the warehouse ceiling.*
>
> *R.J. the Third*

(who was played by the stunning English actress Meliza Canford)

> *squealed in alarm and cried out, "Freeze him again— before it is too late!"*
>
> *"She's right," Champ said to Sagesse. "How do we turn on the liquid nitrogen?"*
>
> *The French fellow jammed his left thumb into the mannequin's*

right aural canal, and something within its head clicked. Looking at the garbage man, he said, "Duplicate."

Champ thrust his thumb into the opposite ear, poked around and elicited a click.

The mannequin stood at attention and dropped to its knees. Ice covered its head as Sagesse and Champ withdrew their thumbs. Epaulette bulbs flashed yellow and red, and three piccolo flutes skirled.

The garbage man surveyed his kneeling father, sighed and eyed the French fellow. "Two things: You're gonna fix him, and you're gonna give me a refund."

"No."

"But you broke him—the head didn't even retract like it's supposed to. I waited a year and a half, and look what happened to him. To my goddamn father."

"Machine," said Sagesse.

"That's it!" Champ shouted as he clenched his fists and lunged.

Sagesse reached for the hilt of the samurai sword that was attached to his belt.

The garbage man punched the French fellow in the stomach. Grunting, the big foe stumbled back and withdrew his katana from a scabbard that was decorated with the eyes of owls.

R.J. the Third plucked a migraine pen from her cleavage and pointed it at Sagesse's face. "I'll lance you!" she warned.

The French fellow paused, holding his samurai sword aloft, while nearby, the redheaded woman readied her weapon. Her eyes were severe, and her dress was gorgeous.

Cowed, Sagesse sheathed his blade.

Champ grumbled, knelt beside the mannequin and looked to R.J. the Third. "Let's get my dad out of here."

"I believe that is the most sensible option," concurred the redheaded beauty as she pulled an errant wisp of hair from her lush eyelashes.

Sheathing his sword, Sagesse looked at the ground, where the two striped dreadlocks that he had accidentally severed lay like dead serpents.

"As a result of this incident," R.J. the Third announced, "I must revoke Sagesse's membership in my fan club, and henceforth forbid the inclusion of any person who dwells in the inhabited bowel movement that is otherwise known as New Queens."

Champ double-tapped his lily and said, "Connect to Mikek."

The pixels dispersed, revealing the black limbo of the mote environment walls, and then cohered. Orbiting the couple was the following information:

Spring 2062: Two years later

The pixels dispersed and then rendered, with perfect forced perspective,

a verdant and expansive mountain range, limned white by the morning sun.

A conical black air shuttle that was beaded with silver solar nodes flew above the peaks, its dark shadow speeding like a stingray across the crenulated stone.

Within the craft sat Champ, clothed in jeans and a t-shirt that read never believe what you read…except this.*; R.J. the Third, squeezed into an opalescent dress; Mikek, clad in orange; and the flesh-colored mannequin, draped in a navy overcoat. Sunshine glimmered upon the marbled green and white ice that surrounded the re-bodied man's head.*

Seated in the pilot's throne, Mikek appraised R.J. the Third's curvaceous physique.

Champ asked, "You'd hit her with the shuttle?"

"I'd give her a thruster."

R.J. the Third blushed at the compliment and coquettishly turned her head.

Mikek examined the bugview octagons and scratched his back with a hairy hand, "This is the location Dr. Kwok gave us, but I don't see anything."

"It'll be camouflaged," said Champ. "The CCI scientists who survived August Thirty-first are all in hiding. Just circle around for a bit so she can see us."

"Shit on shit." The driver scratched his hirsute nape and sighed. "I'll go to half power so that the solar cells can—"

"Look over there." The garbage man pointed to an octagon that displayed two mountaintops. Between these sharp peaks floated a bright, glimmering object. "Zoom in."

The driver tapped the octagon, magnifying the glaring curiosity, which was a chromium kite.

"That's it!" Champ and R.J. the Third cried in accidental, but perfect, harmony.

"If you say so." Mikek notched two drift thrusters and pushed the steering scepter to the right.

The air shuttle arced between the mountain peaks, slowed and hovered beside the chromium kite. Below the craft, the ground trembled and cracked, and from a rift arose a forty-meter-tall cylindrical building that was covered with dirt.

An iris opened in the roof of this tower, and a fifty-year-old Chinese woman wearing a sky-blue lab coat climbed from the aperture. Looking up at the air shuttle, she waved amicably.

The motes dispersed, and soon, the following information orbited the couple:

Spring 2063: One year later

The pixels dispersed and then rendered

the air shuttle, which currently hovered beside the top of the dirt-covered tower. Birds wheeled across the blue sky, pointlessly crying out.

The iris opened, and Champ and Eagle climbed outside, both of them wearing jeans, t-shirts and the same face. The sun shone brightly upon the skin-colored latex that covered all of the mannequin's chrome plating.

Dr. Kwok stuck her head through the aperture like a groundhog and watched their departure. The men reached the air shuttle ramp, turned around and waved good-bye to the scientist.

"Thank you," said Champ. "We really, really appreciate all that you did for us."

"You're welcome. This interface fluid should last for a long time."

"Good," said Eagle. "I'm getting pretty sick of dying."

The father and son entered the craft and shut the door behind them.

Engines flashed, and the shuttle sped off, light glinting upon the silver solar nodes that adorned its hull.

Within the vehicle, Mikek said, "If I was desperate—really out of options—I'd land this thing on Dr. Kwok."

The motes dispersed and then rendered, with perfect forced perspective,

the interior of a church.

Immediately before an avuncular female minister stood Champ Sappline, attired in a loose blue tuxedo, and his beaming black bride Molly Rodriguez, who wore a sky-blue dress that was adorned with silk flowers. Foremost amongst the ninety wedding attendees were Eagle Sappline, Potato O'Boyd, Bagel Butch and Pedro Cheung (all clothed in black tuxedos), R.J. the Third (wearing a gossamer slip that had gold filigree), the obese feline Architect (huddled within a floating litter box), the herpetology student (clothed in an alligator-skin dress), the Indian from the fifth floor (draped in a flag of truce) and the entire Mikek Ghentz family (all of whom wore linen sweatsuits).

"I now pronounce you man and wife," the female minister said to Champ and Molly. "You may pledge yourselves to each other with a kiss."

Champ Sappline took his wife's shoulders and pressed his lips to hers.

"Kick the stars!" yelled Eagle.

All throughout the church, the guests clapped enthusiastically.

The newlyweds' kiss deepened. Their chests pressed together and their hearts touched.

Eagle turned his head to his old friends and whispered, "They waited for me to get fixed—Champ and Molly. Delayed the wedding for three whole years."

"Respectful," commented Pedro Cheung, who was almost sober.

The newlyweds pulled their lips apart and embraced each other.

"It's about time we had that kiss," whispered the radiant bride.

"Thanks for waiting," responded the groom.

The clapping increased. Champ looked over at his father.

A piccolo flute pierced the applause.

The wedding guests looked at the mannequin.

"Don't worry," Eagle said, "that's just how I whistle."

The motes dispersed and then rendered

a festooned dancing hall. Beer kegs, champagne pyramids, salad forests, candied chickens and ziggurats of Sandwedish sandwiches lay upon the food trolley. The wedding guests loudly and jubilantly celebrated the marriage.

An austere forty-five-year-old brunette woman who was clothed in a rose-colored spring dress walked up to Champ.

"Congratulations," said Candace, who was his first wife. "Molly seems lovely in every possible way."

"Thanks. And thanks for coming."

The austere woman nodded. "I'm glad that you're happy."

She looked down at the purse in her hands and added, "I hope she treats you better than I did."

"You and I had a lot of good years."

"We did," said Candace, lifting her gaze.

"Those're the ones I usually think about."

"I'm glad to hear that."

The former husband and wife hugged each other and, for a moment, were transported in time.

Soon, they parted and walked toward their respective second spouses.

The pixels dispersed, and the following information orbited the couple:

Spring 2065: Two years later

The motes dispersed and then rendered

the interior of a bar. Booths circled the perimeter of the violet establishment like unmotivated turtles. Champ, fifty, with short silver-blonde hair, and Eagle, clothed in an overcoat and sunglasses, sat upon a bench with Molly, Bagel Butch, Pedro Cheung, R.J. the Third, Mikek, the herpetology student and her fiancé.

Eagle raised a glass of top-shelf Scotch and said, "To Potato O'Boyd."

"To Potato O'Boyd," replied the chorus, holding their drinks aloft.

Eagle dipped his thimble as Champ and the others drank.

The re-bodied man looked at the aged faces of Bagel Butch and Pedro Cheung and then down at his drink. Two tiny bubbles rose from his thimble to the surface like dead fish.

The pixels dispersed, and the following information orbited the couple:

Winter 2067: One and a half years later

The motes dispersed and then rendered, with perfect forced perspective,

Eagle Sappline seated upon an antique motorcycle. The mannequin steered the speeding two-wheeler along a tortuous mountain road.

The roar of the engine was as loud as a war.

The motes dispersed and then rendered

the peach-colored waiting area of a hospital. Upon one of its buoyed benches sat Champ, fifty-two and wearing bedraggled plaid pajamas, and Eagle, dressed in an overcoat and sunglasses.

"I feel like I should be in there with her," said the garbage man, nervously tapping his right slipper.

"No," said Eagle. "If there's one piece of advice I came back from the dead to give you, it's this: No husband should be in that room. Ever. What's going in there—what that looks like and sounds like and smells like—is way worse than death."

"But it's our child she's having." Champ looked at the living wall, where the words "Delivery Room" shone green. Apprehension, anxiety, guilt and joy knotted his fingers together like quiltwork. "Molly said it was my choice, but I just—"

"Don't. There's a reason obstetricians make so much money."

Champ anxiously ran his hands through his short silver-blonde hair. "You were in the room when I was born."

"That experience didn't make us closer."

"But—"

"Learn from my mistakes."

A smiling doctor walked from the wall and announced, "Champ Sappline, you are the father of a healthy eight-pound girl!"

"Great!"

"Kick the stars!"

The father and son leaped from their seats, cheered and hugged each other.

Luminous with joy, Champ turned to the doctor and asked, "Can I see her?"

"Of course you may."

Eagle seized his son's arm and shook his head. "Wait 'til he cleans off all the junk."

The pixels dispersed, and the following information orbited the couple:

Winter 2072: Five years later

The motes dispersed and then rendered

the golden velvet den of a sizable Brooklyn City apartment, where windowalls admitted a view of the solar panes, floatads, stacked flyways and air barbicans that lined the far side of the East River. Champ, fifty-six, with short silver hair, Molly, fifty-one and a little heavier, and Eagle, clothed in a robe, watched a biracial five-year-old girl run across the den. The gleeful child held a stuffed bird in each of her hands.

"Gale's got a lotta life in her," remarked the re-bodied man.

The weary mother affirmed his statement with a sigh. "I've priced tranquilizer darts."

Eagle chirped, and Molly grinned.

Champ stood up and arched his back, grunting as the joints in his spine crackled. Leaning over, he said, "Come here," to his bounding daughter.

Gale made squawking noises as she flew both of her birds toward her father. Champ scooped up his little girl and kissed her on the forehead.

The five-year-old giggled.

Eagle chirped.

The pixels dispersed, and the following information orbited the couple:

Summer 2077: Five years later

The motes dispersed and then rendered

> *the outside of a nightclub named Jolly Molly's. Eagle's antique motorcycle was parked on the nether curb.*
>
> *Hundreds of flashily dressed patrons who clasped mates, oily cocktails and furry drinks filled the dimly lit interior of the club.*
>
> *Seated together in a plush velvet booth were Molly, thinner and with silver hair, R.J. the Third, her beauty diminished, Architect, his fur white, the herpetology student, her tattoos wrinkled, Candace, gaunt, Mikek, bald, and Eagle, unchanged and wearing an overcoat and sunglasses.*
>
> *A spotlight glared, and gradually, the audience quieted.*
>
> *Standing in the middle of the room upon a buoyed dais was Champ, sixty-one years old, dressed in his orange garbage man's uniform.*
>
> *The amateur comedian ran a hand through his silver-white hair, looked at the mirthless crowd and said, "An obese cat goes into a bar.*
>
> *"He climbs onto a stool and says to the grumpy Irish bartender, 'Hey, barkeep. I'd like some cheese.' The bartender looks at the obese cat and says, 'You should lay off the dairy.' The cat says, 'It's not for me, it's for the mouse I ate last week.' The bartender scratches his beard and says, 'I don't believe you.' The cat opens his mouth really wide and a weird little voice says, 'Hey asshole, get me some cheddar.'*
>
> *"The bartender gets angry and says, 'Nobody talks like that to me in my bar—get the hell out!' The cat closes his*

mouth and asks, 'Me or the mouse?' The bartender asks, 'Can you get rid of him?' The cat says, 'Not easily—I swallowed a Chinese mouse the other day, and he's into Orientals.'"

The audience laughed, and one person chirped very loudly.

Champ resumed. "So the bartender says, 'I feel sorry for you,' and the cat says, 'It's not so bad. Last year I swallowed two gay mice and was burping semen for a month.'

"The bartender says, 'How'd you get them out?'

"'Republican mice.'

"'How'd you get them out?'

"'Stomach tax.'"

The motes dispersed and cohered to form

the outside of the nightclub. The lights were turned off, and the word CLOSED shone upon the living wall. Driverless jetbuses sped across the multi-tiered streets as Eagle and Champ walked to the antique motorcycle.

"You did good tonight," said the re-bodied man.

"Thanks." The amateur comedian sucked on a vapor tube, eliciting a trilling B-flat. "A couple of duds in there, but I got some laughs."

"A lot of laughs. I liked that stuff with the cat the best." Eagle turned away and said, "I've decided it's time to stop all this."

Champ did not understand what his father meant. Dragging on his vapor tube, he asked, "You mean coming to my shows? You don't have to come to all of them—I know you've heard lots of these jokes before."

"That's not what I'm talking about. What I mean—what I'm talking about—is living in the robot...being this thing. I want to stop."

The amateur comedian paled. "Is it broken? Is something wrong with it? We could get it fixed if—"

328

"I haven't felt my hands in a few years…but that's not why I made my decision."

Silent and frightened, Champ stared at his father. "What's wrong?" he asked weakly.

Eagle touched his gelware fingertips to the leather motorcycle seat and then slid them to the chrome gas tank. "Potato… Butch…Pedro—my friends are all dead. I watched them go, one after another." The re-bodied man looked at his son and said, "I don't know how long the mannequin will last…but… well…you're not so young anymore and there're some things I just don't ever want to see."

Champ's hands shook. "So you're just going to…to shut down again?"

"No," said Eagle. "I'm gonna end it permanent this time."

"No!" exclaimed Champ. "Please."

The brilliant white light of a passing jetbus inflamed the tableau, illuminating the amateur comedian's white hair, glimmering eyes, and wrinkled face. Soon, the vehicle was gone, and the night returned.

Eagle said, "You enjoy doing these shows, and you've got a great wife, a cute girl and an awesome boy. Seeing you this happy—that's the only thing I wanted before I checked out." The re-bodied man turned his lenses upon his son and added, "There's a reason I named you Champ."

Holding back tears, the amateur comedian protested, "But, Dad, there's—"

"Let's not argue about it, 'cause you're not gonna change anything—I made the decision. It's done. Tell Molly good-bye, and tell Gale and Richard that I went to work in outer space, or something else exciting that makes them happy."

Champ sniffed, wiped tears from his eyelashes and nodded his head.

The father and son hugged each other.

At the exact same time, the two Sapplines said, "I love you."

The motes dispersed and then rendered

Eagle Sappline, seated upon his speeding motorcycle. Sunlight shone like an oily explosion upon the chromium mannequin, model 8M, from which torn-up latex skin trailed in long tattered ribbons. The street was empty.

Eagle Sappline steered his two-wheeler directly toward the Corpus Chrome, Incorporated Memorial. Sunlight glared brilliantly upon the giant chrome kidney, blinding the re-bodied man, but he did not close his irises.

The roar of Eagle Sappline's engine sounded like the proclamation of an angry lion, the growl of an attack dog, the final explosion that destroyed the Empire State Building, three dissonant flutes, the hand of a sixth-floor champion slapping the cheek of a fifth-floor foe, a clenched fist breaking the cartilage in another man's nose, a rocket impacting a gelatinous wall, the mewling of an obese cat, a trapdoor shutting, the gurgle of an upset stomach, the groans of orgasmic lovers, thrusters igniting, the shouts of those who saw the CCI Building fall, the metallic clank of two crossed katanas, a popped champagne cork, a joyous symphony, the applause of an enthusiastic audience, a coffin lid closing, a newborn girl crying, the beating of a heart and the chirping of the last functional mannequin in the world.

About the Author

Florida-born New Yorker S. Craig Zahler worked for many years as a cinematographer and a catering chef, while playing heavy metal and creating some strange theater pieces. His debut western novel, *A Congregation of Jackals* was nominated for both the Peacemaker and the Spur awards, and his western screenplay, *The Brigands of Rattleborge*, garnered him a three-picture deal at Warner Brothers and topped the prestigious Black List. In 2011, a horror movie that he wrote in college called, *Asylum Blackout* (aka *The Incident*) was made and picked up by IFC Films after a couple of people fainted at its Toronto premiere. His horror western novel *Wraiths of the Broken Land* was published by Raw Dog Screaming Press in 2013, and he is currently at work on his directorial debut *Bone Tomahawk*.

A drummer, lyricist and songwriter, Zahler is half of the doomy epic metal band Realmbuilder (which is signed to I Hate Records of Sweden) and the black metal project Charnel Valley (whose two albums were released by Paragon Records). He studies kung-fu and is a longtime fan of animation (hand drawn and stop-motion), heavy metal (all types), soul music, genre books (especially, horror, crime and hard sci-fi), old movies, obese cats and asymmetrical robots.

To learn more about S. Craig Zahler, visit scraigzahler.com and rawdogscreaming. com.

Lightning Source UK Ltd.
Milton Keynes UK
UKHW040628230120
357484UK00002B/558